THE BLACK LILY SOCIETY

April Oaks, Book Two

Alice G. Holmes

A NineStar Press Publication

Published by NineStar Press
P.O. Box 91792,
Albuquerque, New Mexico, 87199 USA.
www.ninestarpress.com

The Black Lily Society

First Edition, August, 2024

Print ISBN: 978-1-64890-796-8

Also available in eBook, ISBN: 978-1-64890-795-1

CONTENT WARNING

This book contains depictions of death, homophobia, past trauma, mentions of suicide, torture (psychological), bullying (recounted), violence, and child abuse (mental and emotional, recounted).

Lyric Morrison is looking to get away. After the Phoenix Coup, she wants to forget all about vampires. She decides to move to New Orleans, the perfect place for a fresh start. However, upon moving into her new apartment, Lyric meets a woman named Heather Campbell. She's bright, she's cheerful, and she's dead. Heather is a ghost, and she wants Lyric to solve her murder.

Suddenly, Lyric finds herself pulled back into the world of vampires and magic by a power she didn't know she possessed. Lyric is a medium, with the ability to communicate with the dead. As she's drawn further into the investigation, she meets Elias—the vampire who saved her life in Phoenix, who is also the number one suspect in Heather's untimely death.

Along the way, Lyric befriends another vampire named Lionel and Verity, a clairvoyant, both of whom have a dark secret tied to Lyric's own past. Torn between her feelings for Elias and her promise to help Heather, Lyric is caught in a tangled web of mystery that may be her undoing.

To my sister Christin and my niece Raven. I love you.

Prologue

I GASPED AS I woke, still in the grips of the nightmare. My heart raced but I couldn't move. There was something on the ceiling, something with fangs that was moving closer. I whimpered, but fear still froze me in place. As the seconds ticked past, I came back to myself. I was safe. I was in my apartment. The vampires were gone. They had been for months.

When I could finally move again, I sat up. I picked up the glass of water I kept next to the bed and gulped down as much of it as I could without spilling. I winced at the temperature of the water. It was warmer than I liked. The air conditioner was still going at high speed. No brownout then. Well, that was something.

Then I looked at my alarm clock. It was only an hour after I'd closed my eyes! And now I was wide awake. There was no way I'd be able to get back to sleep now. I sighed and rubbed my eyes with my hand. The nightmare was the same as always: the night when the vampires almost got me. When *he* saved me. I didn't even know his name.

I put the glass back on my bedside table and reached for my phone. I saw the group chat was still going and I couldn't help a small smile. No matter how bad things got, I could always rely on my pocket friends. So, I selected the right channel on Eris and started typing.

EratoONine: I've had it.

Psychepomp: I thought you were going to bed?

EratoONine: Nightmare.

DidollCarthage: Again?

EratoONine: Yup.

NathanaBoBanna: The same one?

EratoONine: Yup. This is bullshit! I can't do this anymore.

Psychepomp: Do what?

EratoONine: Everything! I can't stay in Phoenix.

NathanaBoBanna: I thought you were gonna talk with your shrink about that, sweetie.

EratoONine: I did but I can't tell her the truth! She won't believe me!

AoiManto: What did she say?

EratoONine: That it's normal to want to believe in the supernatural rather than to face the truth.

DidollCarthage: Rude.

AoiManto: She'd probably think we're all insane.

NathanaBoBanna: We're not insane, just open to life's possibilities.

EratoONine: I said that to Dr. Cade and she blew me off.

I could see several of them were typing in response, so I waited. In my head, I played a little game trying to guess who would say what. Everyone in the chat claimed to have some kind of psychic power. Well, except me. I'm about as psychic as an eraser. But that didn't matter because I believed in the supernatural, just like everyone else in the room.

Psyche was the most likely to be outraged. She was a woman who stood for what she believed in no matter what the consequences. She kind of had to. She had four kids and all of them were queer, autistic, or in the case of her two youngest, both. It's why we were best friends. Psyche could always tell when someone was lying. Even if it was completely innocuous, she always knew.

Nathana on the other hand was always calm and collected. She was childfree like me. But this was because she and her wife pursued careers in academia rather than just not being a big fan of kids like I was. She was definitely the most spiritually in-touch person in the group. Nathana told me once she was a Kemetic high priestess. I looked it up; it means she worships the Egyptian gods. Her specialty was dreams.

Didoll's gift was pretty harmless. She said she did automatic writing. She'd pass on messages to each of us from whichever entity was talking to her that week. Often the messages wouldn't make sense until after the events occurred. But there was an occasion or two where she made my blood run cold with a message from her angel. She was the only one in the group who used her gift to earn a living. She must have been pretty good at it, given she and her parents lived in a mansion out in California.

Last but not least was Aoi, who was our only overseas member. She lived in London with her fiancée and their little boy. The fiancée was a sculptress of some renown, while Aoi was a mixed media artist. They were pretty well off, at least if their flat in Westminster was any indication. Aoi said she could astral project, which is how she got ideas for her art pieces.

> **Psychepomp:** Well, maybe you're right and it's time to move on.

> **DidollCarthage:** Where would you go?

I smiled as I typed out the answer.

> **EratoONine:** New Orleans.

> **AoiManto:** *groan* Really?

> **NathanaBoBanna:** You haven't stopped talking about New Orleans since your vacation.

> **EratoONine:** Because I love it!

> **DidollCarthage:** Yes. We figured that out when you uploaded two thousand photos from your trip.

> **EratoONine:** Don't exaggerate. It was 1723.

> **DidollCarthage:** I wasn't exaggerating, I was rounding up.

> **EratoONine:** It wasn't that bad. And I think it would be great. I could start over. Maybe I could

even make some friends.

Psychepomp: What are we, chopped liver?

EratoONine: Sorry, not what I meant. You're pocket friends, and you know I love you all. I just want to be around people in real life too. Like all of you.

NathanaBoBanna: That's fair. You are the only person here not living with someone.

EratoONine: Oh hey speaking of, how's Gray?

NathanaBoBanna: Great. She's really excited about the next semester. She's up for tenure and I think she has a shot.

Psychepomp: Awesome!

AoiManto: I'm sure she'll get it.

I yawned, then sighed.

EratoONine: I'm gonna try to go back to sleep. If you see me in here again before dawn, yell at me.

Psychepomp: Can do. Go get some sleep.

There were several messages wishing me a goodnight and I smiled. I put the phone on the dresser and got back under the covers. As I listened to the traffic on McDowell Road, faint over the roar of the air conditioner, I started to plan.

New Orleans. Why not? It was as good a place as any

to start over. And I did love the city when I visited. As though for the first time in my life, I was home. I rolled onto my side and closed my eyes. I would set my plan in motion in the morning.

Chapter One

Eight months later

SWEAT POURED DOWN my back. My glasses fogged up from the exertion. My muscles ached, and I grunted as I pushed against the heavy box. I panted as I shoved the box up the steps, until finally it was in the apartment. I wiped my brow and exhaled, exhaustion creeping over me. "That's the last one," I said. No one was around to hear me. It was the last week of August, and the heat and humidity were getting to me.

I sighed, went inside, and closed and locked the door behind me. Thankfully, I'd already assembled the furniture. I stepped around the last box and collapsed, boneless, onto the bed. I winced as I was a sweaty, smelly mess and these were clean sheets.

"Good thing I got the washer," I said. I'd technically moved in a week ago. But there was a delay in getting my boxes from Miss Sophie's in the Bywater to my new place in the Lower Garden District. Not an easy task without a truck. Or help.

The elation I'd felt with a job well done slowly ebbed away. As I stared at the high ceiling of my new studio apartment, I reflected on how I'd ended up there. My original plan to move involved about two years of working and scrimping and saving but two things happened.

Firstly, everyone who'd been in Phoenix during the

coup was given a check for damages from the government. Mine wasn't huge, since it was just me and no one in my family died. As though a check could make up for what happened. A city taken hostage by the undead, people terrorized and killed, and the government just says, "Here, have money to help you forget about it." Still, I wouldn't turn down free money. And it was enough that I was able to pay down some debt. I used the rest to book a stay at a long-term rental in New Orleans and mail most of my belongings there.

The second was my job. In an effort to save money (and because the coup had been hard on everyone) we went fully remote. I was given a company laptop, headphones, and microphone and told not to come into the office anymore. When I asked if I could move and still keep my job, my supervisor discussed it with the company president. They got back to me a few days later and said it was fine.

My therapist agreed a change of scenery would be good for me, though I wouldn't be able to see her anymore. Fifteen hundred miles was a bit far to travel for an appointment.

On our last visit, she'd asked, "Are you still having nightmares?"

I shrugged. "Sometimes."

"And will you still go to therapy once you relocate?"

"I don't know yet. I still have my job, and I can work from home. But my benefits may change."

"I would recommend you look into it as soon as possible."

"Otherwise, I might go crazier? Great."

She gave me a sympathetic look. "Lyric, you're not crazy. You've had a traumatic experience, preceded by a traumatic childhood. Trauma exacerbated by an un-diagnosed neurodivergent disorder. You may be fragile, but you're not crazy."

"Same thing, different name."

I was flippant because I was terrible at goodbyes. I knew despite requests to keep in touch, I wouldn't. It always played out the same in the past. I'd call and email and make a nuisance of myself. Then I'd come to my senses and stop pestering people who wouldn't write or call me back.

It was nice to finally have a name for my "genius syndrome" as my father called it. Autism, I was autistic. Dr. Cade said if it were still in the DSM I would have been diagnosed with Asperger's Syndrome—as though it lightened the stigma surrounding my diagnosis. Though I'm glad I didn't get saddled with that. After reading online that Asperger's was a term coined by a Nazi, I was happy to leave it behind.

Dr. Cade encouraged me to alert my employers, but I chose to keep my diagnosis to myself, and I was glad I did. Otherwise, when those vampires took over Phoenix, they may have dragged me away, never to be seen again.

A constant point of contention between myself and Dr. Cade: She insisted they weren't real vampires but "troubled people who believed they were," I argued they were and showed her footage I found displaying their fangs and their super strength. She dismissed it as trickery. I stopped short of telling her what I'd seen with my own two eyes. I didn't want to end up like my former boss.

"Stop," I said aloud. I knew where my thoughts were going, and it would only upset me. I needed to focus on the joy of the situation. I was hundreds of miles away, in my new home in New Orleans.

Before the coup, I'd gone to New Orleans on vacation with a friend. I fell in love with the city straight away. I had the strangest sensation I'd been there before. The day I had to return to Phoenix was the day I decided I would go back to New Orleans in the fall. I was originally going to visit on another vacation. I ended up relocating instead.

I reached into my pocket and took out my phone. I opened Eris, my favorite chat app. I saw a message from Psyche. She wanted to know how I was.

EratoONine: Finally done.

Psychepomp: About time!

EratoONine: Yeah, sorry for the delay. The boxes were heavy, and I didn't have any help.

Psychepomp: I thought you were going to hire movers.

EratoONine: This was cheaper.

Psychepomp: But not easier.

EratoONine: You got me.

Psychepomp: You're going to hurt yourself.

EratoONine: I'm fine.

Psychepomp: Liar. So, what are you doing tonight?

EratoONine: I'm going to take a shower and head downtown.

Psychepomp: Ooo! Anything fun planned?

EratoONine: Not really. Walk the Quarter, get some dinner.

Psychepomp: You should go to Port of Call! They have awesome burgers, and they serve them with baked potatoes.

EratoONine: I'll put a pin in that for another time. I'm not in the mood for beef today.

Psychepomp: Suit yourself. Take lots of pictures! I gotta go; the kids are home.

EratoONine: Give them my love. See you later.

She sent me a kiss emoji and went offline. I put the phone away and groaned as I got to my feet. I had overdone it because I just had to do everything myself. I admit it, I have difficulty asking for help. And yeah, I still managed to pull it off on my own, but at the cost of aching muscles and smelling like a dead water buffalo.

I showered, mentally checking out as I did. I stood under the spray of the warm water for a long time, until the water went cold and snapped me out of it. I finished washing off then stepped out of the shower and wrapped a towel around myself. As I left the bathroom, I realized I couldn't remember what the hell I was supposed to be doing. Then my phone chimed, and I picked it up from my desk.

Reminder—Get dressed. Bus leaves at 4:13

"Fuck," I hissed, and stumbled as I rushed to the closet to find something to wear. I had fifteen minutes otherwise I'd have to get a taxi. An expense I didn't need.

I hadn't blown the bank with the move, but I had spent the damages check, most of my savings, and maxed out one of my credit cards. Not the smartest financial move but we all do crazy things when we're desperate. And I had been desperate for a change of scenery.

I pulled on a pair of jeans that were once black but turned gray with age. I had to roll up the cuffs because I could never seem to find jeans the right length. Regular were too short but tall were too long—the curse of being slightly taller than the average woman. I chose a loose white V-neck shirt and an olive-green Army vest.

The vest was because I thought the shirt was a bit too thin. I'm not well endowed, but I am curvy enough that it makes me self-conscious at times. I pulled on my favorite combat boots, the ones with purple laces and the roses embroidered on the side. I grabbed a black crossbody bag since the jeans had a hole in the pocket.

I ran a brush through my chin-length teal hair and pinned it back with black heart clips. My bangs were growing out, and I made a mental note to get them cut. I had a sprinkling of freckles on my nose and cheeks, and I considered putting on some foundation. But I decided against it. I thought they complimented my light-brown eyes. I slipped on my fidget necklace, pulled on my fingerless gloves and my cadet cap, and ran out the door.

As I walked around the side of the house, I heard a voice call, "Hey, new girl!"

"Afternoon, gentlemen," I said as I came around the front.

Jaime and Sawyer sat on the front porch. They were drinking bourbon and people watching as usual. Jaime was a Hispanic man who worked as a restoration architect. And his husband Sawyer was a Black man who wrote mysteries. They were both in their golden years, but neither seemed to have the inclination to retire. I'd met them the first day I'd come to view the apartment. They were very social and liked to spend their free days shooting the breeze and drinking.

"And where are you going, young lady?" Sawyer asked in a mock stern tone.

"Downtown," I replied.

I looked at their earlobes as I talked. I hated making eye contact with people, but then again folks would get suspicious if you didn't look them in the face. So, I'd look at their ears, or at a point past their shoulders. It was also why I usually wore sunglasses. I swapped my regular glasses out for my round black sunglasses while I stopped and chatted. Being social with the neighbors was not an activity I was used to. However, I was in the South, and in New Orleans especially, you were expected to talk to people.

"Anything special planned for tonight?" asked Jaime.

"I'm going out to eat and poke around. Not too much though. I still have a lot of unpacking to do."

"If you need any help, you know where to find us," said Sawyer.

"Thank you. Please excuse me, the bus will be here soon, and I don't want to miss it."

"Do you know when you'll be back?" Sawyer raised an eyebrow.

"Around nine. I like to get out of the Quarter before prime intoxication hours."

"Good call. See you later."

I nodded and walked out of the gate. As I crossed the street, I smiled to myself. Sawyer and Jaime were sweet old gentlemen. They worried themselves silly about their neighbors. They knew I was on my own and the nearest relation I had was a sister who lived in California.

A sister I hadn't spoken to in over a decade. I thought I'd made a mistake when I divulged this to them. But upon hearing I was alone they decided to informally adopt me. It was nice, and while I hadn't said so aloud, I appreciated the gesture.

As I approached the church, the location of the bus stop, I couldn't contain a swell of excitement. I lived in New Orleans! I had an apartment! I wasn't visiting; this was my home now. I turned to face the house and I couldn't stop a smile spreading across my face.

The old house looked like something out of a Southern Gothic horror novel. It was a Greek Revival style mansion with a New Orleans twist. It had a big front porch as well as a second-floor gallery above it. The house was painted a soft yellow once upon a time, though God only knew the last time it had a fresh coat. The columns were off white, while the shutters were a faded hunter green. From a distance, the house looked quite grand. Up close, you could see it was elegantly decaying.

The walls were in desperate need of a good pressure wash. Bits of wood were missing from the columns, and rust crept up every bit of the cast iron fence. The front gate was in pieces, and several of the flagstones were cracked or missing.

The courtyard to the side of the house was paved with

interlaced bricks, and moss grew through the cracks. The yard was full of crab grass and wildflowers, though the maintenance man still mowed it once a week. Unfortunately, he wasn't as diligent about cutting back the bamboo, which was starting to overtake some of the oak trees.

At the back of the property was a pool I think was installed sometimes in the 1920s. It was empty and surrounded by another cast iron fence. The gate had been secured with a heavy chain and padlock that had long ago rusted shut. I couldn't see much of the pool itself, but a little green face was carved into the side under one of the ladders. It reminded me of an image of the Green Man, a mythological figure I'd once seen in a book on paganism.

The hall of the main house was where everyone got their mail. It was furnished with a sofa and two chairs I'm certain were scavenged from an estate sale sometime in the 1930s. A large mirror stood on top of an old sideboard. It had two hurricane lamps decorated with brass cherubs. The blue shag carpet was as old as the chairs. And the balustrade on the staircase would wobble if you looked at it let alone touched it.

The old mansion was split into apartments sometime in the 1980s, each one being of a different size. The first apartment I looked at was well out of my price range and was on the second floor—a one-bedroom that gave me a really weird vibe. Especially since even with the curtains open in the middle of the day it was still dark inside. There was a creeping feeling around my torso the whole time I was there. Like someone had hugged me, then let go. It sent a shiver down my spine.

In the end, it wasn't for me, and I said so. I was ready to leave and look elsewhere, until I was told there was also a small studio available.

And they meant small; only 350 square feet. But when I set foot inside, I loved it immediately. It got more light than the other apartment. It was more affordable and was on the first floor. Most importantly, it was at the back of the house so I wouldn't be disturbed by the foot traffic on the main road. The rent was cheap because the apartment was small, and it wasn't even on the market yet. They were supposed to post it later that month. There was no need; I took the apartment.

I was stirred out of my thoughts by the bus as it pulled up to the stop. I took out my phone and scanned the ticket, then went and sat near the rear doors. Excitement was bubbling up. My first outing as a New Orleanian! I made sure my earbud headphones were fully charged and I tugged at my fingerless gloves out of habit. I put on some music and stared out the window so I could memorize the route.

I've never been great at giving verbal directions, but I was good at memorizing landmarks and maps. I shivered as we passed by the streetcar line on St. Charles. I rubbed my arms and frowned. Another chill? In this weather? Strange.

Little did I know, strange was about to encompass my entire life.

Chapter Two

AFTER A SIMPLE dinner of half a muffuletta and Zapp's chips at Napoleon House, I wasn't ready to return home. I knew I had more unpacking to do, but after such a long and arduous day I wanted to enjoy myself. I wasn't interested in drinking or exploring the usual tourist traps.

So I decided to hike along the Moonwalk. It's a scenic path along the Mississippi River. It has great views of Algiers and the Crescent City Connection. It's surprisingly peaceful given its proximity to the French Quarter. I had my headphones in, my gloves on, and I was ready and set. I swapped my sunglasses for my regular glasses again as the sun was going down.

As I strolled beside the river, I couldn't help a giggle. I was in New Orleans; this wasn't a dream or a hallucination. I'd been living here for two months, but now I had my own place. I was where I wanted to be. I could start over from scratch. Maybe I could make some real-life friends for a change, though I wouldn't hold my breath.

One thing people didn't seem to understand, autism doesn't make you antisocial. Some autistic people are, and some aren't. Personally, I love talking to people; the problem is I don't understand nonverbal cues. Or when someone is joking or being sarcastic.

I also have a tendency to be blunt, which I worked on with my online friends. Psyche had been the biggest help in this regard, seeing as she had the most experience with two of her kids. She could explain things to me in a way I understood and help me rephrase what I wanted to say so it was more polite.

Don't misunderstand, I never want to hurt someone's feelings. If I get even a hint that I've hurt someone, I get pretty upset. But growing up, I didn't understand that when someone asks you to be honest it's best to soften the blow. It's a lesson I learned the hard way over the years. I thought I was getting better at it, or at the very least no one had yelled at me for rudeness lately. Regardless, I was still hyperaware of what was considered rude or polite.

I did find the social dance tedious and exhausting. Which was why so many of my friendships were online. Text and reaction gifs, while sometimes confusing, were a good way to communicate how you feel. They were also helpful in deciphering the feelings of others. But as much as I loved my pocket friends, I was still lonely. It wasn't normal for a person to be alone 99 percent of the time. People are pack animals, we need community. Something I was in desperate need of.

I was drawn out of my thoughts as I approached the Moonwalk steps. It's a staircase that leads down into the Mississippi itself. Though sometimes when the river is low it only hovers in the air like some bizarre art installation. Not this time though. The river was swollen from recent rainfall, and I could see something moving around in the water.

I trod carefully as I descended and was rewarded when I saw it was a river otter. I made a very unattractive screeching noise and took out my phone. Quickly I snapped several photos of the little creature.

"Oh my God, you're so cute!" I squealed.

The otter wasn't the least bit bothered, and it seemed as though it was used to humans. Or at least not afraid of me making an idiot of myself while I took pictures. I sat down and watched the otter after I'd taken at least a dozen photos. I couldn't wait to show them to Psyche.

A breeze kicked up, sending a chill down my spine—something one certainly does not expect in New Orleans. I had that strange feeling around my ribs again like someone was embracing me. It raised goose bumps on my arms and shoulders. I hugged myself and rubbed my arms to try to get rid of them.

I knew in my head that the cold breeze was likely from the river, but the hugging sensation? What was behind that? Maybe my vest was on too tight or something.

It wasn't late, but it was dark. Distantly I could hear the jazz band that played on the street corner in front of the Cafe du Monde. Their song was slow but not mournful, and I found myself humming along even though I didn't know the tune. The streetlights were bright, even on the Moonwalk, but it was harder to see. I'd have to move on soon, but I wanted to see what the otter was doing. It would dive down, come back up for a moment or two, then dive again.

"It's after the crawfish," a voice behind me said.

I looked over my shoulder. A young white woman sat near me.

"Pardon?"

"Sometimes crawfish will hang out down there. Otters are crazy for 'em so they'll come over and try to catch as many as they can. Wrong time of year though, it won't be crawfish season until next spring," she said.

The woman wore a sheer coral shirt with little cherry blossoms made of plastic gems on the collar. Underneath it was a white camisole. She had paired this with lacy mint-colored short shorts and white sneakers. Her blonde hair was in a messy half bun, with her forelocks framing her heart-shaped face. She had thin lips, a button nose, and wide, round hazel eyes.

I figured she had to be local, as she wasn't carrying a backpack or anything of the kind. Also, she was talking to me the same way Sawyer and Jaime did. Normally, I would have clammed up. But Dr. Cade did say that I needed to make an effort to talk to people. And one of the social rules of New Orleans was to talk, even to strangers. So, I started talking.

"I like your outfit," I said.

"Thank you, I made the shorts myself," she replied.

"Really? They're lovely."

"Wish my date thought so. I'm not sure where he is."

"Oh? Were you meeting him here?"

She shook her head. "No, at Jackson Square but he never showed. I suppose I'm all dressed up with nowhere to go." She laughed.

"So am I. I mean, I'm not dressed up. But I have nowhere to go," I said. "My name is Lyric."

"Heather," she replied. She didn't offer to shake hands, which I was grateful for. Even with the gloves on, a handshake would be uncomfortable for me.

I smiled. "It's nice to meet you, Heather."

"So where are you staying?"

"Coliseum Street. And you?"

Heather laughed. "Oh, I'm not visiting. I'm originally from Mandeville but I live in the Marigny."

"Are you close to Esplanade or Elysian Fields?"

"Esplanade. I'm living in my stepdaddy's house. He retired to Florida last year. But he didn't want to get rid of the house since it belonged to his great-grandmother."

"Is your mother from Mandeville then?"

"You're quick. Yes, she was. Mama and Daddy moved to New Orleans together when they first got married. But my daddy left after Mama got pregnant. Then she met my stepdaddy and he and Mama fell in love. After I was born, they didn't want me growing up in the city, so we went back to Mama's hometown."

The otter had departed by this time, and it was well past sunset. I had to go home. I got to my feet and offered a hand to Heather so I could help her stand. Her hand was freezing cold. Like a velvet-wrapped icicle. When she stood, she was shorter than I expected. Probably around five foot two.

"I think I'm gonna head home," Heather said.

"Would you like an escort? I could walk you part of the way."

"I'd appreciate that. I forgot my keys at home and my mace is attached."

"Happy to help. Where are we going?"

"Down this way."

We walked, and I asked, "Are you on Eris?"

"What's that?"

"I'm going to take that as a no. It's a chat app, it's how I keep in touch with people."

She chuckled. "You could take my phone number instead."

I shrugged. "Yeah. But I don't use my phone for talking. Strictly texting. I'm on the phone all day for work."

"Telemarketer?"

"Remote business office. We handle financial aid for hospital bills."

"Ah. Sounds frustrating."

"It can be, but it's also rewarding. I like helping people, even if it's only so they're not going bankrupt from medical bills."

"Those add up. I remember when I went into the ER three years ago after my car accident. I only just paid those bills off recently," said Heather.

I sighed. "Yeah, the cost of medical care in this country is ridiculous."

"No kidding. So where are you visiting from?"

"I'm not. To clarify, when I said I'm on Coliseum, I didn't mean I'm visiting from out of town. I live here."

I felt a tingle of pride as I said it, and I smiled.

"Oh yeah? How long ago?"

"About two months. I was staying at Miss Sophie's in the Bywater."

"I know that place. It's run by the gal with the disco suit and the guitar, right?"

"Yeah. She has a long-term suite that I paid the first couple months for until I found my own place. But I just moved into my own apartment this week."

"Cool. I've always been curious about what it's like to move to a new city. But then again, I'm happy in Louisiana. I couldn't see myself living anywhere else," she said, and I caught a hint of pride in her voice.

"It must be nice to have a hometown."

"Where are you from?"

I shoved my hands in my pockets and shook my head. "I don't know how to answer that question. We moved so much when I was a kid, but we did finally settle down in my first year of high school. And as an adult, I seem to have kept the habit. I lived in Phoenix before I moved here."

"Phoenix? Where the coup happened?"

I nodded.

"Were you there?"

I nodded again. I didn't like the direction this conversation was going in.

Heather raised an eyebrow but to my relief, she didn't press further. "So, why'd you move here?"

"As silly as it sounds, I felt as though I belonged."

"I'm guessing you've been to New Orleans before."

"Yes, I was on vacation here with a friend. I'm not sure what I was expecting. I think I assumed New Orleans would be like many of the old cities and towns I've visited in the South. Atlanta, St. Augustine, Charleston, Savannah, Mobile, I've been to them all. There is something very different here. It has an energy that makes me feel as though at last I've found a home. Which is a rare feeling for me."

She giggled. "The curse got you too."

I blinked and paused. "Beg pardon?"

"It's not a literal curse," Heather explained. "It's something I've seen happen before. Not to everyone, mind you, or we'd have a population bigger than New York City. Some folks...they come to town and it's like a spell's been cast on them. Suddenly they have to move to New Orleans, they won't be happy anywhere else, and you can't change their mind. I call it the Crescent City Curse."

"I see. Do you meet a lot of people like me?"

"Enough of them that I know the type. I used to wait tables at the Cafe du Monde. I've seen plenty of folks just like you. Agonizing over returning to wherever they came from while stuffing themselves with beignets."

I nearly laughed. I'd done the same thing on my last day in New Orleans. I told Candace it was only fitting that our last meal be beignets and cafe au lait at the Cafe du Monde. I was convinced I wouldn't have another beignet for at least a year or so. I wanted to savor the meal for as long as I could.

We were approaching Governor Nicholls Wharf. I said, "We're getting close to Esplanade. Where do you want me to drop you off?"

"I changed my mind. I think I'll go to the club. It's in the Bywater, but you don't have to walk with me. It's over a mile away."

"Will you be all right on your own?"

"Yeah, I've walked it before."

I didn't like the sound of that. To get to the Bywater she'd have to go through Seventh Ward and neither location was the safest at night. But when I turned to Heather to offer to go with her, I gasped. She was glowing! A golden light emanated from her, and the overall effect was unearthly. Her eyes widened in horror as she looked at her hands and arms. "What the *hell*?"

"I...I don't know," I stammered.

Heather stepped off the path. She started walking toward the riverbank.

"Wait," I yelled and ran after her. She was moving so fast!

"I can't stop," she shrieked. "Something's got me, it's pulling me in!"

She tripped and slid along the ground as though something was dragging her. I pursued her but then stopped when I saw it.

A body floated in the water. A body in a coral shirt and mint shorts. I collapsed to my knees, my brain grinding to a halt as though I'd blown a fuse. It was Heather's body. For a moment, I had the notion that perhaps she was injured, or in need of rescue. But my experience in Phoenix taught me what a corpse looks like. And I was looking at one. Heather was gone; all that remained of her was the empty shell caught in the pylons of the wharf.

"Not again," I whispered to myself.

For the longest time, I didn't move. I was berating myself inside my head, shouting everything I needed to do. I would need to call someone. After an eternity, I was able to lift my arm.

I took my phone out of my purse and dialed 9-1-1. A wave of calm washed over me as I told the dispatcher to please send the police. I told her what I'd found, where to find me, and that I would wait for the cops to get there.

Then I hung up and sat in the grass. I was shutting down like I always did when confronted with stress. Or trauma. As my brain switched to disaster mode, I lamented that Heather was dead. She would have been a good friend if she weren't a hallucination.

That left one question. How did I hallucinate a perfect copy of a woman who was already dead?

Chapter Three

I STAYED AS revulsion and curiosity warred inside me. I watched as they pulled her body from the water. I wasn't close, but what I could see was not pretty. She was completely white like there wasn't a single drop of blood left in her body. Worst of all was her neck. It looked as though someone tried to chop her head off and gave up halfway through. Her dead eyes stared at me until they covered her with a blanket and took her away.

After talking to the police and giving them my contact information, I wanted to go home. It was difficult as I was experiencing sensory overload and had to communicate with a text app on my phone. I couldn't face taking the bus, but one of the officers offered to give me a ride.

I knew I would probably be "out of words" as I put it for a while. Sometimes, when I'm too stressed out, I can't speak. Dr. Cade said it's not unusual for autistic people to revert to a nonverbal state when they get overloaded. And I was no exception.

When I got into the back seat, I glanced to my right out of habit. I had to muffle a scream.

Sitting next to me in the car was Heather! She looked the same as when I'd seen her on the Moonwalk. Her expression was cold and distant. I took a deep breath and exhaled. She wasn't real, she couldn't be real.

"Where are we going?" Heather asked.

I blinked and shook my head. Maybe I could make

her go away. But no, when I opened my eyes, she was still there. I had to ignore her. If the cops saw me talking to myself, I would spend the night in jail for sure. Luckily, the officers up front were chatting about some game coming up. I'm not a sports person so I had no idea what they were babbling about. I shivered and turned to my phone. I needed to text Psyche; pronto.

EratoONine: You around?

Psychepomp: Yeah, kids are in bed. What's up?

EratoONine: I think I'm having a psychotic break.

Psychepomp: Shit, really? What's going on?

EratoONine: I'm seeing a woman who's dead.

Psychepomp: How do you know she's dead?

EratoONine: I saw her body in the river.

Psychepomp: Jesus! Are you okay?

I snorted aloud, but no one heard me.

EratoONine: No.

Psychepomp: I guess that was a stupid question.

EratoONine: Yes.

Psychepomp: Where are you right now?

EratoONine: In the back of a squad car, cops are

giving me a ride home.

Psychepomp: Is there anyone who can help you?

EratoONine: Maybe my neighbors? But I don't want to put this on them. I only met them a couple days ago.

Psychepomp: Okay, as soon as you get home let me know. We can do a video call to keep you grounded. What about your therapist?

EratoONine: She's not my therapist anymore, remember?

Psychepomp: Right right, I forgot.

The conversation lasted the entire trip home. When the cops pulled up in front of my building, I thanked them as best I could, though I was stuttering so much I'd be surprised if they could understand me. They appeared to infer it anyway and one said, "You're welcome." The other reminded me to call the detective if I remembered anything else.

Jaime and Sawyer were still on the porch when I walked through the gate. I could smell the bourbon from ten feet away, accompanied by the scent of cheap cigars. Sawyer had his tablet out and he and Jaime were watching a video. They laughed so loud it echoed through the night. They'd be no help even if I did ask. They were wasted.

"Hey, neighbor! How was your night?" Jaime asked.

I tried to make myself talk, but it was like trying to force my mouth open after being wired shut. I typed out on my phone, *Exhausted, can't talk. Bed,* then used the speak function to play it for them.

Sawyer said, "Oh, oh! Yeah, okay, get some sleep."

I waved and walked down the flagstone path until I got to the courtyard. A chill raced down my spine, and I knew that Heather was right behind me. My hands shook as I unlocked the door and let myself in. I slammed it behind me and locked it. When I turned around, sure enough, there was Heather.

She sat on my bed and said, "So, this is awkward."

I ignored her and went to my desk. I booted up my laptop, which took longer than I would have liked. As I waited for it to come on, Heather kept talking.

"I can't believe I'm dead! Like, how? Why? And how come you're the only person who can see me?"

I collapsed into my desk chair. I was determined not to look at her or acknowledge her.

"Excuse me, Miss Attitude, I know you can see me. And I know damn well you can hear me."

Finally, I was able to log into my laptop. I pulled up Eris and typed a message to Psyche.

EratoONine: Home

Psychepomp: One moment.

A bell chimed, and the video chat screen opened. Psyche was at her desk in her home office. Her chin-length honey-brown hair was a little mussed, but her brown eyes were focused. She wore a black T-shirt with a red flannel shirt over it, so she likely wasn't on her way to bed. At least I hadn't disrupted her evening routine.

The walls behind her were decorated with various geeky decor. It ranged from Marvel movies to her beloved *Supernatural.* I knew her students loved it. When she wasn't raising her kids or telling off bigots, Psyche was a homeschool teacher.

"Hey sweetie, are you okay?"

I shook my head and signed "no."

I learned ASL a few years back. The idea was when stress rendered me nonverbal, I could still communicate. I wasn't fluent, but I knew enough to make myself understood. Sadly, there aren't many people outside the deaf community who know sign language. So, I often use my phone instead. I was fortunate that Psyche knew ASL, which she'd learned for work.

"What's happening right now?"

"Stop ignoring me! Do you even know how rude you're being right now?" Heather shrieked.

I winced, then signed to Psyche, "She's sitting on the bed and she's yelling at me. I don't know how to make her go away."

"Did you have hallucinations when you were seeing Dr. Cade?"

I shook my head.

"I'm not a hallucination, I'm a ghost," Heather said.

"Have you had hallucinations before?" Psyche asked.

I nodded.

She frowned. "When?"

"When I was a child. And on and off through high school. Dad said it was ghosts, Mom said I was crazy."

"Ghosts?"

I nodded again. "The hallucination says she's a ghost."

"You're talking about me but not to me? Rude!" Heather huffed and crossed her arms.

Psyche pressed on. "You said this hallucination looks like the woman you found in the water?"

I shook my head. "Doesn't look like her, is her."

I explained about the incident on the Moonwalk and what happened at the wharf. When I was done, Psyche frowned.

"Okay so, I'm going to ask you to do something for me."

"Okay."

"Take your glasses off and look at her."

I raised an eyebrow but did as she asked. Heather was still there, but she was fuzzy. Just like everything else when I took them off. I put them back on after a moment or two.

"Was she fuzzy or clear?"

"Fuzzy."

Psyche pursed her lips. "Hm, I was afraid of this. Can she hear me?"

"Yeah," Heather said. "I'm not deaf, though she seems to be all of a sudden."

"She just yelled at you."

"What did you say her name is?"

"Heather."

Psyche moved out of view for a moment, and I could hear her going through her desk drawers. When she was back, she had a compact mirror in her hand. "Heather, would you stand behind Lyric, please?"

Heather rolled her eyes but did as Psyche asked. I shivered. The closer Heather got, the colder I became.

Psyche turned around so her back was facing the camera. Then she held the mirror up so she could see the screen over her shoulder. "That's a powerful ghost right there."

My jaw dropped. I signed, "What's she look like?"

"Blonde hair, pink shirt, green shorts." Psyche turned

back around and put the mirror on her desk. "I'd say you're a medium, Lyric."

"That would explain it," Heather said.

I went still and retreated into my own head. I could hear Psyche talking, presumably to Heather since Psyche had seen me disassociate before.

I've heard it called zoning out, turning off, or as Psyche called it, a mental retreat. How long it lasted and how far I sunk inside myself depended on how much stress I'd experienced. And frankly, I had enough to last a month. The only problem was it could be pretty inconvenient, and it would take a while for me to snap out of it.

Was Psyche right? Was I some kind of psychic medium? If this was true, then it meant that so much of what I experienced as a child was real. It wasn't a figment of my imagination as my mother said. The implication that I wasn't crazy, I could in fact see and speak with the dead, was not comforting.

My thoughts turned toward death itself. Death could get anyone at any time. It could claim me right now, in my home where I was supposed to be safe. A stroke or an aneurysm or something. I could end up like Heather, wandering the Earth, with no one who could see me or speak to me, except for another medium.

My chest hurt, and I knew I was having a full-blown meltdown. I pushed myself away from the desk and went to the closet. I trembled as the tears came. I knocked a few things over as I looked for the right box. I cursed myself for not unpacking sooner. Finally, I found it. I pulled out my weighted blanket.

I dragged the blanket to the bed and collapsed. I curled into a fetal position under the blanket, and I cried.

I didn't know what else to do. Dr. Cade's advice came into my head, and I took a deep breath. Or at least tried to. I was still crying too hard to manage significant respirations. When I did, I breathed in for a count of four, held it for a count of seven, and exhaled over a count of eight.

It took longer than I would have liked to get myself to calm down. By then, I was too tired to close the laptop or even let Psyche know I was okay. It didn't help that I was embarrassed. I always was when I had a meltdown. Grown adults didn't throw tantrums like a toddler. Except I did, because emotional regulation was not something I excelled at. I balked at the negative thought, and I had to tell myself it wasn't a tantrum. I was simply overwhelmed and that could happen to anyone. Everyone handled being overwhelmed differently.

I was so exhausted it was no surprise I fell asleep.

As I drifted between being awake and asleep, I heard footsteps. For a moment, I wasn't sure if it was a dream or if it was real. But when I saw a thick plastic window, a bus seat, and a 7-Eleven going by, I knew. It wasn't a dream; it was a memory. I fought to wake up, but it was to no avail. I would have to ride it out.

It was after dark, and I was walking to my apartment. I was held up at work because I received a call on an important case right before I was supposed to clock out. No one wanted to be out after dark, not since Caleb Blake and his band of psychos took over. I couldn't just leave the client hanging. She was a single mother of four, and the bills for her youngest child's heart surgery could bankrupt her.

Even in the face of unprecedented times, the wheels

of commerce still turned. It made me sick to think about it. A whole city was held hostage by vampires. Yet people still insisted on behaving as though it was business as usual. The only difference being now there was a much higher chance of dying. But I still needed a paycheck and people like Mrs. Randon's son still needed surgery.

I caught the bus home, nervous because the sun was already down. While I wasn't supposed to be on the menu so to speak, I didn't go out after dark anymore. No human did. When I got off at my stop, I slipped into the apartment complex through the back parking lot. I thought it would call less attention to myself. And it might have if it were still daylight.

I turned the corner to go check the mail, and in front of the mailboxes, I saw three vampires. All three wore cowboy hats. So not only were they vamps, they also worked directly for Caleb Blake. My heart sank into my stomach. I pretended as though I hadn't seen them and headed in the direction of my apartment.

The ploy failed. One of the vampires called after me, "Hey, honey, you looking for a good time?"

"Thank you for the offer, but my boyfriend is waiting for me. Please excuse me," I said over my shoulder. I kept walking. The lie stuck in my throat, but it was one I used often enough that I didn't stutter.

Their footsteps crunched on the decorative gravel that surrounded the paths of the complex. They were following me. Fuck!

"Forget your boyfriend, come here."

"No, again, thank you but it's been a long day." I tried to keep my voice calm, but I still picked up my pace.

One of the vampires appeared in front of me. I backed away and bumped into another. My heart was in my throat, and I clutched my purse to my chest. The vampire who spoke to me grinned as he threw an arm around my shoulders. "C'mon, sweetie, don't be like that. We'll be nice."

I screamed myself awake.

For a minute, I couldn't move, but I didn't panic. I'd had night terrors since I was old enough to remember. It was practically routine by this point. I waited until the paralysis passed, then slowly I sat up.

The lights were out. My laptop was closed. And Heather sat in my desk chair.

"You okay?" she asked.

"Nightmare," I muttered. I grabbed the bottle of water I kept by the bed and twisted off the cap. I drained about half of it, then I asked, "So you're not a figment of my imagination?"

"Nope, I'm a ghost. And I'm haunting you."

"Why me?"

"Because you can see me. And I want to know why I died."

I ran a hand through my hair. "I'm not a private eye, I'm a benefits counselor." I frowned. Where the hell was my hat? I wasn't wearing it when I came home. I made a mental note to check my purse. If it wasn't in there, I probably lost it at the Moonwalk.

"I was drawn to you for a reason," Heather replied. "And I think that reason is you can give me closure so I can move on."

I didn't answer. I pushed the weighted blanket off and slowly untied my boots. It had been a harder evening than most. If I drank, I would need a drink. I was careful to watch my breathing so I would stay nice and calm. I didn't need to restart my meltdown.

"I didn't turn off the computer," I said.

"I closed it. Psyche said to message her when you snap out of it no matter what time it is."

I nodded and grabbed my phone, which had been moved to my bedside table. I sent her a quick message to let her know I was resting. There was no reply, which did not surprise me since it was after 2:00 a.m. She was likely asleep.

My throat felt scratchy when I swallowed, and I was sure I was dehydrated. I was barely hanging on by a thread after everything that transpired. The nightmare was the icing on the terrible cake. The revelation ghosts were real, I'm not crazy (at least not about ghosts), and there was an afterlife? I shook my head. I knew when to tap out.

"I'm sorry," I said to Heather. "I can't do it. I can't investigate your death."

Heather crossed her arms over her stomach and glared at me. "We'll see about that."

Chapter Four

UNFORTUNATELY, HEATHER WAS very persistent. At first, she was just a little annoying. She confined herself to snide comments or begging for my help while I unpacked. Once everything was in its proper place, she thought that would be a good time to press the point again. When I still refused, Heather's attitude changed. She became more destructive.

It started off simply enough. She'd bother me during work calls or jump out and surprise me when I got out of the shower. But then it escalated. Late one night, she undid the pins on the hanging rack in my kitchen. Several pots and pans clattered to the floor and scared the living daylights out of me. My pulse raced so much that I thought I would have a heart attack.

This was not helpful as I had nightmares all week. As soon as I closed my eyes, I would be ensnared in past trauma, unable to break free. The strange part was each time I would see something out of the corner of my eye. It seemed to be a flash of gray, but I could never get a good look at it. Heather was indifferent to my lack of sleep. She said, "Dead people don't need to sleep, Lyric," in a sweet tone so fake that it made me gag.

So, the destruction continued. She hid work files, and she threw out spices I needed for cooking. She even threw the remote for my TV out the window and wouldn't tell me what she'd done with it. How I continued to work under such conditions is a mystery. Or a miracle. But I finally reached my limit one morning two weeks after I found Heather's body, which was the first Saturday of September.

I was already in a pretty poor mood. I wanted to go to Southern Decadence, the pride event that New Orleans hosts on Labor Day Weekend. The French Quarter would be filled to the brim with people celebrating being queer in the most colorful and outrageous ways possible. Originally, I intended to go to the parade so I could get out and socialize. But I was so tired from lack of sleep (and Heather's antics) I wanted my bed more than I wanted to go out.

It started when I was once again startled out of sleep. The sun was rising, and light flowed through the transom window above the front door. I hadn't purchased a curtain for it yet, as it was so high up that I had no hope of reaching it without a ladder. I was a bit hazy as I woke, and when I glanced at the alarm clock I sighed. Six a.m. on a Saturday. It was criminal to be awake so early. I decided to roll over and go back to sleep. But then I heard a loud plastic snap, and I sat up.

Heather stood by my music table, where I kept my multiplayer. It was one of those six-in-one jobs that played records, CDs, and cassette tapes. It also had a radio, an aux output, and a Bluetooth hook-up. I had all my CDs, tapes, and records stored in the cabinet beneath the multiplayer. It was a pretty sweet player, but that was nothing compared to my music collection.

I love music. I've always loved music, and at one point I even wanted to be a musician. I could sing and play piano, drums, guitar, and even the flute. But that requires better people skills than I have. And I don't like the thought of being the center of attention all the time. So instead, I collect music. My CD and tape collections were pretty formidable. I had over two hundred CDs and a hundred and fifty cassettes.

I only started collecting records two years ago. I didn't have quite so many, only about twenty, but what I did have I loved. I kept them in the bottom cabinet of the music table so they'd be safe. The cabinet was open, several of the records were scattered about, and Heather had a guilty look on her face.

She'd spent most of the previous night knocking over books, which were still strewn about. But my eyes were drawn to what was in her hands. A vintage record of Maria Callas's greatest hits. I'm not a huge opera fan, however, Maria Callas had a beautiful voice. And that record had a recording of her singing "Vissi d'arte" from Puccini's *Tosca*. It was a work of art, and Heather had destroyed it.

"I'm sorry! I was going to rearrange them. Put them in the wrong sleeves," Heather said.

I tossed the weighted blanket aside like it was nothing and launched myself out of bed. I grabbed the record from her, but it was no use. It was in two pieces, snapped right down the middle. There was no way to repair it. And I wasn't sure I could replace it. I hadn't built my savings back from the move just yet.

"I'm really sorry," she said. Her tone was subdued, but I was too angry to care.

"Shut up," I snapped. I placed the record on the table and turned away. I stubbed my toe on one of the books and I shrieked. The pain was so bad I literally hopped on one foot like a cartoon character. I managed to navigate the rest of the mess and went to my dresser.

I changed out of my sleep shirt and into a violet sports

bra, gray tank top, and black yoga pants. I made sure it was the pair with pockets.

"Where are you going?" Heather asked.

I pulled on my socks and sneakers. "Out, and don't you dare follow me. Or I'm going to ask the preacher at the church across the street to exorcise you," I snapped.

Heather snorted. "Like he'd believe in ghosts."

"Oh, you think not? Well, I'm sure he'd be fine with a house blessing, and I bet that'd get you out!"

This either hadn't occurred to Heather or it genuinely worried her, as her eyes widened.

Then she shrugged. "You wouldn't do that."

"Oh yes I would," I yelled. "Do you have any idea what this has been like for me? Do you think I want you to suffer? I don't! But I also don't want to suffer myself, and out of the two of us I'm the one who's still alive."

"You selfish asshole! You don't care if I can move on or not!"

"You're damn right I don't! If you wanted me to care? Then maybe we should have gotten to know each other over the past two weeks. Instead, you decided to be petty and selfish and now you've broken something I can't fix. And I can't replace it because at the moment I don't have two quarters to rub together." I crossed my arms and glared at her. "So why, exactly, would I want to help you?"

I didn't wait for an answer. I grabbed my keys, headphones, and phone and I left.

I set off down Coliseum at a faster than normal pace. Which is why I tripped on a bit of broken sidewalk. I caught myself on an oak tree before I could face-plant right into the street. It was enough to shake me out of my anger. At least enough to pay attention to my surroundings.

The Garden District was known for its trees, shrubs, and of course, gardens. Most houses had something planted in front of them, even ours. I wondered if it was for show or for privacy. I'd only lived there a short time, but the strangers gawking at the neighborhood day in and day out made me nervous. It was almost as though they didn't realize the buildings they so admired were people's homes. I wondered if Candace and I had been just as clueless.

We rarely communicated since our vacation. The coup hadn't helped. The Bad Hats, as I called them, weren't tech-savvy. But they knew people who were. For my own safety, I'd scrubbed my online presence and asked Psyche's husband Frank to take care of the rest. I was incredibly lucky he happened to be a cybersecurity expert.

Afterward, when I recovered my accounts and got into contact, I made the mistake of telling a few friends what I saw. While they didn't say they thought I was lying, or crazy, we hadn't spoken since. Candace was one of them. Psyche supported me, as did Nathana and a few others. Though sometimes I wondered if they really believed me or were humoring me.

When Psyche used the mirror trick and saw Heather, I knew she believed. And she had some helpful tips to keep Heather in line. I hadn't used any of them as I didn't want to hurt Heather's feelings. She was already so upset that I refused to look into her death. Now I wasn't so worried. She broke something irreplaceable, and I wasn't in the most charitable frame of mind.

I shook my head and walked faster. It was still early, but a local coffee shop was open. A latte would cheer me up, and if it didn't then the caffeine would.

The sun grew brighter, and the neighborhood awakened. The birds kicked up a ruckus well before dawn, but now that it was light out, the crows were cawing and hopping about. There were many of them in the Garden District, and some folks like Jaime liked to feed them. I read somewhere once that crows remember people, which is why I don't antagonize them. Sometimes I even give them little snacks.

Residents were out on their porches or in their yards, picking up newspapers or taking out the trash. It was early enough the tourists weren't out yet. I waved and said "good morning" to anyone I saw, though I didn't take my headphones out. It was considered rude to ignore your neighbors, something I'd learned the hard way in the Bywater. This was why if you were walking anywhere in New Orleans, it was best to have an extra thirty minutes of time to kill. Just in case you ran into someone and had to stop to chat.

I saw a Caribbean-blue-and-white building ahead, the iconic Commander's Palace. I'd only been once while on vacation, and it wouldn't be open so early in the morning. Even if it were, I couldn't afford to eat there right now. As I turned onto Washington and strolled past the restaurant, I glanced across the street.

Lafayette Cemetery stood as gray and desolate as ever. It had been closed for years, allegedly for repairs and restoration work. As far as I was aware no one had actually seen workers inside. I always got a weird feeling whenever I was near it, though not an unpleasant sensation. I stilled for a moment and looked over at the gate. I was almost disappointed to see no one was there.

Then I scolded myself and kept walking until I got to Prytania and Washington. There was some traffic, and the light at the intersection was always out of order. I waited for my opportunity to cross the street, which didn't take long.

I arrived at the Rink. It was a mini mall that housed a few stores and had been around forever. My favorite store was the Garden District Book Shop, which I found quite charming. I tried not to spend too much time there because I would eventually end up buying something. But the bookstore wasn't on the agenda that day, the coffee shop was.

There were three coffee shops within walking distance of my apartment. Starbucks, PJ's, and Morning Brew. I'd never liked the coffee at Starbucks because it tasted like someone was mocking me. And while PJ's was more of a local chain, it was still a chain and their coffee was only so-so. Plus, I'd made the mistake of eating a macaron there once, and it was a mistake I would not repeat.

Morning Brew, however, was locally owned. It had one location, and their coffee tasted like someone loved their job. When I arrived, Delia smiled at me when I came in. She was an older woman with salt and pepper hair, a lot of curves, and a personality as big as her heart. Which was, to say, enormous. I wasn't clear on if she was the owner or the manager, but I'd heard she'd worked at Morning Brew since it opened.

She waited for me to take out my headphones and said, "Morning, Lyric! What can I get you?"

"Caramel latte, please, medium size. And do you have any of those little quiches?"

"Yeah, baked a fresh batch this morning. Which one do you want?"

"Quiche Lorraine, please."

"Coming up!" Delia went to get the quiche, then said, "You're up early."

"Couldn't sleep," I replied.

"I'm sorry. Any plans for today?"

I tilted my head a bit as I thought about it. "You wouldn't happen to know if there are any used record stores around here, would you?" Even if I couldn't afford to replace the record it couldn't hurt to look for one.

"Sure do. Peaches over on Magazine and Napoleon. They've got a good selection."

I made a note of it on my phone and sat down by the front window. Delia appeared with my quiche, coffee, and silverware. I was looking up the address of the record store when a news alert popped up on my mobile browser. Curious, I clicked on it and was redirected to the local newspaper's web page. It was about Heather's death.

I'd set up an alert on her name for any information about her since I was the one who found her body and was haunted by her ghost. Call me an ass if you want, but I wasn't entirely sure her death was suspicious. I thought it best to keep an ear to the ground as a precaution.

The article restated the facts; how she was found at Governor Nicholls Wharf. Then there was an update with a statement from the New Orleans Police Department. They'd held a press conference the previous afternoon. I'd likely missed it due to work and Heather's shenanigans. I recognized the man in the article photo as the detective I spoke with at the scene.

There was a video at the bottom. I looked around, and there were more people in the coffee shop since I'd started reading. I didn't want to annoy anyone. I put my headphones in, connected them to my phone, and played the video. It was short and sweet. According to the detective, Heather committed suicide.

I frowned at that. How the hell had she committed suicide with a neck wound like that? Unless she had a guillotine at home it was pretty odd. And even if she did have said guillotine, how did her body get in the river? Did she give up on chopping off her own head and throw herself in the murky water?

One of the reporters at the press conference seemed to have the same thought process I did. He asked, "How do you explain the wounds on her body?"

"Those wounds were postmortem. We theorize that Miss Campbell took her own life by jumping off the Crescent City Connection. There are reports of a woman matching her description on the bridge two nights before her body was found. The wounds were likely caused by a propeller blade."

"Rubbish," I grumbled, then winced. I'd said it aloud.

I glanced up again to see if anyone overheard me. No one was staring at me, so I assumed they didn't notice. Despite my anger with Heather, the situation still struck me as odd. It didn't sit right with me, and I wanted to be 100 percent sure before I went home. I opened Eris and messaged Psyche.

EratoONine: Hey.

Psychepomp: What's up buttercup?

EratoONine: I need you to do me a favor. Well, I need Frank to do me a favor.

Psychepomp: Name it.

EratoONine: Can he get me a copy of a coroner's report?

Psychepomp: Probably. Give me the details, and I'll ask him.

I sent her the information, and Psyche went offline, presumably to talk to Frank. I went back to my coffee and breakfast. I was not getting involved. I simply wanted the report as a backup for when I talked to Heather. Or at least that's what I told myself.

Chapter Five

I SPENT THE next hour at Morning Brew. I watched people come in and leave and waited for Psyche to get back to me. I had another cup of coffee while I waited and read everything I could find on Detective Peters. He was in the newspaper more than one would think, given his profession. He either loved the spotlight or didn't mind taking the heat for the NOPD.

According to the articles, the New Orleans Police Department had an image problem. Pretty much from the get-go. They were considered corrupt, careless, and downright lazy. I wasn't exactly inclined to trust the police anyway, no matter how good or bad their reputation was. Not after what I'd seen as a kid.

When Psyche came back online, I sighed with relief.

EratoONine: Any luck?

Psychepomp: Check your email. You're signed into your VPN, right?

EratoONine: Always. I wouldn't make this sort of request where any jerk with the same Wi-Fi connection could read it.

Psychepomp: Clever girl.

EratoONine: *raptor noises*

I signed out of Eris and checked my email.

The coroner's report was short and sweet. They hadn't even bothered with toxicology. There wasn't enough blood in Heather's body to test anyway. The wounds to her neck were made by a sharp object consistent with a boat motor blade. But there was some tissue damage they couldn't explain. Photos documented the damage, but I decided to wait until I got home to look at them.

I got up and cleared my table. I passed the plate and cup to Delia.

"Thank you," I said and put a tip in the jar.

"No, thank you! See you later," she said and smiled.

I smiled back and left the shop.

More people were out, and a small tour group stood on the corner where I'd normally cross to get home. I weaved through them and crossed Washington and down Prytania. It would take me right by the cemetery, but it was easier than trying to walk past the tourists. They always clung together like an atom cluster, and if you tried to walk past, they'd speed up.

I slipped my phone into my pocket, my headphones turned off for once. My head was spinning from what I read. Dr. Cade said paranoia was normal after what I'd been through. It would have been comforting, except she didn't believe me. Not about the night I'd been cornered by three vampires.

A violent shudder went through me, and I gasped. It reminded me of one summer when I swam under a waterfall. I hadn't expected the water to be so cold. I thought my lungs would freeze in my chest. I stopped in my tracks and looked to my right.

I was in front of the main gate of Lafayette Cemetery.

I took a deep breath and exhaled to get some warm air into my lungs. I was still cold as an ice cube. The hair on the back of my neck stood up and I froze in fear. What the hell was happening to me?

Fingers combed through my hair. It didn't feel like normal fingers, more like bones touching my scalp. I jumped and ran my own hands back and forth through my hair. I came up with nothing.

"Beware," a voice whispered, so faint I wasn't sure it was real.

My eyes darted about. I looked for any sign I wasn't alone. The tour group was gone. Headed up Washington toward St. Charles Avenue no doubt. No one was in front of Commander's Palace, not this early. It wasn't even eight yet. No one on the street, at least not that I could see. Then I heard it again.

"Beware!"

Something brushed past me and I yelped. The chains on the cemetery gates rattled, and the metal groaned. Footsteps sounded on the path inside the cemetery, then everything was still.

My heart jumped out of my chest and dropped down somewhere in my knees. I ran home as fast as I could. It wasn't very fast. I had to stop running halfway there due to tripping on another broken paving stone. There was so much bad sidewalk in the Garden District. The roads were even worse, but that was throughout New Orleans. It surprised me the city wasn't known for its potholes.

When I reached the house, I went in through the back gate. I walked past the cracked and empty pool and climbed the steps to my apartment. I was sweating and shaking as I unlocked the door and let myself in.

I expected the house would still be a mess. Or even worse since I told Heather to stay away from me. But not only was everything where it was supposed to be, it was clean. The scent of lemon cleanser hung in the air. Heather was staring at the record she'd broken, and when I came in, she said, "Oh, uh, hi."

"Hey," I said. I closed and locked the door. "You cleaned."

"Yeah. I know I've been a pain in the ass. I wanted to make up for it."

"Thank you for the gesture." It didn't fix the record, but I still appreciated that Heather was making an effort. "We need to have a talk, but it's going to have to wait a few minutes while I look something up."

"Okay," she said and sat on the bed.

I went to my desk, sat down, and turned the laptop on. As soon as it was up, I went to my email and downloaded the report. When I opened the photos, I gagged but looked at each one. I found the smaller wound the coroner talked about and gagged again. Just below the biggest cut, so small you could hardly see it, was a fang mark.

I closed the laptop and turned to Heather. "We need to talk about the night you died."

"Is this a trick?" Heather asked.

"No, it isn't. It's important."

"Okay, well..." She looked around as if trying to bring events to mind. "I remember I was getting dressed. I was going out. I think it was a date. The details are fuzzy when I try to remember. I was excited because it was something I was looking forward to. I went to Crescent Park, over the footbridge."

"I thought you said you were meeting in Jackson Square," I said.

Heather shrugged. "That's what I thought at the time, but now I'm pretty sure it was Crescent City Park. Because I remember going over the footbridge."

"That big ugly iron thing?"

"Yeah, that's the one."

"I hate that bridge. It's too steep."

"Wonderful city views though," Heather pointed out.

"You said you lived in the Marigny?"

"Yeah. I could have taken the elevators on St. Peter Street, but I wanted to get my heart pumping. I was feeling sluggish."

"Okay, so you're in the park. Then where did you go?"

"Piety Wharf. There's an observation area there, it's really romantic. Especially at night. You can see downtown and the Mississippi."

"But your body was found at Governor Nicholls Wharf."

"So?"

"So that's upriver from Piety Wharf."

Heather blinked. "Oh."

"Someone went to the trouble to dump you in another part of the river. But why go to all that effort?" I asked. "If this were a crime of passion why not just shove you in the water and wait? The Mississippi has currents strong enough to tear a corpse apart. Wouldn't it have been easier to throw you off a boat or something?"

"Hey!"

I waved my hand. "Sorry, it seems weird they tried to make it look like a suicide."

"Suicide?"

"Oh, apologies, I didn't tell you." I explained about

the press conference, and what I'd read in the coroner's report. Then I said, "There is one wound they couldn't explain."

"What's that?"

"I'm going to ask you straight out, and I want you to be honest with me. Do you know any vampires?"

She frowned and dropped her eyes to my bedspread. "It's New Orleans."

"Please answer the question, it's important."

"Are you joking around or something?"

I didn't respond, I only stared at her.

She sighed. "Yes, I do. This is a tourist town and because of the city's history and pop culture, there are vampires here."

Damn. I suspected vampires were everywhere as it is. This was going to fuel my paranoia.

Heather seemed to sense this, and she said, "It's okay though. They're not like the ones in Phoenix. Our vampires are nice."

"Are you sure about that?" I asked.

"Yeah. All the vampires I know are good people. Maybe a little weird. But if I were super old and trying to adjust to the age of smartphones, I'd be eccentric too."

I tugged on my earlobe, something I often did when I was trying to think. "The coroner does say the slash on your throat is from a propeller. The problem is, there was a puncture wound beneath it. I think it's from a vampire's fang."

She froze. "You think a vampire killed me?"

"Yes."

"Oh, my God." Heather got up from the bed and started to pace. "It's impossible! These people are my friends! Okay, not, like, all of them but at least two-thirds of them."

"Do you know if any of them might want to hurt you?"

She stopped pacing and looked at me. "I honestly don't but...I guess I was wrong."

I yawned.

"Oh, am I boring you?" Heather asked.

I think she meant it as a joke, but I winced at her harsh tone.

"I didn't sleep well," I reminded her. "And even after coffee and breakfast, I'm still wiped out."

"Oh yeah. Sorry."

"Is there someplace the vampires like to hide out?"

"Yeah, but it won't be open until ten p.m. And it's probably going to be crowded because of Southern Decadence. Maybe you should have a nap."

I looked at the clock. It was close to eight-thirty, so not terrible for a morning nap.

"Good idea."

I stripped down to my underwear and tank top. I took the sports bra off without removing my shirt. I crawled into bed and slipped under the weighted blanket. It wasn't a quiet morning. The birds were singing and the neighbors were knocking about. But it was quieter than the night before. I found myself falling asleep within moments.

I was there again. The vampires, my old apartment building, the certainty I was going to die. But then, just like that night, he appeared.

I'd never seen him before. He was six feet tall, with fine wavy brown hair that fell to his shoulders. Heavy-lidded blue eyes, a turned-up nose, plump lips, and a square jaw. He had a trace of stubble, but not in a fashionable way. He looked more like he'd rolled out of bed and forgot to shave. He wore a brown leather jacket, a red checked shirt, a black undershirt, blue jeans, and brown hiking boots. The leather jacket was so old it had worn through in a couple places.

"Excuse me, gentleman," he said. "I believe you're blocking this lady's way."

"What's it to you?" one of the vampires hissed.

"Keep movin', redneck, this ain't your business," the leader added.

"I think you'll find it is," the new guy replied.

He reached behind his back, and there was a freaking sword in his hand!

"I don't want to kill any of you," said the stranger. "Let her go and we'll forget this ever happened. I have places to be tonight."

"Get him!" the leader replied and pulled me away.

The other two vampires attacked, and while I couldn't break the leader's grip, I had to do something. I still had my keys in my hand, and I wrapped my fingers around them. I made a fist with the keys poking out between my fingers. I turned and punched the vampire holding me in the eye. He screamed and pushed me away.

I hit the ground, but within seconds the stranger had me up again. "Run!"

I rushed to my apartment, taking the flight of stairs to the second floor two at a time. However, I couldn't unlock the door. The keys were smeared with blood and who knew what else. I wiped them off on my pants, but I could hear someone coming up the stairs after me. I balled my hand into a fist again, ready to attack. But it was the stranger.

The sword was gone, and he looked completely unruffled.

"It's okay," he said. "They're gone, they won't bother you anymore."

"They're gonna come after me, the other Bad Hats."

He shook his head. "No, they're going down tonight. By tomorrow they'll all be gone. I promise. But you should get inside and stay there."

I was shaking so bad I dropped my keys again. He was a blur, and a second later my door was open. He pushed the keys back in my hand, then gestured for me to go inside. He stood so close I could smell the old leather of his coat.

"Thank you."

"Don't mention it. One more thing."

He took my hand and stared at me. I wouldn't meet his eyes, so he gripped my chin and made me look at him. "You will forget this night and my face. We never met. You got home safely, had dinner, and went to bed. Do you understand?"

My brain spasmed, there's no other way to describe it. I vaguely recall thinking he was trying to hypnotize me. It couldn't hurt to play along, so I nodded. He vanished, and I went inside.

But when I turned around, it wasn't my old apartment. It was my new one. The walls dripped with water. The floorboards were warped and bleached with age. Everything was gone from the room except my bed. It was caked with mud, and the bed frame was rusted. I could smell mildew and rot all around me.

A creature sat on the footboard of the bed. It had withered gray skin and empty eye sockets, and it grinned at me with a hundred sharp teeth. It crawled toward me and pinned me against the door. It sat on my chest, and the pressure was intense. I couldn't breathe! The thing laughed at me, and I screamed.

I woke up to find Heather was standing by the bed. "Are you okay?" she asked.

I shook my head and collapsed against the pillows. Just a dream. A dream that turned into a nightmare. I rolled onto my right side and tried to go back to sleep. This time, there were no dreams or nightmares.

Chapter Six

AFTER MY NAP, it was a pretty standard Saturday at home. I made lunch, read a book, and watched a little TV, though not as much as I normally would. I was nervous about the coming evening and couldn't focus on any programs for more than a few minutes. I went through all my clothes twice. I was trying to find something both comfortable and inconspicuous. Heather was not as helpful as I'd hoped, as she insisted, "You can wear anything. No one will care."

I settled on my black combat boots, eggplant leggings with a black damask pattern, a black tank top, and black arm warmers. I slipped a black ring on my left middle finger, just in case I ran into someone like me. I chose to leave my hair down so I could hide my face if I needed to. I also slipped on my planchette fidget necklace and put a few extra silver stud earrings in. I have three piercings in each ear, but I don't often wear more than one pair of earrings.

As I did my makeup, Heather watched me in the mirror. "So, you're, like, an e-girl?"

"I don't know what that means."

"You know, like, Goth, punk, emo, that kinda stuff."

"I suppose that's one way to look at it," I replied. I'd finished my smoky eye and looked at myself in the mirror. I had my contacts in, and it was always startling to see myself without glasses.

"I don't mean it as an insult," said Heather. "I just never got the appeal."

I didn't answer as I did my lips, a matte kiss-proof lipstick the same dark purple as my leggings. Once I was sure it wouldn't smudge, I said, "For me, it's more of a silent signal."

"How so?"

"The way I dress, the way I do my hair and makeup, it's my way of saying, 'suspend your expectations, they're not wanted here.' Which helps a lot since I'm also queer."

"You're a lesbian?"

"No."

"But you said—"

"I said I'm queer, that doesn't always mean lesbian. We can talk about it later. We've got a bus to catch."

Heather let it drop. I grabbed my purse and we left the house.

Jaime and Sawyer weren't on the porch this time. It wasn't a huge surprise, as I figured they'd be out at the Southern Decadence celebrations. I wasn't a night owl myself so heading out after nine on a Saturday felt weird to me. A part of me wanted to turn around. Go back inside, get in my pajamas, and go to bed. I told myself we needed to figure out which vampire bit Heather, and if they were the one who killed her. It was the only way to get her to stop haunting me.

Was it selfish? Yes. But I was still doing it so who cared what my motivation was?

I had to take two buses to get to the club. There was more traffic than usual on North Rampart due to Southern Decadence. As I stared out the window, I saw people in various states of dress from flashy costumes to almost naked as they drank and danced. Music played so loud it made the bus vibrate. The bars were packed and draped with pride flags of all kinds. While alcohol and crowds are absolutely not my thing, I wanted to get off the bus. Go lose myself among the living who were celebrating what they are and who they love with pride and zest.

But our destination was in the Bywater near Crescent Park. I got off at North Rampart and Esplanade, then stood on the corner until I transferred over. Which thankfully was not long. As I boarded the second bus, it occurred to me the club was actually a stone's throw from Miss Sophie's. I wondered if I should say hello to my old landlady. But she was usually in bed by ten, so I decided to skip it. It was a little weird that there was a vampire club so close to where I lived, and I had no idea.

If the vampire who bit Heather was a regular at the club, it made sense they would want the body found elsewhere. Even the dimmest detective would be able to put two and two together. If a body was found near a bar, it wouldn't be a leap in logic to check there first. Whether or not said dim detective was willing to finish the equation was another story.

I got off at St. Claude and Louisa and thanked the bus driver as I disembarked. She wished me a good night and the bus roared down the street. It was dark, and I didn't see anyone out. It wasn't terribly surprising. Given that most of the Southern Decadence celebrations were in the French Quarter, that would be where most of the action was.

I took a deep breath and started walking. I didn't dare bring my headphones with me this time. While not riddled with back-to-back crime sprees, it wasn't safe to walk around New Orleans at night. It was best to leave the earbuds at home.

When I arrived at Louisa and Dauphine, I paused for a moment. There was a large Spanish-style Creole building on the corner with iron railings and an iron gallery. The building was painted white with royal-blue shutters, while the ironwork was a stark black. As I crossed the street, I saw a sign that said "Bijou" hanging from the gallery beams above the door.

"I think we're in the wrong place," I said to Heather.

"No, we're here. Go inside and turn right, head to where the carriageway gate is. I'll tell you what to do from there."

I nodded and followed her instructions. The bar was, unsurprisingly, packed. I could hear laughter and jazz from outside. There was a tall muscular Black man at the front entrance who wore all black. He radiated an energy I couldn't put my finger on. Not threatening, more like interest. He held his hand out, and I passed him ten dollars and my ID. He looked at it, then me, handed the card back, and stepped aside.

My first impression of Bijou was of a gentleman's club from the turn of the century. The floors were black-and-white tile. The booths and bar fixtures were dark mahogany, while the walls were painted the same royal blue as the shutters outside. There was a giant gilt mirror behind the bar. They had every kind of liquor I could name and more than a few I couldn't. The upholstery of the bar stools and booths was rich brown leather, and I wanted to run my fingers over it.

It was so full of people, for a moment I considered once again going home. I could see people in gorgeous sequin dresses or dapper suits. The jazz I'd thought might be a recording was actually a live band. They were on a stage all the way at the back of the room. A small dancefloor was set up as well as tables with chairs and candles on them. The music fed the energy of the crowd, and I grinned. I loved live music and wanted to stay to watch the rest of the set.

"Hey, c'mon!" Heather hissed.

I sighed and followed her. We walked past the bar on the right side. A green velvet curtain covered what I presumed was another doorway. If the curtain was the same size as the door, then you could drive a car through it.

Another bouncer guarded this door. This one was Hispanic with chiseled features and lustrous dark hair. He wasn't as large as the man out front, but he was more intimidating. He was also dressed head to toe in black and watched me approach like a hawk sighting prey. There wasn't any outright hostility; he even smiled. But I got the impression I was being scrutinized.

Heather said, "Tell him 'I'm a friend of Vlad's.' But don't say it too loud, they don't want everyone to know the password."

Frankly, with the band and the crowd I'd be surprised if he could hear me at all. I gulped, then leaned close to the bouncer and said the code phrase. He raised an eyebrow but stood and pushed the curtain back. He held it open for me and I walked inside.

I found myself in a carriageway turned courtyard. It was quiet, far too quiet given the noise in the bar. The trellis above my head was bursting with wisteria. And there was a fountain in the center with smiling cherubs. I didn't see another door and I turned to Heather, panic rising in my throat. I'd never been here before; did they know I wasn't a real club member?

"This way," she told me and turned to the left. I

followed and spotted a door after all. It was painted to look like the rest of the wall, but it was there.

"Knock four times, then when the guy answers say, 'I'm expected.'"

Once again, I followed her instructions. The door actually had one of those speakeasy peepholes you see in old movies. I nearly laughed when I saw it. The door opened, and the guy standing there didn't look scary at all.

Like the others, he wore all black. He was a white guy, slim, tall, with full lips and big old Bambi brown eyes. The smell of clove cigarettes clung to him, making my nose wrinkle. I had that probing feeling again, like with the second bouncer. But this one stepped aside too, and I smiled and said thank you before heading up a rickety spiral staircase.

This led to a second-floor interior gallery. There was another courtyard below, though this one had far more plants. The fountain was larger as well, and so tall I thought I could reach over the railing and touch it. Though of course I wouldn't, because it was stupid and dangerous.

Heather pointed to the opposite side of the gallery, and I walked where she indicated. Then we were in front of a pair of French doors. I could hear music from inside; it sounded like Depeche Mode. I looked at Heather, who gave me an encouraging nod, so I went in.

It looked like an old parlor in a creepy mansion. The walls were the same eggplant purple and black damask as my leggings, which made me laugh. Everything was lit by gas lamps or candelabra. It was very dim and difficult to see, at least until my eyes adjusted to the lack of light.

The floors were hardwood. The furniture was all overstuffed late Victorian style with more mahogany like downstairs. Instead of brown leather, it was upholstered in either black or purple velvet. There were several wingback chairs, as well as chaises and an honest to God fainting couch.

In the far corner, a small tent was set up, reminiscent of an old-fashioned circus tent. A sign in front of it said, "Master of Mystery and Mesmerism! Palm, Tarot, and Tea Leaf Reading. Learn about your future!" Painted on the sign was a white man wearing a ridiculous turban. He reminded me of the Wizard of Oz.

A door on the far side of the room appeared to lead out onto the balcony outside. I could see a few people through the windows gathered around a table, smoking. While the club wasn't as crowded as downstairs, there were still quite a few people around. I chalked it up to being Saturday night and Southern Decadence.

I went to the bar and sat down. There was no mirror behind this bar, but an even more exotic collection of alcohol. It went from the bar mantel to the ceiling. Given it was a high ceilinged room, that was really saying something. I also spotted a weird contraption that looked like some kind of fancy water fountain. I leaned in to get a better look and a sultry voice asked, "You want to try it?"

A tawny-skinned woman stood behind the bar. She was stunning, and not only because of her all-black leather ensemble. She was tall, willowy, and looked like a supermodel. She had the longest hair I'd ever seen; it went all the way down to her knees. It was black, thick, and straight as an arrow. Her face was also striking, with a hawk-like nose, pouty lips, sharp cheekbones, and large black eyes. She was analyzing me like the others. Her gaze went to my left hand and she raised an eyebrow but didn't comment.

"What is it?" I asked as I pointed at the contraption.

"Absinthe. We import it from Europe."

"Isn't that the stuff that's supposed to make you see pink fairies or green elephants or something?"

She laughed. "Or something. Try it, you'll like it."

"I'll pass. I'm not much of a drinker."

"Kind of funny you're in a bar then."

"Most of the New Orleans social scene is in bars. Either I suck it up or I won't have a social life."

"You got me there. So, what'll it be?"

I thought for a minute, then asked, "Could I get a Shirley Temple, please?"

She kind of rolled her eyes, but she mixed the drink.

"You're gonna attract too much attention if you're not drinking," Heather told me.

"It's a bar," I muttered. I kept my voice low so hopefully, no one would overhear me. "A Shirley Temple is almost completely indistinguishable from a Sea Breeze."

The bartender turned back and handed me my drink. I gave her my credit card and asked her to open a tab, then put ten dollars in the tip jar.

"Oh, thank you," she said. She seemed surprised and gave me a big smile.

"Don't mention it." As we walked away from the bar, I asked Heather, "What was that all about?"

"Most people who go to bars and don't drink usually don't tip. It's why she was giving you the 'oh lord here we go' look when you ordered."

I frowned. "But they're still getting service from the bar. Why wouldn't they tip?"

"Who knows? Maybe they figure a soda isn't worth an extra dollar. Maybe they think since they're not drinking alcohol they don't have to. But I used to bartend, and it was rare that people like you would tip."

"That's silly, it's a service job!"

"You're telling me."

"Bartending, waitressing, what else did you do?"

Heather shrugged. "Hospitality and customer service about covers it. To be fair, I didn't have to work. My stepdaddy paid for everything including my house. But I like to work because it's a great way to get out and meet people."

I found a chair and sat down so I could observe the rest of the room. I wasn't about to question everyone in sight about Heather. She'd just died a couple weeks ago, and I was worried it would raise too many eyebrows. I wanted to scout the place out and get a feel for it. Maybe lay a few traps. To be honest I didn't know what I was doing. After all, I wasn't a detective. Sure, I watched a lot of true crime but I wasn't delusional enough to think it made me an expert.

I could see what Heather meant when she said not to worry so much about my clothes. There were people from all walks of life in the club. A party of smartly dressed Black people looked as though they'd just come from a wedding. Another group of mostly white people wore Hawaiian shirts with cargo shorts and even fanny packs. Two Asian girls near the tent looked like Gothic ballerinas. They wore tulle skirts and tight vinyl corsets.

Most of the people in the club were there with friends or family. I was the only solo flier. Or so I thought. I spotted a gentleman at a table by the balcony doors whose face I couldn't see due to a potted palm plant. But he was definitely wearing flannel which struck me as odd given the locale and the weather. Even though he was on the other side of the room, I got the feeling he was watching me.

"Do you know any of these people?" I asked Heather.

"Just those girls," she replied, gesturing to the ballerinas.

"Friends?"

"We weren't close, but we were friendly. It's still early though, some folks won't show up until later, like midnight."

I shook my head. "I can't say here that late, I'll fall asleep."

"Then order some coffee."

I held back a sigh and went back to my observations. I took out my phone and typed in descriptions of everyone in the club. I also subtly took pictures when I could. I wasn't going to go full cyber stalker but if they were someone Heather knew I wanted to know more about them. It didn't take me long to finish my drink. Exhaustion tugged at me already and I yawned.

"I'm gonna get another drink, watch my seat for me," I told Heather and went back to the bar.

The bartender smiled at me and asked, "Another?"

"Actually, could I get some coffee?"

"Sure. How do you like it?"

"Black with three sugars."

As she grabbed a cup and saucer, she said, "That's a lovely pendant."

"What, this?" I asked and held up my planchette.

"Yeah, where'd you get it?"

"I don't remember. I like it because it does this." I held the base of the pendant and then flicked the planchette, which spun several times.

"Oh, that's cool! Are you interested in Ouija boards?"

"Kind of."

"You know, we're having a séance dinner here next weekend. You should come."

"Oh? How much?"

"Forty dollars. The meal is included along with one drink. Though if you're not drinking alcohol, I suppose I could make it two."

"Is it a popular event?"

"Yep, nearly all our club members go. If you're interested in meeting people, I'd suggest buying a ticket."

"Who's hosting the séance?"

"Emerson. He's our resident medium and showman. That's his tent over there. I'd introduce you but he's not working tonight."

Another medium? This could be my chance to learn more about what I could do. And maybe get Heather off my back. "Okay, add the ticket price to my tab. When is it?"

"Next Saturday at 11:30 p.m."

"I'll be there."

"What's your name, hon?"

"Lyric."

She smiled. "Well, Lyric, I'm Reyna Alvarado. Welcome to the Black Lily Society."

Chapter Seven

I SPENT THE rest of the evening talking with Reyna. She explained she could sense things about people, and she could tell I was gifted. Which I guess as psychic powers go isn't super weird but doesn't seem all that helpful. She claimed she'd had the power since she was human, which made me pause.

"You're a vampire," I blurted out.

She laughed. "Well, yes, isn't that why you're here?"

"Pardon?"

"That's what the private club is for. So humans who are in the know can rub shoulders with vampires without risking injury."

"Oh, no, I had no idea," I admitted. "See, a friend of mine passed away recently. I think she was a member here. But she was always pestering me to come here for a visit."

"So, you're here in her memory?"

"In a way, I guess you could say that."

"I see."

She handed me my coffee.

"What's the Black Lily Society?" I asked.

"We're a safe haven in New Orleans for the outcasts and the not quite human. We find it's best if we stick together, that's what the Society is for."

"But if it's a private club then why do you allow people who aren't members in?" I asked.

"Two reasons. The first is there's a certain kind of person who comes to New Orleans seeking a truly unique paranormal experience. And we've got more vampire fans than you can shake a cross at. Like I said, it's safer for them to encounter a vampire here where I or others can keep an eye on them so they don't get in trouble. There are a few tour guides and shop owners around the city who help us out, and word of mouth from members. They see the right kind of person, and they give them the password."

"Aren't you worried they'll shoot their mouth off and tell everyone vampires are real?"

"Hardly. Most are smart enough to keep their mouths shut. Who wants to go around yelling about vampires? It's a surefire way to get locked up. And we do have a backup. Our system isn't foolproof but we do have a way to keep out the crazies and those who can't keep a secret. The bouncers you passed on your way in here guarantee silence."

Well, that sounded fucking scary. "Then what's the second reason?"

"We have to keep the lights on, and unfortunately our membership dues just aren't enough for that. Our guests get the thrill of admittance, we get their money to pay the utilities."

It made sense to me.

"Do they know that everyone here is…"

"Different? No idea. And you don't have to tell anyone you don't want to either. We never force members to reveal their gifts. But if you're interested in joining, we do ask for a demonstration at the initiation."

I blinked. "A demonstration?"

"Yes, that you're like us."

I gulped. I didn't even know how to demonstrate my "gift" as she called it. Sure, I could see Heather, but I hadn't seen another ghost at all. At least not since I was younger. What the hell was I going to do? I should probably turn her down outright. I was in way over my head already.

Reyna chuckled. "It's okay, I promise it's not horrible. If you're that worried about your gift we can have Verity confirm it and that'll be it."

"Oh, thank you."

"You're welcome."

"So, what do you say?"

Did I really want to join? I'd only come to look around a little, see if maybe anyone knew Heather. I glanced over to the table where she remained seated. She'd taken her hair out of its ponytail so it fell around her shoulders. Then Heather pulled her coral shirt around herself tight, as though she were cold. She looked miserable.

"Yeah, let's do it."

I was given a temporary membership by Reyna once I paid the application fee. She sent me home with a packet to fill out and return the next day. The packet was simple, in that it wanted my name, the general area where I lived, and what level of membership I wanted. I chose the lowest to start with. I added a note I wanted to be sure I liked the club before I fully dedicated myself to the Black Lily Society.

The rest was about what sort of music I liked. Which foods I preferred, if I had any allergies, events I thought might be fun, and which events I would volunteer for. The club was staffed by members who volunteered their time, and they took it in turns. I wrote down that I was willing to help with bookkeeping and anything on the weekends as I work during the week.

The packet also asked if I had any alcohol preferences (I didn't), and if I was interested in speed dating (I wasn't sure).

When Heather read over my shoulder, she asked, "Okay, what is it with you? Do you want to date or not?"

"I don't know," I replied.

"How can you not know? It's a simple yes or no question."

"Not for me it isn't."

"Why not?"

I took a deep breath, held it, and let it out. "I'm asexual. More specifically a sex-indifferent asexual. While I identify as biromantic, it can be difficult to date."

Heather crossed her arms over her stomach. "So you hate sex?"

"I don't hate sex. But I don't like it either. It's pretty 'meh' to me."

"Okay, the 'I don't know' makes more sense now. Why don't you date then?"

"I have in the past. My autism and attitudes toward sex have not been well received. It's why I'm conflicted about dating. I don't need to date or be in a relationship to be happy. They've brought me nothing but misery, but I don't want to give up. Therein lies the conundrum."

"Gotcha. Sorry about picking at you, then."

"Apology accepted."

*

I RETURNED TO Bijou on Sunday morning and dropped the packet off through the mail slot. I received a call that evening from Reyna. She said my payment for the dinner cleared, and initiation would be right after.

"Oh, the initiation." I could hear the panic in my own voice. Guess I was still freaked out by the thought.

"Don't worry, we don't make you sacrifice to Satan," she teased. "You'll be introduced to the other club members, and it's sort of a 'getting to know you' party. Everyone will be in attendance."

"Oh, well..." I wasn't a fan of parties. But my entire cover story depended on me socializing. "Okay then."

I told Heather about the séance, and what Reyna said about initiation. "So if there's a chance of us finding your killer, it's at the séance."

She was on board, and she said, "Now I get to find out if Emerson is really a medium."

"You could find out now," I pointed out.

"I don't know where he lives."

I frowned. "If you knew they have a monthly séance, why didn't you tell me? That would have simplified everything."

"I forgot," she replied. "It's hard to remember stuff now that I'm dead. Things fade in and out, including memories."

I didn't press the matter further. We had a game plan, which was to go to the séance. Heather would contact Emerson, and she'd tell everyone she was murdered. Then we'd try to flush out her killer. It wasn't the best plan, but it was the best I could come up with.

*

I SPENT MOST of the week distracted. Heather stopped waking me up in the middle of the night, which was great. Sadly, I would wake up anyway due to intense dreams or horrible nightmares, the latter of which were becoming much more frequent. To the point I started taking over-the-counter sleep aids in the hope I would have a dreamless sleep. Sometimes it worked, sometimes it didn't.

The nightmares were always about the same thing: the Bad Hat vampires coming after me. Sometimes I'd see the gray creature, either in the background or a brief flash of the decayed room. The real downside of the nightmares was exhaustion. I woke up tired, spent most of my day tired, and went to bed tired. I don't always have the best sleeping habits, but I did what I could to hold down a job. But now I felt like I wasn't sleeping at all even though I knew for a fact I was.

When Saturday arrived, I was a bundle of nerves all over again. I was convinced I would say or do something stupid. Then everyone would know my true purpose and that I didn't belong. My anxiety took me to the worst possible scenarios. Heather didn't help as she continued to theorize who could have murdered her.

"I don't see Lionel doing it, he's too sweet. German maybe, but Jaxon would stop him for sure. Reyna wouldn't, period."

"Are these people vampires?"

"Yeah. Well, Jaxon isn't, he's human, but he and German have a thing going. I mean, I assume we're not suspecting humans otherwise the suspect list would be super long. There's also this new guy who's been hanging around. I think he's a friend of Reyna."

"Do you know his name?"

She shook her head. "No, but he's hard to miss. He's 'to die for' cute."

Since it was a formal dinner and I wanted to make a good impression, I dressed up a little. I picked a black slip dress, a black lace duster, ankle boots, and more jewelry, all of it silver. I curled my hair into soft waves and traded my leather fingerless gloves for lace ones. My makeup was more understated this time. I went with silver eyeshadow, black mascara, and pale-pink lipstick. I did choose to wear glasses this time though, the oval half frames with the purple lenses.

"You look like a hippie witch," said Heather.

"I think I'd need a hat for that," I replied.

I made sure my purse had my phone, keys, and pepper spray, and I was ready to go. We caught the bus over again. And this time when I got off, I felt more confident. This part, walking to the club, I'd done before, so it wasn't a big deal. It was only the dinner and séance I hadn't done. That still made me nervous.

When I arrived, I went through the same routine as before. This time when I walked into the club, the furniture had changed.

There were tables and chairs set out. The tables were covered with black satin cloth. The chairs were straight out of the Addams Family movies. Each table had name cards on them, except for one lone table at the far side of the room against the wall. People were trying to find their seats, so the entryway was crowded. I held my arms close to my chest as I didn't want anyone to touch me.

Thankfully, Reyna met me at the door. "You're right on time. Come this way. Since you're not part of a group I thought I'd seat you with a few other singles if that's all right."

"Perfectly fine, thank you," I replied.

She showed me to a table near the front. I found my name and sat down. The other people at the table were all in formal wear. Like black tie kind of formal wear. And it appeared they weren't the only ones, the more I looked around. While I wasn't nearly as fancy as they were, I wasn't so underdressed as to stand out.

The woman seated next to me leaned over a bit and said, "I love your hair." She was an older white woman, probably about my grandmother's age. She wore a cream-colored gown the same shade as her hair. She also wore what I suspected was a real diamond necklace with matching earrings.

"Thank you."

She nodded, then frowned. "Though I'm not sure that teal suits your complexion. Perhaps you should try something more natural like a balayage."

Heather rolled her eyes. "Ugh. Negging, really? And what's 'natural' about a balayage?"

I had to bite my lip so I wouldn't respond to Heather. Instead, I turned to the woman and gave my fake customer service smile.

Then I said, "Thanks for the tip. But my hair suits my aesthetic tastes fine. Just like your hair suits yours." I made sure to use my most condescending "bless your heart" tone as I spoke.

I did not want to start an argument with a stranger about my hair, but I wasn't going to allow the criticism either. It took a lot of work to get it how I liked it. Thanks to my sensory issues, dyeing my hair was always an unpleasant adventure. But having it in a bright, pretty color was worth the headaches and occasional meltdowns over the feel and smell of the dye. It was one of the few things I was willing to be confrontational about.

She seemed to decide I wasn't worth arguing with, so she smiled back, as disingenuous as my own.

"Oh, well, if you say so." And she went back to talking to the man next to her. He was a skinny older white guy, not as nicely dressed as her but still pretty impressive in his navy suit. He gave me the elevator eyes, and either decided I wasn't worth greeting or he just wasn't interested. Then he went back to talking to his neighbor.

"They're from out of town," Heather said. "She's got money too. Those rocks are worth at least 50K."

"Yes, I noticed," I muttered out of the corner of my mouth, though I wasn't sure why I bothered. The noise of the conversations in the room was so loud I don't think anyone could hear me.

"If it makes you feel any better, that guy just stole her bracelet," she replied with a mischievous smirk. "Looks like he's got sticky fingers so stay away from him."

I chuckled. "Like I have anything worth stealing."

The meal started shortly after. The guy serving our table I recognized as bouncer number three from the previous week. He still smelled strongly of clove cigarettes. He flashed me a smile at one point, and I couldn't help but smile back.

"That's Lionel," said Heather. "He's a sweetheart."

"Is he..."

"A vampire? Yes. My possible murderer? Not even. He's too nice. He cried when he accidentally killed a spider last month."

I spent most of the meal listening to the people around me talk. No one at the table was interested in striking up a conversation with me. While I was still friendly and said "hello," "how're you," "where are you from," and so on, it was a total bust. Given I'd snapped at that woman earlier I couldn't say I was surprised. And after overhearing their conversations, it was clear I was not missing anything.

None of them were members of the Black Lily Society.

They weren't even prospective members—something the wine mom from Cape Cod complained about to her sticky-fingered friend. She spent most of the meal complaining, as a matter of fact. About the food, the service, and the company (I guess I wasn't up to her standards). She would not shut up. I considered holding my breath so I'd pass out and wouldn't have to listen to her anymore. I regretted not bringing my headphones with me.

"It's ridiculous," she said as she swirled the Chardonnay in her glass. Some of it splashed on her dress, but she didn't notice. "I've made nice with the owner. I always make a donation during their charity drives. I visit every time I'm in New Orleans and make sure to send them new business whenever friends or family are in town. It's like they don't want a higher class of person in their club. Not that I can say I'm surprised considering the neighborhood and all."

"Such a shame," the pickpocket said. Even I could tell from his tone he was bored. I hoped the bracelet he'd lifted was worth listening to her whine.

She either didn't take the hint or didn't care. "They're having a ceremony for new members right after the show. It should be me," she lamented. She'd already polished off half a bottle during the meal, and she was growing louder by the moment.

"It's the club's loss, I'm sure," said the thief sarcastically. He was eyeing her earrings.

Lionel happened to pass by at that moment, and he stifled a snort. I couldn't help myself, I laughed.

She turned to glare at me. "Did I say something funny?"

"No, I was thinking about a cat video I saw online," I lied.

Lionel was still behind her, and he was having a hard time schooling his face into a pleasant mask.

She glared at me, then went back to chatting with the thief.

"Where's the restroom?" I asked Lionel.

"Through those doors on the right," he replied. "I'll show you."

I got up and followed him. Once we were through the doors, I was laughing so hard I was sure someone would overhear. Lionel was laughing too.

"Did you see her face? She looked like you dumped dog shit on her plate!" Lionel said.

"I know, right? Can you imagine how angry she'd be if she knew I was the new member? And that guy she's with! She's too dumb to see he's blowing smoke up her ass to rob her blind!"

He chuckled. "I know. But between you and me, I actually stole her bracelet back and put it in her purse. She sucks but she doesn't deserve to be robbed."

"You're a nicer person than I am. I'm Lyric."

"Lionel."

He held his hand out to shake. Ordinarily, I would refuse. But I was playing the part of an eager new member, so I gripped his hand as lightly as I dared and shook. I couldn't feel much of it through the lace gloves, but certainly more than I would if I'd worn the leather ones.

If I hadn't already known he was a vampire, his handshake gave it away. His hand felt like clammy flesh with steel underneath, and it was cold. Not as cold as Heather when I touched her, but still cold. Just like that night, the vampire who'd grabbed me—no, I couldn't dwell on it. Not here, not now.

The memory sent a thrill of fear down my spine, but I had to play it cool. I had a job to do, and after tonight I would make my excuses and decline the membership. Easy as pie.

"You wanna hear a secret?" he asked.

"Sure."

"Even if she met the base criteria, we'd never offer her a membership. No one wants to put up with her entitled attitude. Sure, she's got money to throw around, but she doesn't live here and she's an asshole."

I blinked. "Damn, I must be pretty lucky then. Considering I was here for barely an hour before Reyna asked if I wanted to join."

"Nah, you meet all the criteria. Besides, Reyna says she has a good feeling about you and she's never wrong. And when she brought up the subject of your membership, Elias sponsored you."

"Who's Elias?"

Lionel's eyes widened. "You don't know each other?"

"Should we?" I'd never heard the name before.

"I just assumed you two were friends since he offered to sponsor you. He never does that."

"I'm sorry, I don't know anyone by that name."

Lionel scooted over to the doors and looked out the porthole-style window. He gestured for me to come closer, and when I did, he pointed and said, "Look over at the bar."

I did as he said, and my blood ran cold. I knew him all right.

He was in the same all-black outfit as the rest of the volunteers, so no leather jacket or red check shirt. He'd tied his hair back into a messy half bun so I could see more of his face. The face I'd been dreaming about ever since that night. A face I would never forget. Then it clicked.

Last weekend, the man in the shadows, the one I thought was watching me. It had to be him!

"He's...striking," I said.

"God, I know, right? So handsome he makes you wanna roll over and bare your throat. But you don't know him?"

This felt like a trap. He'd told me to forget. I'd seen what happened to people who didn't. So, I shook my head and said, "No, I'm sorry."

"Huh. Maybe he thinks you're his type then."

At that, I laughed and rolled my eyes. "Oh sure, I'm the prettiest gal here and he simply couldn't resist my charms."

"I've heard weirder reasons to accept new members." Lionel pushed the doors open and added, "I gotta go. Looks like your hater is ordering another glass of wine. Wash up and hurry back, the show's gonna start soon."

I nodded and thanked him, then headed to the bathroom and did my business. When I was washing my hands, I saw Heather standing behind me. She looked as though she were the one seeing a ghost.

"What's the matter?" I asked.

"That guy behind the bar."

"What about him?"

"I think he's the one who killed me."

Chapter Eight

"HE *WHAT*?"

"He was the one I was meeting the night I died," said Heather.

"Why?"

"Why what?"

"Why were you meeting him?"

Heather shrugged. "I don't remember, but I'm sure it was him."

I exhaled. "You realize I have to go out there and pretend everything is fine."

"So?"

"Do I strike you as a particularly good actress?"

"Oh. Shit."

"Yeah."

I dried my hands and told myself I could do this. I slipped my gloves back on and assured myself I could pretend. I simply needed to keep my mouth shut. It wasn't as easy as it sounded, since Heather was still talking to me. Even worse, when I went back into the club, Lionel was at the bar chatting with Elias. Our eyes met, and I shivered. Elias's expression was blank, or at least I couldn't read it. I went back to my table and felt as though I'd swallowed a dozen bees.

The plates were gone, and people were chatting as the servers brought them fresh drinks. Lionel brought me a Shirley Temple and I managed a smile for him and said,

"Thank you."

The lady from Cape Cod, who in my head I started calling Mrs. White, was still talking to Mr. Pickpocket. One of her earrings was gone. I expected the other would disappear shortly. She was too busy losing herself in Mr. Pickpocket's eyes to notice. The other people at the table didn't pay me any mind. It gave me enough time to compose myself.

Then the lights went out and I jumped. Mrs. White laughed at me, then drunkenly whispered something to Mr. Pickpocket.

A soft glow emanated from a hurricane lamp, and a ruddy-faced thin man sat down at the empty table. He had dark hair, amber eyes, manicured nails painted black, and a perfectly trimmed goatee. He wore a three-piece black suit with a violet shirt, red ascot, and black wing-tip shoes. He tossed a fedora on the table next to him.

"That's Emerson," Heather whispered.

"Good evening," he said. His voice had a Southern drawl. He sounded like my mother's cousins from Knoxville rather than any of the Acadians or Cajuns I'd come across in this corner of southeast Louisiana. "To those joining us for the first time, welcome. For those returning, welcome back. So, sit back, relax, and follow the soothing sound of my voice."

Mrs. White giggled. Emerson glared at her, but he continued.

"It's important to attune yourselves to the spiritual energies of the universe. Any doubts you may have, leave them at the door! If the spirits sense your disbelief, they may not cooperate."

This time, Mrs. White snorted.

"I hope you get hit by a bus," Heather snapped at her.

I had to stifle a laugh.

Emerson closed his eyes and placed his hands on the table on either side of his hat. "Now, clear your minds and prepare yourselves." He began to chant. It sounded like he was speaking Spanish.

"Now's your chance," I said out of the corner of my mouth.

"Yeah, yeah, I'm going," Heather replied.

She went up to the table and waved her hand in front of Emerson's face. "Hey, Captain Emo! What's up?"

No response.

She crossed her arms. "Come on, Emerson, I know we're not besties but throw me a bone here.'

"I sense a presence," Emerson said, eyes still closed.

"No shit," Heather grumbled.

"Spirit, if you can hear me, knock three times."

"Why should I? Come on, I'm right here!"

Three sharp knocks echoed through the room. Heather frowned.

"That wasn't me." She was becoming more upset by the minute. "Come on, you know me!"

"Spirit, we hear you, please knock again," Emerson declared.

There was another knock, but it wasn't Heather. We glanced at each other in confusion. What the hell was going on? I looked around, but I didn't see any other ghosts in the room. At least not that I knew of.

Emerson smiled. "Ah, an old friend is paying us a visit. Madame Le Blanc, it is a pleasure to be in your presence once again."

Heather looked around. "Uh, you don't see any other ghosts here, do you?"

I shook my head, too afraid to answer verbally. Mrs.

White was watching my every move.

"I can smell the delightful scent of your rosewater perfume. Can anyone else smell it?"

"I can!" Mrs. White said, waving a little. Emerson still had his eyes closed so he couldn't see her.

I couldn't smell anything, and my nose was quite keen. A few other people raised their hands and said they could smell the perfume. My frown deepened. Were they really smelling something? Or was it the power of suggestion? The only ghost I saw in the room was Heather. If this Madame Le Blanc existed, she was either invisible or a ninja.

Emerson said, "Madame Le Blanc, would you be so kind as to turn the lights down just a pinch? For ambiance, of course."

The hurricane lamp dimmed. I didn't see anyone near Emerson or Heather. Was this a trick? And if so, how was it being played?

"There we are. The fear of darkness is powerful. The only thing more powerful is those who dwell in the dark, as Madame Le Blanc does. Sit a spell, while I tell you a tale. A story of jealousy, betrayal, and murder."

Heather sighed and sat on the edge of the table. "This isn't working."

Emerson continued. "Our darling madame, you see, was the mistress of the blackest of hearts. The Devil himself."

"I love this story," Mrs. White said to Mr. Pickpocket.

Someone shushed her.

Emerson kept talking.

"The Devil never went to Georgia, you see. He set down roots right here in Louisiana, just off St. Charles Avenue of all places. They say a mansion appeared overnight! A strange mansion, with rooms that took up entire floors. Higgledy-piggledy stairs that went nowhere. Gargoyles and parapets galore.

"And while no servant was ever seen, the glass in the windows shone like crystal. The grass was mowed. Not a speck of dust dared linger on any of the furniture. The house was perfectly kept but by whom, none could say.

"In this magnificent yet tainted palace lived a woman. A woman so beautiful, her smile could strike you blind. They say she had porcelain-white skin, raven-black hair, and velvet-brown eyes. A striking figure, and a face like a china doll. She was always dressed in the finest silks and satins, as well as the most expensive jewels. Her name was Marguerite Le Blanc, and she wanted for nothing. Nothing but love.

"While she was surrounded by splendor, she was often alone. The Devil is a busy man, after all, and could only visit once a fortnight. The beauty and wealth, instead of easing her loneliness, only served to deepen it. For this reason, she sought out a lover. She attracted many admirers. But the one who captured her heart was Jean-Pierre Garnier, a rogue just as handsome as the woman he admired.

"For many months, they cavorted in the mansion, heedless of the Devil. Until one fateful evening."

"I hate this story," Heather muttered.

I glared at her but didn't reply.

"Jean-Pierre was late to dinner and Marguerite asked why. He spoke of a strange man he met on the way, who said Jean-Pierre may have Madame Le Blanc as a bride. Jean-Pierre would be gifted all the gold and jewels he could carry as her dowry, on two conditions. The first condition? They would have to leave Louisiana that very night. The second condition, they were to change their surnames to Monsieur and Madame L.

"Marguerite knew what this meant. The L was for Lucifer. The Devil was on to them! A wiser woman might have taken caution from this. But she was not a wise woman. She was a woman blinded by love. She begged Jean-Pierre to take her away and marry her. To her shock, Jean-Pierre laughed. He had grown weary of Marguerite and intended to leave her for a younger, prettier woman.

"I don't quite know what went through her mind at that moment. But it must have been something terrible. She stood up from the table, and without so much as a 'Bonsoir,' she slipped behind Jean-Pierre and strangled him with her napkin. What strength she must have had! She pulled that napkin so tight he bled from his eyes, nose, and ears. He continued to do so even after he died.

"Upon seeing her ghastly deed, Marguerite panicked. She tried to wash the blood from her hands. The stains would not come out, no matter what she tried! It was then the Devil returned home. What happened next remains unclear. Some say he devoured the lovers and demolished the mansion. Others say he dragged them both to hell and the house simply disappeared.

"What is known is that from that day to this, the ghost of Madame Le Blanc is still seen on St. Charles Avenue, her hands as bloody as the day she killed Monsieur Garnier."

Mrs. White yelped, then jumped to her feet. "Something touched me," she exclaimed.

"She is with us now," Emerson said. "She only wishes to be heard and to be understood. After all, is death not lonely?"

"Fuck this maudlin crap," Heather said. She kicked

the legs of the table. "Emerson! God dammit, stop spinning this bullshit story and listen to me!"

Emerson's brow creased. "Is that you, Marguerite? Knock again if you can."

"Oh, I'll fucking knock all right!"

Without warning, Heather picked up the hurricane lamp and threw it against the wall!

Emerson's eyes flew open. The lights came on, and someone yelled about getting the fire extinguisher. People gasped and one person screamed. Heather fumed as she threw every chair, glass, or table lamp she could get her hands on. This caused a panic, and I heard Reyna's voice. "Anyone who's not a member needs to leave now!"

Mrs. White and Mr. Pickpocket ran out together, along with everyone else at our table. I was frozen stiff with fear. What the hell was I supposed to do?

Heather shoved Emerson so hard he fell out of his chair. "You fucking fraud! Wait until I'm finished with you! You're going to be so fucking sorry!"

She looked ready to beat him to death, and that was enough to spur me into action. I leaped to my feet and put myself between Heather and Emerson.

"That's enough," I said. "Stop it, right now."

"*Why should I?* You won't help me. He can't help me because he's a fake! I'm fucked! I'm totally fucked," she said, on the verge of tears.

"It's okay, I'll help you, I promise," I replied.

"Really?"

I nodded. "I've come this far, haven't I?"

Heather sniffed. "Yeah, I guess."

"Okay then. Calm down, okay?"

Reyna appeared, and she helped Emerson stand.

"You didn't tell me she's a real medium," he said to

her.

"I didn't know," she replied.

Now that the lights were bright, I saw they both wore an enamel pin of a black Easter lily outlined in gold. When I turned to look, everyone remaining in the room wore the same pin.

"I'm really sorry," I said. "She thought Emerson was able to see her but—"

"Oh, honey, I cannot see or speak with the dead," he said. "I'm a telekinetic, and one hell of a storyteller if I do say so myself."

I frowned. "Then why are you pretending to be a medium?"

"Showmanship. You can't tell people you're a telekinetic, they'll call scientists. And they like to poke and prod at people like us. But this little charade of ours allows me to demonstrate my powers and put on a good show at the same time. I must say though, your ghost is damn powerful. I thought you were just having a bit of fun with me."

"No, not fun. She's upset because—"

"Wait!"

I looked at Heather. "What?"

Heather pointed at Elias. "My murderer is in the room! Do you really want him to know who you've been talking to?"

Elias was on the edge of the dance floor, watching me.

"Tell them I'm the real Madame Le Blanc," said Heather. "And I was angry about the lies he was telling."

I repeated what she said.

Emerson blinked and exchanged looks with Reyna. "Is that so?"

"Yeah, she haunts the house I moved into. She follows

me around sometimes." The lie made my throat feel tight.

"Where's your house, honey?" I gave the address and he nodded. "That's pretty close to the address the legend gives."

"Like I said, the story was inaccurate. And the whole ordeal of her death was very upsetting. So, when you made it sound so lurid she lost her temper."

"Then I apologize, Madame Le Blanc."

"I'd say that's enough of a demonstration," said Reyna. "Wouldn't the rest of you?"

I heard various murmurs of assent.

Reyna stepped close and said, "Welcome to the Black Lily Society, Lyric Morrison. We haven't had a medium with us in a long, long time."

The room exploded with applause as she handed me a lily pin. I carefully pinned it to the collar of my duster. Unsure of what to do next, I turned and bowed to the rest of the members. Heather squeezed my shoulder.

"You're doing great. And you said you can't act."

I couldn't help myself, I laughed.

Lionel came up and gushed as he introduced me to people. The members were respectful, and no one tried to shake my hand or touch me, for which I was grateful. There was only one fly in the ointment, so to speak.

Elias slipped back behind the bar. He didn't introduce himself or even say hello. Instead, he watched me, like a guard dog unsure if I was friend or foe. While it did make me anxious, I wasn't able to dwell on it for long. The party to welcome me started, and for the rest of the evening, I didn't think about murder or revenge. Or vampires who rescue damsels in distress.

Chapter Nine

THE PARTY CONTINUED into the early hours of the morning. I met all the members of the Black Lily Society who were currently in town. It was when I met Elias formally things got a little weird. Reyna had me stand at the front of the room and everyone came up to say hello. I was glad no one insisted on shaking hands. Mostly it was waves, nods, and the occasional bow.

Then it was Elias's turn. He said, "A pleasure to meet you, Miss Morrison." His gaze was heavy and piercing. Like I was a rare butterfly and he was a determined entomologist with a jar of formaldehyde and a pin.

"Uh, you too, sir."

"Elias."

"Mr. Elias."

"Just Elias is fine."

"Then you can call me Lyric."

"I think not, Miss Morrison."

I snorted. "Double standard."

"As you say."

Then Elias bowed and walked away. Okay, weird. He didn't even wait for me to curtsy back or something.

I'd already been introduced to a lot of people, and I was told there were more I'd have to meet someday. Not everyone was able to make it to the club that night. Reyna told me some resided in other parts of the country, but most of the members lived in Louisiana.

"We get people who come down from Baton Rouge or Shreveport about once or twice a month. Everyone shows up for the Mardi Gras balls," she said. "We don't have a krewe but we're not altogether different from any other social aid and pleasure club."

I sat at one of the tables near the balcony windows, which were open. It was a warm night but a cool breeze coming off the river was pleasant enough, though I didn't want to go out on the balcony with the smokers. Lionel nipped out there once or twice to have a clove cigarette between serving drinks.

"Do those even do anything for you?" I asked as he passed me.

"Nah, I just like the flavor."

Other society members were dancing or drinking, but I was taking a time out for a little bit. I was still overwhelmed with all the strangers, and I wasn't sure how much longer I would want to be out. Lionel was finished with his drink-serving duties and came to sit with me. A petite white woman with white-blonde hair in a black peasant dress joined us. She introduced herself as Verity.

"I've never heard of a social aid and pleasure club," I said to her as she sat down.

"It's mostly a Southern thing. I know I hadn't heard of it before either. Not until I moved here," said Verity.

Lionel nodded. "They grew out of the old benevolent societies in New Orleans. They're all about charity and having a good time. You get to meet some great people this way too. Many of the clubs have criteria for membership that vary depending on the club's goals."

"I'm still not clear on that," I said. "What's the criteria for the Black Lily Society?"

"You have to have some kind of psychic power, and

you have to be part of the queer community," Lionel said.

"Or you have to be a witch," Verity added.

"Or a vampire," said Lionel.

"Good thing you're a vampire or they'd never let you in," Verity teased, and pinched his cheek.

"How long have you been a vampire?" I asked.

Lionel ran a hand through his hair. "About sixty years now."

"And you're..." I wasn't sure how to ask about his sexuality.

He grinned. "Oh, I'm a trans man. And I'm gay."

"Intersex lesbian," Verity said with a smile.

"Oh, uh, asexual. But I guess you knew that already."

"Reyna noticed the ring you had on," Lionel said.

"Are there a lot of vampires in this club?" The thought made me nauseous. They didn't seem to mind the abrupt change of subject.

"We have a lot of vampire members but not many who show up consistently. The regulars are me, Elias, Reyna, and German. Sometimes Gino comes down from Mid-City but for the most part, he's happy where he is," said Lionel.

I tilted my head. "So, you're from here? Louisiana, I mean."

"I was when I was human, but I had to move when I was turned. Everything went kind of pear-shaped for me for a while, so I decided to move back here," Lionel explained. "I needed a fresh start but on familiar ground."

"We both did," said Verity.

"And you're... Oh, I guess you wouldn't be a couple, huh?"

Lionel and Verity looked at each other and busted up laughing.

"No, not even a little bit," said Verity. "We were… roommates, for a while. Lionel moved to New Orleans first. Then when my girlfriend and I broke up I needed a change. He offered me a place to stay, and I said yes. So, we're roommates again but under much better circumstances than before."

I wondered why the hesitation about "roommates." Had something else happened?

Heather was sitting next to me, and she said eagerly, "Ask her about the breakup." I was learning that Heather loved to gossip.

"You are so nosy," I admonished.

"Who is?" Verity asked.

"The Madame. She wants to know why you broke up."

Verity sighed. "It just didn't work out. We were separated for a long time, and when we got back together, I thought everything would be wine and roses. But then we started a business together and our whole lives revolved around the shop. I would have to book an appointment just to see my girlfriend. And one day, I woke up and realized we didn't love each other anymore. The business consumed everything.

"I said we should sell the shop and go to counseling. She refused. I offered a compromise and said we take a vacation from the shop and still go to counseling. She still refused and said I was being stupid because I was jealous of the store. Then we got into a huge fight because she said that my time away changed me and I wasn't the same woman she remembered. And she was right. So, I left. She bought me out of my half of the business, and I called Lionel to come get me."

"Sounds like she was cheating on her girlfriend to me," Heather said derisively.

"Stop it," I said. "What happened to her?"

Verity shrugged. "We haven't spoken since I signed the papers. I still get updates from mutual friends, she's doing well. The shop is making more money than ever."

"Ouch," I said.

"Don't worry, you'll find someone," Lionel assured her.

"It's not a concern at this time," Verity said. Then she stood up. "I'm going to dance. Tell the Madame I said good evening."

"She said she can hear you and thank you."

Verity smiled at me, then tossed one of her pigtails over her shoulder. A floral scent came off her, though what it was I couldn't say. Verity said it was nice to meet me and went to the dance floor. She was beautiful, she kind of reminded me of a doll. That she wasn't dating anyone shocked me.

Lionel sighed. "It was pretty messy, and I only heard about it. But she's been happier since she moved here. She said she likes the vibrations of the city."

"Where were you two before?"

"Uh, Seattle."

There was a hesitation again. Were they lying? Why lie about something so insignificant? Then again, if anyone asked me where I moved from, I wouldn't say Phoenix. Especially not in a room with vampires, one of whom I'm not supposed to remember. And who was still watching me from behind the bar any time I happened to glance over.

I tugged on my earlobe and asked, "That guy, Elias? Is he...okay?"

Lionel glanced at the bar, then back at me. "Sure. Why?"

"He's been watching me all night."

"Oh?" A grin spread across Lionel's face.

"Not like that," I corrected.

"He's a bit wary of new people. You should have seen him when Verity first arrived. You'd think he was a cop and she was a jewel thief or something. The way he followed her around. He did that to me for a bit too, even though we know each other! Then we all had a nice long talk and he eased up. I thought maybe he wouldn't go through the Columbo routine with you. Seeing as he sponsored you and all. I guess I was wrong."

Reyna appeared next to me and said, "Lyric, may I borrow you for a few moments?"

"Uh oh," Heather muttered.

"Uh, yes, of course." I stood. "Watch my drink?"

Lionel picked up the glass and downed the rest of my Shirley Temple.

"You ass."

He smiled.

I followed Reyna out the French doors and onto the gallery. We pushed past a few people gathered there to smoke. There were several doors along the east side of the gallery, and she led me to the last one. Reyna held the door open for me. I walked in and found myself in an office.

It was decorated with Victorian furniture. Rather than having a Gothic feel like the club, it was more like the Bijou downstairs. Lots of mahogany, but instead of leather the chairs were green velvet. I took a seat in front of the desk while Reyna settled herself behind it. I wasn't great at reading expressions at the best of times, but Reyna's utterly blank face made me nervous.

"I'm really sorry about earlier."

"It's all right, it's not the first time a poltergeist has had a temper tantrum in this building. As a matter of fact, it used to be quite common. Remind me to tell you about Monsieur Renard sometime." Reyna sat up straighter. "I want to speak with you about your club duties. As you're aware, every member also must perform service duties to the club. Lionel, for example, is a waiter."

"I've done food service before."

She shook her head. "I have something else in mind. I would like to preface this by saying you can refuse."

"But she'll be pissed if you do," said Heather from where she stood in the corner.

"Okay?"

"I want you to take over the séances for Emerson."

I stared at her for a minute, then shook my head. "I can't. I've never performed a séance before. I wouldn't know where to begin."

"You're a natural medium, and that is a rare gift," said Reyna. "You could do a lot of good with your power."

"But I don't know anything about it! I didn't even know I had any powers until I met the Madame."

The barest flicker of surprise flashed over Reyna's face. "What do you mean?"

I was torn between wanting a fresh start and my tendency to overshare. Something I worked on with Dr. Cade. In the end, oversharing won out.

"I used to see things when I was little. Then when I hit high school, it got a million times worse. My mother and teachers said I was crazy. Dad was the only one who believed I was seeing ghosts. But...he and my mother were going through a messy divorce. So, he wasn't around much. Then when the police got involved, I didn't want to see ghosts anymore."

This time the surprise was more evident. "The police?"

"Holy shit, the cops were after you?" Heather exclaimed.

"Yeah. It happened during my sophomore year. There was this girl I went to school with. She went missing. Her ghost appeared to me in the girls' locker room. She told me the coach for the basketball team killed her. He hid her body in the rafters of the gym. Everyone was looking for her, so I told my guidance counselor what happened. She reported it to the police, and they found her. But then they thought I'd killed her."

"Oh my God," Heather gasped.

"I presume you weren't convicted," Reyna said.

"No, but I was arrested and questioned for a whole day. Everyone knew me as 'the lesbian girl' so to them, it wasn't a stretch that I'd murder someone. Because all queers are perverts, right? Or at least that's what everyone in town thought." I couldn't keep the bitterness and anger out of my voice.

The injustice of it still enraged me, even nine years later. Just because I was different, they treated me like a criminal.

Heather rolled her eyes. "Jesus, where were you living? Alabama?"

"I was living in April Oaks, California. It's a small town out in the Trinity National Forest between Eureka and Lake Shasta. I know everyone thinks that California is so progressive and liberal. But that's only the big cities. The small towns, especially up north? They're not quite so enlightened."

Reyna nodded in understanding. "What happened to the coach?"

"He was arrested and sent to prison after he kid

napped another girl. After that, most folks stayed away from me. But the people who didn't were the worst. They called me a witch, and a freak. Some of them wanted me to contact their dead relatives and they were not kind about it."

I sighed, then continued. "I don't know if you know this, but ghosts aren't interested in your mental health. I was still seeing them, and some were in such horrid condition... I'd scream, or faint. Mama threatened to have me committed if I didn't 'stop with that ghost nonsense.'"

"If you'll forgive me for saying so, in light of the circumstances it was foolish of you to move to New Orleans."

I looked down at the floor. She wasn't being mean, I knew that. But Reyna's words made my cheeks burn with embarrassment.

"I wasn't criticizing you. It was an observation."

"I know. It's... I'm autistic. One of my symptoms is rejection sensitivity."

"I see. I'm so sorry."

"Thank you. You didn't know."

I took a deep breath and looked up. Reyna was still watching me with interest and sympathy.

"When I came to New Orleans the first time, it felt like coming home. I can't explain it. My friend, the one who died, said it's the Crescent City Curse."

Reyna laughed. "I've heard it called that before. I've lived in New Orleans my entire human life and most of my vampiric one. Misfits and outcasts are at home here because they're the norm rather than the outlier. And perhaps a part of you wants to explore your powers. I won't make you, of course, but it may be good for you. Though...what is your relationship with your mother now? If you don't mind me asking."

"We haven't been on speaking terms for some time. My father and I still talk, but not often since he remarried."

"I see. Well, if you would like, you could take one of the wait staff roles. Or perhaps the coat check."

"Oh, don't even," said Heather. She was leaning on the desk. "This is perfect! You can learn to use your powers and look into my murder at the same time."

She had a point. "I mean, maybe you have a point about learning how to control my powers. But I'm worried about a repeat of tonight. What if something happens?"

"We have witches well versed in banishing spirits. You won't be hurt," Reyna said.

Heather tensed at that. "Say what?"

"Don't worry," I said to Heather. Then I looked at Reyna. "Okay, I'll do it. But I need someone to teach me how to perform a séance."

"I know just the person," Reyna replied. "Come back tomorrow."

"Yes, ma'am."

Chapter Ten

SUNDAYS WERE ALWAYS a bit of a gamble in New Orleans. Sometimes they were quiet. Other times they were bustling and you couldn't get anywhere because of traffic. This Sunday was the latter. Southern Decadence was still going, but there was a funeral second line at Esplanade. It's why I had to make sure I left the house before the parade started. While it wouldn't be along the same street as my bus route, there would be plenty of people going to watch the parade and party after.

I had more nightmares about the gray creature, and I would wake up with my heart in my throat. My chest felt so heavy I expected to find a dumbbell pinning me down. It worried me enough to look it up online.

According to various medical websites, I was likely experiencing sleep paralysis. The easiest treatment would be to sleep on my side. I set a reminder to try side sleeping before bed that evening. I wouldn't recall otherwise.

Most of my Sunday was spent in bed reading. I pulled up several books on mediums and séances through the library's online catalog. Most of them were not helpful. However, I did find one interesting book. It was about séances and the spiritualist revival movement in the early 1900s in New Orleans. I would have to pick up a physical copy from the library, so I put in a hold request.

I was still worn out, and in the back of my head, I counted down to when I would have to leave. I ate a little and ignored Heather as she tried to distract me. It was rude, but I needed to learn more about what I could do. Besides, I did not have the energy to placate her. Around one o'clock I dragged myself out of bed, showered, dried my hair, and dressed.

I went for comfort over fashion this time. I selected hunter-green leggings, a black tunic top, and black sneakers. I left my hair down and grabbed my khaki mini backpack. I brought my black leather gloves this time. While the lace gloves had done their job, I still felt raw from the previous evening. The fewer things I had to touch with my bare hands, the better.

I know it probably sounds like a style decision, but the reason I wear gloves is due to sensory issues. Strange textures and strangers' hands touching mine were enough to set my teeth on edge for days. I couldn't wear full-finger gloves as they made me feel claustrophobic. So fingerless gloves were a good compromise. I had dozens upon dozens of pairs of them in various colors and materials for nearly any occasion.

Sawyer and Jaime were on the porch again, and I stopped for a few minutes to chat with them. They had a pitcher of Bloody Marys and wore large sunglasses. Sawyer declared the drinks "hand of the dog that bit me."

"Don't you mean 'hair of the dog'?" I asked.

He blinked. "Oh, I guess that would make more sense, wouldn't it? You seem in good spirits for someone who was out late."

"I wasn't drinking last night. How did you know I was home late?"

Sawyer said, "I don't sleep anymore, honey."

"I'm sorry, I didn't mean to disturb you," I said.

"You didn't. Everything okay?"

"I joined a social club. I'm attempting to make some new friends."

Jaime grinned. "Good for you!"

"What's the name of the club?" asked Sawyer.

"It's a secret." In truth, I didn't want to tell them. What if they knew about the club? Worse, what if they knew the sort of people who frequented it?

They didn't question further but they did exchange worried looks. I bid them goodbye and walked out the front gate. I didn't like how comfortable I was becoming with lying. Not that I'm some paragon of virtue but I hate lying to people. It makes me ill, both metaphorically and sometimes literally.

I took the bus out to the Bywater, my darkest pair of sunglasses on and wincing at the noise of the engine. My headphones had run out of batteries, so I wasn't able to wear them on my commute. And this time, Heather wasn't with me. After the party, the nightmares, and waking up at dawn, I was not in a good mood. So, I asked her to stay behind.

"What if you learn something important?" Heather asked.

"Then I'll tell you when I get back. Please, I have to learn how to perform a séance and I can't do that with you chattering away the whole time."

Reluctantly, she stayed home. I felt light as I got off the bus. I didn't realize how tense I'd been with Heather around 24/7. That plus the exhaustion was wearing on me. When I checked my phone, I noted I was almost an hour early. Maybe I'd been a little too cautious in avoiding the parade crowds. I didn't want to annoy someone by showing up at Bijou and demanding entry when they weren't even open yet.

I decided I could do with a cup of coffee, so when I got to Louisa and Dauphine I turned left. I passed a second-hand store with bizarre mannequins out front. The owners sat at the entrance and greeted passersby. I waved to them as I walked along, careful not to run into a mannequin as I'd done once before. Next was the wig shop/salon with the garish wigs in the store windows. Past the wigs, I could see the beauticians inside chatting and laughing.

Then I arrived at the cafe. I hadn't visited there since I moved to the Garden District. But I recalled they were usually open until mid-afternoon. I was glad I remembered their hours correctly.

As I walked in, the leaf of a banana plant brushed my legs. The number of plants inside the cafe was astonishing, more like a nursery than a coffee shop. There was indoor and outdoor seating, but I chose indoor as it was a warm day. I ordered a bagel sandwich and coffee, then found a table at the back of the dining room. A stone angel mounted on the wall looked as though she'd been torn from a cathedral.

The service was quick and in no time, I was feasting on a fantastic bagel and washing it down with subpar coffee. I'd yet to find a cafe in New Orleans whose coffee I liked more than Morning Brew, which was a shame. I'd been avoiding them ever since the incident in front of Lafayette Cemetery.

My thoughts went back to the previous night. Everyone seemed to like me, and I'd told Reyna about my autism without hesitation. After so long keeping it under wraps, it felt good to tell someone. Well, someone who was alive anyway. Or at least not a ghost. I wondered if Dr. Cade would be impressed or shocked. Most likely both.

There was another reason I wanted to learn more about my ability. After so long thinking I was crazy, validation felt good. I wasn't insane. I could see ghosts. People believed me. A part of my mind, the part that sounded a lot like my mother, said they were all crazy too. Everyone at the Black Lily Society might be completely nuts.

Another part of me felt like I was finally on the right path. The first step was moving to New Orleans. This was the second step. I couldn't gauge the destination, at least not yet. Sure, I was scared of where it may lead. But also hopeful.

While I dwelt on the subject of sanity, I thought of my old boss. I knew what happened to her, and I'd made the mistake of telling Dr. Cade. She didn't say I was crazy, but her reaction certainly indicated she thought so. She assured me people don't all of a sudden lose their memories. Likely she was mistaken and took steps to correct herself.

Except Cynthia knew the truth about the Phoenix Coup. But unlike me, she was vocal about it. She had an entire YouTube channel dissecting footage and audio proof—until they'd come for her and erased her memories.

One day she didn't show up to work, then the next day she posted a video on her channel saying she'd been mistaken. She removed all her videos except the "apology" one. Then she moved on to another job and I never saw her again. At least not in person. She updated her Facebook page with photos of her son and her dogs, so at least she wasn't dead. But still, I hadn't seen her in forever.

Elias tried to do that to me. I had no doubt he'd done

the same thing to Cynthia and who knew how many others. Maybe it was a weird thing to brood on. But since I was about to go into a vampire lair with no protection, I was justified in my paranoia. I checked my phone again after I finished my coffee. Five minutes. I left a tip on the table and walked out of the cafe, my heart in my throat. "I can do this," I muttered to myself.

When I arrived at Bijou, Verity waited for me at the door.

"Good afternoon," she greeted.

"Hello. What are you doing here?" I asked. I was under the impression it would only be myself and the mysterious teacher.

"We need people for the séance, so I volunteered," she replied, then led me inside.

"Is anyone else here?"

"Lionel, German, and Jaxon too. I don't think they want to contact anyone from the spirit world, they're just curious."

I frowned. "I have to summon a specific person?"

"No not at all. Think of this as on-the-job training. They wouldn't make you do something like call a specific spirit your first day."

There was that floral scent again, and I asked, "Hey, do you smell flowers?"

"Oh, that's me," she said.

"What kinda flower is that? I've never smelled anything like it."

"It's called sweet tea olive. It's a shrub that blooms in New Orleans in the wintertime. You'll see places covered with these tiny little flowers and they smell like heaven. I loved them so much I bought a perfume made from them at a little shop on Chartres."

"It's lovely."

"I can take you there sometime if you'd like."

"I'm not big on wearing scents. I'll just have to enjoy it on you."

She laughed.

We made our way upstairs and into the club. Heavy curtains were drawn over all the windows so it was pretty dark even though it was the afternoon. I paused to swap my sunglasses for my regular glasses. Otherwise, I'd be completely blind, even with the gas lamps on. I saw the tables and chairs from the night before were gone, except one.

Lionel was there chatting with the muscular bouncer from my first night at the Black Lily. Next to him was the Hispanic man from the same evening. He still had an air about him that said he wasn't to be crossed.

"There she is," said Lionel, and he waved to us.

"You're early," the Black man observed. He had an English accent, but not the posh kind you'd hear on TV.

"She was here an hour ago. She went to the cafe because she thought she'd be intruding if she showed up early," said Verity.

I looked at her, my eyes wide with surprise. "How did you—?"

"I'm clairvoyant," she said.

"Oh."

That could be a problem for several reasons. If Verity knew where I'd been, what else did she know? She could easily rat me out to Reyna and Elias.

Either she used her powers or was good at reading faces because Verity laughed. She said, "Don't worry. I don't look into a person's past or future without their permission. At least normally, I make an exception for emergencies. The present, however, can't be helped. You happened to pass by as I arrived. I wondered where you were going and the answer popped in my head."

"I see."

I sat down across from the men, while Verity took a seat next to Lionel.

"I don't believe we've met," said the Black man. "I'm Jaxon, and this is my partner, German."

"Hello," I said and gave a small nervous wave. "I don't shake hands."

"That's fine, neither do I," German said.

"So, you're a medium?" Jaxon asked.

"Apparently."

"We don't get mediums in New Orleans, at least not often."

I tilted my head. "Yes, I've heard. What do you two do?"

"You'll see what I can do later." Jaxon gestured to himself. He put a hand on German's shoulder and squeezed. "German was a witch before he became a vampire." He frowned. "Wait, are you a witch or a *brujo*? Should I say *brujo*?"

"No, because I don't practice *Brujeria*," German replied. He had a voice as beautiful as his face, but he still made me nervous.

"You're scary," I blurted out.

German raised an eyebrow and everyone else laughed.

"I am?" he asked.

Was that hurt in his voice? Oh no, I'd hurt his feelings. Why could I never keep my stupid mouth shut?

I backpedaled and said, "I used the wrong word. Intimidating? That fits better."

"That's just his aura, it sets everyone on edge. I promise, when you get to know him, he's a teddy bear," Jaxon replied. He sounded more amused than anything.

"It's true. He's one of the few Runed vampires in the Western Hemisphere. And the only one in North America. At least at present," Lionel added.

"A what now?"

"You're confusing Lyric," said Verity. "She's new to all of this."

Lionel nodded. "Gotcha. Sorry, I forgot. German's Runed. Those are vampires turned by magic. Most vampires are either born or turned by a blood exchange, like me. And sometimes you'll get the really fancy ones who do magic and a blood exchange. This guy"—he waved at German—"became a vampire all on his lonesome with a spell he invented."

"I didn't invent it, I translated and then adapted it," German said. "I was actually looking for a way to cure cancer."

"I mean, technically it worked," Jaxon pointed out.

German snorted. "Yeah, it sure did."

"You have cancer?" I asked.

"Had," he replied. "The vampirism cleared that up. And a few other things."

I was about to ask a follow-up question, but then the doors opened and two cloaked figures walked in. The first was Reyna, and to my surprise trailing behind her was Elias. My heart leaped into my throat. Maybe I should have asked Heather to come with me after all.

"I apologize for our tardiness," Reyna said and sat on my right. She undid the clasp on the cloak and let it fall on the chair behind her. "We ran into a dispute that had to be resolved right away."

Elias sat on my left, his expression blank, and he made no move to remove his own cloak. He had a book in his hand. He opened it, flipped to a certain page, and began to speak. "This is a trial run, we don't want a repeat of last night." Then he glanced at me.

I gulped, but I had to do this. I needed answers. Heather needed answers.

"If you show me what to do, I will learn it. I'm a quick study."

There was the briefest flicker in his eyes, an emotion I couldn't even begin to guess. "As you say."

Elias passed the book to me. It was old, at least a hundred years. The leather was cracked, and the spine was broken. The binding seams had popped, it was a miracle the book was still in one piece. Gingerly, I ran my fingers over the weathered paper and read aloud, "How to perform a séance."

"Jaxon, would you fetch the candles from behind the bar, please?" Reyna asked.

"On it." He was up and back so quickly I almost thought he was a vampire too. But he didn't have the same energy about him as Lionel, Reyna, Elias, or German. What had Jaxon called it? Aura, he didn't have the same aura.

Jaxon placed the candles in the center of the table, and with a snap of his fingers, they were lit.

"You control fire?" I asked.

"I'm a conjurer," he replied.

"We can go over the specifics later," said Elias in a tone that did not broker an argument. "Let's get started."

Chapter Eleven

THE SUN HAD set by the time we finished. I felt as though I'd been running a marathon for the entire day, even though all I'd done was sit in a chair. Still, I expended mental energy while I tried to connect with a power I didn't understand and didn't know I had until recently. I was beginning to regret not taking Monday off from my day job.

It started simply. Elias walked me through how to do the séance. It was pretty basic. We lit candles, joined hands, then I called to a particular spirit. To be honest, it was as though I were reaching around for something in the dark with a blindfold on. But then I felt a peculiar sensation, like someone put their hands on my shoulders. Much like with Heather, it felt like ice wrapped in velvet.

A chill went through my whole body, and I shivered. Then something clicked in my head. I knew what to do. I was still reaching around in the dark, but the blindfold was off. When I looked up, a ghost stood on the table. A middle-aged man in eighteenth century clothing, complete with wig. The true difficulty lay in trying to make out what the ghost was saying. Unfortunately, he couldn't speak English. And while I know a little French, it wasn't enough to translate what he was telling me.

Reyna, however, was fluent in French. I haltingly repeated what the ghost said, and she would translate it for me. Thankfully, much like Heather, this ghost could see and hear everyone in the room. The most interesting part of the séance came at the end.

You see, the ghost we summoned didn't want to leave. He made that very clear even if I couldn't understand what he was shouting at me. I wasn't sure what to do, and the icy feeling was gone. I was second-guessing myself.

"Order him to leave," Elias said.

"What if it doesn't work?" I asked.

"It will."

"Does it have to be in French?"

"No."

He sounded awfully certain for someone who couldn't even see the ghost. I took a deep breath and did as Elias said.

I looked at the ghost and said, "That's enough for today. Leave now and don't return unless summoned."

The ghost faded from view and was gone.

"Oh, thank goodness," I muttered.

"The spirits are at your command, not the other way around." Elias blew out the candles and stood. "You may keep the book. I daresay you have more use for it than I do."

"Thank you."

Elias left the room without replying.

"That was so cool! Which, thank you, by the way, I'm glad this one didn't wreck the place," said Lionel.

"Same." I closed the book and slipped it into my bag.

"How do you feel about weekly counseling?" Reyna asked.

"Come again?" Did she mean I needed to go to therapy? Did she know about Dr. Cade?

"The séance dinners are once a month. But you could come to the club on certain days. Make yourself available for psychic counseling to club members and visitors. You could help a lot of people."

"And make money in the process," Jaxon added.

"I'm not sure how I feel about that. I do have a day job. Also, wouldn't summoning ghosts for profit be kind of exploitative?"

"Those of us with extra gifts take it in turns to offer our services on behalf of the club," German explained. "It would only be exploitation if you couldn't do what you say you can."

He had a point. "If that's the case, why do any members bother waiting tables or bouncing?"

"Sometimes you don't have the energy," Jaxon admitted.

"Some of us don't have gifts that are useful," added Verity.

"And some of us can only do something super banal," Lionel pointed out. "I don't have any special powers aside from, you know, being a vampire. So, I'm always waiting tables."

"You're still special to us," Verity teased.

Lionel chuckled. "Love you too."

"I'll have to think about it," I said. "This is still very new to me. I'm okay with doing the séance dinners though."

Reyna nodded. "Thank you for taking the time to consider my offer. Also, I should mention, if you are going to attend regularly, we do have a dress code for members."

I looked down at my clothes. "What's wrong with this?"

"There's nothing wrong with it per se. But there are standards we like to meet."

"She wants us to match the aesthetic," German said.

"So, something black and Victorian-esque."

"Oh well…I guess I could go shopping." I'd been meaning to update my wardrobe anyway. Most of the clothes I owned I chose for comfort. I didn't give much thought to style unless I was buying for a particular occasion.

"I can take you. There are a few places in the Quarter that are still open," said Verity.

"Ooo, me! I wanna go too! I wanna get that one jacket I'm in love with," Lionel exclaimed.

We got up to leave. German and Jaxon had moved behind the bar and were talking about something in hushed tones. Lionel hopped up from his seat to speak with Reyna. She smiled, shrugged, and handed him something. Though I didn't see what, as Verity passed in front of them during the handoff. He gave her a quick hug.

I turned to Reyna and said, "Thank you. I know it may not seem like it, but this is very exciting for me."

"You're welcome. Call me Wednesday and let me know what your decision is."

I nodded and left with Lionel and Verity.

"Do you drive?" Lionel asked.

"No."

"Me neither. And Verity didn't bring her car."

I took my phone out and pulled up the app for the bus. "If we hurry, we can catch the number eight over to the Quarter."

"Perfect."

We had to run up to St. Claude, but we got there barely in time. Once we disembarked at North Rampart, Lionel sighed and threw his hands in the air.

"Home at last!"

"You live here?" I asked.

"Sure do. When I was human, I was born here. Before they renovated the French Quarter into a tourist trap? It was popular with poor immigrant families because of the cheap housing. The buildings were falling apart back then. My family was one of them. But then we didn't move out when the French Quarter was reborn. We held on to our building which was technically passed down to me three years ago. Of course, I was passing it from me to me."

"Did you stay over at the club today then?"

"Yeah. Elias said they needed people and there's always a spare coffin at the club just in case so him, me, Reyna, and German slept over."

"He seems...nice."

Verity smiled. "He's very guarded, but he's kinder than you may think."

"Enough about Elias, let's go shopping."

He led us to a store named Road Kill, and with such an unpleasant name I wasn't certain what to expect inside. A Black girl with dreads in punk couture greeted us and asked if we were looking for anything.

"Just browsing," Verity said.

Lionel made a shooing gesture with his hands. "You two go on."

Most of the clothing was pretty typical of underground subcultures. Gothic, punk, cybergoth, steampunk, Victorian, cottage-core, and several other styles I couldn't name.

"You need a gimmick. Something that says otherworldly but isn't an offensive Romani stereotype," Verity said. She selected a dress from the rack and held it up to me. I could see it was some sort of blended fabric.

I shook my head. "Not that, I would be itching the whole time."

She put it back and selected another dress with a high collar. I declined that one too.

"Is there a specific style you like?"

"Hard to say. I mean I do like Goth stuff and maybe some punk, but I usually pick my clothes by how comfortable they are."

"Not a believer in suffering for beauty, huh?"

I sighed. I wasn't sure how to explain my issue, not without either outing myself as neurodiverse or coming off as insanely picky. I decided the truth was better, and it might explain any "odd" behaviors while I was investigating. Wouldn't "I have autism" be better than "I'm undercover to investigate a murder"? Besides, Reyna already knew.

"I'm autistic," I said. "So, something that might be a mild irritation to most can be the absolute worst for me."

"You're autistic?"

I jumped. Lionel was standing behind me. He wore an iridescent green and blue sequin tuxedo jacket. One he definitely didn't have before we arrived. "What do you think?"

"It's lovely, but you know Reyna won't let you wear that when you're working," Verity said.

"Yeah, but this would be really great for date night. If I can ever convince Elias to go out with me."

I stared. "You and he—"

"Not yet but someday," Lionel said. "I know he's bi or something, but he's also stubborn as fuck."

"Maybe if you didn't bother him so much, he might be more willing to go out with you," Verity said.

"I'm not bothering him. I'm trying to get him to come out of his shell."

"How many times have you asked him out?" I asked.

"Once. But then he threatened to cut my head off and stake me so I haven't asked again. But never mind that, what do you think?"

"It's—"

"Keep in mind you can't talk me out of it because I paid for it already."

Verity giggled. "If Felix comes to visit, he's going to steal that from you."

"I will stab him if he tries."

To say I was surprised was an understatement. They didn't care, or at least they didn't make a big deal out of it. "So, it's...okay?"

"Hm?" Lionel glanced at me. "Oh, that you're autistic? Yeah, it's fine. It's not a bad thing, it's how you were born."

"Also, we have a dear friend who has ADHD," Verity added. "We'll have to introduce you someday."

"Oh, well, ADHD and autism are often comorbid, so we'd get along," I said.

Lionel grinned. "That's the spirit. A stranger's a friend you haven't met and all that shit."

I sighed in relief. They didn't care. They didn't think I was weird. They didn't ask me a thousand and one questions about my disorder and what my symptoms were. I could relax, even if only a little bit.

"I'm guessing you have texture sensitivities, so can you name what fabrics work for you and which ones don't?" Verity asked.

I thought about it for a minute, then nodded. "I love soft or smooth fabrics like velvet or satin. I'm okay with lace if it's stretchy lace since that's usually soft. I can't stand corduroy and certain kinds of denim. I'm okay with real leather but I hate faux leather and rubber."

"And nothing touching the neck?"

"Yep, I hate that, it's why I keep my hair short."

"I know just the thing," Lionel said and led us to the back of the shop.

There were more clothes on display. But unlike the ones out front, they were quite expensive.

"If you're gonna be a professional medium you need a costume that says, 'I can speak to the dead, but I also have taste.'" Lionel disappeared behind a clothing rack.

"Do you get stage fright?" Verity asked.

I blinked. Bit of an odd question but I shrugged. "Not sure. Though I was in drama club when I was younger. That usually went okay."

"Then think of the séances as though you're acting out a part in a play."

I blurted out, "But then I'll feel like I'm lying to people. I get nervous and uncomfortable when I lie. Sometimes I stutter too."

I wanted to punch myself in the face. Why did I say that? And to a clairvoyant? Oh God, they'd have me figured out in a fortnight, then they'd kill me and throw my body in the river just like Heather.

"Relax," said Verity. "Everyone lies on some level or another. What's important is putting a barrier between yourself and customers. If you give too much of yourself in this work, you'll burn the candle at both ends. Physical and emotional burnout is not something you want to experience, believe me. Treating it as a role to play will help. I'm something of an expert on the subject."

I'm not the most insightful person on the face of the planet. But I could tell Verity was talking about her ex and the shop. Verity's eyes had fallen to the floor, and there was a palpable air of grief around her.

"I'm sorry," I said.

"For what?"

"You look sad, I'm sorry you're sad. Wait, are you sad? I'm not always good at reading faces."

She gave me a small smile. "You were right, I was sad. Maybe you're a little empathic."

"Not likely," I replied. "I don't have much empathy. Or sympathy for that matter."

Lionel appeared behind Verity. He had something hidden behind his back, but I couldn't tell what.

"But you're such a caring person," Lionel observed. "You were tying yourself up in knots because you were worried you hurt German's feelings."

I tugged on my earlobe. "You don't have to be empathetic for that. I may have zeros in the sympathy and empathy columns, but I have a three hundred in compassion. It's like what Dr. Cade used to say. Empathy is, 'I feel your pain.' Sympathy is, 'I'm sorry for your pain.' Compassion is, 'You're in pain, how do I fix it?' and that's where I'm at most of the time."

"Wow, that's deep," said Lionel.

"Who's Dr. Cade?" Verity asked.

"My therapist. Or she was. She was teaching me how to unmask. But she definitely wouldn't approve of me performing séances and talking to ghosts. She would think it wasn't normal."

Lionel snorted. "Normal is overrated and anyone who says otherwise is boring. Time for a subject change. What do you think?"

He held out a dress to me. It was made of black velvet, off-the-shoulder scoop neck with Juliet sleeves. The bodice ended in a sharp V. The skirt had a black velvet overlay and an underskirt of black taffeta. The rich fabrics were subtle but lovely.

"It's beautiful," I said. I took the dress from him, but my heart sank when I saw the price tag. "I can't afford this."

"Let me see," Verity asked. When she saw the tag, she frowned. "Oh, dear."

"Try it on," Lionel insisted.

"Why? I can't possibly pay for it."

""Oh please, it's for the club. Also, Reyna gave me her credit card and said, 'Go nuts.'"

"I couldn't accept."

"It would be rude to refuse a gift," Lionel countered.

He had me there.

It fit like a glove, and I did end up buying it. Along with some jewelry, and a pair of Victorian-style boots, Verity also found some fingerless gloves. They were silk crochet lace so they were very comfortable. We completed the outfit with a black silk organza veil so I could hide my face and my lack of eye contact. They took great care to make sure I'd be comfortable both physically and emotionally.

After we finished shopping, we stopped at a cafe on Jackson Square so Verity and I could have dinner. Lionel had coffee. I thanked them over and over, but they brushed it off and insisted they were happy to help. The cafe was almost empty, though occasionally people would come in to visit the bar. They would get a drink in a go cup and leave. Unlike most US cities, it was completely legal in New Orleans to open carry alcohol, so long as you didn't try to take your cup into another bar.

When we finished eating, Lionel used Reyna's credit card to pay. When I protested, he wouldn't hear of it and declared it was a club expense so not to worry about it. I was about to reply when I heard something.

"Is that a brass band?"

"Sounds like," Lionel replied.

"Let's take a look."

We walked outside and around to Chartres and St. Peter Street. It was indeed a brass band, playing lively jazz music as they marched behind a wedding party. There were two brides in front, each of them carrying a parasol as their guests walked behind them waving handkerchiefs. There were two horse-mounted cops clearing the way for them as they turned up St. Peter Street. The people who were still out stopped and stared or took photos.

Lionel on the other hand was bouncing on the balls of his feet and grinning. He yelled his congratulations at the happy couple then blew them kisses. Verity swayed to the music and laughed at Lionel's antics. I couldn't help but be swept up in the music too. I'm not much of a dancer, but I was bobbing my head along. The party passed, then the brass band in their white shirts, caps, and black bow ties. A patrol cruiser brought up the rear.

"God, I love second lines," Lionel said. "I gotta say, pretty ballsy to schedule a wedding right after SoDec. But I guess if I were gonna get married that's when I'd do it too."

"Always fun to see the first wedding of the season," Verity said. "And lucky too. It means you'll find love."

"Says who?" I asked.

Verity smiled. "I do."

"What do you mean by 'first wedding of the season'?" I asked.

"It's too hot in the summer to get married," Lionel said. "Most people who marry in New Orleans get hitched in the fall or winter."

"Ah. Makes sense."

*

WE PARTED WAYS after dinner, and guilt made my stomach turn. They were being so kind to me, yet I was lying to them. They didn't know the real reason I put myself through all of this. The shopping bags seemed to weigh more as I dwelt on it. Could guilt make objects heavier? It sure seemed to.

I could only imagine what Heather would say. Especially as I was several hours late. I should have been home by six. Not to mention I hadn't checked in with Psyche all day. I'd been too embroiled in research and ignored her messages. There was a lead bowling ball in my stomach where my delicious dinner had been as I got off the bus at Coliseum. Heather was going to be pissed. Psyche was going to be worried and disappointed.

When I walked through the gate, I braced myself for an argument. And as I approached my door, I could hear things moving inside. Heather was having a fit. I sighed, then let myself into the apartment.

Chapter Twelve

I WAS RIGHT, Heather was pissed. After I got her calmed down, I logged into Eris to read the messages from Psyche.

Psychepomp: Hey I haven't seen you online today. Are you all right?

Psychepomp: Message me when you get this.

Psychepomp: I will drive out to Louisiana and bust down your door if you don't contact me soon.

The last message was received while I was shopping.

EratoONine: Hi.

Psychepomp: There you are! Where have you been?

EratoONine: I went shopping.

Psychepomp: For three days?

EratoONine: A lot happened. I'm sorry.

Psychepomp: Catch me up.

I explained everything that happened at the séance dinner and my membership with the club, including performing my first séance that afternoon. When I was done, Psyche would type for a few seconds, stop, then start up again.

She either had a lot to say or wasn't sure what to say, which for her was unusual. To be fair, I was dumping a lot on her at one time, including the bit where I agreed to investigate a murder on behalf of a ghost.

> **Psychepomp:** So you got a second job?

> **EratoONine:** I guess I kind of did, huh?

> **Psychepomp:** Are you sure this is a good idea? If this vampire did kill Heather, you should stay away from him.

> **EratoONine:** I'm not sure he did. It's why I'm undercover. To find the truth.

> **Psychepomp:** Then why did you leave Heather at home today?

> **EratoONine:** She's kind of a lot. She would have been too distracting. Also, I didn't want her throwing tables around again.

> **Psychepomp:** Yes, that has me worried.

> **EratoONine:** Why?

> **Psychepomp:** Most ghosts can't affect physical objects. Poltergeists can, but they're usually manifestations of latent psychic ability. If you

hadn't seen her body, I would think Heather wasn't human at all with how strong she is.

EratoONine: What, like a demon? You've gotta stop watching those Conjuring movies. They're not good for you.

Psychepomp: Fuck off, I like them. Also, they're not accurate anyway.

EratoONine: So "based on a true story" is in fact bullshit?

Psychepomp: Always has been. So how are you going about this?

EratoONine: I have to be careful because the humans at the club all have some kind of psychic ability. Or they're witches. Or both. Verity in particular could be a problem since she's clairvoyant. She says she doesn't pry but I'm not so sure.

Psychepomp: What kind of clairvoyant is she?

I raised an eyebrow.

EratoONine: There are kinds?

Psychepomp: Some can see the future or the past. Others can read minds or sense emotions. Then there are the true clairvoyants. They're almost omniscient but they're also pretty rare.

EratoONine: She said she can see the future and the past if she tries. Mostly she sees the present, like what's going on around her.

Then I described how Verity knew where I was going and why when I arrived at the club early.

Psychepomp: Damn. She sounds like a powerful one. That's scary.

EratoONine: Actually Verity's nice. Pretty, too. She kind of reminds me of a china doll because she's got a heart-shaped face and these really puffy lips. And she's always wearing these cute clothes with lots of ruffles and stuff.

Psychepomp: Don't get a crush on the suspect, Lyric.

EratoONine: I don't have a crush! I can't help but notice is all.

Psychepomp: Right. Do you in fact have a plan?

EratoONine: Make friends and ask questions until I get a lead.

Psychepomp: I've heard worse plans.

EratoONine: I also need to see what I can dig up on Elias. It might be difficult since I don't have his last name. It may not even be his legal name. I've never met an Elias, have you?

Psychepomp: Nope. But your name is Lyric. Sometimes legal names are unusual.

EratoONine: I guess. Also, Reyna wants an answer by Wednesday about the readings.

Psychepomp: I say go for it. What's the worst that could happen?

EratoONine: Aside from being horrifically murdered myself?

Psychepomp: Yeah, besides that.

EratoONine: I get another victim's ghost clinging to me and can't get rid of them either?

Psychepomp: ...Fair point. You said Elias gave you a book, right?

EratoONine: Yes.

Psychepomp: Then study your little butt off. If it tells you how to use your powers. I wager the book has information on banishing ghosts too.

EratoONine: I'll read it and get back to you.

Psychepomp: Good. And if you're going to disappear, please tell me first. I was scared out of my wits.

EratoONine: I'm sorry, I will next time.

Psychepomp: You should get in the chat. Nathana is worried too.

I did as Psyche asked and logged into the main group chat. Nathana and a few others flooded me with questions about where I disappeared to. I said I was taking care of some business and making new friends. I didn't want to be more specific since I didn't know how everyone would react to me joining a vampire club. By the time I logged out, it was time to get ready for bed.

Heather sat on the sidelines the entire time. At one point she vanished and had only come back in the last twenty minutes. "Is this what you do every weekend?"

"Talk to my friends? Yeah."

"They're not your real friends," Heather said dismissively.

"They're real people I talk to, and we've known one another for years. They've supported me through hard times and I've done the same for them. They are real friends." I couldn't help being defensive. I hated how often people would chalk up online friendships as somehow less valid. Just because we weren't in the same city and didn't speak face to face.

"Jeez, touchy."

I sighed and ran a hand through my hair. "I'm sorry. They are my friends. If I didn't have them, I wouldn't have anyone."

"You know, Verity's pretty great. What little I hung out with her," said Heather. "Lionel's high energy but he's a good guy. And Reyna's the most awesome boss lady you'll ever come across. Maybe when this is all over you should stay with the Black Lily Society."

"I'm not sure they'll want me to. I don't plan on

keeping my intentions hidden forever. I've been lying to them the whole time."

"Once you explain why, they'll forgive you. Believe it or not, people don't judge lies as harshly as you do."

I frowned. "Excuse me?"

"You are super judgy about lying. I can tell by the way you talk about it. But everyone lies, Lyric. Even you."

"Every lie I've told this week has been because of you."

Heather raised an eyebrow. "Oh? And I suppose you're not attracted to Elias?"

I frowned. "What the hell are you talking about?"

"You were staring at him most of the night! You're into him."

"Must we have the asexual talk again?"

"I looked it up. There's also romantic and aesthetic attraction. Maybe you don't want to fuck him, but you like looking at him and you want to get close to him," Heather concluded.

I didn't answer, so I went to the bathroom to take a shower.

What kind of person was I becoming? Heather was still a stranger, but she could read me like a book. Should I tell her about Phoenix? And how Elias saved my life? It was pretty personal, and I wasn't supposed to remember anyway. Heather had to be wrong about him. Why would he kill her but save me? Assuming he had.

Perhaps when she went to meet him that night, someone else followed. Someone who wanted her dead. Then again, she could also have a point. My judgment was clouded, but not for the reason she said. After I finished and dried off, I put on my favorite night shirt and sleep shorts, the pink ones with purple stars. Then I dried my hair and left the bathroom.

Heather was sitting at my desk and watching TV.

"I'm sorry," she said. "I crossed a line."

"No, it was an observation, nothing more." I grabbed a notebook and sat cross-legged on the bed. "We need to write a list of suspects."

Heather frowned. "But Elias killed me."

"Just in case," I added.

"Oh, so since I can't remember—"

I cut her off. "I'm not saying Elias didn't do it. I want the truth as much as you do. But if we're going to get the truth, I need to make sure we cover all our bases. We can't only follow the clues that lead to him. That's why so many cases go cold. The investigators are so fixated on one theory of the crime they won't follow any unrelated leads."

"Since when do you know police procedure?"

"I don't. But I like true crime podcasts. My favorite happens to be about cold cases. I figure we can learn from their mistakes."

"I guess you have a point."

"And I want to go over the whole week before you died. Everything you did, anyone you talked to. As many details as possible. I'm also going to need your social media information. It'll help establish your movements."

"Okay, let's get to work."

We spent the next two hours establishing a timeline, helped a great deal by Heather's social media. She had a profile for almost every site and had a lot of followers on each platform but no close friends. I found that unusual, but I didn't comment.

It was when I was looking at pictures of her at Bar Redux on Instagram that a thought struck me. "Hey, what was your power?" I asked.

"Pardon?"

"Lionel said every human admitted to the club is either a witch or a psychic. Which were you?"

"Oh! I was psychic."

I tilted my head. "What kind?"

"I was an empath. Nothing impressive. Enough to get my foot in the door."

"Oh. Do you still have your power?"

"Nope. It's hard to feel other people's emotions when you don't have a body anymore."

I wondered what her identity was. She had to be part of the LGBTQIA+ community to join. Was she bi or trans maybe? I didn't dare ask. After Lionel and Verity both told me their identities, I felt like I was intruding by outright asking. Heather didn't appear to be out, at least not on her social media. So, I wanted to give her time to come out to me. If she ever did.

"Why did you want to join anyway? It doesn't seem to be your scene." Most of the pictures of Heather were on Frenchman Street or at various other bars around town. A lot of them were nightlife hot spots for people around our age, mid to late twenties.

"It's kind of dumb. But there was this guy I liked who was a member. But then when I joined, he moved to Tallahassee. I couldn't believe it! But it was kind of nice to be around people like me, so I stayed. Then I got the biggest crush on Elias, so I had even more reason to stick around."

The way she talked about him sounded as though she still had a crush on him. Maybe that's why she was so sure I had a crush; she was projecting. I kept that thought to myself. I didn't want to start another fight.

Once I was satisfied with the timeline, I went to bed.

I wasn't ready to sleep, I just wanted to read for a while. I knew I would nod off soon after. I turned out the lights except for the bedside lamp and settled in with the book Elias gave me.

It was called *Piercing the Veil of Tears*. It was all about mediums, the history of mediumship, and contacting the dead. I'd always found mediums fascinating when I was younger. Many well-known mediums confessed to being frauds later in life, but I still found their stories comforting. Even if they were fakes, it meant someone out there might have the same affliction as me.

Affliction... That was the word I used when I was a kid. Because I didn't view my ability as a power or a gift. It was a curse. But the way everyone at the séance behaved that afternoon, I was beginning to wonder if I was mistaken. I put it out of my mind. I needed to finish the chapter I was on before I fell asleep. I read aloud.

"'A true medium is a person who can bridge the divide between the living and the dead. To see past the veil of tears and into another realm. They are able to call individuals back from the beyond, to speak with us once again. Mediums can become possessed by the spirits of those who have passed. And those who were never human to begin with. This is called channeling.' Well, that'll be a fun party trick someday."

Heather laughed.

Then a certain passage caught my attention. This one I didn't read to Heather.

It is good to note, mediums are not born. They are made. Only a truly depraved person would attempt to create a medium. This would require a psychic child to pass into the next world. Then the child must be brought back to life. Whether through the miracle of science or the miracle of God. The child is thus clothed in the veil they so briefly passed through. The veil clings to their life force and corrupts it. The result is the child has a connection with death few possess.

I shivered and closed the book. I had a near-death experience when I was four. I couldn't remember it, but I knew the story well. It was a hot day, and the adults were outside for a barbecue. I wanted to cool off and loved to swim, so I jumped in the pool. But I jumped into the deep end and sank like a stone. My father dove in to save me, but I'd already inhaled so much water. Dad said it was a miracle I pulled through.

Another thought occurred to me. Why did Elias even have this book? It was a first edition, and I'd tried to find another copy online but there was no trace. It wasn't in the best condition, but still pretty good for a book that was almost two hundred years old.

Then I remembered what Elias said at the end of the séance. He was so sure ordering the ghost to leave would work. Was Elias a medium as well as a vampire? That didn't make sense. If he were a medium too, why would Reyna say they hadn't had one at the club in a long time? And wouldn't he be able to see Heather?

When I glanced at the clock, I froze and did a double-take. It was two in the morning! I'd have to be up in a few hours. I slipped the book under my bed and turned out the light. I hoped I wouldn't have any nightmares. Thankfully, this time, I enjoyed a peaceful night's sleep.

Chapter Thirteen

IN THE END, I decided I didn't want to do one-on-one readings and called Reyna on Wednesday to tell her. I explained I didn't want to offer appointments until I had better control of my abilities. She said she understood, and to come by the club again on the weekend so we could plan the next séance dinner. My stomach flip-flopped at the thought, but I agreed.

What I needed to do was practice, but that was difficult. I wasn't unwilling to practice; I was unable to. We were getting into the busy season at work, and I was swamped. This was nerve-racking enough without adding "learn to control ghosts" to the list of tasks I had. At the top of the list was "solve Heather's murder."

I was still reading and rereading *Piercing*, and I copied down as much information as I could. I didn't want to highlight any of it or I would damage the book. Though I was worried I was doing that already since I wasn't reading with white gloves like you saw at museums.

Heather was surprisingly patient in this regard. I thought she would be annoyed or upset that I wasn't fully devoting myself to the investigation. But she agreed I should learn to use my powers. She even offered to help.

"Becoming more powerful is the only thing that will keep Elias from killing you," she said. "And I think you need to learn some self-defense too. Like karate."

"I already know how to fight," I told her.

"Really? You don't look the type."

"My father wanted sons. When he didn't get one, he decided gender equality is the way of the future. He taught my sister and me basic fighting and survival skills."

"You have a sister?"

I rolled my eyes. "We haven't spoken in twelve years. She's older than me and went no contact with the family when she turned eighteen. I used to wonder why, but now I want to know how the hell she did it without losing her mind."

"Oh, bummer," she said. "Hey, did your dad teach you how to use a gun?"

"Yes, but I'm not good with one. I'm pretty good with a bow and arrow though."

Heather rolled her eyes. "Bullshit. You don't have a bow here."

"No, I don't. Because I sold it before I moved. I haven't replaced any of my archery equipment since I don't have the money."

"Oh. So, you were good?"

"Yes."

"Olympics good?"

"No."

"Fine, Katniss, you don't have to be so crabby."

I sighed and looked up from the book. "I am not being crabby. I'm trying to concentrate as I find reading archaic English difficult. I can't do that when you're asking me a million questions."

"Then I guess I'll just leave!" she snapped and vanished.

I closed the book and rubbed my temples. Heather was, to my great misfortune, prone to dramatic fits. I thought perhaps it was due to the circumstances under which we met. Until I discovered the many videos she filmed for YouTube. In most of them, she did her makeup while complaining about some recent drama. Drama she either started or threw herself into headfirst.

Ordinarily, I wouldn't watch something so childish. Yet I put myself through several hours of "content" in the hopes of finding a clue. There were none, or at least none I found useful. She wasn't famous or even particularly well known. She had what I consider a lot of followers. According to Nathana, three hundred is actually pretty small potatoes.

There was also the matter of Heather's memorial service, which we attended earlier in the day. It was a Thursday, so I had to take the morning off from work for it. Heather was buried in Lake Lawn Cemetery in Metairie, in the Campbell family tomb. The service was held at the mortuary in the cemetery.

Heather's stepfather was there along with four of her cousins. Only two of her friends attended the funeral. I spoke with everyone and introduced myself as a former coworker. What I learned was not helpful.

The most anyone knew, she wasn't depressed nor were there any signs of suicide—at least as far as they knew. None of them had spoken to Heather in months. According to her stepfather, she had requested privacy during a difficult time. Then she stopped returning his calls. Though the way he said it was like he was holding something back. I didn't want to press, given he'd just lost his stepdaughter.

Heather was upset when we left and had been ever since. I didn't ask about it, but I knew I would have to at some point. I may be a compassionate person, but other people's emotions are difficult for me to deal with. Under normal circumstances, I wouldn't have attended the funeral at all. I was always awkward around people who were grieving, I didn't want to make a bad situation worse for them.

I went back to the book, and an hour later Heather returned. She was still fuming as she sat on the edge of the bed. She glared at me. I was at my desk, still clocked in for work, but I hadn't received any calls since I'd finished up my case list for the day.

"You're still reading?"

"I'm almost done." I placed the bookmark on the page I was on and closed the book. "Are you all right?"

"Yeah, fine. Why?"

"You've been more angry than usual since the funeral."

Heather bit her lip. "It's nothing."

"If it's nothing then I hate to see what you're like when you're really angry."

"You don't have to be such a bitch!" Heather snapped.

"And you're being defensive," I pointed out. I knew all the signs from my sessions with Dr. Cade. I'd been like that myself when I didn't want to open up. "What's bothering you? I'd like to help if I can."

"Yeah, well, you can't. Not unless you can make people miss me."

I paused, unsure of what to say. I couldn't argue with her either. She was right. Her family hadn't been sad or happy, or at least her cousins weren't. They'd been indifferent at best. Her stepfather seemed sad, but he hadn't cried or said much. Her so-called friends were only there to "mine content" for their YouTube channels.

"So you're upset because you think no one misses you?"

"They don't! I know I'm not perfect, but I deserve a real funeral where people are sad I'm dead. No one even shed a tear!"

"About that, why do you think no one from the Black Lily Society came?"

She sighed. "It's Society policy that club members don't attend funerals. You get a wreath and that's it."

"Seems like a strange policy."

"Yeah, well, considering there are a few vampires at the club and the service was during the day it's not a big surprise. Maybe they feel guilty because Elias killed me."

I frowned. "Could they be covering for him?"

"Maybe. I suppose if anyone would be it would be Lionel. Those two are close."

It made sense to me. Out of everyone I met the first night, Lionel was the one who talked the most.

"I should see what their connection is," I said. "Just to be on the safe side. And for the record, I'm sorry. If I had known you before you died, I would miss you."

Heather snorted. "Sure you would."

"I would. You're a little dramatic but that doesn't make you a bad person."

We left it there.

I finished the book that night, but I still had more questions. Sadly, I didn't have another medium to answer them. And I wasn't sure how I was supposed to practice. Was there another psychic I could talk to? Were most powers the same? I didn't think so. Especially as the book stressed that while a medium could practice on their own it was best to have a teacher. Since I was the only medium I knew, that was one hell of a roadblock.

I went to the Black Lily Society on Friday night and Saturday night. It would have been suspicious if I didn't, and I did need to plan with Reyna. Besides, I liked the club. Most of the members were nice and the ones who weren't were at least polite.

I learned more about Verity and Lionel. And despite

the circumstances, I could see myself becoming good friends with them, even with some of their more unusual quirks.

For example, Lionel was a world-class snoop. He could find out anything about anyone if you asked. Or sometimes even if you didn't. This alarmed me when I first heard about it. Then I saw his talents in action on Friday.

Verity and I were having drinks after I met with Reyna, and Lionel appeared at our table and said, "You can't date Nora."

Verity pouted. "Why not?"

"She's pretty enough but her credit score is in the double digits. Nora voted against increasing the library budget but voted for the 'more cops' initiative. Oh, also? She hates cats and she's a slob," he said as he sat down.

"How do you know what she voted for?" I asked.

Lionel held up his phone. Of course, social media. Was there anyone who didn't have an online footprint these days? Granted I was one to talk. I was always on Eris and spent more time than I cared to admit on Tumblr.

"How do you know she's a slob?" Verity asked.

"She left her back window unlocked."

I was stunned. "Did you break into her place?"

"Of course not, I'm not a burglar. I can't get in anyway—she would have to invite me in. But since I was in the neighborhood and the window was right there, I figured I might as well take a look. Her bathroom is a mess."

"Oh my God," I muttered. "Why does it matter if her bathroom is a mess?"

"It doesn't," said Verity. "But I can't date someone who hates cats, that's unacceptable."

Lionel nodded. "Damn right. Anyone want a refill?"

*

ON SATURDAY NIGHT, I brought *Piercing* with me to the club. I didn't really want to speak with anyone, but I also didn't want to go home. I sat at the end of the bar near the wall and read. Most people were considerate enough to leave me alone. Heather tagged along this time but didn't talk my ear off as usual. She was preoccupied, but I didn't ask why. Heather wasn't the type to play something close to the vest, she'd tell me one way or another. I just had to be patient.

Then, to my surprise, Elias sat next to me. He was in his red flannel shirt again, so he was off duty.

"How do you like it?" he asked and gestured to the book.

"Very informative," I said. "Though lacking in practical application."

My heart was pounding so hard I was sure the whole room could hear it. I thought that would be the end of our interaction. But Elias didn't budge.

"How?" he asked.

"The exercises assume the reader already knows how to use their powers. I don't."

"Is that so?" He didn't sound as though he believed me.

"I told Reyna I never actually tried to use my ability before. The ghosts I've seen are entirely accidental."

Elias nodded. "I see. Come with me."

I gulped. "Uh, to where?"

"Where we won't be disturbed."

"I've got your back," Heather whispered in my ear.

I finished my Shirley Temple and followed Elias out of the room, the book shoved in my bag. I was so nervous I knew he could hear my heart racing. He led me out to the inner courtyard gallery, then to the spiral staircase. But instead of going down into the yard as I expected, we climbed up until we were on the roof.

Most buildings in New Orleans have slanted or semi-slanted roofs due to all the rain. A flat roof means that water can gather and that in turn could lead to the roof collapsing. While the Bijou's roof was indeed slanted, someone had added a widow's walk as well. It wasn't huge, about six by ten. But it couldn't be seen from the street.

"Oh wow," I said. It wasn't the most impressive view in New Orleans, but I could see most of the Bywater. And the river, and of course the skyscrapers downtown.

"Focus, I'm not a patient teacher and I'd prefer it if I didn't have to repeat myself," Elias said. His voice wasn't mean or angry, but it was stern.

"Uh, yeah, sorry."

We faced each other, and he said, "I'm going to teach you how to connect to your powers. It's different from most psychics. Their powers aren't always in their control, like with Verity. And you can't simply meditate on it like a witch. I presume you have read that part of the book."

"Yes."

"Good. Do you know what sort of power runs in your family?"

"No. As far as I'm aware I'm the only person with any psychic ability."

"Unfortunate. That would make this much easier." Elias looked me up and down, then asked, "Do you always wear glasses?"

"Except when I wear contacts, yeah."

"I see. Take them off."

I shook my head. "Nuh-uh. I need them to see. I'm almost blind without them."

To my surprise, Elias explained himself.

"Glasses are used to correct your vision. Many visually impaired psychics are unable to tap into the visual elements of the ethereal with their glasses on. I think you can see the Madame because she's a particularly strong ghost. But you could see more if you took your glasses off."

"Would I have to go without my glasses forever?"

"No. This is just to practice. Once you're more familiar with your powers, you should be able to see ghosts with or without your glasses. It's a bit like exercising. You struggle at first but over time you're able to do more as your muscles build."

"Damn, that's actually really good advice," said Heather. "Wish I'd thought of it."

"Okay, but if I'm gonna do this, shouldn't we go somewhere that's haunted?"

Elias chuckled. "This is New Orleans. The entire city is haunted."

"Right, I keep forgetting that's in the brochure."

I reached up and took my glasses off. I fumbled a little when I closed them and hung them from my shirt collar.

At first, I didn't see much of anything. My eyesight is terrible, so I couldn't even make out Elias's face and he was only two feet away. Heather was to my right, and when I glanced at her I paused. A glow emanated from her like the night I found her body. I could see the glow more than her. I narrowed my eyes. "Madame, could you move please?"

"Uh, okay," Heather said and took two steps to the left.

The glow was actually coming from behind Heather, as it didn't move when she did. It was a faint outline of a person. I moved closer but had to watch my step. Being on a dark roof late at night without your glasses made walking more of a hazard than usual.

The closer I moved, the more distinct the figure became. "Can you hear me?" I asked.

The figure turned to face me. They were too faint; I couldn't make out anything about them except they were there.

"Miss Morrison," Elias said, and I turned toward his voice. Between one blink and the next, he was at my side.

"Jesus!" I swore. "You startled me."

"I'm sorry. May I take your arm? It will be easier for you to move if I guide you."

"Uh...sure." At least he asked first.

I wasn't the biggest fan of being touched. As a matter of fact, I hate it. And it's always hard to explain why. No, that wasn't true, people just don't like the explanation. The closest thing I can compare it to is petting a cat the wrong way: not agonizing but irritating and uncom-fortable. The worst part is, I was also touch starved, which does tend to screw with my mental health.

But that didn't happen with Elias. When he touched my arm, it was soothing. Nice, even. He helped me to the other side of the widow's walk, the one that looked down on the street.

"What do you see?" Elias asked.

The streetlights were on, bathing the pavement in their eerie blinding light. I expected the streetlights in New Orleans to be like everywhere else: the soda-orange that makes the world look like a post-apocalyptic hellscape. But no, the streetlights in New Orleans were a bright white. I was grateful for them now as I stared at the world below us.

Silver figures fluttered up and down the street. In and out of buildings, around cars, and even floating in the air on the river breeze. Some were faded and formless. Others were just as substantial as Heather. So detailed that even with my glasses off I could make out their faces and clothes.

"Oh my God," I whispered. "This really is a haunted city."

"If you want to see a ghost, come to New Orleans," Elias said.

"What about Savannah?" I asked.

"Don't mention Savannah around the locals, you will regret it." I could hear the amusement in his voice.

"I'm starting to get a headache," I told him. I put my glasses back on. I was disappointed to see the ghosts vanish. "Aw. Ghosts go poof."

"As I said, you need to practice. The more you practice the better you'll see."

"You know a lot about mediums," I observed.

He looked away. "Yes, I do." Elias let go of my arm. "Good evening, Miss Morrison."

"Thank you," I called after him.

Either he hadn't heard me or didn't bother to answer. Elias vanished.

Chapter Fourteen

I DID AS Elias suggested, and I went without my glasses. Not for long periods, but enough that I could see how many ghosts were around. A lot, it turns out. I also discovered that some had staying power while others faded over time. I even worked my practice sessions into my daily routine. Now each morning when I went to Morning Brew, I would get my coffee and ghost-watch.

There were two bay windows in the front of the cafe that had a great view of the Lafayette Cemetery. I would sit with my coffee at one of the windows, glasses on the table in front of me, and observe. I could see ghosts and spirits bustling around the cemetery and even going inside or leaving. It was fascinating. Like watching a colony of ants who had no idea they were being perceived. But I made sure to stay away from the gates. I didn't want a repeat of what happened the last time.

After a few weeks of this, Delia asked, "Are you okay, hon?"

"Delightful. Why do you ask?"

"I thought maybe your glasses were bothering you."

I was about to deny it but then thought better of it. "I got a new prescription. They work okay but they also give me headaches on occasion."

"You should try those ones that block out blue light. My neighbor works from home too and he says they do wonders for him."

"I'll consider it. Thank you."

I would typically spend an hour with my glasses off and write down my observations. There were so many ghosts I began to tabulate them into a category system I devised. The book had no such system. I still hadn't received the book I placed on hold at the city library, but I doubted it would have one.

Sometimes, it's unclear to me if I do things a certain way because of my autism or simply because of who I am as a person. I don't think the two can be separated, as autism does shape how I see the world. And how I adapt to it. Regardless, I called my system the Ghost Directory. And used it to categorize spirits based on what I could observe.

For example, level one spirits were ghosts I could see a vague outline of, like heat rising off a summer road. But they were otherwise invisible and couldn't speak. Level two were spirits who had a faint light, but they lacked any features or defining characteristics and were also mute. Level three had a brighter glow and more definition but like the previous two couldn't make a sound.

Level four was a shade brighter and more defined, and I could hear them but not well. And level five was the brightest with the most distinguishable features. They were able to talk whether you wanted them to or not.

Level six had only one ghost, and that was Heather. She was completely different from all the others I'd seen. For starters, most of the time she looked like a regular person—unless she was enraged, then she was sur-rounded by a golden glow. Not the same silver light I'd seen around other ghosts. She could affect her environment with ease, like when she broke my record. None of the others could do that.

I wasn't sure what made her so different. Or how she appeared to have so much vitality when she was, in fact, dead. There was nothing like her in *Piercing*. I assumed her psychic abilities in life contributed somehow, though in what way I didn't know. I would need to do more research. In the meantime, I was occupied with practicing my powers. Both in my own time and at the club.

My first public séance was coming up shortly, and I wanted to be as prepared as I could be. I was lucky that Verity, Lionel, Jaxon, and German were more than willing to help me practice. We commandeered a dark corner of the club, and Reyna even set up a private table for us. She'd placed a privacy screen in front of it with a sign that said "reserved." This was so no one would actually see me practicing.

I was still nervous about my first performance, but the more I practiced, the more confident I felt. Though the feeling didn't last. Usually, the first time I do anything is a mess. I'll convince myself it will be an abject failure and I'll only humiliate myself. This is rarely the case as I am more capable than even I know. Though you certainly can't convince my anxiety otherwise.

Lionel decided to be my hype man, while Verity was quiet in her reassurance. Jaxon was always sure I could do anything. German didn't say as much as the others, but he did say he believed in me. He would also sometimes offer his own opinion about whether this or that wording was a good idea. And he always helped me open and close the circle.

One night he even helped with an eighteenth-century merchant. The ghost spoke rapid-fire Spanish and I couldn't keep up with most of it. German was able to translate, though we had to go the slow route much like with the French ghost at my first séance. Eventually, I ordered the ghost to leave. It took some doing. While Elias said I had to be confident, I still felt ridiculous ordering ghosts about.

When the merchant was gone, Verity said, "You're getting better at this."

"Sure doesn't feel like it. I'm not the most assertive person," I replied. It was a flaw, and one I tried to resolve with Dr. Cade's help. While I wouldn't change my mind, I would often stop arguing or acquiesce to others so I could avoid a fight. It wasn't lost on me that this summed up my entire relationship with Heather.

"You're still getting better," she assured me.

I smiled in return. Verity wasn't the type of person to say empty words to make you feel better. She would state facts in straightforward, plain language. No exaggerations or frills. It was, in my opinion, one of her best qualities. And probably the one that made me want to spend as much time with her as possible.

"We should celebrate," said Jaxon. "Who's for burgers? We could go to Port of Call. Or maybe the Clover Grill."

"You just want an excuse to go to the Cardinal," German teased.

"What's the Cardinal?" I asked.

"The Cardinal Apothecary and Lapidary," he replied. "It's a magic shop. They sell herbs, books, candles, and all sorts of stuff. I stop in there a few times a month for ingredients. But the reason Jax wants to go is because the owner has a corgi she brings to work with her."

"You won't let us get a dog," Jaxon said. He then stuck out his bottom lip and whimpered like a puppy.

Verity and Lionel laughed. German rolled his eyes,

but he hid a smile behind his hand.

"Incorrect. Our lease won't let us get a dog. We're not getting evicted because you want a pet," he said. "And stop that. Pouting doesn't work on me."

Jaxon whimpered again and hugged German. "Please can we get a dog? Our neighbor has two."

"He has a note from his psychiatrist saying they're emotional support animals. Stop begging. I promise when we buy a house, we can get all the dogs you want." German paused. "Within reason. The limit is fifteen."

Jaxon grinned and kissed German's cheek. "I love you."

"I love you too, even if you are a pain in my ass."

"We should still go to the Cardinal anyway," Lionel said. "They're doing free readings tonight."

Verity frowned. "You don't need to go to the Cardinal for that. I can tell you your future."

"Is that the sound of professional jealousy I hear?" Lionel asked, his hand cupped around his ear.

"That's not what I meant. You know I don't do that anymore. Not for profit anyway."

"What do you do? When you're not here, I mean," I asked.

"I'm a dancer, or I'm trying to be."

"Oh? What kind?"

"Burlesque. But I don't have a following and it's difficult to book gigs since I don't have a theme."

"I still say sexy psychic would work," said Lionel.

"No," she replied. "I don't want any of my income tied to my gift. Even in a joking way."

Verity was glaring at Lionel, who looked more uncomfortable by the minute. My guess was this was a pet peeve of hers, and I made a mental note not to bring it up again.

Lionel sighed. "I'm sorry, I don't mean anything by it."

"I know. You're forgiven."

"Come on, let's go get a bite," said German.

We left the club and headed over to the French Quarter. It was easier to take the bus as there was hardly any parking in the Quarter at the best of times. But in the early evening during the dinner rush? Not a chance. We did end up going to the Clover Grill, a cheap greasy spoon diner on Bourbon Street that was open twenty-four hours. The five of us commandeered a table near the back where we ate and talked.

Well, Lionel and Jaxon did most of the talking with occasional input from Verity and German. I don't like to talk while I'm eating. Though I noticed something interesting. Lionel didn't eat food, that was all part of his vampire thing. But German was a vampire too, yet I saw him scarf down a tuna melt with no problem. Was it because he was magic? I wasn't sure, and it would probably be rude to ask.

I got a bacon cheeseburger with fries, and a flood of nostalgia hit me with the first bite. It was good, but it tasted exactly like the sort of burgers I'd get at Irena's Diner back home. I wondered if the line cook had ever been to April Oaks. Or perhaps all diner burgers taste the same.

When I was done eating, Jaxon asked, "Are you ready?"

"For what?"

"The Cardinal! You'll love it, I promise."

"You must really want to pet this dog."

Lionel and Verity laughed. Jaxon shrugged but

smiled.

"Okay, let's do it."

We paid the bill, added a big tip, and we left.

Jaxon led the way. He turned down Dumaine and walked down until we hit Chartres. The conversation carried on, though I continued my silence. I was once again struck by the fact I lived in such a beautiful city, with some of the oldest buildings in America that were miraculously still in one piece. Given the general US attitude of "new is better" it was astounding that the French Quarter has lasted so long.

We ended up crossing in front of St. Louis Cathedral on our way to the shop, and I paused for a moment. The palm readers and magicians who entertained the tourists for sweaty dollar bills were long gone. Returned home for the night so they could peddle their wares again tomorrow. A few homeless people were curled up near the gates of the Cabildo. They would sleep for a few hours until the vampire and ghost walking tours would wake them.

It felt strangely empty, despite the fact there were still people out. Teenagers clad in black sat on the Jackson Square gate steps. They were smoking cigarettes and passing a bottle of something in a brown paper bag back and forth. They cracked jokes and laughed about passersby. I remembered when I was that age and the illicit thrill of being out somewhere after dark and away from the house. I silently hoped they had a great night and got home safe.

I looked up at the stained-glass windows of the cathedral, illuminated from within. The lamps in Jackson Square had a soft, warm glow to them, in sharp contrast to the bright streetlights elsewhere in the city. The lights didn't take away from the stained glass, or the hands on the clock high above the cathedral doors.

Fog rolled in off the river, carried by a cold wind that sent a shiver right through me. It was late September, and the weather was just beginning to change. A little earlier than expected since it normally didn't cool down until late October. At least according to Sawyer. I had yet to spend an autumn or winter in New Orleans, so what did I know? The ambience of the square made me curious. Was it really so abandoned? I slipped my glasses down my nose and looked around again. It wasn't a surprise to see ghosts were everywhere. I pushed my glasses back in place.

"Are you coming?"

German stood next to me, while Jaxon, Verity, and Lionel waited on the other side of the square.

"Yeah, sorry." As we walked to catch up, I said, "I love it here."

"The cathedral is beautiful, isn't it?" German smiled. "I heard the gates were made from melted-down torture devices used in the Spanish Inquisition."

"The way I heard it, they're from the blades of the guillotines from the Reign of Terror," said Jaxon.

"Historically speaking, neither of those would be a viable option," I replied.

"Yeah, but you'd be surprised. In this town, there's always a kernel of truth in every tall tale," Lionel said.

We walked two more blocks until we found ourselves in front of a three-story Spanish colonial. It was terra cotta orange with dark-green shutters and a cast iron gallery on the second floor. A wooden sign hung above the door. It was in the shape of a mortar and pestle with a male cardinal bird painted on it.

"Here we are," said Jaxon and held the door open.

"Ladies first."

Verity and I walked in, followed by Jaxon, German, and Lionel. They'd already been to the store and the sight of it was lost on them. For me, it was overwhelming.

There was a huge line of ebony shelves in the back, with every kind of herb you could think of. To the left behind a sales counter were more shelves. They held wands, gemstones, cauldrons, pendulums, candles, incense, and many other objects. I couldn't name them all, but I had seen them in new-age catalogs growing up. The right side of the room had the same floor-to-ceiling shelves, but they were stocked with books. An arch in the center went over a black marble fireplace.

The entrance floor was black and white tile, and probably older than my grandparents. It gave way to beautiful hardwood flooring that went to the back of the shop. To the side of the herb shelves, I could see a courtyard with a moss-covered fountain and many banana and elephant ear plants. Chandeliers wired for electricity lit the room.

"Can I help you?"

I turned and saw a plump, middle-aged white woman in a pink sundress standing behind the counter. She wore mint cat eyeglasses and just a hint of black eyeliner. She had rose-gold hair that was pink at the ends and fell to her shoulders. And she had on a white apron with the red cardinal from the sign embroidered on it.

"Oh, um, my friend came to pet the dog," I said.

She laughed. "Yes, I know. Shorty's happy to see them."

She gestured and there was Jaxon, out in the courtyard with the corgi. The dog lay on its back while he cooed and rubbed its tummy. Verity, Lionel, and German were making silly faces and fawning over the dog. I couldn't help laughing.

The woman stared at me for a moment and asked, "Are you Lyric Morrison?"

I froze, anxiety creeping up my torso and clasping around my throat. "Yes, why?"

"My cousin Delia owns Morning Brew," she replied. "She mentions you quite a bit."

"Oh! Yes, I like the coffee there. But...how did you know it was me?"

"She said you have teal hair and laugh like a super-villain."

I wish I could say it was the first time someone said that about my laugh.

"Oh, I'm Amy, by the way," she said but didn't offer her hand to shake.

"Hello, it's nice to meet you."

Amy tilted her head. "If you don't mind me asking, how are you sleeping?"

I frowned. "Why do you ask?"

"I'm not as talented a witch as German, but I can read people. And you..." Amy pushed her glasses down her nose, much like I would do to see the ghosts around me. She stared at me for a moment and nodded. "Are worn out."

I tugged on my earlobe. This was not going some-where I wanted it to. "I'm not sleeping," I blurted out, then winced. I really, really needed to keep my mouth shut. Whose business was it that I hadn't had a full night's rest in weeks?

"I can help you with that."

Amy turned to the shelves behind her. She gathered a couple of shiny-looking rocks and put them on the counter. Then she picked up a bowl and went over to the herbs. She had to climb the ladder to get to the ones she wanted, and I said, "You don't have to go through so much trouble."

"It's no trouble at all," Amy replied and scooped out the herbs she wanted. She brought the bowl back to the counter and set it down next to the rocks. I stepped closer to the counter, curious about what exactly she was doing.

Amy picked up a small bottle of oil and a little lavender candle. She took the oil, rubbed it on the candle, then put it behind the stones. Now that I could see them better, I realized they were chunks of amethyst. She sprinkled the herbs on the candle and lit it. She dribbled a little wax on the stones and put them in a tiny purple velvet bag. Then she blew out the candle.

"Here," she said and handed the bag to me. "Put this under your bed. You'll sleep more soundly, and I guarantee you won't have another nightmare."

"Thank you," I said. "How much do I owe you?"

"Ten dollars."

Sounded like a bargain to me. Shops in the Quarter sold gris-gris and talismans for forty bucks a pop at minimum. I gave her the money and slipped an extra dollar in the tip jar by the register. Then I put the little pouch in my purse.

Shorty the corgi had apparently had enough of Jaxon's attention and wandered off. The others came back inside. We stayed for another few minutes as German wanted to get some ingredients for a ritual and Verity found a book she wanted to read about clairvoyants.

When I asked Lionel about his reading, he shrugged and said, "I didn't need it."

I stared at him for a moment. I didn't understand.

"You didn't?"

"No, but you did." He gestured at my purse where I'd stored the bag Amy gave me. "You've had these bags under your eyes for weeks now." He put his fingers below his eyelids, then pulled down and made a face. "I figured if anyone could fix you up, Amy could." Then he grinned.

"Oh." I was a little annoyed that he tricked me but touched that he was worried about me. "Thank you."

Lionel winked at me and smiled.

It was only when I arrived home, I realized I never told Amy I was having nightmares. How did she know? I chalked it up to a lucky guess, I was too beat to think about it further. Heather wasn't around, which was odd. Usually, if she didn't come with me to the club, she'd be waiting for me when I got back to hear all about it.

As I kicked off my shoes, a wave of exhaustion hit me so hard I grabbed my bed's footboard so I wouldn't fall. I swore under my breath. I needed sleep. Good, uninterrupted sleep. I stripped out of my clothes, shoved the rock pouch under the bed, then crawled under the covers. I fell asleep right away and didn't have a single nightmare.

Chapter Fifteen

"DO I LOOK okay?" I asked as I fussed with my veil.

"You look like an extra in *Penny Dreadful*," said Heather.

"I don't know what that means."

"Because you have zero taste in TV shows."

I sighed and looked at myself in the mirror again. I wore the dress Lionel picked out along with the jewelry Verity selected. I curled my hair and brushed it out a little, creating a halo of soft teal curls around my face. I also switched to my silver wire-rim glasses with round lenses. While they might not have matched perfectly, they were the only non-tinted lenses I owned.

Heather's hands were on her hips and she was frowning. "So, what's the plan this time?"

"Perform the séance," I said.

"And this gets you closer to Elias how?"

"I'm still working on that."

I'd been going to the club for weeks and the only time I'd spoken with Elias was on the roof of the Bijou. He was difficult to get close to. Any time I approached him or spoke to him, he would stare at me until I clammed up. Or if I was being particularly chatty (something I can't help when I'm nervous) he would walk away. If it weren't for Lionel, I would think he hated me.

"He doesn't talk to anyone," Lionel said.

This left me perplexed. Why did he sponsor me? Was

it because of the night we met? He saved my life; he didn't owe me any favors. If anything, I owed him.

"Hey, space cadet, you're going to miss your ride if you keep zoning out," said Heather.

"Sorry, I'm nervous. I'm not a strong performer."

"I'll be there, you'll be fine."

"I'm not sure that's a good idea."

Heather frowned and crossed her arms over her stomach. "You're leaving me behind again?"

"I'm worried about you. I don't want you to strain yourself."

Ever since I'd gone to the Cardinal with my friends, Heather was in and out. I knew she wasn't disappearing voluntarily either, since she vanished in the middle of an argument. Heather didn't so much love to fight as she knew she was good at it. She was also particular about getting her way. When she came back, she said she wasn't sure where she'd gone or how long she was there.

Even more disturbing, the glow around her was beginning to fade. It was still gold, and she was as detailed as ever. But like an old TV losing the signal, she would flicker and vanish when she manifested too long. If she weren't already a ghost, I would have thought she was dying.

"It's fine, I can handle it."

I sighed. "And if you disappear entirely?"

She pursed her lips. "Okay, fine. I'll stay here."

"Thank you."

My cell phone vibrated, and there was a text from Verity.

We're here.

"I'll be back before two."

"Be careful."

Heather sulked as she flopped on my office chair. I waved and walked out. I made sure to lock the door behind me.

I had to pull up my skirt so I could walk around the back of the house. The bricks were uneven, and I didn't want to trip. When I got to the parking lot, I laughed. Verity was behind the wheel of a sleek black convertible. But that was the only thing normal about the sight before me. I knew that Verity and Lionel wouldn't be waiting tables, so I shouldn't have been surprised by how they were dressed.

Lionel was in the iridescent sequined tuxedo jacket. He'd paired it with a black mesh shirt, black leather pants, and boots. The mesh was thin enough that I could see his top surgery scars. He either wanted to show them off or just didn't care who saw them. His hair was slicked back into a pompadour and he'd accentuated his brown eyes with a hint of eyeliner. He was in the back seat checking himself out in the rearview mirror.

Verity on the other hand wore a Gothic Lolita dress. It was light purple with white lace, white tights, and lavender Mary Janes. Her hair was done in huge doll-like curls, and she even wore a purple velvet headband with white lace ruffles and lavender bows on both sides of her head. Her makeup was very simple. Just some mascara and white eyeliner to make her eyes look bigger, and a hint of peach lip color.

"You both are going to stand out a mile," I said as I got in the car.

"We like to be a little theatrical sometimes," said Verity.

"Can you put the top up now?" Lionel asked. "Lyric

will lose her veil and I don't want to mess up my hair. I don't know how yours is still in one piece after driving on the freeway."

Verity gave him a beatific smile. "Aqua Net."

She did put the top up as he asked.

On the ride over, Lionel and Verity chatted about the dinner and what fun it would be. I vaguely wondered if Mrs. White and Mr. Pickpocket would be there. I hoped not. Wouldn't that be awkward? Then again, they may not recognize me. My costume was more extravagant than my normal wardrobe. Plus, the veil would help obscure my face.

My phone buzzed again, this time due to a message from Psyche.

Psychepomp: Everything okay?

I figured it wouldn't hurt to chat, so I swiped the notification and replied.

EratoONine: I'm on my way to a séance.

Psychepomp: Another one? Why?

EratoONine: I'm hosting it, remember?

Psychepomp: Oh God that's right. Is that why you disappeared on us?

EratoONine: Yeah I've been practicing. Also, I made some new friends.

Psychepomp: Are these friends from the club?

EratoONine: Yes.

Psychepomp: Okay, be careful.

EratoONine: They're good people, don't worry.

Then I muted my phone and put it on "do not disturb."

The closer we got to the Bywater, the more nervous I became. By the time we got to Dauphine and Louisa, I was close to trembling. Verity managed to find a parking space close to the Bijou, but when she parked, I didn't move to get out. She and Lionel exchanged glances.

"You're going to do great," she said.

"Yeah! And if you don't, we can provide a distraction so you can run off screaming into the night," Lionel added. "Hey, you want the dirt on some of tonight's guests?"

I frowned. "Wouldn't that defeat the purpose of the séance?"

"You're there to talk to ghosts, not get the hot goss on the attendees."

"Save it for later in case I need cheering up."

I inhaled, held my breath, and exhaled. I counted each second as Dr. Cade taught me. Then I opened the door and got out of the car. I quickly made my way up the street before I could change my mind. We went upstairs, and I was happy Jaxon and German weren't working that night. They sat at a table close to the front of the room.

As I lingered outside the French doors to the club, I was surprised to see it was jam-packed. Even more so than the first séance I attended. Verity noticed too, as did Lionel who let out a low whistle.

"Looks like the entire Society has shown up," he said.

"Oh, dear lord in heaven," I muttered.

Verity frowned. "That's a funny thing to say. I thought you were an atheist?"

"Old habits die hard. Just, uh... I'll see you later."

Even though no one turned around, I felt as though every eye in the place was on me. I quickly walked down the gallery to Reyna's office but stopped at the door. Elias was there. He was leaning on the railing and gazing down into the courtyard below. He looked up as I stood frozen just a few precious feet away. Far too close for me to make a hasty exit. My pulse pounded in my ears.

"Oh, uh... Sorry, just looking for a place to hide."

He turned to leave.

"It's okay, I can find another spot if you need to—"

"I'm not hiding," he said. So quick I almost didn't catch it.

"Did you need to use the restroom?" I winced. God, how stupid could I be? The restrooms were inside the club and nowhere near us.

He paused and turned to look at me. "Vampires don't need bathrooms."

"Right, sorry, uh, I guess I didn't think of that. I'm not uh, I'm not very bright about some things."

I was praying to a God I didn't even believe in to strike me dead so I would shut the fuck up.

"I doubt that," Elias replied. "If anything, you're too bright. You're observant. Don't think I haven't noticed."

My heart jumped into my throat and did the tango with my tonsils. *What the fuck?* "Oh, I, uh..." I didn't know what to say. Was I busted?

Elias didn't comment further. He walked away.

I did my breathing exercise and pulled my necklace out from under my collar. I spun the planchette at least two dozen times as I paced the gallery. Waiters ducked in and out of the club, carrying food or rushing to get a bottle of wine from the wine cellar. It wasn't underground because basements aren't really a thing in New Orleans. Reyna converted the old stables into a temperature-controlled wine cellar. It was some years back, or so she told me.

Then I did something I really wished I hadn't. I slipped my glasses down my nose and looked inside the club. Every person had a ghost sitting next to them. Some had two or three. And they would all probably want a chance to speak. This was going to be a long night.

At last, Reyna appeared and said, "It's time."

I gulped but stuffed my fidget jewelry back under my dress. I nodded and followed her inside.

As I approached the empty table, my nerves intensified to the point I wasn't sure I could keep walking. But I made my way to the table. Everything was set up as I requested, and I breathed a sigh of relief. At least this part I knew.

Part of the preparations for the séance involved finding a suitable ghost. We didn't want to summon poor Julie from the Bottom of the Cup or the horrible Madame LaLaurie. And I didn't want to summon "Madame Le Blanc" for fear she would fully manifest and the jig would be up.

Instead, we went through a few ghost guides and found one ghost who seemed to fit the bill. Not entirely malevolent but not a victim either. I hadn't tried to summon her yet, and I prayed this would work.

The house lights dimmed, and when I took my seat I said, "Good evening, and welcome to the Black Lily Society. As you're aware, this evening we will be conducting a séance. Tonight, we are going to attempt to contact Marie-Anne, the famous Witch of the French Opera. And hopefully, she can give us her side of the story."

I paused because I couldn't remember my next line. When I looked over at where Lionel and Verity sat, she mouthed, "Tell the story."

Oh, right.

"Not many are familiar with the story of Marie-Anne, at least not anymore. More well-known New Orleans murderesses like Delphine LaLaurie dominate the various ghost tours. And movies, and television shows. Marie-Anne's story is both understandable and quite sad. But we won't get into the lurid speculations of her life and her death. Instead, we will stick to the facts."

I paused for a moment. Everyone was staring at me. I curled my hands into fists, hidden in the folds of my dress. I could do this.

"Marie-Anne was many things: a businesswoman, an actress, and an opera singer. She had a career at the French Opera for many years. When she retired, she opened a bakery close to the opera house on the Rue Royale.

"It was said she had a special sense for what people wanted. She was never short of the pastries and chocolates that would soothe the souls of her customers. There were rumors as well of a side business. One involving potions and concoctions that would cure any illness, but that's all they are. Rumors.

"At this bakery, she employed a pastry chef who, frankly, couldn't bake a loaf of bread let alone all the fancy treats demanded by her customers. Why would she employ a baker who couldn't bake? Simply put, she was blinded by love.

"Santiago and Marie-Anne became partners both in the bakery and in life. Though they never formally married, they were together day and night, both at the bakery and in Marie-Anne's Royal Street townhouse. They spent many happy years together. Until Santiago's eyes began to wander. They fell on the lovely Camille, a soprano at the Opera and a regular customer. This set a series of events in motion that would end all their lives.

"At first, Marie-Anne was none the wiser. But then Santiago made his intentions known. He left Marie-Anne and moved in with Camille. Marie-Anne dwelt in despair until she couldn't take it anymore. She hung herself, cursing her unfaithful lover and his paramour in the process.

"Rather than feeling guilt, Santiago was elated. Marie-Anne did not have time to change her will. The bakery and her estate would be all his. He and Camille celebrated late into the night. It was said at midnight is when the ghost of Marie-Anne appeared. She cried tears of blood and howled for justice. Then her specter marched down the Rue Royale to the abode of Santiago and Camille.

"No one knows for sure how the fire started. It could have been an overturned candle or an improperly tended hearth. Regardless of where the first spark came from, the love nest was soon in flames. Neither Santiago nor Camille escaped; the lovers perished in the fire only three days after Marie-Anne herself passed from this world. And now, we will be calling on the Witch of the French Opera herself."

Perhaps I didn't have the same panache for storytelling as Emerson, but no one seemed to notice. There was just the slightest trembling in my hands, but I clasped them together behind my back to hide it.

"We will be deviating from the routine, and as such, I would like to ask for volunteers to join me at the table."

Every hand in the room went up.

Okay, maybe I should have thought this through.

To my shock, one of the volunteers was Elias. Not wanting to waste the opportunity, I gestured for him to join me. He did, and he chose a seat to my left. I then selected five other people at random, none of whom I knew on sight. This meant they were either irregular members or guests of the club. It was hard for me to say.

When everyone was seated, I took my glasses off and slipped them into my pocket. Yes, each person had a spirit with them. Even Elias.

The ghost clinging to the vampire was indistinct, I'd say probably a level two at most. I wanted to know more about them. Were they a victim of Elias? A friend? Perhaps even a family member? I couldn't be sure. Elias either didn't know about their presence or he didn't care. He looked at me and raised an eyebrow.

Oh, right, the séance.

I lit the candles on the table and said, "Please join hands."

I still didn't like being touched, but the lace gloves helped. I was surprised by how warm Elias's hand was. Before, his hands were cold. Did he feed recently? I shuddered at the thought. Even through the lace, I could feel calluses on his palm. I couldn't help wondering where they were from. I pushed the thought to the back of my mind. I had work to do.

"Spirits of the dear departed," I said. "Hear me. We are here tonight to contact the spirit of Marie-Anne, the Witch of the French Opera. Marie-Anne, we are joined in perfect love and perfect trust. We ask you to join us. Join us and tell us your story."

I felt more than saw the ghosts moving about the

room, drawing closer. I kept my eyes on the candles. The tremble in my hands hadn't abated; if anything, it was growing worse. To my surprise, Elias squeezed my hand. Was he trying to reassure me? Could he feel how nervous I was? Did that mean the person on my right could feel it too?

Then I heard a gasp and looked up. A fog descended on the middle of the table. A silver fog in the vague outline of a woman. Gradually she appeared. She was transparent, but there was still definition to her. She was dressed in fine green silk, and her white hair was perfectly styled in sausage curls. The echoing gasp through the audience was all the confirmation I needed. They could see her too.

"Thank you for joining us, Marie-Anne," I said.

"I come only for you, I will not entertain this prattle," she said, her French accent sharp.

"For me? Why?"

"To warn you! You are in danger!"

A cold wind gusted through the room. I heard various gasps and cries from the attendees, but I didn't turn to look at them. I kept my eyes on Marie-Anne. I knew if I broke eye contact, I would lose her.

"In danger from what?"

Marie-Anne seized my face in her hands, and I felt as though I'd been sunk in an ice bath. I was so cold I could hardly breathe.

"The Night Hag," the ghost exclaimed, "she has her eye on you! And you will meet the same fate as I if you do not heed my warning!"

The ice in my veins was painful, but I had to get past it. This was the second time a ghost had warned me, and I needed to know more. "What fate? Are you saying I'll die?"

"Beware, little medium," Marie-Anne replied and faded.

"Wait, come back!"

It was too late, she'd disappeared. The ice was gone, and the candles were blown out. Someone turned the lights back on. Candles and gas lamps lit with inhuman speed. People stared at me in awe, though a few looked disappointed or even angry.

"That sure didn't last long," someone muttered.

There was murmuring and my stomach sank. I failed. I couldn't do the one thing I promised. I was about to apologize to the audience, but then Elias squeezed my hand again.

He leaned close and whispered in my ear, "Don't break the circle. We can summon Pere Antoine for them. He would be more likely to cooperate."

"That's...actually, that's brilliant."

Pere Antoine was another famous New Orleans ghost: a friar who they said had the voice of an angel. As a matter of fact, one of the alleys next to St. Louis Cathedral was named after him. It was said that any time it rained in New Orleans, you could hear Pere Antoine sing at the cathedral. I often thought you must be able to hear him sing every day in springtime.

"My apologies, everyone," I said. "As you're probably aware, we cannot force a spirit to appear or perform. However, if you would indulge me for a few minutes. I may be able to summon a gentler soul that all of New Orleans is familiar with. Pere Antoine."

More murmurs, but this time they were positive instead of dreadful. The lights were dimmed again, and the candles reignited on their own. It drew a surprised gasp from the table sitters. I made a mental note to thank

Jaxon for that later.

I closed my eyes and concentrated, so I could call Pere Antoine from the void. It was more difficult this time. Pere Antoine was a much older ghost, and not inclined to travel as it turned out. Elias held my hand, and his resolve inspired me to keep trying. Then a dim shade appeared above the table, speaking in a gentle voice.

After that, it was smooth sailing. Pere Antoine graced us with a beautiful rendition of the Kyrie. It was enough to satisfy both members and guests of the club. I thanked him for his appearance, and he departed with little prompting from me. When the séance was over, I excused myself to the balcony outside. I needed to breathe. And in truth, I was terrified.

Marie-Anne's warning echoed in my ears. The Night Hag... It sounded familiar.

"Are you all right?"

I jumped. Elias was at my side once again.

"Jitters. I thought I really screwed up in there."

"I would say you were fortunate. Marie-Anne Dupont was not known to be kind. As a person or as a ghost." His eyes narrowed. "Do you know what a Night Hag is, Miss Morrison?"

"No."

"I see." He took a business card out of his pocket and handed it to me. "Be at that address tomorrow night at nine. We need to talk."

Before I could ask any further questions, Elias was gone. Again.

I stared down at the card, both anxious and elated. What had I gotten myself into now?

Chapter Sixteen

THE NEXT EVENING, I was in the Quarter, vulnerable but unafraid. I'd opted for something simple. The dress I'd worn to the séance caused some sensory issues toward the end of the evening. The weather was hot again, though not as bad as the summer. Still, it did make picking out an outfit pretty easy.

I selected a black tank top, blue denim shorts, my planchette necklace, and black Converse shoes. My hair was pinned back from my face, and I wore my violet glasses. I was indistinguishable from the throngs of tourists, and I liked it that way. I felt like I was undercover. I found Elias's home easily enough. Convincing myself to approach and knock was the problem.

For someone who was intensely private and didn't seem to like people, it was weird his home was on Bourbon Street. Specifically, near Bourbon and St. Philip which was a pretty busy section. I wasn't a fan of Bourbon Street myself. Not only because I don't drink but also because I hated the smell and the noise, especially in the warmer months. I was quietly glad we were starting to get into the cooler seasons, and fall was only a few short weeks away.

I stood on the sidewalk in front of a large canary-yellow Spanish colonial. It was a two-story building with royal-blue shutters and a wrought iron gallery like so many buildings in the French Quarter. I could see why people called it "iron lace." It was so intricate yet looked delicate at the same time. I snapped a picture of it with my phone.

Heather wasn't with me; she faded hours ago, and I wasn't sure when she would be back. She was excited I was invited to Elias's place as she thought I'd get some good evidence there. I didn't have a chance to tell her about Marie-Anne's warning of the Night Hag. I doubted that Heather would care. She didn't seem to care about much aside from her case.

Psyche urged caution when I told her what I was doing. But she agreed there would be evidence galore at his home. This made little sense to me. How cautious could I be in this situation? I was walking right into the lion's den with no protection. I didn't dare ask Lionel or Verity to come with me.

And it wasn't as though Elias would leave me unattended so I could go through his things. For all I knew he was luring me into a trap to kill me. I was praying he wouldn't murder me like he did Heather. Well, allegedly. There was still no proof either way. And he had a really big mark in the "probably innocent" column.

Elias was willing to help me, and he'd saved my life. This didn't match with someone who would murder without a thought. But what did I know of him really? We weren't close friends. We were barely acquaintances. Perhaps I was only seeing what he wanted me to see.

I had to know for sure. I screwed up my courage and went to the side gate. I rang the bell as the card instructed and waited. The gate creaked, then slowly opened. I didn't see anyone around. I let myself in and carefully closed the gate behind me. When I heard the gate slam shut, my heart dropped down to my knees. No turning back now. But as I walked further into the property, I gasped.

I found myself in a courtyard garden, but not like any I'd seen before. This one was teeming with plants that weren't tame but were pruned back. The brick paths were close to being crowded out by ferns and plants I couldn't identify. A fountain bubbled somewhere. Dozens of flower beds lined the walls of the courtyard. I could smell star jasmine and roses, and I smiled.

Overhead were several strands of blue and violet fairy lights. They twinkled softly and cast a calming glow over the garden. Alongside them were iron lanterns on shepherd hooks, with candles burning behind colored glass. By each lantern stood stone furniture, overgrown with moss. Each bench had silk damask pillows and throws draped over them. It gave the feel of a space both ancient and civilized.

There was a garçonnière to the left, though it was crumbling and didn't appear lived in. I doubted anyone had even been inside in the last hundred years. At the back of the courtyard was a small two-story cottage painted in the same yellow and blue as the main house. The French doors at the front of the cottage opened, and Elias stepped out.

He wore the same black T-shirt as always, though the red flannel shirt was missing this time. He was barefoot and had on a pair of olive cargo shorts. His long chestnut hair was in a half bun, the shorter strands framing his face which was now clean-shaven.

"Right on time," he said.

"I'm late," I replied.

Elias frowned and took his phone out of his pocket. "It's nine on the dot."

"If I'm on time that means I'm late."

"I see. Please, follow me."

I did, and Elias led me down a path that took us past a beautiful fountain with a fairy. She was pouring water from a vase into the basin, frozen in stone for eternity. The fairy and the fountain were both covered in a thin layer of moss. Red impatiens had been planted all around. Elias moved the leaves of a fern aside and gestured for me to sit down.

The stone bench was carved into the wall of the courtyard itself. More moss clung to the stones, but here too were the silk pillows and damask throws. I thought the feel of the moss and silk against my bare legs would be irritating, but it was quite comfortable. Elias sat on my left again, his elbows on his knees and his fingers knit together.

"This place is beautiful," I said.

"Thank you. It took a lot of work to get the plants to a more manageable level, but I'm pleased with it."

"You did all this?"

"Yes, I like gardening."

"You've recreated the Garden of Eden on Bourbon Street. If you 'like' gardening, then I only 'like' music."

Elias chuckled. "You must have quite the record collection at home then."

"I do. And CDs, cassette tapes, I even have a couple 8-tracks, but I don't have anything to play them with."

"That's wonderful, though you should add more vinyl to your collection. There are a few shops I could recommend."

"Thank you, I'd appreciate that. I don't listen to music as much as I used to, but I still like to play some before bed every night."

Elias tucked some of his hair behind his ear. "To get to the point, you told me you don't know what a Night Hag is, correct?"

"Yeah. I tried looking it up last night. But all Wikipedia says is something about sleep paralysis and I already have that."

"What?" Elias sat up a little straighter.

"Relax, it happens to people who sleep on their back. It's a problem I've had since I was a kid."

"The Night Hag is different," said Elias. "It's a creature that feeds on the psychic energy of others."

I pulled my legs up onto the bench, turned to face him, then sat cross-legged. "Go on."

He copied my movements but scooted back a little so our legs wouldn't touch. "Legends say the Night Hag was born from those who were corrupted by demons."

"I don't believe in demons."

"I bet you didn't believe in vampires either."

I gulped. "Uh, fair point."

"As I was saying, Night Hags are the souls of those who are corrupted by demons. Whether that's figuratively or literally, no one is quite sure. Ordinarily, those who are so tainted would be taken to hell after their death. But on rare occasions, some of those souls slip their demon's grasp. Yet they have nowhere else to go. They're too tainted to move on to the afterlife. And without a body to sustain them, they're in danger of decaying into nothing. They latch onto a victim and drain them of energy until the victim dies in order to sustain their own existence."

"Sounds...vampiric." I winced. Apparently, between last night and tonight, I still hadn't learned to shut up.

Elias actually smiled. And wow, that was a beautiful smile. Too bad it disappeared within seconds. "I believe humans nowadays call them psychic vampires. It isn't entirely true, however. The Night Hag feeds off a specific form of energy. Can you guess what that might be?"

I thought back to the Wiki article. I could probably recite it word for word if I felt like it. But I doubted Elias would be impressed, so I said, "Fear."

"Very good. They're not unique in this. There are many beings that can and do feed off fear. As a matter of fact, some ghosts can manifest more easily when the person perceiving them is afraid. However, the one aspect which sets them apart is their ability to cause and create nightmares."

I shuddered as I recalled my nightmares. The ones I had soon after this whole mess started. Though they didn't trouble me anymore. Not since I went to the Cardinal.

"I'm good, then."

"What do you mean?"

"I got some magic rocks that keep bad dreams away. I haven't had a nightmare since I got them."

"Good, that will keep you safe for the time being. I would recommend speaking with German about a cleansing ritual, just to be safe."

I frowned. "Why?"

"Because as a medium you're going to attract many spirits, not all of them good. Regular cleansings of your home would prevent them from latching on and causing trouble."

"Oh, right. I think I read something about that in the book you gave me."

"German is a powerful witch; he would be able to help you."

"How do you know so much about this?" I asked.

"Were you a medium before you…"

Elias shook his head. "No. But my lover was. He was the one who wrote the book I gave you."

"Oh. That's handy."

"Handy?"

"That he was able to write a book. I don't have the attention span to write an email let alone a book."

"Yes, Reyna told me about your condition."

I knew Reyna let it be known among the club members, as I didn't want to say anything myself. The thought stressed me out. I knew from my experience online I would get a lot of well-meaning but quite rude or invasive questions about it. The one I hated the most was if I was "high functioning," whatever the hell that meant.

"Uh, yeah. My brain wiring was not performed by a licensed contractor. And while it still works, the on switch is somewhere in the basement and if it rains the power goes out."

Elias stared at me, then laughed. "A unique metaphor."

"I'm good at those. I used to read a lot of Neil Gaiman and Douglas Adams. I also just started reading Sir Terry Pratchett."

"I have heard of Gaiman and Pratchett."

"It should be illegal that you've never heard of Douglas Adams. He's one of England's national treasures."

"I haven't been back to England since the mid-1800s. And it's no more illegal than it is to be American and be unfamiliar with Stephen King."

"Wait, you're from England? You don't have an accent."

"As I said, I haven't been to my home country in some

time."

"Makes sense. And I know who Stephen King is, by the way. But I'm not a fan of his writing."

"Oh? And why is that?"

How did I explain this in a way that made sense to someone outside of my head? Elias hadn't run screaming yet, and we were developing a rapport. But sometimes I had difficulty explaining a concept that felt normal to me. And could possibly be weird to others. Still, nothing ventured, nothing gained. So, I charged ahead.

"So, when I read, I usually picture the events in my mind. It's like I'm watching a play, but I also experience it in first person so it's kind of like a dream. The ones where you're outside your body but inside it at the same time. The words in the story contribute to how the scene looks and feels to me. I don't like the words he uses; they don't create a picture I want to see or feel."

"Let me see if I understand you correctly. You don't like his books because the experience it creates in your head is unpleasant?"

"Yeah."

"Is it the language he uses?"

"Nope. Like, don't get me wrong, the frequent use of racist and homophobic slurs in his earlier work is not the least bit fun. And I'm not against swearing, I'll cuss up a storm myself, especially when I'm worked up. But like when I tried to read *It* and one of the kids was getting bullied? I saw it in my head and also felt it, and I didn't like it."

Elias nodded. "I see. Though wouldn't that mean he's good at drawing you in?"

"I'm not saying he's not talented, he is. I'm just saying his work isn't for me, and there's nothing wrong with that."

"Is it because you're autistic you feel like this?"

"I don't know," I admitted. "It could be an autism thing. It could be a 'me' thing. It's not something I think about often and the few times I've brought it up with other people they look at me like I'm..."

"Insane?"

"Yeah. It's not a fun feeling."

"Does this happen only when you read fiction?"

I had to think about it for a minute. I had never considered the question before. "Come to think of it, yes. But when I read nonfiction it's more like watching a true crime documentary. One that happens to be playing in my head."

"I see. Do you prefer nonfiction then?"

"Oh hell no. It's a startling experience but I do prefer fiction. It's like escaping the world for a little while to a completely different one. I like Alys Arden's books especially. They're still kinda nitty gritty at points but her words paint a much more pleasant picture in my head. Plus, they're all set in New Orleans so it's easier to imagine what's going on in the background."

"I don't believe I'm familiar with her work."

"She's a local author. If you go to the vampire store over on St. Ann, you can get her whole series."

Elias snorted. "I believe I'll pass but thank you."

"They have a vampire speakeasy too."

"Yes, I've been there. It's quite lovely," he said. "I prefer the Black Lily."

"Suit yourself." I smirked. "And being a real vampire, how do you feel about vampires being so heavily associated with New Orleans?"

"Given the city's history, it isn't surprising," said

Elias. "Many of the stories humans tell about vampires are based around xenophobia. With New Orleans being a port city, that occurred here more often than most places in the United States."

"Yeah, but does it bother you?"

He shook his head. "No. While it may make things inconvenient at times, it doesn't bother me. Most are unaware we exist. Even after recent events, we're nothing but fairytales to humans."

I nodded but then stifled a yawn. "I should go. I have to be up early for work tomorrow."

"Let me walk you."

"I live in Uptown. I'm not walking, I'm taking the bus." I checked the time on my phone. Only fifteen minutes to get to the stop and I'd have to navigate around drunk tourists to do so.

"Then let me escort you to the bus stop."

I didn't see a problem with it, so I agreed and we left.

We went up to Dauphine, then over to St. Anne. We kept walking until we hit North Rampart and reached the bus stop outside Armstrong Park.

There weren't many people around, but the entrance to Armstrong Park shone like a beacon. It was a white arched gateway with "Armstrong" spelled in all capital letters. There were lights behind the letters and the arch itself reminded me of a Ferris wheel. When it was lit, you could see the arch all the way down to St. Ann and Chartres, as though inviting you to come to the park for a late-night stroll. This of course would be impossible as the park closed at seven.

"Do you do this often?" Elias asked.

"I don't have a car, so yes."

"And the possibility of being mugged doesn't bother

you?"

I shrugged. "Of course it bothers me, but I don't carry cash, I can cut off my cards as soon as I get to a computer, and my phone is insured. I don't necessarily want to be mugged but if I worried about it all the time, I'd never leave the house."

"I see." Elias was staring at me again, a small frown on his face.

"Hey, about the book." I turned toward him. "I'm sure it's precious to you, given who wrote it and all. Would you like it back?"

"It's yours now, you'll make more use of it than I will."

I blinked. "Are you sure? I mean, I've already memorized it. You can have it back if you want."

"Consider it a gift."

Before I could press the point, the bus pulled up. I fished my phone out of my pocket and showed my pass to the driver as I boarded. I found a seat near the back, then looked out the window as the bus pulled away. Elias was gone like he'd never been there at all.

Chapter Seventeen

I CRASHED THE minute I got home. While I wasn't having nightmares anymore, I was still tired most of the time. Briefly before I went to sleep, I thought Elias might have a point. Maybe I needed a cleansing. The ghosts were becoming clearer, and as they did my energy seemed to always be at about seventy out of one hundred. Why was that?

Unfortunately, due to falling asleep so fast, I forgot to set my alarm, which would have been a problem if I weren't a light sleeper. I startled awake around 2:00 a.m., the cobwebs of a dream about orcas sticking to my brain. Why orcas? I didn't like homicidal sea cattle.

I looked at the clock on my bedside table and stared for a moment. I was so foggy for a moment I said, "How did it get to be 2:37 in the afternoon? I'm late for work!"

Then I woke up fully, figured out the actual time, and realized I hadn't set my alarm. I corrected the mistake, rolled over, and tried to go back to sleep. My brain, however, wasn't having it. My meeting with Elias kept running through my head.

I felt completely relaxed in his company. If he killed Heather, I should be able to feel it. Shouldn't I? I realized my thoughts were not going to stop racing. I rolled again to turn my bedside lamp on. Maybe I could lull myself back to sleep with a good book.

"You know, for someone who lived through a vampire

cult taking over a city, you sure have a lot of books on vampires."

I jumped. Heather stood by my desk.

"I used to love vampire stories," I replied. "I still do. Books, movies, television shows, if it's got a vampire in it, I'll probably watch it."

"How is that even possible? Vampires try to kill you and you're like, 'Oh, but you're still so sexy'? That's not okay, Lyric."

Great, she was in another one of her moods. I sighed and put the book down. "There's enough separation between fictional and real-life vampires in my head. I don't feel triggered reading about them like you."

"I'm not," Heather said in a huffy tone.

"Could have fooled me. Plus, it seems like every time I see you lately you're mad about something. Are you trying to drive me away?" It was a routine I'd used myself when I was young and convinced no one would love me because I was weird. I tried to burn the bridge of every good relationship I had because I was "crazy." Then I did the same thing again when I received my autism diagnosis as an adult. I thought it was kinder to those around me because they deserved a better friend.

Thank God I didn't succeed. At least not with the people who really mattered.

"I'm trying to understand you," Heather exclaimed. "You lived in Phoenix. You told me yourself vampires took over the city and yet here you are buddying up to them. Did you even get anything useful from Elias tonight?"

"Yes."

"And?"

"And there's nothing to report. He's not the type to confess to anything because he keeps himself to himself.

If I'm going to get the truth out of him, I need to build a relationship with him, so he can trust me enough to divulge his secrets. And stop changing the subject, why are you being such a brat lately?"

She rolled her eyes. "Oh, I don't know. Could it be because I'm dead? Didn't you promise to help solve my murder? Or are you too busy cozying up to your undead boyfriend?"

I sat up and swung my legs to the floor so I was facing her. "You're hiding something."

Heather snorted. "I am not."

"We may not be best friends, but I can tell when you're lying. You like to misdirect and put me on the defensive, so I stop asking questions. Obviously, I can't make you tell me what's wrong. I can, however, ignore you until you go away."

"No, you can't. I'll break everything in the house."

I opened the top drawer of my bedside table and pulled out *Piercing the Veil*. "I've been studying, remember? I can ignore you. Or I can call German and have him banish you."

"You're blackmailing me into telling you what's wrong? You're unbelievable!"

"You're still avoiding the question. Also, it's not blackmail, I'm threatening you. There's a difference."

Heather scowled and crossed her arms over her stomach. "Oh hell, fine! It's not fair you have such an easy time making friends with these people! I was at the Black Lily Society for months and never got as close to everyone as you. They like you more than me."

"If you behaved this way when you were alive, I think I might know why," I said. I rubbed my temples. My head didn't hurt, but I was getting the "brain full of bees" feeling, meaning I was close to sensory overload.

"So you're saying it's my fault?"

"I'm saying you're high maintenance as a ghost. I can't imagine what you were like in person. Don't forget you're the one who bullied me into this investigation in the first place. You keep insisting you were murdered. And the only proof we have is a possible fang mark on your neck and nothing else. You're so fixated on Elias that you can't seem to consider any other options. And I haven't been able to turn up any evidence supporting your theory."

"And you're determined to prove him innocent because you're infatuated with him."

I sighed. "I am not. What I know of him doesn't match up. Not with the sort of person who would bump off some girl he hardly knew. Which is by your own admission, by the way. Can you at least give me a motive as to why he would want you dead?"

"I would if I had one." Heather's eyes watered. She was on the verge of tears. "I can't believe you're being so judgmental! I thought you'd know better than to blame the victim!"

"I'm not victim-blaming. I'm saying there's no proof. You can't remember the night you died, and Elias isn't out hacking up other girls—at least not that I can find. And no one at the club has so much as mentioned you." I paused. I knew what I was going to say next would hurt her feelings, and as much as it pained me, I wanted to get the truth. "If I didn't know better, I'd think you weren't a member at all."

Heather sobbed. "But I was! I knew the passwords to get in!"

"Which you could have gotten at any time because the club frequently has guests."

"I was friends with Lionel, Verity, and Jaxon. Okay, not so much German—he wasn't fun to be around. And they don't miss me at all! Do you know how much it hurts, knowing that none of the people you loved give two shits about you?"

"Where's your pin?"

"Excuse me?"

I got up and went to the bathroom. I pulled my jewelry box off the top shelf, grabbed what I wanted, and put it back. Then I showed Heather the enamel pin I was given my first night at the Black Lily Society. "If you were a member, you should have one of these."

"I lost it," she replied.

"Where?"

"On Bourbon Street. I was at that European jazz pub over on Bourbon and St. Ann and it popped off my jacket."

I knew the place she was talking about. It was the same building as the "vampire" speakeasy I mentioned to Elias.

"When was that?"

"Like a couple weeks before I died."

"Then what about your number?"

She frowned. "What?"

I showed her the back of the pin. "They're numbered. Mine is 1132. And that's where you'll find me in the membership ledger."

"How should I know that?" Heather demanded. "It doesn't matter because you're still trying to prove Elias didn't do it and I know he did."

"He saved my life," I blurted out.

Heather's eyes widened. "What?"

I sat on the bed again. "In Phoenix, the night the coup ended. There were some vampires at my apartment building, and I was stupid enough to get home after sunset. Elias saved me."

"You two know each other? Why didn't you tell me?"

"Because you were so insistent he was the one who killed you. I thought you'd have a fit if I told you he saved my life."

"How did it even happen?"

So, I told her. I explained about the night in Phoenix and how Elias saved me. Except I left out the part where he tried to erase my memory. The fewer people who knew about that the better. And sure, Heather was dead and I was the only person who could see her. But I still didn't want to tell her about Elias's hypnosis. It would only fuel her conviction that he was guilty.

When I finished talking, Heather let out a low whistle. "Shit, no wonder you're always staring at him. If a handsome vampire with a sword saved me from being munched by other vampires, I'd get a little starstruck too."

"Yeah, well, there's also the bit where I can't talk about what happened in Phoenix. Cynthia shot her mouth off and she paid for it."

"Who's Cynthia?"

"My old boss." I looked at the clock. It was past 3:00 a.m. But we needed to clear the air, so I decided to explain. "She was my floor supervisor at my old job. When the coup was lifted, she posted a video to YouTube. It was of vampires feeding on people and killing them in Phoenix. She said the news and the government lied to everyone and vampires were real."

"Oh my God."

"Precisely. I knew she was telling the truth and I wanted to support her. But then the day after posting the video, she made another one. She apologized for 'perpetuating the hoax' and said the footage was fake. When I confronted her about it, she had no idea what I was talking about. It was like she was brainwashed."

"Oh shit." Heather slapped a hand over her mouth, eyes wide with horror. "Do you think…"

"I think a vampire hypnotized her. They do not want word about vampires to get out to the general public. Which is hilarious given the kind of guests they have at the club. And Elias has been careful not to mention it, but he did save me that night. If I breathe a word of it, I could end up like Cynthia."

Heather bit her lip, then asked, "But wouldn't Reyna or German stop him?"

"I don't know," I admitted. "Look, I've got to try to get back to sleep. I'm asking you to please be patient while I get this worked out. I don't think Elias is completely innocent but I don't think he's guilty either. Which is the entire point of my going undercover. To find the truth one way or another."

"I guess," she said, her lower lip thrust out in a pout.

I put *Piercing* back and felt something against my foot. I moved the bed skirt aside and felt around, then pulled out the baggie from the Cardinal. "Huh, that's strange, I thought I put this closer to the center."

"What is it?" Heather asked.

"Something a witch made for me so I'll sleep better. Though it doesn't seem to be doing the job tonight."

"What's in it?"

"Rocks and herbs." I put the bag back and pushed it back into place with my foot.

Heather frowned again. "You brought home some random junk from a hoodoo witch doctor without even asking what's in it? For all you know, it's a gris-gris that'll turn you into a zombie!"

I silently counted to ten before I answered. "There are so many things wrong with what you just said I don't know where to start. One, she's a witch. Two, it wasn't hoodoo. Three, you can't just turn someone into a zombie with a gris-gris. As a native Louisianan, you should know better."

"Oh, excuse me for not using the latest PC woke language," Heather snapped. "Just get rid of it."

Great, she was mad again.

"I watched her make it, and Amy is Delia's cousin. She's a nice person. And German trusts her so that's good enough for me."

Heather glared at me. "Wow. You know, they could all be in on it. Luring you into a trap so they can kill you like they did me. And you'd be too stupid to see the knife coming until it's lodged in your back."

"As if you're actually worried about me," I replied. I laid down and pulled the covers over me.

Heather got up from the chair and sat on the side of the bed. "Think about it! You said they never mention me. It's like I've never been to the club but clearly, I have. I know everyone by name and I know the layout of the place."

"Mm." I turned the light off. I hoped Heather would take the hint to drop it.

"So, if Elias killed me, maybe they were his accomplices."

"Why would a vampire need help from two other vampires, a magic vampire, a conjurer, and a clairvoyant to take out an empath? Or a hapless medium who can't even control her powers?"

"I don't know. But you saw how weird Reyna was

about your powers. Everyone at that club is a total freak about it."

"Mediums are rare." I snorted. "Heh. Medium rare."

"Hilarious. I'm just saying don't trust them so easily. Or maybe you'll—"

Heather broke off. She was flickering again, and I couldn't hear her voice.

I sat up and concentrated. "Heather, stay with me. Follow the sound of my voice."

She continued to flicker, then she faded from sight. She was gone. Again. I sighed, flopped back on the bed, and stared up at the ceiling. Even with the lights off, I could still see. My blackout curtains were spaced too far away from the window to block out all the light. And I still hadn't found a covering for the transom window. The light from both the streetlamp and the lamp in the courtyard always burned so brightly.

My head was swimming. What if Heather was right? What if these people weren't my friends at all? I admittedly wasn't a good judge of character, which was proven time and again. I'd had people I thought were friends talking about me behind my back or worse. Using me for their own gain, then tossing me aside like trash.

What would they have to gain though? Did Elias want my blood? Did Reyna envy my powers? Maybe that was why she continued to press me about solo appointments at the club. I glanced at the clock again—3:30 a.m. Fuck. I grabbed the clock and adjusted the alarm forward an hour.

I wouldn't have time to visit Morning Brew, but the extra hour of sleep was better than a cup of coffee any day. Then I rolled over and fell into a fitful sleep. I dreamed about fangs, ghosts, and blood.

Chapter Eighteen

HEATHER WAS ABSENT for a while. I couldn't say I blamed her. We'd been fighting so much lately, and every time we fought, she would run out of energy and disappear. It worried me because I was no closer to solving her murder. Maybe she was right and I didn't want to believe Elias did it. But if that were the case, shouldn't I have found some evidence?

Even more troubling, when I went to check Heather's social media for more leads, it was all gone. Every single profile was missing, and I couldn't recover the information from any of them. I tried using the Wayback Machine, but none of it was archived. I even asked Psyche's husband Frank if he had any ideas, but he said the only way would be to appeal directly to the social media companies. That was definitely out.

So, I poked around the Black Lily Society and dropped Heather's name a few times. If she was there as frequently as she said, someone would know her. In this, I had no luck. I mentioned her to Verity and Lionel, but they said they'd never heard of her. When I asked Jaxon and German, they said the same thing. When I went to Reyna and asked about Heather, she said she didn't know who she was.

"Is this the friend you said passed away?"

"Yes."

Reyna took out a thick ledger with a red leather

binding and black pages. "Do you know when she would have joined?"

"Sometime around May, I think."

Reyna flipped through the pages and shook her head. "If she was here, I don't think she was ever an official member."

"She was an empath if that helps."

Reyna checked again. "We haven't had any new empaths join the club since 1994. I'd remember, I like to keep an eye on them."

I raised an eyebrow. "Why?"

"They can be trouble." She put the ledger away in her desk drawer. "As a matter of fact, the empath who joined in 1994 is no longer welcome here and was expelled."

"Really? What did they do?"

"He used his powers to stir up trouble. Pitting members against one another, amplifying negative emotions, things like that. He also gossiped about everything and everyone. We had to change the name of the club because of him."

"He sounds unpleasant."

"He was."

"What was it called before it was the Black Lily Society?"

"The Magnolia Social and Pleasure Club. Not terribly original I admit, but they are lovely flowers and we have so many of them here."

"So why switch to the Black Lily Society? They're not flowers native to Louisiana, are they?"

At that, Reyna smirked. "It was to mock the Lily-white Movement."

"I'm not familiar with that," I admitted.

"It was a political movement in the Fifties. Its goal

was to keep Black people and other people of color out of, well, everything. As I'm an Afro-Latina myself, I'm not a fan of the concept. However, lilies aren't only white, they come in a variety of colors including black."

I laughed. "Very clever."

"I thought you might appreciate it."

"Well, thank you anyway for looking," I said and stood.

Reyna did the same. "I am sorry I couldn't be more helpful. Though, if you'll forgive me for asking, why don't you summon her?"

"I tried, but she isn't responding." Technically, it wasn't a lie. I did try to summon Heather before going to the club. It irked me that I was unsuccessful.

"Perhaps she's passed on then. Oh, have you reconsidered my offer?"

After the happy disaster at my first séance dinner, Reyna renewed her request. She thought I could really help people with private readings. She sweetened the pot by offering to split the proceeds with me sixty/forty. She also offered to waive my yearly membership dues.

"I have, and I can do it but only on certain evenings."

"Excellent! Which would you prefer?"

"Wednesday and Friday. Maybe some Thursdays but it will depend on how I'm feeling."

"I can do that. How long would you be available for?"

"Ninety minutes."

Reyna pulled out another ledger. This one was black with red pages. She opened it and wrote something down, then asked, "When can you start?"

"Next week."

"Thank you, we could really use another draw. We're not necessarily in trouble. But given the current state of the economy, every little bit helps."

"I do have a request."

She looked up and raised an eyebrow. "Yes?"

I sighed. "First off, I don't want to be booked solid for every day through forever. Please try to keep the number of appointments limited. Secondly, I understand the people I'll be seeing are likely going to be grieving. Is there someone here who can help them? I'm not much of a counselor and I have a tendency to put my foot in my mouth. So, I think it would be a good idea to have a grief counselor or someone like that on standby."

Reyna didn't flinch. She didn't even seem surprised. "Done and done."

"Thank you."

"You've got a good heart, worrying like that."

"More like cautious. I know myself and I...I'm not rude but not polite?"

"You're blunt."

"That works. I don't want to say the wrong thing and end up emotionally destroying a grieving friend or relative."

"I understand. I'll take care of it."

"Thank you."

I left the office and went home. My phone buzzed a few times, but I ignored it until I got back to the house. When I walked through the front gate, I saw Jaime sitting on the porch by himself.

"Good evening," he greeted.

"Are you okay?" I asked.

Jaime shrugged. "Just a little tiff with Sawyer. He's not sleeping much so just the littlest thing sets him off."

"I'm sorry," I said. "If he's having trouble sleeping, I have an over-the-counter sleep aid he can take. I can bring it over later."

He shook his head, his salt-and-pepper hair sticking to his forehead. "I don't think it would help. He's been having nightmares, something fierce. He wakes up screaming and then he can't get back to sleep."

I took my phone out and looked up the information for the Cardinal, then said, "I'm going to text you an address. I talked to a lady downtown when I was having nightmares and she helped me."

"He won't see a therapist. And we don't have money for one at the moment."

"She's not a therapist. I don't know if she's a witch or a priestess or what. But she made me a charm and it helped a lot with my nightmares. Maybe she can make one for him." I sent him the location and business hours.

Jaime gave me a considering look after reading the text message. "Are you..."

"Yes?"

"Are you a cat person?"

"What?" What did that have to do with anything?

"I mean, cats. Do you like them?"

"Yeah, of course. I don't trust anyone who hates cats. Those people are always mean and weird." Which was true, but then I remembered when Verity said she couldn't trust anyone who hated cats and I smiled a little. I briefly wondered how Elias felt about cats.

Jaime chuckled. "That they are. I mean, can you sense things? See things, maybe?"

"Sometimes." I didn't elaborate. The last thing I needed was everyone in the neighborhood knowing I was a medium. I'd never get any peace.

"Sawyer is a cat person too. Every cat person I've ever met has a little something about them. Sawyer can talk to animals.”

“Everyone talks to animals,” I pointed out.

“I mean talk to them and they talk back. He’s a regular Doctor Dolittle.”

It sounded pretty far-fetched to me. But I could see and talk to the dead. Who was I to say what Sawyer could and couldn’t do?

“I hope he feels better. But definitely head to the Cardinal and ask to speak with Amy. She can help.”

“Thanks, darling. Going to bed?”

“Nah, my friend is blowing up my phone so I should text her back before she calls the National Guard or worse—my dad.”

“Okay. Sleep well when you get there.”

“You too.”

I went inside, unsurprised to see my apartment was empty again. Where the hell was Heather hiding? I took my phone out and saw ten messages from Psyche and sighed.

EratoONine: Hi, I’m not dead.

Psychepomp: WHERE THE HELL HAVE YOU BEEN?! I WAS WORRIED SICK!

EratoONine: Could you please not yell at me? I’ve had a long day.

Psychepomp: And I’ve been having a heart attack thinking the vampires ate you!

EratoONine: Rest assured they have not. What’s so important anyway?

Psychepomp: Nathana had a dream.

Well, that wasn't good news. To be clear, it was well-known among our group that Nathana's dreams were prophetic. If she had a dream about you, then you'd best listen up. Same for if Didoll had a message for you. Aoi had ignored one of Nathana's dreams once, and she paid the price for it.

EratoONine: Is she online?

Psychepomp: Yeah, get your ass in the group chat.

I took a deep breath and switched over to the chat.

NathanaBoBanna: Oh thank goodness, you're alive.

EratoONine: Aren't I usually?

DidollCarthage: Not funny.

AoiManto: We've been worried.

And many more messages like that poured in. I didn't read them all; my eyes glanced over them and all I could take in was they were angry, and it stressed me out. This, along with my deceptions at the club, and my day job not being ideal, didn't help. I tried my breathing exercise, but the messages kept coming in. I snapped.

EratoONine: WOULD YOU FUCKING STOP ALREADY?! I'm fucking busy okay?! The only way I'm going to get rid of this ghost is by finding her murderer and I've got NOTHING to go on! I can't even find proof she was ever at the club! And these people are actually really nice! I feel horrible about lying to them! And work is stressing me out and now I'm going to be giving readings at the club and I have a LOT going on! I am doing the best I can to be here, but it is a LOT! GET OFF MY BACK!

I should have taken a second to breathe, but I hit send. And you know you're in trouble when "Several people are typing" pops up at the bottom of the chat screen. Instead of waiting for their replies, I muted the chat. If I didn't, I'd check every message and I was not in the headspace for their yelling. I tossed my phone to the side and went to find something to make for dinner. I forgot to eat before I went to the club and my food reminder sounded twice while I was there.

Figuring with the mood I was in I probably couldn't screw up ramen, that's what I made. After slurping down artificial chicken flavor noodles, I was calm enough to resume.

Instead of messages calling me out for being a bad person and a worse friend, there was one message from Nathana.

NathanaBoBanna: We know you're overwhelmed right now. This is important. I was sleeping this morning and I had a dream about you. I saw you standing on the banks of the Mississippi with fishing nets wrapped around your neck and wrists. You were pale and waterlogged, and asking for help. You said the Night Hag had you and then you were dragged under the water. I saw a blonde woman in a fishing boat, she was pulling the nets in. She pulled you onto the boat and took you away.

My blood ran cold.

EratoONine: Did you get a look at the blonde woman?

NathanaBoBanna: I couldn't see her face, just her hair. Why? Do you know a blonde?

EratoONine: Two, actually.

She could have seen Heather or Verity. But without more details, I couldn't be sure which. I sighed and saw another message from Nathana pop up.

NathanaBoBanna: I see. This was a warning then. You should back off.

EratoONine: What about Heather?

At this, the others spoke up.

Psychepomp: Is this ghost really worth putting your life in danger?

AoiManto: We didn't mean to gang up on you like that. We're scared for you. I think Nathana's right. You should leave it.

DidollCarthage: Besides, these people you're dealing with! They're vampires! You've told us how dangerous vampires are. It'd be better for you if you cut all contact with them and this club.

EratoONine: Maybe but...I like these people. Verity and Lionel are actually pretty cool.

NathanaBoBanna: You don't have to cut off all contact. But I would recommend you drop the investigation.

EratoONine: I'd still have Heather to deal with.

Psychepomp: If she becomes troublesome, have someone cleanse you and the house.

EratoONine: I'll think about it.

NathanaBoBanna: That's all we ask.

I didn't reply. I powered off my phone and went to bed. My brain was full of bees and my heart was made of lead. I still didn't know what I would do, but I wouldn't rush into a decision. Not without considering the consequences. I was in too deep to be rash.

Chapter Nineteen

MY BRAIN WASN'T any better the next day. Or the next. I was performing my day job tasks like a sleepwalker, and my boss actually called me to see if I was all right. After I made up an excuse about lack of sleep, he cautioned me to be more careful or I might make a mistake that would be detrimental to my cases. I assured him I would do everything I could to prevent that from happening.

Heather finally showed herself again and was apologetic as always. I didn't blow off her apology, but I didn't need to accept it either. I told her what the investigation was doing to me mentally and said she needed to back off. She accepted, but only time would tell if she would abide by my wishes. She was stubborn and had a mean streak a mile wide. It wasn't a wonder to me anymore why so few people were at her funeral.

I also asked her why the club had no record of her.

"They should, I paid my dues."

"Reyna doesn't have any membership information under the name Heather Campbell. She also said they haven't had any new empaths at the club since the mid-nineties."

Heather bit her lip. "Maybe he made her forget about me."

"Excuse me?"

"You said Elias tried to erase your memory and failed, right? Maybe he erased Reyna's and removed me from the books."

I frowned. "I never said that."

"Yes, you did! After you said why you were afraid of him!"

"I never said I was afraid of him, I said he saved my life."

"And then he tried to erase your memory."

I didn't mention that Elias tried to hypnotize me, at least not to Heather. How would she know about that? I didn't press the point; instead, I went back to my research. Nathana's dream indicated the Night Hag was a blonde woman. It didn't escape my notice that Heather's hair was blonde. She wasn't the only one I knew. The other suspect was Verity. I didn't get the feeling it was her, but I could be wrong. I had been so often in my life.

I went to the club that night just to hang out. I needed to get out of the house for a while. Heather was with me, but she drifted off as soon as we arrived. I sighed and sat at the bar, where Lionel was working.

"Hey, sweetie. You want a Shirley Temple?"

"Yes. With an extra cherry, please."

"Extra cherries cost extra."

I went through my pockets and found some change and a slip of paper. "I can give you eighty-three cents and a coupon for a free sno-ball at Hansen's. Though we're outside of sno-ball season so you won't be able to redeem it until next year."

"Ooo, good deal."

I raised an eyebrow. "Can vampires eat sno-balls?"

"No, but humans can, and Verity is depressed. It's why she's not here watching me do my best Tom Cruise impression."

"Did something happen?"

"Tali called."

I blinked. "The ex?"

"The one and only. She called to apologize and wants her to come back."

"I'd think she'd be happy then. She's been mooning over that girl forever."

It was obvious to everyone Verity was not over her ex, despite the attempts of men, women, and people outside the gender binary to ask her to dance or go to dinner. She turned them all down politely. Or viciously if they didn't take no for an answer. The other day a guy tried to kiss her. She told him how he would die, and it scared him so badly no one had seen him since. Which is just as well since I'm pretty sure Lionel or German would have killed him if he showed his face at the club again.

Honestly, it hurt to see her so distraught. Between my duties as a medium and my day job, I'd done my best to cheer her up. Mostly we texted and a lot of it was silly memes or corny jokes I found online. She was actually pretty funny when she wanted to be.

Lionel rubbed the back of his neck. "She says she can't go yet because she's got something to do. They had a fight about it, and it got pretty ugly. Then Tali said she'd changed her mind and hung up on her."

"That sucks, I hope Verity will be okay. Let her know I'm thinking about her."

"I will. Here you are."

He handed me my Shirley Temple and I passed him the money for it plus the eighty-three cents and the coupon. There was indeed an extra cherry.

"Does she want to go back to Seattle?"

"To tell you the truth, I'm not sure. She loves it here and she's a great roommate. I just wonder if she's doing this for herself or me. I really hope it's not for me, that would be pretty shitty. And I wouldn't want her to make herself unhappy just for my sake."

"How so?"

Lionel shrugged. "Verity is one of those people who will give you the shirt off her back. She's a little too nice for her own good. It's how she got in trouble back home."

I snorted. "Trouble? What kind of trouble? She's pretty well-behaved. I wouldn't think someone so soft-spoken could get in trouble if they tried."

"It's her story—if she wants to tell it she can. What about you, Miss Morrison? Rumor has it you went to Elias's house not too long ago."

The abrupt subject change nearly made my head spin. Unfortunately, it caused me to choke on my drink. I coughed up soda mixed with grenadine and it spilled all over my white David Bowie shirt as well as part of the bar. Lionel leaped into action and handed me a wet towel, then went to work to clean off the bar.

"I expected a reaction but not an explosive reaction," he teased.

"There's nothing going on between me and Elias," I replied. "Fuck. My shirt's ruined."

"I can help."

We both jumped. I glanced over my shoulder to see Elias. "Come on," he said and left the room. I followed him out onto the gallery and to Reyna's office. She wasn't there, but Elias seemed to know his way around. He went to a wardrobe in the corner and opened it, looking for something. He dug out a black T-shirt and tossed it to me.

"Go to the bathroom, get cleaned up, and soak your shirt in the sink. Wring it out and give it to me."

"Uh, sure." My face felt very hot. "How much did you

hear?"

"Of what?" He tilted his head to the side, his chocolate tresses catching the light.

"Never mind." I fled the office and locked myself in the bathroom.

I was horrified when I saw myself in the mirror. My shirt was fucking see-through! And of course, I was wearing the Hello Kitty bra underneath. I felt like an idiot. Still, at least I had something to change into. I wet a paper towel and used it to scrub the soda and grenadine off, then dried myself and put the black shirt on. I left my Bowie shirt soaking in the sink while I did. Once I felt presentable, I wrung it out and left.

Elias was waiting outside. "I'll give this back to you tomorrow."

"Thank you. I would be really disappointed if it were ruined. I love David Bowie."

"Most people do."

"Do you like his music?"

"I'm not most people. Some might argue I'm not even a person."

He didn't say it like he was bragging, more like he was reciting a boring fact.

I frowned. "I'd say you're a person. I mean, you're standing right here, aren't you?"

Elias didn't reply.

"Okay. Well...I'll see you later."

"Goodbye, Miss Morrison."

I'm pretty sure my face was still on fire when I went back to the bar. Lionel was serving drinks to a couple I didn't know. My glass was gone. I considered going home, but when I checked my phone, I realized I'd already missed the bus. There wouldn't be another one for forty-five minutes. So, I sat down and waited for Lionel to finish.

He bounced over like Tigger from Winnie the Pooh, grinning from ear to ear.

"Did you two go necking in Reyna's office?"

"It's not like that, he was just helping me."

"Oh, I'm sure he was. Another drink? It's on the house."

I nodded and he got to mixing. When he finished, he passed me another Shirley Temple and he was still grinning.

"You like him," said Lionel.

"He's nice."

"No, I mean you *like* him." He drew out the "i" so it sounded like eight or nine syllables.

"I don't know if I like him. I don't date, remember?"

"Neither does he, and I know because I have tried. But he seems to like you well enough. Elias doesn't talk much to anyone. If I'm being honest, I'm not sure why he's a member here. He doesn't socialize and he doesn't have any friends. Besides me, and that's because I annoyed him into it."

"Seriously? He doesn't talk to anyone?" I asked.

Heather said Elias flirted with her before he asked her out.

"Nope. No one."

"What about four months ago?"

He shook his head again. "No. Actually, I'm not sure he was here then. Sometimes Reyna sends him on these little errands and he's gone for a while. I think this is the longest he's been in residence. Maybe she ran out of errands. Or maybe he's sticking around because he *likes* you." He drew out the word "like" again and grinned.

Another part of Heather's story that didn't add up. Not much of a shock. So little of what she told me turned out to be true.

Could they all be covering for him? I doubted it. I didn't believe in conspiracies. For the same reason, I don't believe in confiding in people offline. I know exactly how ridiculous that sounds given the Phoenix coup cover-up but that's different. Besides, I knew the cover story wouldn't hold forever. The truth about Phoenix would come out someday and for one very simple reason.

People talk, literally all the time. In the information age, it's harder than ever to keep a secret. I made an exception for online friends because they were scattered throughout the world. I'd confirmed no one in the group chat was within six hundred miles of me. So even if they did spill the beans, it was unlikely to ever affect my offline life.

It's not as though Psyche knows my boss's name or where I work. She and the rest of our group chat don't even know one another's full names!

Lionel was still staring at me, and I sighed. "It's just, I'm ace. I don't really do the whole dating thing."

"Oh, are you aro as well?"

"I'm... Not sure? I don't think so but since dating is a challenge on so many other levels and I'm indifferent to sex I simply go without."

"I see." Lionel leaned against the bar and looked at me. "I could ask him out for you."

At least this time I didn't choke on my drink. "I don't know..."

"This is the first time Elias has shown interest in anyone. Whether it's as friends or more it's pretty momentous. And if I can't go out with him, I need to live vicariously through you. Besides, it's for your own good and his. You don't know if you're aro? This would be a good way to find out."

"I'm still not sure."

"Look, if he's not interested, I'm gonna make another pass at him. He's so beautiful it's unfair. But in the meantime, let me set you up. If I don't have a chance at least you do."

I didn't like the sound of that; it made me wince. Though I wasn't sure why it bothered me. I wasn't interested in Elias, right? At least not as anything other than a murder suspect.

"Oh my God, you are too shy for your own good," Lionel declared and threw his hands in the air. "Will you just talk to him?"

"I'll think about it."

He rolled his eyes, then walked to the other end of the bar. The couple was dry and were waving at him for a refill.

I finished my drink, left a tip on the bar, and went home.

Maybe Heather was right. Maybe I did have a crush on Elias. That would complicate things for a number of reasons, the biggest of which being he was a vampire. Had I compromised my own investigation? In my defense, it was hard to look into someone's death if they couldn't tell you how they died.

There was also Heather's theory that Elias erased everyone's memories to cover his tracks. Could he really do that to everyone? The club had well over a hundred members who were in and out all the time. Not to mention guests of the club, who only needed the cover charge and the password to get in. That would turn one hundred memories erased into over a thousand. Then again, I only had to recall Phoenix and all the people who forgot about the vampires, convinced it was only a cult of crazies instead of the undead who took over the city.

It was a lot to mull over. Unfortunately, I wouldn't get a chance to think about it for long. When I got off the bus and crossed the street to my house, I saw Elias standing by the front gate.

"Good evening, Miss Morrison. I think it's time we had a chat."

Chapter Twenty

HE'D CHANGED HIS clothes. Elias wore a black button-down shirt, gray slacks, and black wing-tipped shoes. His hair was tied back, except for a few wisps of forelocks framing his face. He'd shaved too, the usual stubble nowhere to be found.

I walked past Elias and said, "I'd rather you didn't come in, but we can talk on the porch." No way was I inviting him into my apartment.

Heather stood on the steps to the porch and I walked through her. "Oh, classy," she snarked.

"Don't stand in my way then," I replied.

"Is someone here?" Elias asked. He walked through Heather too.

"Just a ghost."

"Are there a lot in this neighborhood? I confess I am curious."

I shrugged. "It depends on how you define 'a lot'. Not as many as the French Quarter, the Marigny, or the Bywater."

"What about the Ninth Ward?"

"I haven't been down that way."

"Are you afraid?"

I sat down in the chair Jaime usually occupied, and gestured to the other chair, which Elias took.

"I don't know that it's fear so much as I don't want to disturb anyone. I read an article a while back about tour groups who still go to the Ninth Ward on Hurricane Katrina tours. They point out damaged buildings and tell sensationalized stories about the ferocity of the storm and how many people died. It turned my stomach. People still live in the Lower Ninth. And that area may never recover from the damage of Katrina. It feels gross to exploit something both painful and relatively recent in history, especially just to sate my own curiosity."

"Hm, yes, I see your point." Elias gestured across the street to a large Greek revival mansion. "I imagine you get a lot of tourists here as well."

"Yes. Four houses on the block are on several different walking tours so there's a lot of foot traffic. I don't begrudge tourists who want to see the houses. I just wish they'd remember this is a neighborhood. And a majority of the buildings are private residences."

"What do you mean?"

"We've had an incident or two. I found a couple girls in the courtyard last week taking pictures of the rose bushes. They got all indignant when I asked if they were guests of any of the residents. Then my neighbor Jaime came out to see if everything was okay. They told him I was threatening them when I did no such thing. Jaime said he heard the whole conversation. Then he declared they were trespassing, and the girls needed to leave."

"Perhaps that is why I frequently see signs that say 'be nice or leave.'"

I laughed. I knew exactly which signs he meant. They were made by an artist named Simon of New Orleans. He had a shop on Magazine Street where he sold garishly painted signs with the motto painted on them. As a matter of fact, there was one two blocks away nailed to a telephone pole.

"I assume so. I mean, tourists as a group aren't bad. But there's always one or two bad apples who act as though this is Disneyland and they can do whatever they like."

"Ironic given you can't do whatever you like at Disneyland. Wait until you've lived here longer, you'll end up hating them no matter how nice they are."

"I doubt it. I was a tourist myself once, and now I'm a transplant. And there are plenty of native New Orleanians who think transplants should pack up and leave."

"Touché."

"Admittedly, I see where they're coming from. Because some people move here and then just do whatever. And New Orleans has a culture all its own which is why it appeals to visitors in the first place. But as they say, 'When in Rome, do as the Romans do.' Or at least as the New Orleanians do. So, when someone tells me, 'Hey, don't eat king cake outside of Mardi Gras season,' then I don't. Hasn't steered me wrong yet."

"Are you done babbling?" Heather asked.

I ignored her.

"So, what did you want to talk about?" I asked.

"I overheard your conversation with Lionel."

My blood froze in my veins. We weren't bad-mouthing Elias, but since most of the conversation was about whether he liked me? Yeah, not ideal.

"Oh?" I managed to say, my voice shaky just on that one syllable.

"Yes. In the future, I would recommend that if you are going to talk about a vampire, do so when they're out of earshot."

"Got it."

"And I do like you. Or at least I find you interesting."

"Thank you? I think."

"I also heard about your difficulties in romance and love. Therefore, I have a proposition for you."

I groaned and got up. "No thanks, I don't need you to fuck me straight. Forget it." I walked through Heather and was ready to go back to my apartment.

"Excuse me?"

I turned to look at him. Elias's eyebrows were practically in his hairline with how wide his eyes were.

"I've heard more than one guy say he can fix me if we have sex. Hell, I've had women say that to me! I'm asexual, not broken, not stupid, or immature. And dick isn't going to change anything about my sexuality or who I am as a person. I'm not interested." Even I could hear the disgust in my voice.

"No, it's not like that, I assure you," Elias replied. "Please sit down."

"No way, go home," Heather hissed in my ear. "It's a trap."

I glared at her and sat down again.

"I'm sorry, I phrased that incorrectly. I should have taken into consideration how it might sound." Elias rested his elbows on his knees and laced his fingers together. "Let me start again. You stated you don't date because of your disability and lack of interest in sex. Is that correct?"

"Yes."

"I'd like to ask you out on a date. As friends."

I blinked. "Excuse me?"

'We would go on a date, the same as any other couple. However, if you're ever uncomfortable we can simply remain friends."

A platonic date? I liked the idea immediately. I wouldn't freak out the whole time about whether I was doing something wrong. Or feel as though I were leading him on.

"You won't be mad if I decide we're better off as friends?"

"Not at all. You remember I told you about my lover?"

"Yeah, the one who wrote the mediumship book."

"Yes. I only felt an attraction to him after we'd become intimate. Emotionally, not physically."

"Are you demisexual?"

Elias nodded. "Yes, though the term didn't exist when I was human. One of the things I love about this century. So many new words."

"So you're aspec too."

"I am."

"Cool! Always pleased to meet another ace."

He chuckled. "I suppose I am too."

"Okay so like... We date, and it's strictly platonic unless I indicate otherwise? And you're okay with that? Because if you're just gonna get mad about no sex later I'd rather not."

Elias tilted his head to the side. "I take it this is something that's happened to you before?"

I nodded. "Yeah, a few times. I can appreciate you're demisexual which means if this does go further you may want to have sex. I'm not... I don't hate sex. But I don't like it. I'm indifferent to it."

He held his hand out to me. I could take it or ignore it. Elias knew I hated people touching me without permission, or just in general. It was clear he was allowing me a choice. I took his hand.

"I promise you I will never pressure you for sex. If I need satisfaction physically, I can take care of myself."

"Don't do this," Heather said. "He'll kill you like he

killed me." Her listless tone drew my gaze to her. Her face scrunched up with worry, and she fiddled with the hem of her overshirt. "Please? I don't want anything to happen to you. I know we've been fighting and I'm sorry but don't do this. It's not worth it."

I looked at Elias again.

He was still, patiently waiting for my decision. There was no frantic energy about him and I didn't get the sense he was lying.

I was second-guessing myself so much lately. Especially since I'd met Heather and discovered my powers. But this? It felt right. So, I said, "Okay. Where should we go?"

A smile bloomed on Elias's face. It was the first time I'd seen him smile showing teeth. His blue eyes glittered and there was a dimple in his right cheek I hadn't seen before. He really was beautiful.

"How about dinner and then a walk up Esplanade? Have you been to Cafe Degas?"

"No, not yet."

"Then that is where we shall go. Unless there was another restaurant you'd like to try?"

"There's Commander's Palace down the street. They serve a pretty good brunch from what I hear."

"I don't think I'd make it to brunch," he said with a laugh.

"Oh God, I'm sorry, I didn't think." I wanted to kick myself.

"Don't be, I know it can be easy to forget we're not human. Besides, it's not as though I'll be eating at dinner." Elias squeezed my hand, then let go. "May I have your phone number?"

"You're not going to call me, are you?"

"I believe that is the purpose of a phone number.'

"I'm on the phone all day at work, I don't like getting phone calls. I'd prefer it if you could text me."

"I see. I'll confine our correspondence to text messages then." He took his phone out of his pocket.

We exchanged numbers, and Elias got up to leave. I walked him to the gate.

"Thank you," he said.

"For what?"

"For giving me a chance."

I smiled. "Don't mention it. Text me the details when you get them. Oh, wait! What's your surname?"

He raised an eyebrow. "Why do you ask?"

"I already have an Elias in my contacts list."

"Rothschild."

I edited the contact information. "Thank you, Mr. Rothschild."

"Of course, Miss Morrison. Good evening."

And with that, he was gone.

"Are you insane?" Heather shrieked.

I ignored her and walked the flagstone path to the courtyard, then climbed the steps to my apartment. I let myself in and locked the door. Heather pushed through and stomped around, throwing her hands in the air.

"Hello? Lyric? You just accepted a date from the guy who fucking murdered me? What is *wrong* with you?"

"Stop screaming."

"I won't until you tell me what the hell you were thinking!"

I smiled as I showed her my phone. "I don't know anyone else named Elias."

Heather stared at me. "So?"

"So that means I can do research on him. And I can

use the dates to dig up dirt.”

“Wait, really?”

“Yup.”

“But you like him.”

“Yes, I do,” I replied. “But this investigation is not going well. I’m out of leads, so I need to try a different approach.”

Heather stared at me for a moment, then sighed. “You’ve got me there.”

“I need to get some work done. I’ll see you later.”

“Yeah, later,” Heather said, and she vanished.

I logged onto Eris and messaged Psyche and Nathana. I was going to find out once and for all if Elias was innocent or guilty. No matter how I felt about him.

Chapter Twenty-One

IT TURNS OUT, even with his last name, it was difficult to find anything on Elias Rothschild. While not a common name, it didn't stand out much. You couldn't type it into Google and get his entire personal history. Given he was likely over a century old, this could take a while. I was disturbed by how much I could find with what little I knew of him.

He wasn't registered to vote, but he paid taxes and didn't make waves. I wasn't surprised he didn't have any social media accounts. Psyche wasn't able to get far, even with her husband's help. She found about as much as I did, which is to say nothing. Frank tried using the phone number to see if there were hidden accounts, but he couldn't find anything. I didn't tell either of them I was going on a date with Elias. I didn't want a lecture from Psyche or anyone else.

"It's kind of weird he doesn't have any social media," Psyche commented. I personally didn't see it as a bad thing as I didn't have much myself.

A high school bully once tracked me down on Facebook and that was enough for me. I swore off the entire platform and anything like it. What little online presence I did have outside of Eris was all under pseudonyms and all my profile pictures were things like shoes or trees. Not an easily identified human face. God knew I did not need someone like my mother finding me.

As far as she and her family knew, I was still in Arizona and it was going to stay that way. Though to be fair it wasn't like she was able to operate a laptop or a smartphone. But sometimes a little paranoia goes a long way.

It was Nathana who finally found something in the city archives. You could access the New Orleans archives online, but certain sections were restricted. You had to make an appointment at the main library to see them in person or be an academic with an accredited university to view them online. Thankfully, Nathana was a graduate student at a prestigious midwestern university; one I sadly could never remember the name of.

She sent me an article to look over with a note that read, "I've actually heard this story. I thought it was an urban legend."

The article was from the late 1800s after the Civil War. The headline made me freeze, and I said, "Heather, get in here."

She poked her head through the bathroom door. "What?"

"I might have something on Elias."

Heather walked through the door and looked over my shoulder. She read the headline, "Massacre at Sultan's Mansion."

"Why would a sultan be in New Orleans?" I wondered aloud.

"We've totally hosted royalty. And we almost had an emperor here once too."

I raised an eyebrow. "Really?"

"Yeah. You know that restaurant Napoleon House? That's where Napoleon Bonaparte was gonna live. At the time it was the governor's mansion or something and they renovated it for him but then he got sent to Elba," she said.

"Wasn't Napoleon the one who sold Louisiana to the United States in the first place?"

"Yeah."

"Shouldn't they have been, like, super pissed at him? Why would they want to help him?"

"Maybe they thought if they brought Napoleon here, they could be part of France again. I don't know. People are weird."

"You can say that again."

I clicked back to the article and read aloud.

"Six in the morning on Tuesday the second of March. Two maids and several workmen were outside the mansion at 716 Dauphine Street. No matter how many times they rang the bell, none were granted entrance. This was cause for concern, as it was known there was a soirée that took place the previous night. And yet, not a sound was to be heard.

"No one had entered or left the building. Which in itself was suspicious. The mansion was known to be home to a sultan who threw lavish parties and frequented the opera and the theater. He had an entourage of nearly twenty people and, as a sultan, a taste for the finer things in life. He employed a sizable but ever-changing staff. They were paid handsomely to do their work and remain silent about what they beheld.

"But the workers were unable to enter the residence that day. They were aware their master would not want a police presence. But unsure of what else to do, both of the maids went to fetch a policeman. They were spared the gruesome sight that greeted the workmen only minutes later. Blood gushed from beneath the locked gate, as though from a mighty river.

"When the patrolman arrived with the chamber-maids, he summoned his superiors. They forced the door open. Inside, they discovered the dismembered corpses of the sultan's entourage. Men and women in pieces, strewn about the courtyard and inside the mansion. The sultan himself, however, was nowhere to be found. The only trace of him was his bed, which was set ablaze.

"Witnesses in the neighboring homes reported hearing screams throughout the night. They assumed the noise was yet another party held by the Sultan. Few could imagine such a gruesome crime would occur within a stone's throw of their own homes. Obviously, this has set many on edge.

"One witness claimed to see a man clothed in black leaving the mansion sometime before dawn. However, the person in question was Elias Rothschild, who has an alibi for the evening. Upon further questioning, the witness admitted they may have mixed up the nights.

"Mr. Rothschild of Bourbon Street stated he was previously a guest of the sultan and was shocked by the murders.

"'It's simply incredible,' he said. 'To think, a man like that slaughtered with such fury! One cannot help but wonder what crime would have deserved this savagery.'

"At this time, it is unclear who could have done this, though rumors abound. Some say he was an imposter, and he and his party were killed by the real sultan's men. Others say he stole the paramour of a powerful rival, and her retrieval resulted in the massacre. The only conclusion of which we are certain is that no single person could have carried out such a heinous act.

"The police have no suspects. But they have assured this reporter the investigation is ongoing."

I sat back in my chair, staring at the photograph accompanying the article. The sultan's mansion. I recognized the building. It was on the corner of Dauphine and Orleans in the French Quarter. Elias lived only a couple blocks away. They didn't have a picture of him in the paper, but they did have a sketch. It was definitely him. They'd even captured his dimple.

"Jesus Christ," Heather said, clutching her shirttail in her hands and twisting it.

"I mean, he's a vampire. He could have killed everyone single-handed."

"And that doesn't scare you."

"It should."

"But it doesn't."

"No."

Heather circled around so she was leaning against the desk and looked down at me. "You need to call off this date."

"No fucking way."

"But—"

"This is the first bit of proof we have that he's not what he seems," I insisted. "You see that building? He lives down the street."

Heather looked at the picture then back at me. "So, what, he decided to mass murder his noisy neighbors?"

"Fuck if I know. I've heard the story before though. According to Nathana, so has she."

"What do you mean?"

I leaned back in my chair. "It was on an episode of some haunted house show on the History Channel way back in the day. I remember because I thought it was made up. They talked about the massacre and how the murderers were never caught. They also say the place is haunted. Oh! And the fountain in the courtyard fills with blood on the anniversary of the deaths."

"Ew."

"Yeah, my reaction too. Supposedly you can hear the screams of the victims as they're dismembered on the night of the full moon."

"Charming. What does a full moon have to do with the murders?" Heather asked.

"Probably nothing. People love adding little details like that. Like how they say the coldest night in December is when you can see the ghost of Julie. They say she will appear stark naked on the roof of Bottom of the Cup over on Chartres Street."

"You've heard that story too, huh?"

"It was in the same episode and gets repeated a lot around town. Though what they don't mention is that her ghost is at the original shop location at 318 Royal Street and not the current location on Chartres. I'm kind of looking forward to December now because I want to see if she really appears."

Heather snorted. "You're a medium, you could literally see her any time."

"Oh, shit. Yeah, you're right."

"You're still determined to go on this date?"

"Yeah. We need more information. But first I need to find someone who knows more about the sultan and his buddies. If there's an article about their deaths, there must be a paper trail somewhere."

"Makes sense."

I emailed my thanks to Nathana, then went to the New Orleans library website. I made an appointment to go to the archives. While making the appointment I received a notice that my book was ready for pickup. I figured I could do both at the same time. When the form requested a reason for the visit, I claimed I was researching an old urban legend for a book. Once that was done, I stretched.

"I should get a cat," I said.

Heather grimaced. "Ugh, I hate cats. They're fucking weird."

"They're cats, they're not snakes or anything. I mean, I'd like a tarantula or a milk snake someday, but I think my landlord would have a fit. He'd probably be okay with a cat."

"No way. Cats are mean. They scratch you for no reason and piss and shit everywhere."

I crossed my arms over my stomach. "Have you ever had a cat?"

"No, but my cousin Amora did. I hated that little jerk and she hated me right back."

"Gee, I wonder why," I muttered. "I love cats. I still want to get one."

"Okay, fine, if you want your furniture destroyed and cat hair everywhere. Be my guest. Enjoy the smell of ammonia."

I glared at her but didn't press the point. Once this was over, I probably would get a cat. But this was yet another strike against Heather. Verity said it herself.

"Dogs are blindly loyal and give their love unconditionally. Cats, however, have their own set of standards and rules. You earn their love, and you do it on their terms. Now there's nothing wrong with disliking cats or preferring dogs. But if someone says they hate cats? Run. They're not the sort of person you want to befriend or fall in love with."

Considering my mom loathed cats, and the worst

people I'd ever met hated cats too? It was a good rule to live by.

When Heather left, I pulled up a document on my computer: one she didn't know about, at least not yet. It was my evidence against Heather. I'd recorded her inconsistencies, her outright lies, her outbursts, everything. To the list, I added "hates cats" and saved and closed the document.

I opened my document where I kept my evidence against Elias. There was so little there. But I transcribed the article and took several screenshots of the pictures. When I'd saved and closed it, I heard the text alert on my phone.

Speak of the devil.

Elias Rothschild: Cafe Degas, Saturday, 7:30PM. Let me know if you would prefer a different time.

Lyric Morrison: That's fine.

Elias Rothschild: Would you like me to pick you up, or would you prefer to meet there?

Lyric Morrison: I'll meet you there. That reminds me, how did you know where I live?

Elias Rothschild: I asked Lionel.

That made sense. He and Verity picked me up the night of the séance so of course they knew my address.

Lyric Morrison: I'll see you Saturday.

Elias Rothschild: Goodnight.

I looked at the clock and sighed. It was close to my bedtime. I shrugged and put the phone away, then got ready for bed.

Chapter Twenty-Two

I WAS PRETTY bummed out when I heard back from the library, as they denied my request to go through the archives. They were simply overwhelmed with requests. Unless it was for academic purposes my request could not be granted. I guess writing a book doesn't count unless it's for a dissertation.

However, not all was lost. When I explained what I was looking for, the librarian recommended a couple books: one about French Quarter history and one about urban legends. I could pick them up with my mediumship book. I had just enough time between when I left work and when I needed to be at the club to get them. And so I did.

When I arrived at the club I changed into my medium dress, which I stored in Reyna's office. She'd offered to pay to have it dry-cleaned, for which I was grateful. Once I changed, I went into the bar and headed for the tent. The sign with Emerson in the turban was gone, replaced by a poster of a crystal ball and ghosts that declared in bold letters, "The Medium of the Black Lily! Speak with your departed loved ones, reconnect with the dead!"

I think people expected more theater, but in truth, I wasn't great at it. Not like Emerson, who tried to give me a few tips and tricks to put on a show for the bereaved. But to be honest, this was already a very delicate situation. I didn't want to make it worse by treating it like a sideshow attraction.

The first appointment was for a widower looking for closure. He was in his seventies, and he'd been married for almost half a century. His wife was, sadly, haunting him. So for half an hour, I told him what she was saying.

He was pretty sad and cried a few times. But he managed to smile in the end when she told him she would be waiting for him when he passed. She also berated him to take better care of himself, which he promised to do. He left a small tip, which I thanked him for.

I took a break for another half hour so I could recover and read my books. The mediumship one was interesting and contained some pretty great local history. I was so engrossed in it that I still had it out when my second appointment arrived.

This time it was parents who'd lost their son in an accident. He died so suddenly they were convinced he had to be haunting them. "He was so young, just out of high school!" his mother wailed. I wasn't able to summon him, and I told them that he'd crossed over and was in heaven.

I thought they'd be angry, but they were in fact relieved and left a very large tip. I split it with the people working that night, one of whom was Verity. I presented the money to them after I changed back into my regular clothes.

"Wow, they must have been really happy," Verity said.

"I suppose. They were distraught when they came in. They miss their son so much."

"It's natural for a parent to miss their child."

I snorted.

Verity raised an eyebrow. "You don't agree?"

"I haven't talked to my mother in so long I don't

remember what her voice sounds like. Though that's my choice since I never want to see or speak to her again. My dad is so busy with his new family he forgets I exist most of the time. And my sister... She left home at eighteen and never came back. The most I know is she's in California and doesn't want contact."

"Okay, then I amend my statement. Most parents miss their children."

"Thank you. Where's Lionel?"

"On a date. There was a gentleman from Atlanta who took a fancy to him. They're attempting to drink their way through Frenchman Street."

I laughed. "Gonna give his beau alcohol poisoning, is he?"

"I don't think that's his intention, but it'll happen if they're not careful." She frowned at the floor as she said it.

I leaned over the bar and muttered, "Did you see something?"

"No, not to do with Lionel."

I looked around. The club was deserted since closing time was fast approaching. They didn't stay open late on weekdays. "Hey, do you want to go somewhere?"

Verity looked up at me, her eyes watering.

"What's wrong?"

"Can we talk? Like friends?"

"We are friends," I said. "Come on." I got up and opened the bar gate for her. She took off the apron she wore to keep her black dress clean and put it aside.

I saw Emerson over by the gallery doors and called, "Hey, come watch the bar, I gotta take Verity home."

"As you wish," he said but stopped and looked at Verity. "You okay, sweet child?"

"I just want to go," she said.

Emerson and I exchanged worried looks. I'd never seen Verity cry before. Hell, I'd never seen her upset. Judging by the look on his face, neither had he. I led Verity downstairs and outside. We walked down Dauphine, then turned onto Piety and headed toward the river.

This likely won't come as a surprise but I'm not great at comforting people. I always feel like I'm doing something wrong and making any given emotional situation worse. Did I hug Verity? Offer her my hand? I settled for walking in silence.

Given it was Wednesday, we didn't see a lot of people out. But then I had an idea.

I stopped outside a pizza restaurant and said, "How about we get a couple slices and go to the park?"

"Won't they be closed?"

"The pizza place?"

"No, the park."

I checked the time on my phone. "No, it's open for another two hours. What do you say?"

Verity smiled, but there were still tears in her eyes. "Sure, why not?"

She wiped her eyes and we went into the pizza parlor. We each ordered two slices and a soda, then headed to Crescent Park.

The park is a little difficult to get into, but there are three entrances. There's one in the Marigny on North Peters with an elevator and one on Alvar that leads into the dog park. But both would have required we walk at least a mile, and I wasn't in the mood. I doubted Verity was either. So, when we reached Piety and Chartres we approached the Rusty Rainbow Bridge. The same one I'd complained to Heather about.

I would like to state for the record, again, I hate that bridge. More specifically, I hate walking on it. It's beautiful and there's one hell of a view at the top. But crossing it involves climbing about three flights of very steep stairs, then descending three more to get down. This is because Crescent Park is surrounded by a levee wall, which means you either take the two main entrances or you climb the bridge.

I hoped a little physical activity would get Verity's mind off whatever was bugging her.

We trudged up the steps, and I kept a death grip on the handrail as we went. I was panting by the time we reached the top.

"Are you okay?" Verity asked.

"Just not used to the altitude."

Verity laughed.

We paused at the top and took in the sight of the city.

The sun had set hours ago, which wasn't surprising in mid-October. The weather was getting colder and the nights longer. It was why the club opened earlier in the evening now rather than ten p.m. like in the summer. It was a clear night, and we could see the skyscrapers of the business district and even part of the Quarter.

"God, I love this place," I whispered.

She didn't say anything.

We descended to the other side and into the park itself. We walked the paths, which were thankfully well-lit, and we made our way over to Piety Wharf. It didn't escape my attention this was where Heather said she was the night she died. Maybe I should have been afraid; someone with more sense would be.

But Verity was so upset. I doubted she was capable of luring me into a trap. If that was foolish of me, well, so be it. I wanted to take a chance, I wanted to trust her. I wanted us to be friends.

Verity found a bench near the water and I joined her. We ate our pizza in silence while we watched the lights of the city twinkle on the water. I cracked open my soda can and sipped ginger ale, then asked, "So, is this about your ex?"

"Kind of. She wants me to go back to...Seattle."

"I heard. Why don't you?"

"It's not my home anymore. Besides, there's something I need to do." Her voice was mournful as she spoke.

"Lionel said you guys were fighting."

"Lionel has a big mouth and should mind his own business."

"That would be a miracle. What do you have to do exactly?"

"It's complicated." She finished her pizza and dumped her trash in a garbage can nearby.

I followed suit, and we both sat down again.

"Wanna tell me about it?"

"No," she said venomously.

I winced at her tone, and Verity looked at me.

"Not because I don't like you. Or that I don't appreciate that you're trying to help. But there's...a lot I haven't told you."

"I suppose that's fair. I'm not exactly an open book myself."

She nodded. "I knew you'd understand."

And I did. I wasn't about to spill my guts about Elias or what I was doing at the club. Besides, she wasn't crying anymore so I considered that mission accomplished.

"Hey, do you know anyone who works at the New Orleans library?"

"No, why do you ask?"

"I need to get into the city archives so I can look into this urban legend thing. It's kind of bugging me and I wanna know how much is true and how much is stuff they made up for the tourists."

Verity smiled. "You're in luck, then. I happen to be a tour guide."

My jaw dropped. "You're fucking kidding! I thought you were a burlesque dancer?"

"I am, but I told you I haven't established myself yet so I don't have any paying gigs. I give ghost tours every other day of the week."

"Oh shit! That's so cool! Is it fun? I bet it's annoying."

She laughed. "Why would you say that?"

"I don't really like dealing with the public and that's very much a 'dealing with the public' kind of job," I pointed out.

"I suppose you have a point. Which legend were you trying to research?"

"The sultan's mansion." I took the books out of my bag and showed them to Verity. "I mean there's some stuff in here but it's not really specific."

"I know the story. It's one of my favorites."

"Is there any truth to it?"

"As a matter of fact, there is." Verity grinned. "My boss, Jason, put together the tours based on his own research."

"No shit? So can you tell me if they ever found out who did it?"

Verity shook her head. "No. Though according to him, there was a group of people who 'looked foreign'." She made quotations with her fingers. "They checked into the Hotel St. Louis the night before the massacre and checked out the next day."

"How many?"

"Maybe four or five? No one's sure. But here's what they won't tell you on the tour. I don't think even Jason knows." Verity looked around, and I did the same. We were alone on the pier, but she leaned close and whispered, "The sultan was a vampire."

"What?" I explained and pulled back to look at her. "How do you know?"

"They say they didn't find a trace of him except for a burned bed. Well, the most effective way to kill a vampire is by staking them, beheading them, and then burning their body. Once you set them on fire, there's nothing left of them."

"But that doesn't mean he's a vampire. Human bodies burn," I pointed out.

"They do but at much higher temperatures. And for several hours and there's some trace left behind," said Verity. "Despite what they say in murder documentaries, it takes a lot to burn a corpse to ashes. If the sultan's body had been burned that hot and that long the fire would have engulfed the whole mansion."

"Holy shit," I murmured.

Verity nodded. "Exactly."

"Have you been to the building?"

"Yes, it's on the tour."

Did I tell her what I found? Or that Elias lived nearby? In the end, I decided against it. I would simply have to file the information away.

Verity looked at me expectantly, so I asked, "Is it true you can hear the ghosts screaming?"

"I haven't heard anything. Shouldn't I be asking you that question?"

I chuckled. "Good point. But I've been there. I haven't seen or heard anything yet."

"Perhaps the ghosts have moved on."

"Yeah maybe. Though if I were murdered, I don't know that I could move on."

Verity sighed and twirled a strand of her platinum locks around her finger. "Neither could I. Not right away."

We fell into a comfortable silence as I considered the possibilities. Had Elias killed another vampire? Then I said aloud, "But if the sultan was a vampire, why kill the people in his entourage? It doesn't make sense to me."

"What do you mean?"

"Well, think about it. The only body they didn't find was the sultan's, right? So that means the rest of the people in his entourage were humans. Why kill them? What was there to gain?"

"Maybe they were protecting him."

"But why?"

Verity's eyes widened with surprise. "Can't you guess?"

I thought about it but shook my head.

"What would you do if someone showed up to the club tomorrow intent on killing Reyna? Or Lionel?"

"I dunno. I mean, I'm not as skilled at hand-to-hand as I used to be. But I would probably try to stop them." I may have joined the club under false pretenses, but that didn't mean I didn't care about Reyna or Lionel. I was fond of everyone there, even the people I didn't talk to much.

"You'd want to protect them, right?"

Then her point clicked. "I see your point. Who could have done it? Vampire hunters?"

"Could be. Or maybe someone from the Court."

"The what now?"

She slapped a hand over her mouth and looked at me, terror in her eyes. She moved her hand away and said softly, "Forget it."

"I don't think so," I replied. "What Court?"

"Drop it, Lyric. You're not ready for that conversation yet." Verity stood up and added, "Shall we go? It's getting late."

I checked the time on my phone. She was right. The park would close soon. I tried to bring the conversation back around to the Court. But Verity refused to say anything further on the subject. As we ascended the bridge, my mind was buzzing. What the hell was the Court? What did they have to do with the massacre? And how was Elias connected to all of this?

Chapter Twenty-Three

I DID RESEARCH as soon as I got home, but I couldn't find information on a Court or what that could mean. I asked Psyche, Nathana, Didoll, and Aoi if they had any idea what the Court was. They said they didn't.

NathanaBoBanna: Why? Is it important?

EratoONine: It might be linked to murders Elias committed in the 1800s.

NathanaBoBanna: From the article I sent you?

EratoONine: That's the one.

AoiManto: Did she use any quantifiers?

EratoONine: Nothing. She wanted to drop it as soon as she let it slip.

DidollCarthage: It's not much to go on, is it?

EratoONine: I suppose not.

Psychepomp: Sounds like a dead end to me.

EratoONine: It is literally my only lead at this point.

Psychepomp: Then you need to reinterview your witness.

EratoONine: Yeah, about that...

Heather was fading faster than ever. I couldn't figure out why and she wasn't around long enough to tell me. It scared me that I might lose her soon. Yes, she was a pain in the ass, and I wasn't sure I could trust her, especially after she lied to me. That didn't mean I wanted her gone forever or that I didn't want her to find peace.

I explained to the group what was happening to her.

Psychepomp: I was afraid of this.

EratoONine: Of what?

Psychepomp: Sometimes, even with unfinished business, a ghost can't hold on. She may be transitioning to the afterlife. Whether she wants to or not.

EratoONine: Maybe that's why her glow is changing.

AoiManto: Her what now?

I wrote out how I saw ghosts and how I categorized them. And how Heather was different.

NathanaBoBanna: That's weird.

DidollCarthage: Really weird.

EratoONine: Thanks, guys. Totally makes me

feel like less of a freak.

Psychepomp: We're not calling you weird.

NathanaBoBanna: It sounds like you can see auras too.

EratoONine: Oh yeah, because I need more weird shit on top of everything.

NathanaBoBanna: It's actually a handy gift. You can tell a lot about a person by their aura. And I've read that ghosts have them too. The glow you're referring to is likely Heather's aura.

It made sense when she said it, since *Piercing the Veil* said mediums occur when psychic children have a near-death experience. And Elias asked what powers my family had. That must have been it. Perhaps I'd been able to see auras all along.

AoiManto: You know, there's a chance she's not a ghost at all. She could be a spirit.

EratoONine: What's the difference?

AoiManto: You know the story behind my username, right?

EratoONine: Yeah, it's an urban legend you liked as a kid when you and your parents lived in Japan. One I still find fucking weird because what kind of ghost haunts a fucking bathroom? And where does one even get red or blue toilet paper?

AoiManto: Cute, but don't get sidetracked. Technically Aka Manto or Aoi Manto isn't a ghost. That's the difference between him and, say, Teke Teke or Kuchisake-Onna. He's an evil spirit whereas Teke Teke and Kuchisake-Onna used to be people.

EratoONine: Don't follow.

NathanaBoBanna: What Aoi is trying to say is, it's possible Heather was never a human being.

EratoONine: Interesting hypothesis. One problem. I saw her body. I went to her funeral and met her family.

Psychepomp: That's a good point.

DidollCarthage: What did she say her power was again?

EratoONine: She said she was an empath.

Psychepomp: Ew.

AoiManto: Seconded. Ew.

EratoONine: What is it with people hating on empaths?

NathanaBoBanna: It's not so much that people hate empaths. It's more to do with the fact a lot of toxic people will claim to be empaths when actually they're master manipulators.

DidollCarthage: Yeah, like my sister. She does that all the time. "I'm an empath!" And then she acts like a mean girl in a high school movie.

AoiManto: It's true. I've met her sister. She's a total Regina George.

EratoONine: I don't know what that means.

DidollCarthage: From Mean Girls.

EratoONine: I've never seen it. I've never been to New York.

DidollCarthage: Huh? What does that have to do with never having seen Mean Girls?

I took a deep breath and rubbed my face. This happened sometimes as I wasn't up on every bit of pop culture in existence. Thankfully, Psyche came to the rescue.

Psychepomp: I think Era is thinking of the Broadway musical based on the movie. Mean Girls is a movie that came out in the mid-oos. It's about a trio of girls at a high school who are very popular but very mean. Then a fourth girl comes along to rock their shit.

EratoONine: Why would anyone want to watch that? I didn't like girls like that in school. I wouldn't want to watch a movie about them.

DidollCarthage: It's actually pretty funny.

EratoONine: It doesn't sound like my sense of humor.

NathanaBoBanna: Folks, could we focus? The point is, it sounds as though Heather may not be what she says she is.

EratoONine: Yes, I'm rather worried you're right.

Psychepomp: Why?

I bit my lip. Did I tell them? They wouldn't be able to help me if I wasn't honest. So, I spilled the beans. About Heather's lies, and her other inconsistencies. When I finished typing, I groaned. "Several people are typing." Great, now I was in for it.

NathanaBoBanna: Are you sure you want to help her? If she's lying to you, she's definitely hiding something.

Psychepomp: She could also be confused. Dying is traumatic.

AoiManto: I think you should get rid of her.

NathanaBoBanna: Agreed. This is bad, Era. I think it's clear you can't trust her.

While everyone else chatted, I frowned at the screen. It kept showing "DidollCarthage is typing" for a longer time than I thought possible. Then her message popped up.

DidollCarthage: The power of the Demon Mistress grows with the Dark Season. Beware the time of the Light.

I realized she was automatic writing. Didoll's angel or spirit guide or whatever responded instead of Didoll.

I didn't get a chance to ask what that meant, as I heard behind me, "Whatcha doing?" I jumped and closed my laptop and turned to see Heather standing by my bed.

"Discussing the case with my friends," I said.

Heather frowned. "Why'd you close the laptop?"

"Force of habit. My mother used to barge into my room whenever I was on the computer."

"Oh. Yeah, my stepdaddy did that too."

I slid my glasses down my nose and took the chance to really look at Heather. She was translucent, and the golden glow around her was almost gone. When I pushed my glasses back into place, she frowned at me.

"What is it?"

"You're fading."

"I know."

"Psyche says you could be transitioning to the afterlife."

Heather snorted. "I doubt it."

"Then where do you go?"

"What do you mean?"

"When you disappear, where do you go?"

Heather paused and hugged herself, then her eyes closed. "I don't know. But it's dark and cold. I think there's wind? But I don't know. It's like being between dreams."

"Sounds like the twilight world."

"You know what that is?" Heather asked as her eyes opened again. Their hazel color seemed gold in the low light of the studio.

"That sensation between being awake and asleep. Where one dream has ended and another is about to start. I call it the twilight world."

"Huh, I guess it kinda is."

"I used to spend a lot of time there when I was sick."

"Sick?"

I shook my head. "I'd rather not talk about it just now, but the short story is I was ill for a long time a few years ago. So I slept a lot."

"Guess that makes sense." Heather crossed her arms over her stomach and sat on the bed. "Any progress?"

"Nothing yet. I might have a lead from Verity but to be honest it's looking like a dead end."

"New plan then?"

"Yep. Try to get more information out of Elias on Saturday. And..." I sighed. "I need you to tell me the truth."

"Excuse me?" She glared at me. "What do you mean by that?"

"You haven't been straight with me. No one at the club knew you. I've talked to everyone. I've even tracked down guests and none of them remember you. Were you ever at the club to begin with?"

Heather shot to her feet. "Of course I was! I knew the password, didn't I? I told you how to get there! I told you how to get in!"

"That's the only part of your story that panned out," I replied. "No one remembers you and you're not in the society's member book. And I asked around at the cafe and the bar you used to work at. No one remembers you there, either."

"It's Elias, he's erasing their memories to cover his

tracks!"

I rubbed my temples. I wasn't in the mood for this, but I had to get this out. "One vampire isn't going to be able to erase the memories of hundreds of random people."

"You certainly gave him enough time to do so, since you've been trying to prove he's innocent the whole time!"

"How did you know he can erase memories?"

Heather threw her hands in the air and started pacing. "Because you told me! He saved you then he tried to wipe your memory! How could you forget?"

"I didn't."

She stopped pacing. "What?"

"I never once mentioned he tried to erase my memory. I only told you he saved my life. So how did you know he could erase memories?"

"But you told me he can! You told me it didn't work on you!"

I signed and spun around in my chair so my back was to Heather.

"Lyric?"

I didn't answer.

"Hello? Earth to Lyric? Hey, don't ignore me! That's rude!"

I picked up my headphones and put them in, then connected them to my phone. I pulled up my music and pressed play with no regard to what it was. I just wanted to block her out. She was too weak to affect anything physically. I knew it wouldn't take much before she would lose her temper and go away. I decided to play a word search game while I waited for Heather to disappear.

After about twenty levels, I figured it was safe to take my headphones out. When I did and turned around, she was still there. Heather was more translucent than ever and she was pouting. I was amazed she could hold on; it couldn't have been easy.

"I want the truth," I reiterated. "Or I'm going to ignore you and you're going to fade out of existence."

"I won't, I'll keep haunting you until you fulfill your promise."

"And I will do just that if I can. But if you're not willing to tell me the truth then I won't be able to."

I hated the very thought of breaking a promise. If I made a promise, I had to keep it, no matter what. The problem was, if Heather wasn't being honest, the promise itself was no good. Why should I keep a promise to someone who lied to me over and over?

Heather bit her lower lip, her eyes darting between me and the window. I wondered what she was looking at, so I peered outside.

Sunset was several hours ago, though it wasn't late just yet. I could see the streetlights were on. The light filtered through the leaves of the giant oak trees lining the street. Standing in the parking lot were several ghosts, a couple of whom I recognized from readings at the club.

"Ugh, go away," I said.

They didn't move.

"Shoo." I gestured with my hand, as though I were attempting to get rid of a pesky dog.

The ghosts still didn't move.

"I suppose I'll have to get used to them."

"You could ignore them like you were doing to me," Heather pointed out in a bitter tone.

"I was ignoring you because you were doing what you always do. Redirecting the conversation and not addressing any of my concerns. You're just like my mother."

Heather snorted. "Oh, sure, lay your mommy issues on me."

I glared at her. "My mother is a narcissist. She uses the same tactics you do and frankly, I'm tired of it. I had no problem cutting her out of my life. What makes you think I won't do the same to you?"

"Why are you being so mean to me?" Heather demanded.

"This is exactly what I'm talking about," I said. "You've lied to me, and instead of being honest like I asked you're changing the subject."

"I am not! You don't know what it's like! I'm dead, I can't affect anything, I can't do anything. And I'm going to die again!"

I took my glasses off and rubbed my eyes. "Which is unfortunate. But until you tell me the truth, I can't pursue my investigation. You're on your own."

Unsurprisingly, Heather went from pleading to pissed off in less than a second. "Oh yeah? We'll see about that!"

And she stormed out.

I collapsed into my chair, exhausted. Why the hell did I keep trying? Heather was never going to tell me the truth. And if Elias did kill her, which I doubted, how would I prove it? I was at a dead end.

Chapter Twenty-Four

HEATHER DIDN'T REAPPEAR again. There wasn't even a hint of her presence. I wondered if she moved on, or perhaps she was looking for another medium to pester. I wished her the best of luck in finding one, seeing as mediums were a rare breed and all. Secretly, I hoped she did because I was angry at her for lying.

To the surprise of no one, when people start acting like my mother it has a tendency to turn me against them. I don't hate Heather, mind you, but her behavior had gone from suspicious to triggering. The sad part is the more a narcissist tries not to get caught the worse their behavior becomes, especially toward whoever they're trying to sucker in. At least that was my experience with my mother.

I saw the cycle repeat itself over and over. The more she wanted to keep Dad with her, the more she drove him away with her lies and manipulation. When she realized she couldn't keep him in her thrall anymore, that's when he became a villain. She would cry about how he'd never loved her, he always cheated on her, and he treated her as less than a dog. She did the same thing when my sister went no contact with our family. I'm sure she spun an equally absurd yarn about me when I eventually followed suit.

Heather was the least of my worries. More ghosts were appearing around my house, and it was getting to be a pain in the ass. While I did my best to order them away, I was about as adept at banishing as I always had been. Which is to say, I'm terrible.

When I finally sat down with *Spirits and Mediums of New Orleans*, the book I'd been waiting for from the library, I hoped I would find an answer. Maybe I would discover a way to locate a medium who could help me with my powers. Sadly, it was a dead end. It mostly talked about the history of spiritualism and how it had come to New Orleans from the North East and the famous mediums who would visit the city. Though I did find one interesting tidbit.

There was a passage about a medium from England named Jonas Remington. It wasn't much, simply that he'd emigrated to New Orleans around the 1890s and was a gifted medium. It further stated he could be found on Bourbon Street. The name sounded familiar, and I knew I'd read it somewhere before. It was later in the evening I realized where. Jonas Remington was the author of *Piercing the Veil of Tears*. Elias's ex. How long had he lived on Bourbon Street?

It was still on my mind when I came home from returning *Spirits and Mediums* to the library. Jaime and Sawyer were back to sitting on the porch and people watching. Whatever troubles they'd had appeared to be over. I climbed up the porch steps and leaned against one of the columns.

"How're you doing?" I asked.

"Much better, thank you for the recommendation," said Sawyer. "Haven't had a single nightmare since."

"That's great.'

"Oh, Amy had a message for you," Jaime said.

I raised an eyebrow. "Did she? I'm surprised she

remembers me. She must get hundreds of customers a week."

"We got to talking about you because she asked who referred us," Sawyer explained. "She said to tell you the charms don't last forever and you'll have to come in to get a new one, about every few months or so."

"I'll keep that in mind."

I wrote a note in my phone but promptly forgot about it a few minutes later when I walked into my apartment. Not my fault, as I was surprised by several ghosts standing around when I came in. I told them to get out, but they didn't listen until I yelled at them. I hated it when someone invaded my space without permission.

I was reading *Piercing* over and over again in the hopes I would find a way to get rid of them. Preferably in a way that didn't involve "willing" them away. I didn't know what that meant. If it meant yelling, it didn't work for long because I did that a lot.

In the meantime, life was getting back to normal. Or as normal as it was for me. Despite the ghosts, I was getting my tasks done at work with no incident. I performed readings at the club, though I kept the time limit. What I made in tips I stuck in my savings account.

While I wasn't officially employed by the club, I knew I was pulling in enough I'd have to declare it on my taxes. So I didn't spend any of my savings. I wasn't sure how much I'd have to give back at tax time, something I complained about to Lionel, who stared at me like I was insane.

"It's in cash! Don't declare it, there's no paper trail! They can't prove anything."

"I'm not committing tax fraud because I'm afraid of a little paperwork," I replied.

"You are so weird," he muttered.

I rolled my eyes. "This coming from one of the undead."

"Low blow. I still say don't declare it."

"Your opinion is noted."

Verity was sitting next to me at the bar, and I expected her to chime in. She didn't say anything, so I asked, "Hey, are you okay?"

"Just tired," she replied. "I've taken on a few more tours and I have an audition for a part in a show next week. One of their usual dancers had to drop out at the last minute."

"Which show?" Lionel asked.

"L'Amour de la Danse." Verity didn't sound thrilled.

Lionel, however, grinned. "That's great! They're one of the most popular burlesque shows in town! They perform in the Quarter, right?"

"Yes, at Le Petite Theatre."

"Oh hey, I've been by there. I love that building," I said. "Do they perform there a lot?"

"No, just once a month. If I get in, I get a cut of the ticket sales and tips."

Verity was talking about it as though she were going to be executed. Lionel and I exchanged glances.

"Ver, is there something wrong?" he asked.

She shook her head. "No, just...tired. Like I said. I promise I'm really excited about it."

We didn't press, but I could tell Lionel was just as worried as I was.

"Let's change the subject. Do you know what you're wearing tomorrow?" Verity asked.

"Oh! Right, your date with Mr. Rothschild," Lionel said. His face lit up like a kid on Christmas.

I groaned and stood up. "I'm going home."

"Oh no you don't, get back here."

Lionel blocked my exit.

"Hey, no fair using your speed."

"Cry me a river. Sit down and tell us what you're wearing tomorrow."

"Why? I'm not letting you pick out my clothes."

"Hey, I did a great job with your performance outfit."

"Back when I didn't know you. I'm not showing up to my date in a halter top and bedazzled booty shorts."

Lionel opened his mouth to answer, probably to give a smart-ass comment, but Verity cleared her throat.

"We're just curious," she assured me. "We're not going to judge you."

I took out my phone and showed them a picture. I'd taken it so Psyche and the others could see and tell me what they thought. Judging from the smiles Lionel and Verity sported, they approved.

"He's gonna love it," Verity said.

"I don't care if he does. I want to be comfortable." I put my phone away and stepped around Lionel. "I gotta go, don't wanna miss my bus."

"We want details!" Lionel called after me.

As nonchalant as I pretended to be, I was really worried. I hadn't been on a date in forever, and the few experiences I had were not great. Rejection sensitivity was something I'd dealt with for years. It was only with Dr. Cade's help I managed to cope with it. I hoped I wouldn't need to break out those tools again.

I spent Friday refreshing my hair color. I hadn't found a beauty parlor yet that suited me, so I had about an inch of dark roots growing out. Not to mention the teal was so faded it was more of a tint than anything. I applied the dye and let it soak for two hours before washing it out. My hair was getting longer, and my bangs were getting on my nerves. I wouldn't cut them myself, but I was going to have to pin them back or curl them so I could see.

Saturday arrived and I spent most of the day reading. It wasn't a good distraction, but it was something. Heather wasn't around at all, and the other ghosts weren't invading my space. It helped that I'd snapped at them the previous day to stay the fuck out of my place.

Two hours before I needed to leave, I showered, my hair under a shower cap so the dye wouldn't bleed. I ended up curling my bangs so they rested on my forehead. I even managed soft curls for the rest of my hair. I slipped on a black Alice band for a bit of style. But I had to angle it so it wouldn't pinch the stems on my glasses. I picked my favorite pair of violet-tinted glasses and looked in the mirror. Not bad at all.

Satisfied, I got dressed. I picked a black velvet babydoll dress that stopped at two inches above my knees. I'd opted for the same lace gloves and black boots I wore to séances. I wasn't sure what I wanted to do for jewelry, but I settled on a black beaded necklace I'd picked up at a shop on Magazine.

I went easy on the makeup. My hands were shaking so much from nerves I couldn't manage anything elaborate. A little mascara, some lip ink, and just a hint of eye shimmer. I looked at myself in the mirror and did a small spin. I looked pretty good.

I opted to take the bus again since it was a Saturday and a rideshare was going to be expensive. One time I was quoted sixty dollars for a one-way ride on a weekend. Sounded pretty exorbitant to me so I opted for the bus. Besides, the bus route on Jackson went right up

Esplanade and had two stops near Cafe Degas.

When I got off the bus at Esplanade and Grand Route St. John, I took a deep breath and let it out. While not the Quarter, Esplanade wasn't exactly empty. Several restaurants and cafes were open, and people strolled up and down the avenue talking and laughing. I was about to walk up the street to the cafe when a shadowy figure stepped out from behind a tree.

"Allow me to escort you."

"Elias!" I pressed my palm to my chest. "You nearly gave me a heart attack!"

"My apologies." He offered me his arm.

I debated for a moment but then linked my arm with his. I was more comfortable with Elias touching me than anyone else. When did that happen? I couldn't recall. Maybe the night he showed me how to use my powers.

His hair was loose and flowed around his face and shoulders in waves. He wore a burgundy button-down with tight black jeans and motorcycle boots. So not super dressy but not casual.

"You look great," I said.

"Thank you. You're a vision of loveliness," he replied.

"I'd accuse you of teasing me but I don't think you have a sense of humor."

"Nonsense. Simply because I don't find everything funny like you Americans do."

"Did I touch a nerve?"

A small smile tugged at his lips. "Perhaps."

"If it makes you feel any better, I kind of agree. Dry humor is so underrated."

"Then I believe we will get along just fine, Miss Morrison."

"Thank you, Mr. Rothschild."

The smile turned into a grin.

When we got to Cafe Degas, my jaw dropped. There was a tree in the middle of the dining room! Like someone decided to build the restaurant around the tree rather than remove it. I didn't have long to gawk at it, as we were escorted to one of the outdoor tables. More trees lined the outdoor patio, strung with fairy lights. But from our table, I could see the wine bar and a little grocery store across the street. It was a great spot for people-watching.

I let out a low whistle. "This is lovely," I said.

"I'm glad you like it." He was staring at me as he spoke. His face was blank again, but there seemed to be something in his eyes. Amusement? I couldn't tell.

We didn't speak much after that. I ordered, opting for the French onion soup as an appetizer, and the duck entree. Elias ordered wine and a salad.

When the waiter left, I asked, "You can eat salad?"

"No, but I can shuffle it around my plate to make it look as though I'm eating," he said. "It was brought to my attention that it would look strange if you were the only one eating. I asked Reyna about it. She had some recommendations to make it appear as though I am eating. I haven't been to a restaurant in...a while."

"I bet," I said.

When the food arrived, I was a little hesitant. I took a spoonful of soup and popped it into my mouth, metaphorically crossing my fingers.

The flavor was fantastic, and I didn't gag! I cheerfully finished the soup with a smile on my face.

Elias watched this with intrigue. He asked, "Are you all right?"

"Texture issues. I always worry about eating new food. French onion soup sounded like something I could handle but I've been wrong before."

"I've never heard of such a thing."

"It's pretty common with autistic people. You should see the face I make when someone tells me to eat a banana. I think it looks something like this." I thought about the texture of a banana, and the taste, and gagged.

Elias laughed. "I see. Then no Bananas Foster for you, I take it?"

"You've got a better chance of me stripping naked and going for a swim in Lake Pontchartrain."

He laughed again. His eyes lit up as he did. And it was...nice.

The rest of dinner went much the same way. We talked, not about anything significant, and I didn't get any new information out of him.

But I did get to see him laugh quite a bit. And by the end of dinner, he was grinning.

After dinner, we stopped at the grocery store. I got a popsicle and he got a soda. We then decided to walk down Esplanade. We both pointed out houses we liked and architecture we each found interesting. When we got to Broad Street, he put his arm around my shoulders and it made my heart leap in my chest.

This was nice. One could almost forget he was a vampire.

When we were close to North Tonti Street, I said, "Wait! Look!"

I grabbed his hand and we crossed the street to the Degas House. Really, it was two houses, one that Degas himself had occupied and the house next door that acted as a bed and breakfast. Lights were strung up between the two, connecting the properties. I'd gone on the breakfast tour with Candace when I first visited New Orleans as I loved Degas's work.

As we looked at the house, I had an idea.

"Do you know this place?" I asked.

"I think I've seen it in some silly television show," Elias replied.

"Probably has been, I have no idea. I just wanna check something real quick."

I took my glasses off and waited. Ghosts came into view, but they were faint. I couldn't hide my disappointment.

Elias asked, "Trying to see if Degas is haunting his old home?"

I sighed. "I figured it wasn't likely. I mean, the dude was only here for five months. But it was worth a shot."

We decided to call it a night after that. Neither of us was interested in the bar scene and there wasn't much else to do that time of night. Elias escorted me to the N. Tonti Road bus stop, and once I was on my way home, I sighed.

I really did like him. Well, fuck me.

I said to myself, "God, please, do me a solid. Let him be innocent."

Chapter Twenty-Five

WHEN I GOT home from the date, several ghosts greeted me. I didn't know them and I hadn't summoned them but word had gotten around the underworld. One begged me to call her sister, and another wanted me to pass a message on to his wife. It took me half the night to get them sorted out and even when I did, they didn't disperse.

It was an issue I was running into more and more. It was my own fault, really. Reyna had approached me about increasing my appointments at the club. Instead of only Wednesdays and Fridays, I worked on Thursdays and Sundays too. Saturdays were still reserved for the séance dinners which were now bi-monthly.

This was fine. I could handle the workload and the money was too good to say no. Reyna was right, it was a money maker. I'd never had so much disposable income in my entire life. Not only that, but it gave me the chance to spend more time with Elias, Lionel, and Verity. I'd been on two more dates with Elias, and the others were always at the club. I could see them whenever I liked.

So, when I wasn't summoning ghosts, I was sitting at the bar with one of them. Elias was really coming out of his shell. Lionel was as funny and nosy as always. And though Verity was still tired more often than not, her calming presence was always wonderful to be around. It got to the point I was going to the club almost every night even when I wasn't working.

Then, the weekend before Halloween, we all went to the Krewe of Boo parade in the French Quarter. It's much like a Mardi Gras parade, in that there are floats, marching bands, and things like moon pies and beaded necklaces thrown at you. But it's much more fun because everyone from the marchers to the spectators are in costume.

We weren't terribly original with our costumes, to be honest. I dressed up as a witch complete with the stupid hat and long black dress. Verity chose to be an angel, and she did look quite angelic in her white dress with feathered wings and silver halo. Lionel picked a dime store vampire get-up because he thought it was hilarious. Elias refused to tell us what he was dressing as.

In the early afternoon, Verity and I picked a spot on Decatur near Barracks. She said it was close to where she and Lionel lived. We sat in chairs on the sidewalk and waited. Once the sun was down, Lionel and Elias joined us. Lionel looked ridiculous in his cheap costume. While Elias...didn't appear to be wearing one. He wore a flannel shirt and jeans as always, but his hair was down.

"And who are you supposed to be?" I asked.

He smiled and said, "Sam Winchester."

"From *Supernatural*?"

"It was Lionel's idea."

"You're a little short to be Sam, aren't you?"

He sighed. "I wanted to dress as Dean but he said my hair is too long."

Lionel grinned. "I was gonna dress up as Castiel so we could get a little Sastiel action going but I don't look good in a trench coat."

"Maybe we can do it as a group costume next year," I replied.

We had a great time watching the parade. We caught so many throws I was glad I'd brought a backpack with me. The thrill of catching a string of plastic beads one handed is a heady feeling that can't be accurately conveyed in words. The music, lights, and crowds should be enough to drive me into sensory overload. Instead, it sent a vibration of pure joy right through me.

Best of all were my friends. We laughed and teased one another mercilessly. We all experienced the triumph of a good catch, and the wail of defeat when a throw was dropped. I danced to the pounding music with each of them in turn. The delight I shared that night with Elias, Verity, and Lionel brought us all closer. Not just as friends; there was the sense we were becoming family.

But there was a downside. I was running out of ways to placate the dead while remaining anonymous.

For example, one ghost was murdered like Heather. But he actually knew who killed him. It was his cousin. After looking the ghost up, I discovered he'd been missing for three years and his case went cold. The ghost told me he was buried on his cousin's property under the shell of an old Chevy truck.

I was reluctant to go to the police. I'd seen more than one TV psychic insert themselves into an investigation for clout or attention. I did not want to be that person. There were also my own memories with the police force I didn't care to relive. Instead, I wrote out what the ghost told me, set up a temporary email through the VPN, and sent it off to the police. They'd never be able to trace me.

"How do you know they'll take it seriously?" the ghost demanded.

"I don't. But they'll have the information they need to find your body."

"That's not good enough! I want justice! Ron should fry for what he did to me!"

I turned and glared at him. "I'm not going to become a contract killer just to make you happy. I did all I could. Leave."

I thought he'd press the issue. Many of the ghosts had. But either I finally had enough force behind the statement or he could tell I was spoiling for a fight. He left.

Another ghost came after him. And another. And another. Finally, I declared I needed to sleep and to leave me alone. Fat chance of that. They kept coming and I couldn't make them stop. Everywhere I went in New Orleans they turned to stare at me. They'd follow me or demand to speak with me.

I was beginning to wish I'd never unlocked this stupid power.

Whether they meant to or not, the ghosts were causing problems, the worst of which was sensory overload. Because they wouldn't shut the hell up and let me have some alone time, my brain was usually toast by lunch. It was difficult to concentrate at work which caused me to be short with people, both at my day job and with people who booked séance appointments.

After I snapped at a woman who wanted to contact her grandmother, I felt awful. I apologized profusely and said her grandmother had already passed through the veil. I also gave her her money back and apologized again. She understood but she was still hurt and I felt awful. I told her to speak with Emerson since he was the counselor Reyna chose.

I walked out of my little tent and went outside to the balcony for a breath of fresh air. Every little noise was getting on my nerves. Every smell caused nausea. The lights, soft as they were, hurt my head. My clothes felt constrictive and every time my hair touched my face or neck, I wanted to scratch myself. The thought of being in close proximity to another person made me want to scream in frustration.

There were ghosts around me, but I said over and over, "Go away." I knew I said it out loud, and I didn't care how crazy it made me sound so long as it worked.

"Lyric?"

"*What*?"

Reyna stood next to me. She raised an eyebrow. "You want to dial back that tone?"

I covered my face with my hands. "I'm sorry."

"Do you need a minute?"

"I need to go home."

I couldn't look at her. There was no way in hell I could continue with my appointments. I wasn't even sure I could take the bus home. I'd have to call an Uber and that had its own complications. Trapped inside a small vehicle with a stranger who would talk my ear off the whole way. I shuddered.

"Why don't you come with me to my office?"

I moved my hands away from my face. Reyna had walked away. Fuck, I was in trouble. I had to be. I'd snapped at a customer and at Reyna. She was probably pissed, even if she didn't look like it. My stomach sank down into my shoes and my skin prickled with heat. I'd fucked this up, so I had to face the music. Reluctantly, I followed her.

When I walked into her office, Reyna turned the lights off and left some candles burning. It helped relieve the pressure in my head for which I was immensely grateful.

She sat behind her desk, and I collapsed into a wing chair by the far window. "I'm so sorry."

"Thank you. But what's with the attitude?"

I covered my eyes with my hands. "Sensory overload."

"Oh, that explains it."

I moved my fingers away from my face. "What?"

"Why you went from pleasant to raving in the blink of an eye."

"Oh God, I'm so sorry, I really didn't mean—"

Reyna cut me off. "You're not in trouble, relax. You informed me of your disability and that this might happen. I'm a little surprised it took this long."

I let out a sigh of relief. I tried to run my hand through my hair, but the veil got in the way. I growled and tore it off, then tossed it aside.

"It's the ghosts," I said. "They're following me home and they're a fucking menace! I can't sleep or get any rest because they're like, 'Lyric, help me' and 'Lyric, do this' and 'Lyric, say that' and I'm fucking sick of it! They're even more self-centered than the living. They don't give a shit that I have a job to do! And maybe I don't want to devote my entire fucking life to helping people who died a long time ago. They're so selfish! It's like I don't get to have a life anymore just because I can fucking see them!"

I ran out of steam as I said it and had somewhat calmed down by the end of my rant.

Reyna steepled her hands together, her dark eyes on me. "And this is a recent phenomenon? I was under the impression you've had your powers since childhood."

"I have but I kind of...suppressed them."

She raised an eyebrow but didn't respond.

This was enough to induce me to info dump. "My

mom is a super scientist type of person. There's a logical explanation for everything and all that shit. I fell into her line of thinking, especially after the murder at my high school. I thought ghosts were hallucinations and I was being stupid and weird. Then when I got diagnosed with autism later in life, I thought maybe they were a side effect."

"Are autistic people prone to hallucinations?"

"Not that I'm aware of, but I couldn't shake my mother's mindset. I was either stupid or crazy. Eventually, they stopped appearing and I thought that was the end of it. I thought I was getting better."

"Until you moved to New Orleans."

"Yeah. That might have been a slight miscalculation on my part."

"What does your mother say about all of this?"

"I haven't talked to her in years. She's currently in a nursing home."

Reyna's eyes widened. "How old is she?"

"Middle-aged. But she's had a problem with alcohol since her teens so she has the mind of an eighty-year-old with dementia. To be honest, if I did visit her, I'm not sure she would even know who I am. Her second husband's kids visit her sometimes, and they say she doesn't know who he is or that she even has children."

"Is that why you no longer speak?"

"No. I went no contact because she's a rampaging narcissist. I feel terrible for cutting her out of my life but she wouldn't seek help and I..." I took a deep breath and let it out. "I dropped out of college to help her when her drinking got bad. I'm not a very good nurse. But I was the only one who could help her when she couldn't take care of herself. I cooked, cleaned, and when she came home drunk, I would put her to bed. The whole time she'd tell me how lazy and useless I was. Then one day I realized she was never going to get better no matter what I did, so I left."

"How long were you doing that for?"

"A while. I'd rather not say how long."

Reyna nodded. "You must feel like you're taking care of your mother all over again."

"A little, but at least the ghosts are sober." The pressure in my head was increasing. I didn't have much time. "I have to go."

"Let me give you a ride."

"You don't have to."

"No, I don't, but I want to. Come along."

I followed her outside. It turned out Reyna had parked on Chartres. I heard a boat whistle in the distance on the river. It was only after we were in the car that I realized I left my veil in her office. I was too overwhelmed to retrieve it.

Reyna drove me home. The only time she said anything was when she asked for my address. When we arrived, she looked up at the house and said, "It must have been grand in its heyday. It certainly doesn't look like the Devil himself built it."

"I think that house was demolished. This one was built on the same spot."

"Have you seen Madame Le Blanc at all? Since the séance?"

I almost asked her what the hell she was talking about. Then I remembered the lie Heather and I cooked up. "No, she's been gone for a while now. I think the other ghosts scared her off."

"I see." She took out her purse and extracted a

business card. She handed it to me and said, "Here. If the ghosts are becoming troublesome, call German. He can cleanse the property for you."

"And that will work?"

"It would keep them from waking you up at the very least." Reyna stared at me for a moment. "Just so you know, it's normal."

"What is?"

"Being overwhelmed the way you have been. If your power is new to you then there are some growing pains. But keep practicing. It's the only way you'll perfect your control."

I got out of the car and said, "Thank you."

"You're welcome. Seriously, call German. He's done a cleansing for each of my rental properties and he's the best."

I raised an eyebrow. "You have rental properties?"

She smirked. "I'm an entrepreneur, my dear. I have been for over a century now. I have my fingers in more pies than you can count."

"Awesome. Good to know."

"Goodnight."

"Night."

I closed the car door. Reyna drove away.

I looked at the business card. It had German's name, an address, a phone number, a website, and a Facebook account. I smiled a little at the thought. A vampire witch with Facebook. The twenty-first century was fun. I tucked the card away in my pocket and promptly forgot about it when another wave of pain hit. I needed to lie down.

Chapter Twenty-Six

I DIDN'T DO any more readings for the rest of the week. And Sunday night I didn't go to the club. I couldn't face everyone. While I knew Reyna said she wasn't upset, that did nothing for my anxiety. I got a few phone calls asking if I would come in, but I declined and stated I wasn't well enough. It felt like a lie, even though it was 100 percent true. The thought of facing anyone when I felt delicate made me nauseous.

Interestingly, Heather wasn't around, and I tried to summon her but without success. What was she doing? Did she finally move on? I doubted it. She was stubborn, she was mean, and would do anything to get her way.

She wasn't the only one absent. I hadn't seen a single ghost the entire day. Did they decide to give me the day off? To be honest, I was so stressed out and tired I didn't care why they weren't around. I was glad to have a reprieve from the constant aggressive demands. I didn't want to waste such an opportunity, and when I realized I was on my own, I had excess energy to burn.

So I decided to clean the apartment. I'd been neglecting my chores because, well, I hate them. I don't like the smell of most household cleaners. I don't like having wet hands. I especially hate sweeping, dusting, and mopping. Mostly for sensory reasons, but partly because it reminds me of living with my mother. Though in this case, I wasn't taking care of a voluntary invalid.

I winced at the thought and shook my head. It was cruel to think that way, even about someone who made me so miserable. I chastised myself for it because it wasn't fair. Addiction was a disease. It was one of the reasons I refused to drink alcohol. What if I turned out like her? Unable to experience joy without abusing substances that would rot my brain and my liver in the long run. It didn't help that all alcohol tastes awful to me.

After I finished cleaning, I curled up in bed to read. It was a rainy day, very common in New Orleans no matter the time of year. I would take that over the heat any time. Of course, rain didn't automatically mean a cool and breezy day, simply that the humidity and precipitation would cancel out any extreme heat waves.

After sunset I felt antsy. I was a homebody by nature, and all the time at the club was draining me. But I was now more used to being out than not. I still didn't want to return to the Black Lily Society, at least not this week. So I decided an evening coffee might be in order. An advantage of my particular neurodiversity is caffeine won't keep me up all night.

I dragged myself out of bed. I pulled on a pair of jeans, boots, fingerless gloves, a velvet burn-out ruana, and a tank top, all black. I had to look under my bed to find my umbrella. It was a pagoda-style black umbrella with black ruffles on it that I thought was pretty cute. Once I'd located it, I was out the door and on my way to Morning Brew.

Unusually for a Sunday evening, the pitter-patter of rain against the oak leaves was all I heard as I walked up Coliseum. Tourists didn't often stray into the Garden District after five but there were still the people who lived there, and I didn't see anyone. It was starting to creep me out. Many restaurants and attractions were closed on Mondays and Tuesdays, so Sunday was the Friday night of the food and hospitality industry. And yet, the street was abandoned.

"Did I miss a party or something?" I asked aloud.

Only the sound of the rain answered.

I checked the time on my phone. It was just after five-thirty and Morning Brew would close at six. I needed to hurry.

As I navigated the uneven sidewalk, I had the most peculiar sensation someone was watching me. I paused, turned around, and slid my glasses down my nose. Nothing. Not even a ghost.

"Hello?" I called.

No response.

I kept walking, unnerved and wishing I'd brought my headphones with me. I'd left them at home so I could listen to the rain. There were no further incidents as I reached Commander's Palace. Several people were absconding from a limo, dressed like they were going to prom. The men in tuxes, the women in gorgeous evening gowns. They must have been pretty important because they had security with them.

When I tried to walk around the party, one of the security officers stopped me and asked, "Can I help you, miss?"

"Just going to get some coffee," I replied.

"All right, but don't dawdle."

I waited until the finely dressed people were on their way inside. Then I dashed up Washington. They must be having a private party or something at the restaurant. Finally, I reached Morning Brew and I let myself in. I closed my umbrella and left it in the stand by the door. I'd still got a bit wet from the rain, but not too bad. I vigorously wiped my feet on the welcome mat and looked around.

The coffee shop was empty, except for a familiar face behind the counter.

"Nice to know you haven't died."

"Uh, hello, Delia," I said sheepishly and rubbed the back of my neck. In trying to avoid a confrontation with Reyna, I hadn't been going out at all. So now I got to have one with Delia since I hadn't been getting my morning coffee each day. This evening was not getting any better.

"I was worried. Where have you been?" she asked.

"I got a second job," I replied. It wasn't a lie.

"You work full time as it is, what are you doing for a second job?"

"Could I order before you interrogate me? I don't want to accidentally make you work late."

Delia blinked, looked at the clock on the wall, then at me. "Considerate of you. What would you like?"

I ordered a white chocolate mocha with caramel. She gave me a look but didn't argue. As she made the drink she asked, "So what are you doing these days?"

"Telling fortunes at a private club." Not my actual job but close enough.

"That wouldn't be the club out in the Bywater, would it?"

I raised an eyebrow. "That depends."

Delia, without missing a beat, said, "I know all about it. I'm a friend of Reyna's."

I didn't comment. The rules said not to talk about the club unless someone gave you the password, and she hadn't.

She seemed to realize her mistake and she said, "Le

lys noir c'est belle."

"Aussi beau que la rivière."

"I knew it! Amy told me you were at the shop with her best customers."

"I didn't know you were in the club. What can you do?"

"I'm your garden variety kitchen witch."

"Is that why your coffee is so good?"

Delia chuckled. "Maybe."

"What about Amy? Is she in the club?"

"She's a green witch, she works with plants and herbs and things like that. But she's not a member, just an associate."

"Oh? Why is that?" It was clear Delia was a member so why was Amy shut out?

Delia smiled. "Unfortunately, Amy is cis and straight."

"Ah." That would do it.

"Yeah. But Amy's got a green thumb and has an affinity for crystals. Which isn't surprising since she's an earth sign."

I made a face which Delia raised an eyebrow at.

"Something wrong?"

"I'm not a fan of astrology. I've run into too many people who use it as an excuse to be rude or completely write others off."

"You're an unpopular sign, I take it?"

"Gemini."

"Yep, that would do it."

My coffee was finished by then, and she handed it to me. "So, what are your plans for tonight?"

"I'm going to go home, read a book, and go to bed."

"You're not going out?"

"No, should I be?"

"It's Halloween!"

I blinked. "Is it?" I took out my phone and saw that, yes, it was indeed October 31st. "Huh. Considering I went to the Krewe of Boo parade you'd think I'd have realized what today was."

"Not a big fan of the holiday?"

"Actually, I am. I've been so busy lately that I've lost track of time." I sighed. "I suppose it's too late to do anything now. I don't have a costume."

"You don't have to dress up. If you like, you can come with me. Amy is having a party at her home in Mid-City. A mellow party, and then we'll make offerings to the dead."

"What for?"

"Just to let them know we're thinking of them."

I looked around. Still no ghosts in sight. "I suppose. But I'd rather go home. I'm bushed. Maybe next time."

"Suit yourself." Delia wrote a phone number on a piece of paper and handed it to me. "Text me if you change your mind."

"Sure."

I paid for my coffee and left. Delia closed the door and locked it behind me. It was only after I crossed the street that I realized I forgot my umbrella. When I turned around, the lights were out. The rain had stopped, so it wasn't a big deal. I could go back for it tomorrow. Or later in the week.

As I looked down Washington, I saw a crowd. There were more well-dressed and likely well-to-do people outside of Commander's Palace. One woman caught my eye. She had beautiful auburn hair, wore a yellow satin dress and diamonds at her throat. She smiled and laughed as she went inside the restaurant. She was on the arm of an equally gorgeous brunette in a white jacquard gown, but I was too far away to make out the pattern.

Self-consciousness hit me like a bus. I was wearing clothes that were held together by home stitching and a prayer. Suddenly, I didn't want to be seen by anyone. I decided to cross at Washington and walk around Lafayette Cemetery. If I did a full circuit around the cemetery, it would take me right back to Coliseum. I wouldn't have to push my way through the elegant people outside the restaurant.

The temperature dropped as a breeze rustled through the trees. I wished I had brought a proper jacket rather than a ruana. But I had my mocha, and I sipped it as I walked. I had to go even slower than usual. The sidewalk around the cemetery wasn't just uneven, it was an obstacle course. The roots of the old oaks in the cemetery caused the sidewalk to rise and crack nearly a foot up from street level. It made walking a challenge.

I hummed a song to myself as I went, and idly wondered where all the ghosts were. Little did I know I was about to find out.

I rounded the corner and moved onto Sixth Street, where the sidewalk was a little less hazardous. I'd just finished my mocha and went to throw it in the garbage near the gate. The peculiar sensation that once again I was being watched crept up my spine. When I tossed the cup in the trash can by the cemetery gate, I looked up and yelped.

Several ghosts stood behind the gate. They stared at me.

"Let us out," one wailed.

"Please, it's Halloween, I want to see my family," said another.

"I'm sorry, I don't have a key," I said, then winced. If a living person was watching me, they would think I was crazy and talking to myself. I had to get out of here.

"Please let us out," a third ghost begged.

I slipped my glasses down my nose. They were more distinct now, and something was strange about the specters. They had the same golden aura I'd seen with Heather. But unlike Heather, they were wearing clothes from different eras. This struck me as odd, as one man appeared to be dressed for a ball in the early 1700s. It didn't make sense since the Lafayette Cemetery wasn't incorporated until much later.

"I'm really sorry, I can't open the gate," I said.

One of the ghosts, a woman in a dress straight out of a Victorian fashion plate, threw her hand out and grabbed my arm. I gasped with pain as her nails dug into my flesh. Her face contorted in fury and her eyes burned with hate.

"Let us out!" she screamed.

I tried to wrench my arm away but only succeeded in drawing my own blood. I was so scared, but I couldn't scream or call for help.

Then a cool hand pressed into my arm and a voice said, "You have to push back with your mind."

Elias. It was Elias!

I inhaled and exhaled, picturing a hammer coming down on the ghost's arm. She screamed and released me, and I fell back against Elias. The rest of the ghosts were yelling and demanding I release them. He put his arm around me and said, "Come on," and we walked down the street.

When we got to Sixth and Chestnut, he said, "That was a very foolish thing you did."

"What? Walk home?"

"No, walk by a cemetery on Halloween. The veil between the living and the dead is thin tonight. Ghosts and spirits are at their most powerful. They could have hurt you."

I blinked. "That wasn't in the book."

"Some things are so widely known that most do not think to commit them to paper," Elias pointed out. He stared at my arm as he spoke.

I looked down. There were bloody scratches from my elbow pit down to my wrist. "Fuck," I said.

"Let's get you home," he said and did his best to ignore the blood.

Chapter Twenty-Seven

ON THE WAY home, Elias explained what happened. The veil between worlds is thin on two days of the year. Halloween in the fall and Hexennacht in the spring, which is on April 30th.

"Whenever the veil is thin, ghosts are much more powerful. Surely you've noticed no specters have bothered you today?"

"Yeah, I thought it was weird."

"It's the best day for ghosts to visit their families. Or to pursue their enemies."

"Then why were those ghosts stuck in the cemetery?"

"They weren't ghosts," he said. "They were malevolent spirits bound to hallowed ground. They receive power from this day too. It's why they were able to hurt you. But not enough power to escape their bondage."

I frowned. "Oh, well that makes sense. Why bind them to the cemetery though?"

"I'm not sure, you would have to ask whichever witch or medium bound them. Ah, here we are."

We'd reached my house. We went in through the back gate. When we got to my door, I scolded myself. Elias knew which apartment was mine now. But we walked the whole way from the cemetery to my home and not once did he rush me or make me feel unsafe. In fact, quite the opposite. I got the door open and stepped in, and he remained on the front steps.

I looked at him for a moment, and he said, "I should go."

"You can—"

He cut me off. "Think carefully. I'm a vampire. If you invite me into your home, you won't have any protection from me."

I bristled at that, as though I didn't know the risk. I wasn't an idiot. Still, he had a point. I didn't know if an invitation could be revoked once given. But I figured it was too late now. He knew where I lived and if he was clever, he would find a way in without an invitation.

"Come in, Elias."

He stared at me, and I wasn't sure he would move.

"Either come in or leave. And close the door, you're letting the heat out."

He climbed the final step and came in, then closed the door gently behind him.

The ghost had gotten me pretty good, and I'd bled most of the way home. I was still bleeding sluggishly as I went to the sink to rinse it off. I'd have to clean and sterilize the wound before I could dress it.

"Could you grab the first aid kit out of the bathroom for me please?" I asked. "It's on the top shelf to the right. Next to the window."

He disappeared for a moment, then came back. "This?" He held up the green bag with the red plus sign on it.

"Yes. There should be a tube of antiseptic in there. Would you hand it to me, please?"

I heard some rustling, then he said, "I don't see it."

"Blue and white tube that says antiseptic wash."

"It's not here."

I looked over and frowned. He'd emptied the contents of the bag on the counter. Yep, it was gone.

"Oh, God damn it. Well, soap and water it is. I hate doing that. I always think I'm going to get an infection." This of course was ridiculous and my anxiety rearing its ugly head.

Elias stared at my arm again. I was still bleeding.

Then it clicked. "I'm sorry, this must be terribly uncomfortable for you. I didn't think. If you'd like to leave—"

"I could clean it."

"Come again?"

"If you'll permit me, I can clean it and heal it for you."

I acted before I thought, something that was becoming a habit as of late. I turned the water off and offered my arm to Elias.

He gingerly took my hand and guided me out of the kitchenette to sit on the bed. "This is going to be intense. If at any point you want me to stop, tell me, and I will. Do you understand?"

I nodded.

Elias lowered his face to my arm and brushed his tongue along the wound. Then his lips fastened to one of the scratches and I gasped. He was gentle as could be, but other sensations promised to overtake me if I let them. I focused on what I was seeing. A vampire was feeding on me, and I was letting him. No, my friend and potential boyfriend was offering to help in the best way he knew how.

He switched to another of the gashes. He drank from each one before running his tongue along them. I felt hot, confused, and... Was I aroused? It had been a while, so I wasn't entirely sure.

When he sat up, there were traces of blood on his lips.

My blood. His pupils were dilated, and slowly, Elias wiped the blood away with his thumb and licked it off. I was panting and my face was hot. But when I looked down at my arm, the gashes were gone.

"Holy shit," I whispered.

"Are you all right?" Elias asked.

I nodded. I didn't trust myself to talk. At least not at the moment.

The silence was awkward, and I didn't think I could speak again. I was overstimulated, but it felt different this time. More good than bad. My mind hurtled through a hundred thousand thoughts, most of them incoherent. I had to remind myself to keep breathing.

I signed "a lot," then winced because Elias probably didn't know ASL.

To my surprise, he said, "It can be, yes. I was a little worried that taking your blood might have that effect on you."

"You know ASL?"

"Yes, though I'm out of practice. I had a deaf colleague for a time."

"Were they a vampire?"

"Yes."

"Surprised."

"There are vampires with disabilities." Elias tucked his hair behind his ears. "I feel it's only fair to warn you, I know."

I stilled, and my heart slammed to a stop. I decided to play dumb. "Know what?"

"I know you remember that night in Phoenix."

If I thought I was blushing before, my face must have turned into an inferno. I got up from the bed and walked toward the bathroom. I needed out of this conversation.

"Wait, please."

I stopped and turned to look at him.

"I've known since the night we met. Our mesmerism doesn't always work on people such as yourself."

"Mediums?"

"The neurodivergent. Mesmerism can be hit and miss but with those who are neurodivergent most of the time it doesn't work. Once Reyna mentioned your autism, I knew it failed. And there's a slight tell we look for."

"What tell?"

Elias sighed. "I can't tell you."

I rolled my eyes.

"Not because I don't want to," he clarified. "I can't tell you because it's imperceivable to humans, even gifted ones such as yourself."

"Why did you change my boss's memory?"

"What boss?"

I gave a quick summary about Cynthia.

"I'm not familiar with her. But any human who attempts to expose vampires to the world is stopped."

"By murder?"

"No, there are other ways. Mesmerism is one, but when that fails most humans respond to bribes."

I recovered enough to respond with my words. "That's insane. What happens if someone takes your money but then shoots their mouth off anyway?"

"They don't get a second chance."

"I don't even want to know what that means."

Elias raised an eyebrow. "Is that why you were so afraid of me? Did you think I would hurt you if you told the truth?"

"It would be pretty stupid to say 'no' now," I said. "Also, you're kind of intimidating. You're the strong silent type but sometimes you get this look on your face that's..." I struggled to find the right word. But then went with my first instinct. "Dark."

"I can't help that. There are things I've done I'm not proud of. But I take responsibility for each one."

"Like killing people?"

"Yes. Humans, shapeshifters, fairies, demons, angels, witches, and vampires. Other vampires especially. We are a quarrelsome race by nature, and the events in Phoenix have only exacerbated it. Now there's talk of separating the species and disbanding the Court."

"Verity mentioned that. What Court?"

Elias was quiet for a moment, having his own silent debate. "I can't say, not yet."

"She said that too."

"Verity knows many things, it's her gift and her curse. It's why I was outside Lafayette Cemetery tonight. I was waiting for you."

"She told you I'd run into trouble."

"Yes."

"And you dropped everything to help me?"

"Of course."

"Why?"

Elias frowned. "Why?"

"Yes, why? We're not intimate. We hardly know each other. I've been lying to you this whole time! You should be furious with me!" I grew louder the more I talked, and I ended up shouting, "You don't know the first thing about me. I'm dishonest, and a handful. I'm several neuroses wrapped up in one box. I'm autistic, I have PTSD, I work a dead-end job! Then in the evenings, I extort mourning people for money so they can talk to dead loved ones. Who does that? Not a very nice person, that's who."

I was crying. Everything was pressing on me. I wanted to tell him about Heather and her death and why I even joined the Black Lily Society in the first place. But I couldn't get the words out. I wrapped my arms around myself and backed away. I bumped into the bathroom door.

I was approaching a meltdown. I knew that distantly in the logical part of my brain. I didn't want Elias to see it. I was humiliated as it was. I didn't need more heaped on.

Elias surprised me when he grabbed the weighted blanket off my bed and offered it to me. I snatched it from his fingers and wrapped it around myself. Then I flopped on the bed like a worm. I'd gotten the king-sized weighted blanket so it would cover me from shoulders to feet.

When I'd wrapped myself in my cocoon, Elias asked, "Would you like me to hold you?"

The extra weight would calm me down. At least he hadn't run screaming yet. "Yes," I whined.

His arms wrapped around me, cold but strong. He didn't speak, he was silent as he held me.

It took a long time for me to calm down. I spent most of it crying and occasionally I would grab a tissue off the dresser to blow my nose. I'm not sure when I fell asleep, but I remember when I woke up.

It was three in the morning, and I jolted awake like someone pinched me. I looked at my alarm clock, saw the time, and that I had my alarm set. I was ready to roll over and go back to sleep. I was warm and safe, and someone held me from behind. Elias.

I turned my head to see he was awake and watching me.

"Hi," I said. My voice was hoarse.

"Sleep well?"

"Kind of. I'm really sorry."

"No, don't be sorry. I get the feeling that was pressing on you for a long time."

I nodded. "I don't freak out as often as I used to, but that was a bad one even by my standards."

"Would you like me to leave?"

I shook my head. "No, but I do need to use the restroom. Maybe change into my pajamas."

"As you wish."

He let me go. I untangled myself from the weighted blanket and headed for the bathroom. I grabbed a nightshirt out of the closet as I went. Once there I used the toilet, washed my hands, brushed my teeth, washed my face, and got undressed. I left my clothes and boots in the bathroom. I could deal with them in the morning.

When I came out, Elias was waiting. He'd turned the light on for me and made the bed.

"Thank you."

He nodded but didn't give a verbal response. I crawled into bed and got under the covers, then I shut the light off. Elias remained on top of them and lay down beside me.

"A gentleman," I muttered.

"As much as I can be."

"I'm so embarrassed. I haven't had a blow-up like that in front of another person in...let's just say it's been a while."

"I imagine you don't have many guests."

"I don't. I mean, the apartment is pretty small."

"Is that the only reason?"

I sighed. "No. To tell you the truth, I thought you'd get weirded out and run. Everyone who sees me like that does."

"Then the loss is theirs." He slid closer. "May I touch your hair?"

I nodded, and he ran his fingers through it. I sighed, goose bumps marching up and down my neck and arms.

"How did you know what to do?" I asked.

"When you were upset?"

"Yeah."

"We didn't know what autism was when I was human. But my little brother would have fits. They were most unbecoming for a child of his rank."

"You guys were royalty?"

"Nobility. I think the last royal of our family line was several centuries back. Around when Henry VIII was terrorizing every woman in England."

"That guy sucked."

"Indeed."

"What happened with your brother?"

He didn't answer right away. Then, in a quiet, low tone he said, "My parents thought he would benefit from a good whipping. Our governess thought otherwise. I loved my brother; I would never hurt him. So, between the two of us, we devised a system to help him. Through trial and error, we discovered what would calm him or what would make him worse."

"When was this?"

"Around what is now called the Regency period."

Definitely before anyone knew that autism was a thing then.

"So, you have experience with autism."

"Some, but I'm aware it can differ from person to person."

"I'm glad I didn't scare you off."

"I am glad you aren't scared of me."

"You're too nice to be scared of."

He chuckled, but his eyes remained closed. "I hope you will always think so."

I yawned and shut my eyes too. The sensation of his fingers gently grazing my scalp was lulling me to sleep. "Thank you."

"My pleasure."

Chapter Twenty-Eight

ELIAS WAS GONE by the time my alarm woke me. He'd left a note on the bedside table, but I didn't read it right away. After the incident at the cemetery and the meltdown, I was overwhelmed. I knew I had work. The thought of being professional and pretending nothing was wrong made me nauseous.

What was worse, all the ghosts who disappeared on Halloween were back in full force. My apartment was crowded, more than I'd ever seen. I demanded they leave, but not a single one of them budged. I tried again, but still nothing. I wouldn't be able to work with dozens of ghosts bothering me. When they realized I was awake their litany of demands started all over again. I was already back to the threshold of sensory overload, and I'd only been awake for twenty minutes.

I called in sick. My manager probably thought I was insane because I was using much more formal speech than usual. It was a trick I'd learned when I was worried I would either stutter or be unable to speak at all: pretend that I had a role in a period drama and act it out. He said he hoped I felt better and hung up. I also made sure to send a text to Reyna to say I wouldn't be in this week. She didn't text back since it was daytime.

I left the curtains closed, curled up under my weighted blanket, and used the pillows to try to block out the ghosts. Unsurprisingly, they were not happy about it.

Still shaken after the ghost at the cemetery hurt me, I didn't dare try to force them out. It wasn't working anyway.

Then I remembered there was a passage in *Piercing* about banishing. I removed the pillow from my head and opened the nightstand drawer. I took out the book and flipped through it. I did my best to ignore the ghosts while I read. When that didn't work, I went in search of my headphones.

"You can't ignore us forever!" a woman hissed.

"You're so selfish. You won't do anything, but we need help," a man yelled.

I didn't respond. I didn't have the words to. I found my headphones on my desk, but the buds had been torn off, and who knew where they were.

"Oh God damn it," I muttered.

Something shoved me from behind.

"Hey! Fucking cut it out."

"Then help us," someone yelled in my ear.

"Let me read and I'll see what I can do."

Okay, not the best idea. The last thing I wanted to do was compromise. Otherwise, the ghosts would turn out like Heather. Give an inch, they'll take a mile, and I'd never have another moment's peace. I missed Elias. Even with the run-in at the cemetery, last night was blissful. And traumatic, but for the most part blissful.

I picked up the book and flipped to the section on unwanted ghosts. I did my best to block the book with my body so they couldn't read over my shoulder.

If phantoms continue to accost you once the séance is complete, enforce your will and banish them. Any medium can do this, though this skill comes more easily to some than to others.

The passage was no help at all, since I'd tried to make the ghosts leave and they ignored me. One ripped the book out of my hands and threw it across the room.

"Help us," it hissed.

I closed my eyes and put my hands over my ears. This did nothing to block out the sound as the ghosts gathered around me. They were screaming, crying, and carrying on. They demanded my energy and time, to bend to their will.

"What kind of selfish brat are you?" an old woman snapped.

I'm not sure what it was about that sentence, but those words ignited in my chest. Raw pain and rage coursed through me, as though a dam inside me had burst. I dropped my hands and opened my eyes. I was pissed.

"Selfish? You're calling *me* selfish? You all fucked up your lives so bad you're haunting me and expect me to tidy up your unfinished business! Do you really think if I tell your son you always loved him it will give you or him peace? Do you believe you'll go to heaven if I give your last words of spite to your ex? Look at all of you," I demanded and gestured wildly around the room. "Some of you are so damn old I can't even see you. What gives you the right to—"

"How dare—" the old woman started to say.

I howled in her face, "I am talking, do not interrupt me."

She looked ready to argue, but then it was like someone glued her mouth shut. Try as she might, she couldn't pry her lips apart! Carried on waves of repressed anger, I pushed back at her with the full force of it. She was thrown backward and through a wall.

Internally, I was awash with guilt. What if I'd hurt her? But I was so angry I didn't care if I did. The ghosts hurt me plenty.

"What the fuck is wrong with all of you? Do you think I want this power? I'd give it back in a heartbeat. All you care about is what I can do for you. No wonder you're ghosts, I bet none of you ever did a single thing in your lives you didn't have to. Now it's too late and you want me to clean up your mess. And you have the nerve to call me selfish? Look in the mirror! Oh, that's right, you can't. Because you're dead and you don't have a reflection."

The ghosts were silent. Several glared at me, though they'd all backed away. I wasn't done, not by a long shot. I'd been too polite, and let them trample all over my boundaries, just like Heather. I'd reached the end of my rope. I was sure another meltdown was coming, and on the heels of the last one it was going to suck. I didn't care; in the moment the only thing I wanted was for them to stop pushing me around.

"I'm not going to do a goddamn thing for any of you until you learn to ask me properly. You will be respectful and you will accept it if I say no. You don't get to pitch a fit and act like a bunch of raving lunatics when I turn you down. This is my life, and I am not going to sacrifice my health, happiness, or sanity for someone else ever again. Especially not a bunch of dead people. Now you can either accept this and ask me again politely or I swear by all the powers that be I will have each and every one of you exorcized and that is a promise. Now get the hell out of my house!"

Most of them faded while I screamed at them. The remaining few looked at one another, then disappeared.

"Took you long enough."

I jumped and spun around. Heather lay on my bed inspecting her nails. She sat up and smirked at me. "Finally grew a backbone, I see."

"And where have you been?" I was still too pissed off to play nice.

"Away."

I snorted. "Yeah, well, I'm telling you the same thing I told them. No more pushing me around. Elias is innocent until proven guilty and I'm not taking any more of your shit."

Heather held her hands up and said, "Hey, calm down."

"Don't you tell me to calm down, Heather Campbell! Not after what I've been through!"

"No, I mean like calm down because you're right."

I was ready to read her the riot act too, but that made me pause. "Excuse me?"

"I said you're right. I was treating you like shit because I'm scared of disappearing forever. I thought maybe if you busted Elias or found out who actually killed me, I'd be happy. But last night I realized something."

"Last night? I haven't seen you in weeks."

"My bad. Look, would you sit down with me for a minute? You look like you're about to blow your top and it's kinda scaring me."

Guilt gnawed at me again, but I sat down on the bed. My back was against the footboard while Heather was propped up against the headboard.

"So, Halloween, it turns out, is a big deal for ghosts."

"Yes, I found that out."

"Okay, but let me tell you what it's like from our end."

I sighed and gestured for her to continue.

"I went and saw my stepdaddy," said Heather. "I

figured with the veil being thin and all that shit he'd be able to see me. And he did. You know what he said?"

I shook my head.

"He told me to go away. He said I was dead and I needed to move on. I can't stay here on Earth." Heather grimaced. "He didn't care that I was murdered. Or as he saw it, committed suicide. He only cared that I was still hanging around and that I may never be at rest. I tried to tell him about Elias and my death too. He said…"

"He said what?"

"He said I needed to let it go or I'd never be able to go home and be with God."

"What did you say?"

"I left. Didn't seem there was any chance I could talk sense into him. And I wasn't the only person out either. I saw ghosts everywhere. They returned to their loved ones, or where they died. They tried to talk to people or make them pay attention. The few people who did see them were afraid or thought it was a prank because it was Halloween. That's when it hit me. It doesn't matter, it never did."

Heather stared down at the bedspread; she wouldn't look at me.

I tilted my head and frowned. "What do you mean?"

"It's what you said just now. Let's say you do prove Elias killed me. And by some fucking miracle, he was arrested and punished for it. Then where does that leave me? Do I stop existing? Do I go to heaven? Or do I end up like all the sad fucks we see around here, wandering around without purpose or somewhere to go? I could end up on one of those stupid ghost tours if I'm not careful."

"Unlikely, they seem to prefer older murders."

"Eh, most of them. Some don't give a shit about living

relatives and friends. Those kinds of people will take advantage of a tragedy if it makes them a few dollars."

"I suppose you have a point. What do you want to do now?"

"I still know in my heart Elias is the one who did it. And...I know you like him a lot. I like you too, as a friend. I don't want you to choose between us. If you don't want to investigate anymore, I won't make you. Just promise me you'll be careful."

I nodded. "I will be."

"Great."

Heather got up from the bed. "Now that that's out of the way, what do you wanna do today? I've got a clear schedule."

"I want to go back to sleep. It's been a pretty intense couple of days. I actually called out of work."

"Wow, someone alert the authorities. Lyric Morrison called in to work! It's a national emergency."

I laughed.

Then I picked up the note from Elias. I could finally read it now that things had settled down.

Miss Morrison,

I had to return home as the sun was rising. I hope this letter finds you well. I would like to see you again. This weekend, if you are free. Please let me know at your earliest convenience.

Elias Rothschild

It was very sweet, and I couldn't help clutching the note to my chest. I showed it to Heather, who admitted it was nice of him. She even complimented his handwriting.

Heather seemed better. Not angry or bitter. Definitely not the vengeful harpy she'd been over the past couple of months. Maybe if I couldn't solve her murder, I could at least be her friend. And maybe this would all work out.

I wish I'd known how wrong I was.

Chapter Twenty-Nine

I WAS IN my Phoenix apartment again. It was the night I met Elias. I sighed as he stood in my doorway, happy to see him. He smiled at me, the same smile he gave when I said something funny. I was about to invite him in when to my surprise he grabbed my arm and pulled me out onto the porch.

He had me in his clutches, and his smile turned to a feral grin. He grabbed my hair and yanked my head to the side, so hard I could feel the bones in my neck pop. His teeth sunk into my throat, and I couldn't draw breath to scream. The pain was too intense.

Elias growled as he fed on me and crushed me to him. My bones broke and tendons popped. No matter how hard I tried, I couldn't get enough breath to scream. There was a pressure on my chest that hurt so much I thought my rib cage would explode. Then he dropped me to the floor, blood on his lips and pupils dilated.

I heard laughter. I managed to turn my head just enough to see the gray wraith was back. It was perched on the arm of my sofa and watching with a maniacal grin and fathomless black eyes. It crept closer to me, then it sank its claws into my scalp. As the creature's nails thrust into my brain, I screamed again.

My eyes snapped open, and I was paralyzed. A black mass loomed over the bed, undulating over me. Finally, I had enough air in my lungs, and I screamed so loud I was sure I'd woken up Sawyer and Jaime. The mass vanished, and I wasn't sure it had been there at all.

I turned on the bedside lamp and bolted out of bed. Not a ghost in sight, not even Heather. I rubbed the side of my neck, but there were no bite marks. It had been a nightmare. An intense one at that. I was breathing too hard and the logical part of my brain knew I was hyperventilating. I couldn't make myself stop. I stumbled into the kitchen and while I didn't have a paper bag, a plastic one would work just as well.

After breathing into the bag for a few minutes, I finally calmed down enough to register how tired I was. Exhausted, actually. Like I'd run a marathon in my sleep. My arms were like jelly, and it took more strength than I would have liked to expend to get back into bed.

*

I ENDED UP taking the next day off from work too. Verity texted me that evening to check-in.

Verity Archer: Still sick?

Lyric Morrison: Yeah. Thanks for looking out for me. And for Halloween.

Verity Archer: You're welcome. Elias will be disappointed you won't be in tonight.

Lyric Morrison: I wish I could come say hi but I'm kind of hanging on to my own sanity by a thread.

Verity Archer: I know. I'm sorry.

I realized I hadn't spoken to her since the parade. I decided to change the subject. Something Dr. Cade would remind me of is that I am not the only person in the world. If I want to make friends, I have to show interest in others, even though I tend to talk about myself the most. It wasn't that I didn't care about other people. It simply didn't occur to me to ask as I figured people would talk about themselves unprompted. I had to remind myself to be mindful of others.

Lyric Morrison: How have you been?

Verity Archer: All right I suppose. Some nightmares, but those aren't unusual for me.

Lyric Morrison: You too? I wonder if there's something in the water.

Verity Archer: What do you mean?

Lyric Morrison: I was getting them a lot until Amy over at the Cardinal made me a little sweet dream bag. But I think it must have worn off or something because I'm having them again.

Verity Archer: Oh, I'm sorry to hear that. What are they about?

I bit my lip. Verity still didn't know about Phoenix, and it wasn't something I wanted to talk about via text.

Lyric Morrison: Just some stuff from my past. Not worth getting into. What are you having nightmares about?

Verity Archer: Tali.

Lyric Morrison: Your ex?

Verity Archer: Yes. I keep having nightmares that she's in trouble. Or dead. And it's all my fault.

Lyric Morrison: That sucks. But like, how would it be your fault? You two aren't together anymore.

Verity Archer: It's complicated.

There seemed to be a lot neither of us were saying. I glanced over at Heather, who sat at my desk reading a book. She'd come back that afternoon, and she would sneak glances at me when she thought I wasn't looking. No, not at me. My phone. She was trying to read what I was texting. I rolled over so I was facing her and my phone wasn't. Heather blinked, then went back to the book I left out.

Lyric Morrison: Maybe we should get together to clear the air.

Verity Archer: Oh?

Lyric Morrison: I've been keeping something to myself for a while. And I suspect you have too.

Verity Archer: You're right, I have.

Lyric Morrison: We should discuss it in person.

Verity Archer: Shall we invite the boys too?

Lyric Morrison: The boys?

Verity Archer: Lionel and Elias.

I shivered.

Lyric Morrison: Lionel yes, Elias no. At least not yet.

Verity Archer: Okay. Well, when you're ready to talk, I'll be ready too.

Lyric Morrison: I will.

I put the phone away and curled up again, then closed my eyes. I dozed for a time but every time I felt myself being pulled down into sleep I would jolt. I didn't want to sleep, not right now. Before I knew it, the sun was down. I was in the twilight world between dreams and waking when I heard a gentle tapping.

I opened my eyes and sat up. My ears strained to pick up anything else. The neighborhood was freakishly quiet. I saw Heather puttering around and another ghost hanging around the apartment. I couldn't hear anything.

"What was that?" I asked.

"What?" Heather replied.

Okay, clearly she hadn't heard it.

I got out of bed, grabbed a robe from the bathroom, and pulled it on. I wasn't naked, but if there was someone outside I didn't want them to see my Sailor Moon pajamas. Some things you just don't want to show off in public. Adorable pajamas are one of them.

I opened the door, and to my surprise, there was a basket on the bottom step of my stoop. Curious, I picked up the basket and brought it inside.

"Whatcha got there?" Heather asked.

"I'm not sure."

The contents of the basket were wrapped in green velvet fabric, tied closed with a gold silk ribbon. An envelope was pinned to the front. My name was written on it in a gorgeous curlicue style. It reminded me of old journals and historical letters. I carefully opened the envelope and extracted a card.

It was from Elias. I read it aloud.

"My dear Miss Morrison,

"I have been advised by Miss Archer you have fallen ill. If not for a full work schedule I would love to be there to nurse you through this malady. As it stands, I have included several items you should find useful. If you would like to request my company once I have concluded my business, please don't hesitate to reach out.

"If you would prefer to keep your own company, I understand. Perhaps we can meet again once you are on the mend. You may disregard the invitation for a date on Saturday. Either way, please don't hesitate to contact me.

"Lovingly yours, Elias."

I sighed and held the card to my chest. He was too kind.

"Wow, some boyfriend," Heather said and rolled her eyes.

"He's giving me options instead of insisting he be here. I appreciate the effort and that he respects my personal space," I replied. "He's not acting as though he's the boss of me or as if I'm some frail helpless maiden who can't function without him."

"If this is all it takes to impress you, your love life must have sucked before coming here."

"No argument here."

I pulled the ribbon off the basket and let the velvet fall away. I smiled when I saw the contents.

There were two pints of soup from Bywater Bakery. He also included a loaf of their challah bread which I was crazy about, a container of earplugs, a bottle of aspirin, and a six-pack of Gatorade. He'd added a blindfold I was delighted to discover had headphones wired into it. They operated via Bluetooth. I'd be able to listen to whichever ambient sounds or music would relax me.

I also discovered the green velvet was actually a weighted blanket cover. It was the same size as the weighted blanket on my bed. I couldn't stop myself from grinning.

"This is the best gift I've ever received," I said.

Heather looked at me like I was nuts. I ignored her.

I wondered how Elias had gotten the soup. He couldn't go out during the day, and the bakery was only open from 7:00 a.m. to 3:00 p.m. Then I remembered in the note he mentioned Verity. He must have asked her to get it for him. When would he have had the time?

I wanted to call Elias and ask him to come over right after work. I had my phone in my hand, but paused and thought it through. I was still pretty fragile from the meltdown and the nightmare. I probably wouldn't be up for visitors, especially after the Black Lily closed for the night. I didn't want to invite him over while I was excited, then ask him to leave later. That would be kind of rude.

So, I had some of the soup and bread for dinner and looked around online. I admittedly didn't know too much about Elias except for the fact he liked plants. I wanted to get him something that would show my appreciation.

When I came across a very interesting nursery online, I knew what I would get him. A local business, they specialized in carnivorous plants. I wasn't sure if Elias would like them, but who didn't? Bug-eating plants seemed pretty damn awesome to me. One would at the very least keep the bugs off his other plants and flowers.

Satisfied this would do, I paid for a pitcher plant and selected local pick-up.

When I went to bed that night, I felt better, as though a burden had been lifted from me. This time there were no nightmares.

Chapter Thirty

THE CARE PACKAGE from Elias did wonders. I was ready to return to my regular job as well as work at the club by the end of the week. There were still too many ghosts flitting in and out of my house. But hard as I tried, unless I was truly angry, I couldn't get rid of them. It was as though they delighted in ignoring me, or that they didn't take me seriously until I blew my top. Neither of which was ideal.

When I returned to the Black Lily Society, I went straight to Reyna's office to talk to her. I'm not the confrontational type, and I was pretty sure she would be upset by what I had to say. I was making a lot of money for the club. The kind of money where I was taking home a thousand dollars a night. That much cash was hard to say no to.

When I let myself into her office, I said, "I need to scale back my readings."

Reyna was reviewing the ledger and didn't look up. "By how much?"

"I can do three a week and that's it."

"Why three?"

"Four felt like too much and two felt like too few. Also, I wanted it to be a prime number."

Reyna didn't respond for a few minutes. She crossed something out in the ledger and looked up at me.

"Are you okay?"

"I'm burned out," I admitted. "I bit off more than I can chew and it's why I haven't been around as much."

This was the truth. It wasn't just the investigation and work. The investigation was on hold until I sorted out my feelings for Elias and my suspicions about Heather. We were friendly again, but I didn't know how long that would last. Heather was not a patient person and she was pushy by nature.

I expected we'd have another fight any day now, especially when she found out I'd gone back to the Cardinal for another dream charm. I couldn't find the old one, so I picked up another one on my way to the club that night. I decided to keep it a secret from her since she'd been so pissed the first time. She'd find out eventually, but I wasn't about to tell her.

"You've still got commitments for the next two weeks. You'll have to keep them as it's too short notice to cancel. And there are the people who were rescheduled for this week. That's including another séance dinner. After that, I can rearrange your schedule. I'm not canceling any appointments but I can at least space them out."

"That's fine. Please extend my apologies to the customers."

"I will." Reyna rested her elbows on the desk, knit her fingers together, and placed her chin on her hands. "You know, if you are having difficulties, I can help."

I raised an eyebrow. "How?"

"Financial counseling. You make enough tips here that you don't really need to work at your day job anymore."

It wasn't until she said it that I realized she was right. I could leave my job tomorrow without a problem. No more corporate America with its confusing pitfalls and protocols. I'd strictly be in entertainment and tourism. It wasn't exactly a dream of mine, but it would free up my schedule for something that was.

"I don't need counseling," I said. "It just...didn't occur to me I could quit."

Reyna chuckled. "Is that so?"

"I'm an idiot," I muttered.

"Don't talk about yourself like that. You're not an idiot. I'd say you're overworked and stressed out."

"That too."

Reyna frowned. "Are you still having trouble with the ghosts?"

"Yeah. Hey, do you know if German is here tonight? I have his card but I keep forgetting to call him."

"He is. Do you need to speak with him?"

"If he's not busy."

"He isn't, he's here with Jaxon. They're hanging out in the bar."

"Awesome, thank you."

Reyna waved me off and went back to her ledger. She was probably trying to figure out who to put where now that I'd kind of screwed the pooch on the schedule. I felt horrible. I still wanted to help people and I was being selfish. I seemed to think that a lot lately. It didn't help that the ghosts screamed the same sentiment at me constantly.

German and Jaxon were indeed at the bar, and I paused in the doorway when I saw who was behind it. Elias was drying some glasses and putting them away. His hair was loose this evening, and the all-black uniform made him look paler than usual. I admit, I missed his usual flannel shirt.

I approached and asked German, "This seat taken?"

He looked over and grinned. "Hey! Where have you been?"

"Oh, meltdowns galore due to stress and sensory overload. The usual."

"I'm sorry to hear that," said Jaxon.

I shook my head. "No worries. If anything, I should be apologizing. I'm the one who keeps missing work."

"Because you were ill, we understand," German replied.

I almost corrected him. My only illness was in my head and it didn't count. Except, he was right. It wasn't the same as having the flu or a cold, true. But a meltdown could knock me right the hell out like one. Most people, especially the neurotypical, didn't understand that. Admittedly I had a hard time with it myself since I was always expected to pull myself together. To keep going, even if I was a complete trainwreck.

It was nice to be understood by others without having to overexplain. I thought I was going to cry, I was so touched. I coughed a little and swallowed to clear the lump in my throat.

"Thank you," I said.

"What can I get you?"

I looked at Elias. His expression was as closed off as ever, but I could see a little glint in his eyes. He was happy to see me.

"Ginger ale with a twist of lime please."

"You got it."

I turned to German. "I want to speak with you about a problem I'm having if that's okay."

"Sure, what do you need?"

"I'm having trouble banishing ghosts from my apartment. They're uh...following me around. I can summon them but I'm terrible at banishing them. The only time I've gotten close is when I go ape shit and start screaming at everyone. And I can't do that all the time. I'll lose my voice."

"Or your mind," Jaxon teased.

I shrugged. "You said it, not me."

"I can cleanse the place for you," German said. "It's my specialty."

"Why is that, by the way? I mean, you can't see ghosts." I paused. "Wait, can you?"

German shook his head. "No, I don't have that particular gift. But I was raised to believe in ghosts and spirits and I followed in my mother's footsteps when I took up magic. Cleansing is extremely important because evil spirits can infect a physical space. Kind of like a disease but the effect is entirely on your emotions and mind. They'll make everything in your life go from bad to worse and it takes shockingly little effort."

"Oh, I didn't know that."

"It's something that's common knowledge among witches, *brujas*, and *mambos*. Or anyone who practices magic."

"Which I don't."

"Precisely. But since your gift has to do with working with spirits so much, I assumed you knew how to banish."

Jaxon leaned around German to look at me. "It's kind of weird. You can't make them leave at all?"

I shook my head. "Not unless I've lost my temper. And I don't want to be angry like that all the time. It's exhausting."

"What does happen when you try to banish them?" Elias asked. "More specifically, what do you feel?"

He'd returned with my ginger ale. I put a five on the counter, but he shook his head and pushed it back toward me. He put a finger to his lips and winked. My face heated up. I bet I looked like a tomato wearing a teal wig.

I sipped my drink and thought about it. "I feel guilty."

German and Jaxon exchanged glances, then said in unison, "Excuse me?"

"I can't help it. Yeah, I bitch about the ghosts being selfish. But I feel bad that they're dead and no one can see them. It's terrible being ignored. It's like if you were shipwrecked and instead of someone responding to your SOS, you see everyone sail past without a care in the world. Any time I try to banish a ghost I think about what that must be like and how lonely it is. It makes me feel awful. Which is kind of hilarious because I also feel like they're being pushy and demanding way too much of my time. But then that starts me feeling guilty all over again."

Elias crossed his arms over his chest. "Miss Morrison, you can't think like that."

"Why not? Isn't that what it's like for them?"

"It is, but you're forgetting that they're dead and you're not. They'll consume your life if you let them. You can't let ghosts take over your life."

"He's right," said German. "I get you want to help, you're compassionate and it's sweet. But you have to be able to put your foot down. You have to establish a safe space and boundaries for yourself. Or you won't be able to help anyone."

"What, like, I'd lose my powers?"

"No, but burnout is a thing. It happens to therapists and counselors all the time," Jaxon pointed out.

Elias held his hand out to me. "May I?"

I nodded.

He took my hand in his. There was a chill like he'd just pulled his hand out from the ice bucket.

"Think of it this way. You can't help anyone if you're burned out. Which is already happening. You have a good heart, and I know you would see it as a failure. But it isn't. Just like you aren't failing any of these ghosts by establishing boundaries. It means you'll have enough energy to help more of them."

"I suppose you're right."

German tossed back his drink and placed the empty glass on the bar. "When do you want to do the ritual?"

"I have one more question first."

"Shoot."

"Would a friendly ghost be able to still access my apartment?"

He frowned. "I don't understand."

"There's one ghost I'm friends with. Would you be able to make it so she can still enter my home?"

"No, the spell would banish all ghosts and spirits from the space."

I didn't say no right away. Yes, Heather was a pain in the ass and I wasn't sure we were friends anymore no matter what she said. She was dramatic, took up a lot of my time, and frankly, her presence was draining. But I'd discovered my powers because of her. And I still hadn't found her killer.

"Then I need to figure something out first," I concluded.

"Okay. You have my number. Call me when you're ready."

Elias had to get back to work, but he gave me a kiss on the cheek before he did. I smiled as he walked to the opposite end of the bar to talk with Emerson. I knew I was making a stupid face, but I couldn't help myself.

When I turned back to Jaxon and German they were

on the verge of laughing.

"What?" I asked and frowned.

"Nothing, we're just happy for you both," said German.

"Yeah. Elias has opened up a lot. It's nice to see."

I blinked. "Yeah?"

"Yeah. He talks to people now. Before he'd do his job, not say a word, go home, and come back the next night. Same old routine, and he was pretty stoic," Jaxon said and did an impression of Elias's blank stare. "But now he socializes. We love to see it."

"I think he's been alone for a long time, he just needed someone to help him come out of his shell," German added.

I looked back at Elias and said, more to myself than anyone, "So have I."

I stayed for a little while. I chatted with German about his magic, and how being a vampire affected it. Jaxon also talked about himself and said he wasn't a witch but a conjurer, which made little sense to me. He did break it down for me, but it still sounded like witchcraft. He swore it wasn't the same, but German teased him and called him pretentious.

When I began to tire, I figured it was time to go home. But before I did, I asked Elias if I could speak with him.

He looked at me, then said to Emerson, "I'm taking a break."

"Ooh, don't do anything I wouldn't do," he replied and winked at us before switching places with Elias behind the bar.

We went up to the roof, and once we were alone Elias asked, "Are the ghosts what caused your meltdown?"

"Kind of, but actually a lot of things. Work and the

club together it's like having two full-time jobs so...I think I'm going to quit my day job."

His eyebrows furrowed. "Are you sure?"

"No, that's why I have to think about it."

"I see." Then Elias smiled. "By the way, thank you for the pitcher plant."

I grinned. "You liked it?"

"Yes, very much. It will be put to good use."

"I'm happy to hear it. But that's not why I wanted to talk to you."

"Then what is it?"

I held my hand out, and he took it and squeezed. I had to stand on tiptoe to do it, but I leaned close and kissed his cheek. His stubble felt weird against my lips, but not in a bad way.

"Thank you for the care package."

He brushed my bangs back and traced a finger down my cheek. He narrowly avoided my glasses. He grazed the pad of his thumb over my lips, his eyes searching mine.

"May I?"

I couldn't speak, but I nodded.

Elias kissed me. A brief peck on the lips, but it was enough to make my heart soar.

"Would it be terribly crass of me to ask you out again?"

"We have a date on Saturday. If you'll recall, I didn't cancel."

"Another after?"

I smiled. "I'd love to."

"Wonderful. Will Thursday evening suffice?"

"I have to work that night. But after?"

"After that would be fine. Come, let me escort you to the bus stop."

Chapter Thirty-One

I HANDED IN my resignation at work. When my boss asked why, I simply said I was having personal problems. He said he understood and to use my PTO for the last two weeks since company policy was "use it or lose it." I was surprised since Thanksgiving was coming up and the holiday season was normally when all hands were on deck.

He also said if I wanted my job back to call him any time which surprised me. I wasn't under the impression that my boss liked me, let alone thought well enough of me to offer my old job if things didn't work out. I thanked him for the opportunity and turned over my case files. When I logged out for the day, for the last time, I sighed. I felt much lighter, a great weight lifted off my shoulders.

I packed up the equipment to mail back, then tried to figure out what I was going to do with all my sudden free time. I was a little worried about taxes. But I'd asked a local accountant about it, and she'd given me instructions on how much to set aside. Even taking that into account, I was still making enough from the séances I'd be comfortable.

Heather, however, was not enthused by this turn of events. "Are you sure? I mean you have a steady paycheck. Or did. You're gonna be at the mercy of the tourists."

"It's the slow season right now and I'm still making bank," I pointed out. "Even with slowing down my nights at the club each week. I imagine it'll be even busier when Mardi Gras rolls around."

"I still think it's too big a risk."

"Your opinion has been noted."

As calm and collected as I sounded, I was having doubts. What if Heather was right? What if I took a stupid risk? I wasn't sure I was doing the right thing. But I also didn't want to keep working a regular nine-to-five. Not when I was spending so much of my time at the Black Lily Society. It felt as though I was clinging to my day job because it was familiar, not because I actually wanted to do it.

Not to mention how often I worked with ghosts. Reading *Piercing the Veil*, I realized there was more than one way to make a ghost leave. And it was so simple I couldn't believe it didn't occur to me before then.

Ghosts thrived off attention. Not in a "look at me, look at me!" way. But as a form of energy transference. Giving a ghost your full attention was giving them power and your energy. No wonder I felt so tired all the time! The important part was focusing on shielding your aura and energy from them. The easiest way to do this was to picture yourself encased in some kind of force field. I pictured a bubble made of diamond since it's so strong.

This wasn't as easy as it sounded, and some of the ghosts were very persistent. But the more I practiced, the better I got. It also helped that I set ground rules and worked on enforcing them. I wasn't a tool for the ghosts to use however and whenever they pleased. I drew up a schedule and would talk with a few ghosts a day. I'd get their stories, and how I could help them get closure. Once my "office hours" were over I would do research and try to track down whoever or whatever they requested.

Some ghosts didn't want to move on. There was nothing I could do to convince them to. Those ghosts were relegated to either helping with small tasks or hanging about. Some were so indistinct I didn't know their names or what time period they were from.

That Saturday evening as I got ready for my date, I had a strange, nervous feeling. Like something momentous would happen. I brushed it off as best I could. It was just a date. With Elias. That he'd asked me to go on. Perfectly normal.

We were going to City Park, then to dinner. The park is gorgeous, and there are several paths through the old tree groves as well as a beautiful pond. We'd only just gone through the time change, so it was getting darker earlier. It opened up more activities for us, and I suggested we rent one of the light-up swan boats to have some fun. Surprisingly, he agreed, so we made plans to meet at the bus stop and walk in together.

I changed into black velvet leggings, green combat boots, a green sleeveless tunic, and a black mesh shirt with bell sleeves under the tunic. I also picked out black velvet fingerless gloves and a wide-brimmed black fedora. I fished my rectangular green glasses out of my purse and grabbed my black mini backpack in case I decided some shopping was in order. A little black mascara and maroon lipstick and I was ready to hit the town.

"You look like a cartoon character," Heather said.

"At least I can change my outfit," I replied. Heather was still in the mint-green shorts and coral shirt she died in.

She rolled her eyes but didn't say anything further.

I left the house and was surprised to see Jaime and Sawyer weren't out. I walked to the bus stop and got there just as the bus was pulling up. Then I was on my way. When the bus got to the City Park roundabout, I saw Elias waiting for me at the stop, as agreed. He was back to his red check flannel and blue jeans, and it brought a smile to my face.

I got off the bus and waved.

"Good evening," he said.

"Hi."

He offered me his hand but I shook my head.

"I'm a little overstimulated right now. I don't want to hold hands."

"As you request."

Elias shoved his hands in his pockets and we started to walk up Lelong Drive. It's a two-lane road with a wide neutral ground in the middle. The sidewalk on both sides of the road is lined with trees. The streetlights were muted by the leaves, so it was dark but not pitch black. There weren't any other people around that I could see and I chuckled.

"For a city known for partying so much this place feels like the town that dreaded sundown," I said.

Elias smiled. "Most businesses cater to tourists. And those that don't have customers who either have odd work hours or don't work at all."

"Huh, you know it just occurred to me that means me now."

"And how are you feeling after quitting your day job?"

"Like I'm committing a crime. Any moment the authorities are gonna arrest me for crimes against capitalism, then force me to go back to work in corporate America. Only this time I'll be chained to my desk so I won't escape again."

"Interesting scenario. Though, isn't working a standard job difficult for you?"

"Because of my disability? It can be, not gonna lie. Some days I would get so frustrated I would start crying at my desk. I think the worst part had to be the fluorescent lighting. I felt like someone was shining a flashlight in my face the whole time I was at work. That's why I've got several pairs of these." I touched the side of my glasses. "The tinted lenses lessen the effect of fluorescent lighting. It doesn't work for everyone, but it does work for me."

"Clever, though unfortunate that it was even necessary."

"Most big companies kind of suck at ADA compliance. It's one of the pitfalls of being disabled enough to need help but not so disabled you're not able to take care of yourself. Well, really, it sucks either way. But it's why I was so happy to work from home."

"So you can make those accommodations yourself?"

"Bingo."

"And now you needn't worry."

"Nope. Reyna has been great. Speaking of, I have a couple questions if you don't mind."

Elias raised an eyebrow but said, "Go on."

"You said your brother was autistic too, right? Whatever happened to him?"

He grimaced. "He fell into a lake and drowned while I was away on the Continent. My parents considered him too old for a nursemaid and often left him to his own devices with little to no supervision. It was sadly the death of him."

"Oh gosh, I'm so sorry."

"Thank you. I drifted from my parents after that. I don't remember much about them. However, after David's death is when I met Jonas."

"The guy who wrote the book you gave me?"

"Yes."

"Were you a vampire before you met him?"

"I was turned shortly after we met."

"Bet that complicated things."

"Just the opposite as a matter of fact. Jonas was understanding and helpful. Especially as my sire was a contemptible person and I'm lucky to have escaped him. If not for Jonas, I don't think I would have."

A light breeze started up, tossing my hair around. I shivered. I felt as though someone was walking just behind us. I pushed my glasses down my nose and looked over my shoulder. There was a vague outline, but that was all. I slid my glasses back into place.

I frowned. "How was he contemptible?"

Elias shook his head. "I can't discuss it. You should ask Lionel."

"Why?"

"We were turned by the same vampire. Unlike me, Lionel didn't have anyone to pull him away from our sire's influence."

I made a mental note to ask later, then changed the subject. "What happened to Jonas?"

"The same thing that happens to all humans."

Well, that made sense, but I still pressed the issue. "Then how did he..."

"Die? A Night Hag drained him of his energy."

Damn, now more pieces were coming into place. That must have been why Elias seemed so afraid for me when the Witch of the French Opera warned me about the Night Hag—who I still hadn't located or knew the identity of. A cool wind blew through the trees and I shivered. We were approaching the New Orleans Museum of Art. We'd have to turn onto Collins Drive which circled around the museum, then take Enrique Alferez Drive to get to the dock.

I couldn't help feeling as though I'd crossed some kind of line, so I said, "Sorry again."

Elias sighed. "Thank you, but he would have died eventually anyway. He didn't want to become like me."

"I can't say I blame him."

Elias suddenly turned off the path and crossed the street, which took us to the fountain in front of the museum. Then he paused and looked at me.

"Why is that?"

Crap. Had I insulted him? "Oh, I just, I mean—" I was tripping over my words before I could spit out a full sentence.

"I'm not offended, just curious. You wouldn't seek immortality?"

"No," I replied. "I just... Look, I don't want to die. But the thought of living forever? I hate it. The world is already so bright and noisy. And it's only going to get worse the longer we go on. There's climate change and racial injustice. Let's not forget homophobia and so many other crappy things! And we have no guarantee those are going to be eradicated anytime soon. If ever! For all we know it could get worse. I hope it doesn't, but I don't want to stick around to find out."

"Essentially you feel the world will become too turbulent for you to exist in comfortably."

"Well, yeah. I already feel stressed to the extreme as it is. I don't want to make it worse."

"I suppose I can understand that."

Elias was about to say something more, but he froze. Slowly, his head turned. He then said, "Wait here, please,

Miss Morrison."

And he vanished.

"What in holy hell?" I asked aloud.

I felt weirdly vulnerable, out in the open with no one around. I jogged across the street to the museum. I walked toward the gates to the Besthoff Sculpture Garden. As I approached, I could hear two ghosts talking, but not to me. They sounded like men. As I tuned into their conversation, I thought my heart would jump into my throat. I kept walking so I could get closer to the conversation until I reached the Dueling Oak.

"Pretty nasty fight, huh?"

"Yeah. You reckon that little guy's gonna be okay?"

"Who can tell with vampires? But that's a damn biggun he's picked a fight with."

"Yep, it looked like he had the little guy on the ropes. Maybe we should help."

"How are we gonna help? Cheer him on?"

At that, I took my glasses off and the two phantoms were clear as day. Two workmen in overalls and boots from the early 1900s was my guess.

"Where are they?" I demanded.

"What in blazes?" the first exclaimed.

The second gasped and asked, "Who are you?"

"Never mind that, tell me where you saw the vampires fighting."

"Don't get your panties in a bunch."

"Yeah, you're interrupting—"

I don't know what possessed me to do it. Something told me to make them talk. I held out my hand, and a surge of cold energy went through me. The ghosts froze and I growled, "Tell me what I want to know. Now!"

"They're at Popp's Bandstand," they said together

tonelessly.

I broke the connection and ran.

It wasn't far from the Dueling Oak. I raced over the bridge, past the Café du Monde City Park, and down Dreyfous Drive. Popp's Bandstand was to the left, and I ran over the grass toward the steps.

Elias had a white man twice his size pinned to the ground. He had an iron stake in hand and said, "Declan Lotz, you have been sentenced to death by the Vampire Royal Court. Do you have any last words?"

"Fuck you," the other vampire howled.

"Noted. I will now carry out your sentence."

Elias drove the stake into the vampire's heart. Then between one blink and the next, the vampire was missing his head! I gasped, my hands going over my mouth.

He looked up. There was no change in his expression except the pinching at the corner of his eyes. "What are you doing here?"

"I—"

"I told you to wait!"

"But the ghosts said—"

Elias was gone. The body of the other vampire had vanished as well. I gulped, confused and worried for more than one reason. Well, the date was definitely over. I sighed, turned around, and went home. I got off a few stops before my own so I could stop at the Brothers on St. Charles and Jackson. I got some fried chicken since I hadn't eaten dinner yet and I was starving.

As I walked down Jackson, my food and an extra soda I picked up bouncing against my leg, I sighed. I was scared for Elias, but also for myself. What had I done to those ghosts back there? More importantly, how did I do it? I hadn't read anything in the codex about mind-controlling spirits. Something like that I would remember.

When I got home, the apartment was, for once, empty. Heather was gone and no ghosts were hanging about. I checked Eris and saw no one was online. It wasn't late, but it was Saturday night. Everyone had lives to live, and I wouldn't begrudge them that.

So, I ate spicy chicken fingers and potato wedges. I drank my Coke. I went through *Piercing* to see if there was any information on controlling spirits. There was nothing. When I threw out the chicken box, I realized I was going through the motions. I continued to see the dead vampire and Elias's blank expression. It made something in my stomach twist.

He was a merciless killer, and I had no idea. God, was Heather right? Had I really been so blind?

I sent a text to Elias.

> **Lyric Morrison:** Get home safe. Text me to let me know you're okay.

I didn't wait for a reply. I put my phone on to charge and went to bed.

Chapter Thirty-Two

ELIAS DIDN'T REPLY to me for weeks. I'd stopped by the Black Lily but he wasn't there either. He'd read my message but didn't respond. Still angry then. I alternated between embarrassment over not listening to him and anger he wouldn't talk to me. I deleted the text convo for fear I would overexplain and make things worse.

It was the week of Thanksgiving that Verity approached me. "Hey, you're looking pretty down. Are you okay?"

I shook my head.

"What's going on?"

"Elias is avoiding me." I rubbed my forehead. "He hasn't been here at the club, he's not texting me back, I don't think he's going to forgive me."

She held her hand out, and I squeezed it. "What are you doing for Thanksgiving?"

I frowned. "That's not for two weeks."

"Lyric, it's tomorrow."

"Oh. Well. Uh... Nothing. I'm not doing anything."

"Well, now you're doing something. Come over to our apartment, we'll have dinner and talk."

"The talk?"

She nodded. "Yes, it's time."

We'd been tiptoeing around the conversation we needed to have. Partially because I was worried about Elias, and partially because I didn't want things to change.

But Verity was still holding part of herself back, and I was too. If we were going to stay friends, we needed to clear the air.

"Yeah, okay. Should I bring anything?"

"Just your appetite."

"Gotcha."

When I arrived at Lionel and Verity's on Barracks Street, I was pretty frazzled. So much so that I actually walked past the building twice. I paused in front of a carriageway gate that had the right address and hit the buzzer.

"Who is it?" Lionel said in a singsong voice.

"It's me."

"Who's me?" Now he was talking in a weird falsetto. What the heck?

"Lyric. How do I get in?"

"One moment please!" And the intercom went dead.

A door in the carriageway opened and Lionel stepped out. He was wearing pajama pants and a Stevie Nicks T-shirt with no shoes. He let me in, and I followed him into the building.

"Careful, the stairs are a little warped."

"And small," I muttered.

"They're wider at the end."

I meant the steps were shorter than what I was used to. It wasn't worth the effort to correct him. There was a loud crack and I looked down. I expected to see a broken floorboard. It looked pretty solid, and Lionel smiled at me.

"That happens a lot, just ignore it."

Up the winding staircase we went until we reached a landing on the third floor. I could see a hallway with two sets of doors on the left, and one set of French doors on the right that went to a gallery. Lionel opened the first door on the left and said, "Welcome to my home."

The walls of the apartment were exposed brick, and so old it made me wonder how the building was still in one piece. There was a small kitchen to the right of the front door with a stove dating to the 1920s and a breakfast bar from the seventies. To the right was a china hutch, a fireplace, and an old writing desk. I could also smell something cooking, though I wasn't sure what. Something savory. Maybe a turkey?

Various knick-knacks were scattered about the apartment. Some looked older than my grandmother, others were tacky as hell and likely picked up from the souvenir shops in the Quarter. The Bourbon fleur de lis flag hung in front of the fireplace.

"Isn't that a fire hazard?" I asked.

"We don't light fires in there so, no," Lionel said.

I could see a bathroom next to the kitchen, and beyond that a large bedroom with a balcony, the door of which had been left open. Interestingly, I only saw one bed in the bedroom. Then I remembered. Lionel is a vampire. He probably hides in an attic or coffin during the day.

Verity sat at the breakfast bar, drinking a glass of white wine and flipping through a magazine. "Evening," she said without looking up.

"Hi, sorry I'm late. The first bus was a no-show." I paused, then frowned. "Are you okay?"

She looked up. There were bags under her eyes and her shoulders were slumped, as though someone had just shot her dog. "Just blue today is all. Don't worry about it. Would you like something to drink?"

"Yeah, lime soda if you have any."

"Coming up," said Lionel.

I sat next to Verity as she closed the magazine. "Were you able to talk to Elias?"

"No. I haven't spoken to him since our date got interrupted."

"By what?" Lionel asked.

He handed me the soda and I popped the tab on the can.

"He..." Lionel stared at me, while Verity fell silent. She had to know what happened. She was a clairvoyant for fuck's sake. God, I didn't want to talk about it, yet I couldn't stop myself. "He killed another vampire. Then he got mad at me and left."

"Wait, back up, he killed a vampire?" Lionel asked. He didn't even sound surprised!

"Yeah. He said some Court sentenced the vampire to death and then he killed him right then and there."

"He did this in front of you? Doesn't sound like Elias."

I sighed. "He told me to wait by the museum. But then I heard these ghosts talking about how two vampires were fighting and I panicked and went to find him. I tried to explain but he just fucking disappeared on me! Now he's not texting me back! I thought we were finally getting somewhere ever since the Phoenix shit."

Lionel held up a hand. "Hold your horses, what about Phoenix?"

Oops. "I was there during the coup."

"So were we," Verity said.

I stared at them, confused. "You were? Wait, how come you didn't already know about Elias saving me?"

"Believe it or not I don't use my powers all the time. And some things I can't see."

"Let's circle back though. Why would you ever talk about Phoenix with Elias?" Lionel asked.

"Because he saved my life. The night the Bad Hats were overthrown he saved me from three vampires who wanted to have me for breakfast. Then he did this kind of...evil eye thing to make me forget but it didn't work."

Lionel and Verity exchanged glances.

"I told you it doesn't work on everyone," said Verity.

"Fuck me running, we have to call Amira and let her know."

"Don't do that, she'll have a heart attack! Let's call Martin."

"Hey, time out," I said. "I don't want my memory erased."

Verity shook her head. "Not about you, we promise. If you were going to tell on us, you would have already."

"You guys were involved?"

They looked at each other again. Whatever silent argument they were having, Lionel must have won because he said, "This is all my fault. Let me explain." He grabbed a chair and sat in front of the fireplace, while Verity and I turned around on the stools to face him. "Don't get mad until I finish talking." His brown eyes darted around the apartment, looking at anything except me.

"To start off with, Elias killed that vampire because Elias works for the Vampire Royal Court. He's the royal executioner. He's not the only one but he is the best there is. I told him to tell you about it sooner rather than later. Doesn't sound like he listened."

I shook my head. "He hasn't said a word about it."

"Figures. But it's why he was in Phoenix in the first place. To carry out Caleb Blake's sentence. Which, despite what Elias thinks wouldn't have been easy. We're damn lucky Kingston and Martin killed Caleb instead."

"Who?"

"Don't worry about them," said Verity, "they're not important to the story. Lionel, you're rambling."

He sighed. "Yeah, I know I am. It wasn't just to kill Caleb that Elias came to Phoenix. He also wanted to save me from our sire."

I had a sinking feeling I knew where this was going. "Who was..."

"Caleb Blake."

"You're fucking kidding me."

"No, I'm not. Before you start yelling, please know that Caleb had the ability to manipulate and control his offspring. He forced me to work for him ever since he first turned me."

"What do you mean 'forced'?" I asked. Maybe if I concentrated on the details I wouldn't scream at Lionel.

"It's not hypnosis. It's more like...if he told me to kill myself, I could fight it for a time. But I would still do it. I'm just thankful he never guessed I was trans or he definitely would have killed me."

"Yeah, I remember his efforts to eradicate anyone who wasn't a cis het able-bodied white person."

"Exactly. Not a great time for me. What really killed me was I knew I'd go the same way if he even suspected what I was. But I kept my mouth shut. I thought to myself, 'I can do more good alive than dead,' and that's how I justified preserving myself. I did everything I could to subvert his rule and help the resistance. It only went so far though. And I wish I could go back in time to fix it. Or stop the whole thing from happening."

I sighed. I knew that feeling all too well. "I did too."

"I beg your pardon?"

"When Blake took over. I pretended to be neurotypical and straight because I didn't want to end up in the cattle yards. But I knew people who weren't as lucky as me."

Verity gasped and put her hand on my shoulder. "I'm so sorry."

"For what? I'm a coward. There's nothing to be sorry about because it's true. There were plenty of people in the Valley who lived their truth and died for it. And I went into hiding."

"You're not the only one," Verity said. She looked at Lionel, then at me. "Plenty of people chose to go into hiding rather than die. There's no shame in being in the closet if being out of it will cost you your life. You're no better or worse than anyone who decided otherwise."

"What about the people who had things they couldn't change? Like their appearance? Or if they were in a wheelchair or something?"

"That one I helped with," said Lionel. "Remember, Blake said any 'undesirable' humans had to have someone to vouch for them. I worked with my friend Tyrone to connect those people with the 'right' type of white people to keep them out of the yards. I couldn't save everyone but by God, I did the best I could."

I blinked, then smiled. "I heard about that policy. I thought that might be why we suddenly had all these new people at work when the coup started. That was all you?"

"Yep. I was in charge of that shit. And when to send patrols out and shit. Caleb never knew because he didn't care about day-to-day operations. He just wanted to terrorize people and be the top boss."

"He sounds lovely," I said with as much sarcasm as I could muster. "So how does Elias fit in?"

"When the Vampire Royal Court was ready to make a

move, they sent him to Phoenix, along with several members of the Royal Guard. Elias volunteered because he wanted to save me. We never met but he knew our sire was as evil as they come, so he wanted to help."

"And he did, I presume?"

Lionel nodded. "He found me before Caleb was killed and restrained me. I was with friends but due to the link between me and our sire, he was the only one strong enough to hold me back. If it wasn't for him, I don't know what I would have done."

"What do you mean?"

"Caleb tried to force me to commit suicide. If he was going down, he wanted me to go with him. He knew he was about to die and one of his last acts on this planet was to will me to stake myself. Thankfully his influence ended with his death."

"That's fucked up."

"You're telling me."

"Is that how you two know each other?" I asked, gesturing between Verity and Lionel.

"Yes. Blake was holding me prisoner and using me for my powers," Verity replied. "Lionel did his best to protect me."

"Thank God for your powers otherwise I don't think we would have gotten out of there."

"This is all so fucked up," I said. "I mean, I never said anything because of Cynthia. She was my boss and she insisted that there really were vampires who took over the city. Then one day she stopped talking about it and just left the company."

Lionel sighed. "Yeah, the Vampire Royal Court decided it was best for everyone if vampires stayed a secret. The US government agreed. Like they thought it would cause massive issues for everyone or something.”

“So that's what happened to Cynthia?”

“Yeah. Probably the same thing Elias tried to do to you. Her memory was altered. I'm surprised it didn't work on you. He's one of the best mesmerists I know.”

I rubbed the back of my neck. “I could feel him doing it but it didn't work. I just played along.”

“I wonder why that is,” Verity said.

“Elias said it doesn't always work on the neuro-divergent.”

Lionel was about to say something, but then his phone rang. He raised an eyebrow. “Speak of the devil.”

“If it's Elias I'm not here,” I said.

“Why would he be looking for you at my house?” Lionel asked.

“Oh. Good point.”

He sent the call to voicemail. “I'll talk to him later.”

“You're still doing the séance dinner on Saturday, aren't you?” Verity asked.

“Yeah.”

“Great. I'll smooth things over so you two can talk,” said Lionel.

“That...would be great actually, thank you.”

“You're welcome. Now, ready for nibbles? I think the pie should be about done.”

“Oh, that's what that smell is!”

Verity laughed. “Yes. For someone who can't eat human food, Lionel is a wonderful chef. I especially love his pastries.”

“What kind of pie is it?”

“Turkey.”

“Sweet, thank you!”

Lionel chuckled and said, “You're welcome.”

Chapter Thirty-Three

SATURDAY NIGHT AT the club was busy. When Lionel, Verity, and I arrived, Elias was already behind the bar. He looked at me but didn't smile or nod. It was only by the slight tension around his eyes that he acknowledged my presence.

I didn't know what to do. So I went to prepare for the séance. It was fairly run of the mill, at least so far as summoning the dead to assuage the curiosity of the living goes. I summoned a notorious New Orleans madame from the days of Storyville named Josie Arlington, then let her entertain the audience with her outrageous stories. Occasionally I would glance over at the bar, but Elias kept himself busy. I did see him and Lionel talking at one point, but I couldn't hear what they were saying.

When I was done for the evening, I was torn between going to the bar or leaving. I didn't get a chance to decide as Elias suddenly stood before me. "Would you come up to the roof with me?"

"Of course."

He offered his arm, which I took. I wasn't sure how angry he was, but I wanted to see this through.

When we reached the roof, he said, "I'm sorry about the other night. Lotz has been avoiding his sentence for months. I never would have gone after him with you so close and I imagine he knew that. Which is why he made his move."

I frowned. "Made his move?"

"He was closing in for an ambush. It's why I left you so abruptly. Once he was dead, I had to return to the Court and give a report of his death so his case would be closed. I only returned last night. Still, I'm sorry I was rude to you. And I'm sorry for ignoring your messages. I hope you can forgive me." His expression was still difficult to read, but I was getting better at it. His blue eyes were full of regret, though his face was blank.

"You scared me," I admitted.

"I know I did, and I apologize for that too."

I took a deep breath and two steps back. I didn't turn my back on him. Not because I was afraid, but because he would take it as a rejection. Once I was sure I wouldn't cry or yell, I asked, "Why though? Why did you do that? I'm not completely helpless, you know."

"I lost my head for a moment," he replied.

He wasn't meeting my gaze. I could see how he struggled with his words. I'd done the same more times than I could count. Was this why he was so quiet? Did he have trouble expressing himself?

"The ghosts said you were in trouble," I said. "I was terrified for you. That's why I didn't listen."

"Then I am fortunate to have a fearless paramour," he replied.

"Are you making fun of me?"

"Not at all. Rather...I'm experiencing emotions that have been alien to me since Jonas died." Elias looked up. His jaw trembled. Was he going to cry?

I stepped close to him again and cupped his face in my hands. "What is it? How can I help?"

"I'm afraid for you," Elias said in a whisper. As though just those little words were being torn from him against his will. And yet, he continued to speak. "I care for you the way I care for him. The thought of you being hurt or killed freezes my heart with fear. So, I lashed out, and I shouldn't have. I'm so sorry."

Well, it was certainly hard to be mad at him for that. Especially when he looked so vulnerable. There were many words I would use to describe Elias but vulnerable wasn't one of them. At least not before this evening. "Thank you, I accept your apology."

He sighed. Tension trickled out of him.

"If you'd be so kind, Miss Morrison, I'd like to continue our discussion. I'm sure there are several questions you'd like to ask me."

"You bet."

"Whenever you are ready."

"Why did you kill him anyway? That Lotz guy. Did he hurt you?"

"No," Elias said. "But he broke the law, and Reyna ordered him killed."

"What? Why would she do that? Wait, how does she have the authority to do that?"

He hung his head and took a breath. "I knew this was coming. You need an education about the vampire world. If afterward you decide it isn't for you, I'll back off."

I didn't like the sound of that. "Why would I want you to back off?"

"Because my work will disgust you."

I reached out and lifted his chin with the tips of my fingers so he was looking at me. "Let me be the judge of that."

He didn't reply.

"Am I correct in guessing that Reyna is somehow involved in this Court you mentioned?"

"She is."

"And what is the Court?"

"The Vampire Royal Court is the governing body of the vampire world. All species of vampire are represented in every region of the world."

"There's more than just the two?" I remembered German hadn't been turned the traditional way.

"Six that we know of but only four are recognized by the Court."

"Fun... Okay, so you work for the Court."

"I do."

"And they were the reason you were in Phoenix. Lionel filled me in on that a bit."

"Correct."

"How does Reyna fit in?"

"She's the mayor of New Orleans. At least as far as the vampire world is concerned. I believe her actual title is along the lines of a landed knight."

"That seems pretty Euro-centric. Aren't there different forms of government around the world?"

"For the human world, yes. In the vampire world not so much. The titles will vary from country to country, but the structure is very much the same. Something I discovered when the Court was in Bangalore for a time. Every country has their own ranks of the high born and the low born."

"*Was* in Bangalore? So, the Court isn't based there?"

"The Court moves, rather than staying in one location and giving the country in question too much power. It's also for security reasons."

"That makes sense. A moving target is harder to hit. So why did Reyna sentence that guy to death? Why not like, prison?"

"Our laws aren't as forgiving as human laws. Imprisonment isn't much of a deterrent when you can live forever. Therefore, it's usually torture, dismemberment, or death."

"I take it you all don't believe in rehabilitation."

Elias scoffed. "Not as such. Not because it isn't possible but because there aren't many crimes that would result in a death sentence in the first place. You would have to kill too many humans, or too many vampires without permission. Or if you're a threat to humans and vampires alike."

"So you don't just kill vampires." Immediately I thought of Heather. Was she right this whole time? Oh God, I could be standing alone on a romantic rooftop with her murderer.

"No. I've killed witches, fairies, and a few human scientists mucking about with our DNA. I even killed a rougarou once. Though I can't give you details."

He was incredibly composed about all of this. I gulped.

"Or what, you'll kill me?"

"No. I'm not at liberty to say because I've been sworn to secrecy."

Okay, that did make sense. "And you're a man of your word."

"One of the only things in this world I will honor no matter what, is my word. If I swear an oath or make a promise, I will keep it."

"Are all vampires like you?"

He shook his head. "It's an aftereffect of being sired by Caleb Blake."

That fucking guy again. I tilted my head to the side. "How so?"

Elias fell silent while he collected his thoughts. I didn't want to interrupt so I waited.

"You see, Jonas knew of the vampire world. He knew enough that when I was taken, he contacted a Court representative. Kidnapping a human and turning them against their will isn't a crime. But as mediums are rare, Jonas offered a favor to a member of the Royal Guard if she would save me."

"And you were rescued?"

"Yes, but not right away. As a matter of fact, by the time my situation became known, the damage was done. I'd been changed in more ways than one. It took Jonas half a decade to accomplish his task. In that time, Caleb turned me into his guard dog."

"What do you mean?"

"Caleb knew I knew how to fight. And how to handle a weapon. When he turned me, he had me trained to be his bodyguard and personal assassin, which the Vampire King at the time took as a personal threat."

I had a sinking feeling about where this was going.

"It was a dangerous situation," Elias continued. "Caleb escaped, but I was captured. There was much talk as to what was to be done with me. Many were in favor of my execution. But the guard felt differently. She convinced the king I could be useful to the Court. Though not at first.

"It took over a year for Caleb's influence to wear off. Once I came back to myself, I was disgusted by what I'd become. Jonas was patient. And Captain Stone gave me further training to join the Royal Guard. Eventually, I worked my way up through the ranks to be an executioner. If only Jonas lived to see it. How proud he would have been."

Elias sighed and stared off into the distance.

I hesitantly spoke. "Does that mean the Court is here in New Orleans? Since you're here?"

"No. I'm not required at the Court all of the time. I'm not even required most of the time. There are so many in the Royal Guard now, my position is mostly an honorary one. From what I've heard they're even employing vampire hunters. I must say that I admire His Majesty's ingenuity in employing them. No one knows how to kill a vampire better than a vampire hunter."

I wasn't sure Elias would say anymore. He darted glances at me out of the corner of his eye. Waiting for my reaction, or perhaps for my rejection. I needed to steer the conversation to figure out if he was the one who killed Heather.

"I have a question, but I'm worried it might upset you."

"Go on."

"Did you kill the Sultan and his entourage?"

Elias's eyes widened, then to my surprise, he laughed. "You are industrious, aren't you? Yes, I did."

"Why?"

"He was sentenced to death. He and his harem were killing humans left, right, and center. They were drawing too much attention to themselves."

"Then why kill the humans? I think the papers would notice if the corpses had fangs."

"The corpse of a vampire won't survive exposure to sunlight. I didn't kill the humans in that house." Elias stared down at the street, hands folded together on the railing. "They were dead before I arrived. The Sultan's nightly ritual. He would invite the dregs of society, people no one would miss. To eat, drink, and partake of opium or other narcotics until they were insensate. Once they were intoxicated, the Sultan, his Sultana, and his concubines would feast. I hoped to get there beforehand but the sentence wasn't passed in time."

That's when it clicked. "The foreign-looking guys at the hotel. They were with the Court."

"Correct."

"Huh. Couldn't you have saved the humans first and killed the others later?"

"I requested to do exactly that, but it was forbidden." Elias looked up at me. "The King still fears me. Each who has sat on the throne since the first spared my life. If I were to kill without permission from the Court or one of its representatives, my life would be forfeit."

"But Caleb is dead. He can't control you anymore," I pointed out. "Surely such a rule is unnecessary."

Privately, I thought it quite a good rule. If Elias really was some kind of vampire sleeper cell operative, it was best he was on a leash. But I needed to see if there were any holes in this edict. Something he could work around to kill Heather.

"His Majesty is aware of that. But he will not reverse his decree and I dare not petition him to do so. Lionel is under a similar decree. If he were to kill, he would die."

"So, this is some kind of unbreakable oath? And you wouldn't just..."

Elias stared at me. "I can smell your fear, Miss Morrison. I know what you want to ask. Just ask me."

"You wouldn't just kill a person with no good reason?"

"I wouldn't kill an innocent human even if ordered. While the decree doesn't specifically protect them, I can't in good conscience do so. But it doesn't matter what my personal feelings are about it."

"Why not?"

"Because Reyna has a no-kill order for New Orleans. Ever since the Phoenix coup, as a matter of fact. Many mayors across the country have followed suit. The coup was successfully portrayed to humans as a cult. But no one wishes to attract that sort of attention again. Vampire kind wants to stay secret, and the best way to do so is to keep us under the radar, so to speak."

A small part of me reasoned he could be lying. He could be telling me what I wanted to hear. But Elias had never lied to me. He'd been as honest as he could be. I was still a little freaked out by the fact he was a royal executioner. That was going to take some getting used to. More importantly, I was sure he hadn't killed Heather. I just had to ask one more question.

"Do you swear to me you haven't murdered any humans since the coup?"

"Not a single one," he replied.

I nodded. "Okay then."

He raised an eyebrow. "Okay?"

"Okay as in I believe you. This is still a lot and I think I need to lie down for a while to process. But I believe you."

The corners of his mouth curled upwards. Then the small smile turned into a grin. He actually grinned at me! I grinned back and laughed. He shifted forward and his lips found mine. I kissed back enthusiastically. However, when I felt we were heading in a horizontal direction, I pressed my hand against his chest. He immediately pulled away.

"Shall I escort you to the bus stop?" Elias asked.

"I think I'd rather get an Uber. Text me tomorrow?"

"Yes, of course."

Elias accompanied me downstairs and waited with me until my ride showed up. On the way home, I felt something inside me relax. Elias wasn't the murderer. He couldn't be. But the question was, how was I going to convince Heather?

Chapter Thirty-Four

AS I PREDICTED, Heather didn't believe me when I told her it wasn't Elias. She was waiting for me when I got home. I'd told her before I went out that I was going to confront Elias about a few things, including the death of the other vampire. Heather was ecstatic and eagerly stayed behind. So, when I came in, I wasn't surprised to see her smiling like she was about to receive a treat.

Heather asked, "So? How did it go? Did you talk to him?"

"Yes," I said as I closed the door and locked it. I took off my veil and went to change out of my costume. Heather of course followed.

"What did he say?"

"He told me about his past. It was sad. Someone tried to turn him into a real-life Manchurian Candidate."

"Ew."

"Yeah, that was my reaction too."

Heather crossed her arms over her stomach, her coral shirt wrinkling as she did. "So that's why he killed me?"

"He didn't kill you."

"Not this again."

"He couldn't have! Reyna has a blanket ban on killing humans in New Orleans and it's been in effect for almost two years. He wouldn't dare go against her; she's his boss."

I changed into gray sleep shorts and a black tank top,

then put the costume in the hamper. I'd have to get it dry-cleaned. I stretched and sighed. "We need to look at other suspects."

"You've said that since the beginning," Heather snapped. "You just don't want to believe Elias did it."

"There is literally no proof," I replied. "I've been investigating for months. There's nothing to tie you to Elias or the club except your word."

"Because they're all in on it! Think about it!" Heather tapped the side of her head for emphasis. "I get murdered and suddenly no one has heard of me? No one remembers me? I'm not on the membership roster even though I paid my dues?"

"Can you prove that? Because I'd like to see it."

I sat down at my desk and turned on my computer. I needed to check in with Psyche since I hadn't spoken to her in a while. We were both so busy it was hard to find the time. Heather stomped after me, clearly not done.

"You can look up my bank statements! I paid in cash but the amount matches!"

"How in the fuck am I going to get your bank statement?"

"My account should still be active. I can give you the login."

"Fine."

I pulled up her bank's website. She gave me her screen name and password. Unsurprisingly, an alert popped up. "This account has been closed," I said aloud.

"That's impossible!"

"Your stepdad probably closed it," I pointed out.

"Ask him then!"

"I'm not calling your stepfather about your bank account. Do you know how suspicious that sounds?"

Heather stomped her feet again. She threw her hands up in frustration. "Why aren't you listening to me?!"

"Because you're wrong," I yelled back.

I took a moment to take a deep breath and let it out so I could center myself. Then I turned to face Heather.

"Listen to me. I have done everything you've asked. I've interviewed people. I've had friends hack the police department's records. I've looked into every nook and cranny of Elias's pitiful life. I tried to find one iota of evidence he ever spoke to you let alone killed you. There is nothing. I don't know what the fuck you have against him, but I'm sick of your vendetta. I'm sorry you died, I truly am. But I'm not going to spend the rest of my life on this. You need to either give me other suspects or move the fuck on."

"You're so full of shit," Heather screamed. "You just want your stupid boyfriend and your new friends! Well, guess what? They'll kill you too! They're just using you for your powers and as soon as they're done, you'll die. They'll throw you in the river just like they did to me. You think they befriended you because they like you? They're turning you into one of them! A dark and evil person, a freak!"

She said a few other things. But after Heather called me a freak I wasn't listening anymore. That was the word the other kids used to taunt me when I was in school. It was what my mother called me when I told her I could speak to dead people. It was thrown in my face by strangers on the bus because of my clothes. It was hurled at me by people on social media, which was another reason I'd given most of it up. Worst of all, it was the favorite word of people who couldn't stand an autistic woman living her truth and being happy.

It was a trigger word for me, but not for my PTSD. It was a trigger for my rage.

Something not a lot of people know about me—if I go quiet, you've crossed a line. Yes, I'll blow my top and yell when I'm angry. But when I'm in a rage? When I'm so pissed off I can literally see red? That's when I lose my words. When I was a kid, I would also black out and start hitting people. As an adult, it's when I start breaking shit if I can't get myself to go for a walk. That's not what happened this time.

I still wasn't sure what aspect of my powers it was. I wasn't even sure I could use it when I actively wanted to. But I wouldn't let Heather bully me anymore, and I had the power to shut her up. I reached out like I had the other night. The cold energy rushed through me. Heather froze and stopped talking. Her eyes went wide and her mouth was open, as though she were trying to scream but couldn't get enough air.

"I've had it with you. You don't get to talk about my friends that way. You don't get to boss me around anymore. Get out of my sight."

"Fine, I will! You'll be fucking sorry you ever crossed me!"

Then Heather vanished.

The few ghosts milling about the apartment glanced at one another. Fear and worry marred their faces.

"Anyone else want to bother me? Or can I talk to my real friends now?"

The ghosts faded, one after another.

I slumped in my office chair and sighed, then rubbed my forehead with my hand. God, this night was not turning out how I wanted it to. Why couldn't Heather take the blinders off? Something else was bothering me. I hated to admit it, but I liked seeing Heather scared. She was supposed to be my friend, or at least friendly, and she called me a freak. It's not like I was happy to punish her for it, but I was pleased I could. As though I'd taken the law into my own hands.

Then guilt hit me like a baseball bat between the eyes. What the hell was I thinking? Did I like hurting someone? That wasn't me at all. I would cry if I stepped on a cat's tail. Sure, Heather was a handful, but I shouldn't like punishing her. Was she right? Was I being corrupted?

I knew one person I could ask, so I logged into Eris.

> **Psychepomp:** There you are. Where have you been?

> **EratoONine:** Finishing the investigation into Elias and disappointing Heather.

> **Psychepomp:** Uh oh. What happened?

> **EratoONine:** Apparently Elias was some kind of Winter Soldier experiment. Except he's a vampire. And doesn't have a metal arm.

> **Psychepomp:** What is even the point if he doesn't have a metal arm?

> **EratoONine:** I know right? But yeah, he didn't kill Heather. He's under orders never to kill without permission or he'll be executed.

> **Psychepomp:** Okay I can see the logic in that. If I had a brainwashed assassin working for me I wouldn't want them killing anyone either.

EratoONine: It gets better. According to Elias, the vampire higher-ups in New Orleans outlawed killing humans.

Psychepomp: ...Ah. So Elias couldn't have killed Heather.

EratoONine: I thought maybe someone broke the law. Elias just killed a vampire for breaking the same rule the other day.

Psychepomp: Maybe you should try to talk to him then. The guy he executed could have killed Heather.

EratoONine: Actually, I'm starting to think I made a mistake.

Psychepomp: What do you mean?

I sighed and ran my hands through my hair. I tugged on the strands as though it would make me think faster.

EratoONine: I haven't been able to find a single fucking thing to support murder. Like seriously, nothing. The autopsy does have the weird puncture mark on her neck but that could have been caused by anything. I was the one who jumped to the conclusion it was a vampire fang. No one at the Black Lily knows who Heather is. I even tried talking to people at her old jobs and no one remembers Heather working there in the past two years.

Psychepomp: Do you think she was living under

an assumed name?

EratoONine: I don't think so. All the news outlets said her name was Heather Campbell. That's the name that's gonna be etched on the tomb in Metairie. I met her stepdad, for fuck's sake. There's something she's not telling me and I don't know what it is.

Psychepomp: What about social media?

EratoONine: Scrubbed after the funeral. I even tried the Wayback Machine but none of it was archived. Which is weird because she was some kind of online guru or influencer or something. She didn't have a large audience, but she had one.

Psychepomp: Friends?

EratoONine: As far as I can find, none. There weren't many people at the funeral. Her stepdad, some cousins, and two other influencers who were there just to make a video.

Psychepomp: Then you'll have to talk to the family.

EratoONine: I can't do that.

Psychepomp: Yes, you can.

EratoONine: How?

Psychepomp: Okay, tell them you're a detective calling from the NOPD. And you have a few questions about Heather.

EratoONine: Isn't impersonating a police officer a crime?

Psychepomp: Only if you get caught.

EratoONine: I don't want to risk it. Wait, I have an idea. Be right back.

I grabbed my phone and pulled up Heather's stepdad's number. I called and waited, mentally preparing myself. This was way outside my comfort zone, but I needed answers.

"Hello?"

"Hi, is this Mr. Campbell?"

"This is."

"Hello, sir. I'm Irene Roberts. I'm sorry to trouble you, but I'm working on a personal interest column for my blog. It's about suspicious deaths in the New Orleans area. Do you have a few minutes to talk about your stepdaughter Heather?"

He cleared his throat. "I suppose I can make time. What do you need?"

"First off, is there any reason to doubt the coroner's finding of suicide?"

"Can't think of one. There was that neck wound but they said it was a boat motor."

"I see. And was your stepdaughter having any problems before her passing?"

"Nothing a little common sense wouldn't have fixed. She was always a bit flaky. Her mother, God rest her soul, used to say that Heather was a free spirit and gifted."

"So she was a genius?"

"Not really, she was never the brightest crayon in the box. But you wouldn't find a sweeter girl in the whole world. At least before her mother died."

I paused and pretended as though I were taking notes. "How did she change after her mother's death?"

"She turned mean. You have to understand, Ms. Roberts, Heather loved her mama. Once she lost her, it was like she lost herself. She went from kind and compassionate to selfish and vain. She would stir up trouble then tell the most bald-faced lies you could think of to try to get out of it."

"I see, that is quite a dramatic turn. Why do you think your stepdaughter took her own life?"

"She was depressed. I asked her to seek help, but she blew me off. That boyfriend of hers had enough of her mind games and threatened to leave her."

I raised an eyebrow. A boyfriend? That was new. "Did she always have turbulent relationships with men?"

He snorted. "I suppose so. It was kind of strange. Before her mother died, she never met a man she liked, even as a fling. She used to say she was a man-hating lesbian and proud of it. After that though, she took up with this asshole from Delacroix for a while. He didn't even come to her funeral, the bastard. I wouldn't have known about him at all if I didn't stop off at the condo one night to check on a leaky faucet."

"This boyfriend, was he about six feet tall, brown hair, blue eyes?" I didn't want to press the issue too much, but I had to be sure.

"No, he was about five-nine, white guy, dressed funny. Never did get his name."

"You don't suspect he could have been involved in her death, do you?"

"No. I wish I could blame it on someone else, Ms. Roberts. But facts are facts. She killed herself. I think it was the guilt from all her game-playing, it finally got to her. I wished she'd come home. Or took a moment to think about what she was doing. Would you mind if I said something? Off the record?"

"I promise it won't go on my blog." It was an easy enough promise to make since I didn't have one.

"That'll do, I suppose. She called me the day she killed herself. She said she was free but worried about being chained again."

"Chained?"

"Yes, ma'am. I asked her what she meant but she wouldn't say. I begged her to come home but she said she had to take care of something first. Next thing I heard she was dead."

I took off my glasses and rubbed my eyes. Fuck, this was heavy.

"I'm very sorry to hear that, sir."

"So was I. She was battling something. I just wish I knew what it was."

"Thank you for your time, Mr. Campbell. And I'm sorry for your loss."

"Thank you."

He hung up and I sighed. Holy shit. If Heather had a boyfriend, why did she have a date with Elias? I went back to the computer and typed out everything Mr. Campbell said.

Psychepomp: So she lied to you.

EratoONine: Looks like. And she's got some boyfriend who wasn't at the funeral and I can't find any trace of.

Psychepomp: Why would she lie? Why wouldn't she tell you about this guy?

EratoONine: Mr. Campbell did say she liked to play mind games after her mother died. If Mr. Campbell hadn't seen him with his own eyes, I probably wouldn't believe this boyfriend existed at all.

Psychepomp: How does someone do a complete 180 personality wise though?

EratoONine: I don't know. I mean, you don't suddenly develop a narcissistic personality overnight. No matter how hard you're grieving.

Psychepomp: I agree. I don't like this. You need to banish her.

EratoONine: Well, she's disappeared at the moment, but you're probably right.

We talked a little more then I signed off. I sat in the dark for a long time, lost in thought. I needed to make my next move. And come clean to everyone at the club.

Chapter Thirty-Five

IT TURNED OUT this was easier said than done. The first week of December I suddenly had more bookings than ever. I had to increase my dates of availability just to accommodate everyone. I was confused by this until, the Sunday before Christmas, Lionel said, "It's the holidays. People get really sentimental this time of year and want closure with their loved ones."

"Not everyone," I said.

Lionel shrugged and said, "Yeah, I get that. Hey, speaking of, I take it you're not going home for Christmas?"

"Nope." There was no point. My father had his new family, I didn't know where my sister was, and I never wanted to see my mother again.

"Great, you can come to our place again. Verity's gonna make her famous peppermint bark cake. Elias is coming too."

I blinked. "You're inviting us over for Christmas dinner."

"Duh, isn't that what I just said?"

"Yeah, I'm just surprised is all. Isn't that a time for family?"

"Elias is my brother in the blood, and you're his girlfriend. Also, Verity adores you and she's like a sister to me. We can't have Christmas without you."

I smiled and said, "Yeah, that would be great. This

time though, I'm bringing my famous garlic mashed potatoes."

Lionel raised an eyebrow. "Really?"

"Hey, it's not toxic to you guys and trust me, they're amazing. So good you don't even need gravy for them. You can live vicariously through Verity and me."

"Sounds like a challenge, I'm in."

*

WHEN I MET up with Elias later, he said he'd also been invited and would be bringing a dish. More specifically he was bringing a lamb roast.

"I find it kind of hilarious you're cooking when you can't eat," I said.

"It was something I enjoyed when I was alive," he said. "I think it's one of the reasons I enjoy botany as much as I do. There is a lot of intricacy in caring for plants, just like there is in cooking a good meal."

I didn't agree, as I thought the two were completely separate, but I kept that to myself. Everything should have been great, but I was a little worried about Verity. She'd become more withdrawn lately, and when Lionel and I invited her to go for coffee that evening she turned us down.

"I'm too tired," she said.

I frowned. "Have you seen a doctor? You've been pretty worn out for a while now."

"I know what's causing it," she replied. "It's not something a doctor can help. I just have to endure it for a little while longer."

"Ver, honey, are you sure you're okay? You're acting really weird, we're worried about you," said Lionel.

She nodded. "I'm fine."

I wasn't sure I believed her, but I also knew we couldn't force her to say anything. Verity was the Fort Knox of secrets. If she knew something and didn't want to share, you'd never get it out of her. I told her if she needed anything to text me right away. She agreed, then said she was going home because she had her audition for the burlesque show the next day. Lionel offered to go with her, which she agreed to. I went home shortly after, still worried about her.

I slept poorly that night. I was having nightmares again, though they didn't feel the same as before. They were more like the stress dreams I'd had after the vampire attack. At least I wasn't waking up to any more black masses on the ceiling or weird demonic gray women biting my head off. But one dream was very odd. I couldn't remember most of it, but it ended with Heather and Verity holding hands. Heather was smirking, while Verity looked afraid.

When I woke up, I texted Verity to see if she was all right. I had a sinking feeling in my stomach something was wrong, but I hoped I was being paranoid. I knew what I had to do, and I'd put it off for long enough. Heather had to go. I knew she'd lied; I just didn't realize to what extent until I'd spoken with her stepfather. I hadn't seen her since she stormed out and I wanted to keep it that way.

*

AS I RODE the bus to the club that night, I reflected on how much my life had changed in just a few months. I'd gone from an ordinary person with a healthy fear of vampires to having the power to communicate with the dead. And now I was dating a vampire. If that wasn't growth, what was? New Orleans was no longer an exotic wonderland of old buildings and strange traditions. It was my home.

When I got to the Bijou, I was ready to go upstairs and ask German for that cleansing. But the lights were off. There was no one in the bar. A sign on the door said, "closed due to emergency."

Oh no, what happened? Was I wrong? Had Heather hurt someone? Or possibly Elias? I ran around to the back entrance and took the stairs two at a time until I got to the upstairs gallery. I let myself in through the servant quarters' door. I dashed from one end of the inner gallery to the other and threw open the doors to the club.

Reyna, Lionel, Emerson, German, Jaxon, and Elias sat at one of the tables with a bottle of absinthe. Each was more morose than the last. They looked up when I rushed in. "What's the emergency? What's going on?"

"Verity is missing," said Reyna.

I collapsed in the chair between Elias and Lionel. "For how long?"

"She didn't show up for her audition this afternoon," said Lionel. "The guy called me after I woke up for the night. I tried calling her phone but there was no answer. It's shut off."

"It doesn't look like she left on her own," Elias added.

"Oh my God," I whispered.

"We haven't been able to locate her at all, at least not through traditional means," German told me.

"We don't know anything right now. And the police won't let us report her missing," said Jaxon. "They say not enough time has passed."

Reyna sighed. "I've contacted the Court. They've dispatched two investigators. They should be here in a matter of hours."

"Court investigators? Why?" Emerson asked. He sounded almost nervous.

"There's something not right about this," Reyna replied. "And Verity is one of us. If she's in trouble, we want to find her as quickly as possible."

Everyone fell quiet. I had an idea, so I took my glasses off and looked around the room. "I don't see her."

"Pardon?"

I turned back to the table. "I don't see her. I'm pretty sure she's not dead."

"That's a relief," said Lionel.

They talked some more, questioning one another if Verity said anything weird in the past few days. Everyone agreed she'd been tired and withdrawn. But other than that, she was her normal self.

Meanwhile, I concentrated. This didn't feel like a coincidence. Verity vanishing so soon after that weird dream? They had to be connected. Especially as Heather said I'd be sorry. Could she have done something to Verity? Without the power from Halloween or Hexennacht, it seemed unlikely, but I was uneasy. I had to know for sure where Heather was.

Whenever I called a particular spirit, I was like a fisherman throwing out a line. I may not get the exact spirit I wanted, but if I used the right bait I could lure them in. And I'd called Heather so many times it should have been child's play. After our fight, I didn't think she would be all that happy to talk to me. Still, I wanted to talk to her. So I zoned out, calling to Heather just like I'd learned from the book. However, when I tried to reach out, I didn't feel anything.

Spirits could disappear. They could leave Earth altogether and head to realms unknown. I'd helped one or two move on when I started holding the séances. But this was different. Instead of "no results found" this was more like "this person does not and has never existed." That more than anything made me nervous.

Reyna looked at the clock on the wall. "We've got some time until the investigators get here. I want everyone to split up and search for Verity in the meantime."

Reyna gave us our assigned search areas. She said she would remain at the club and once they arrived, she would call us back. I thought I would be paired with Elias, but instead, I was placed with Lionel. We were told to search the French Quarter, the Central Business District, and the Treme. Elias and German would check the Bywater and the Lower Ninth Ward. Emerson and Jaxon would take the entirety of Uptown.

"That's still not covering Mid-City, Lakeview, or New Orleans East," I pointed out.

"I'm aware of that, but we're short-handed this evening. Almost all of the other club members are out of town or unavailable due to the upcoming holiday. And I don't want anyone going off alone," Reyna replied. "Stay together and if you run into trouble call me. If you run into any other vampires or gifted humans who may be able to help, deputize them."

"You got it," Lionel replied.

We dispersed and Lionel and I started in the Treme. We didn't talk, he just drove up and down the streets in Verity's car looking for a flash of familiar platinum hair. Then we went to the CBD and were similarly disappointed. Lionel parked in a garage near Canal Street. We decided to walk the Quarter on foot since it was well after dark. Which meant the Bourbon Street ban on driving would be in effect.

Due to people being, well, the way they are, Bourbon Street turned into a pedestrian zone at night. And as much as the two of us balked at the idea of being on Bourbon, we needed to find her. We started at Decatur and walked from one of the French Quarter to the other. Canal to Esplanade and back again. This was not made easy by the weather, which was freezing cold with a strong wind. Each time the wind would gust it was like being stabbed by icicles.

"Do you think we should check the Marigny too?" I asked when we were on Chartres.

"We can, but if we're going to, I should get the car back from the garage first," Lionel said.

I sighed and shook my head. "This is all my fault."

He snorted. "Since when? Look, we'll find her, and she'll be fine." It sounded like he was trying to convince himself more than me.

"Something's been bugging her for a while now," I said. "I've tried to get her to talk about it a few times but the most she'll say is she has something she has to do and to drop it."

"I know. She has these crazy nightmares too, at least when she's able to sleep. Then when I ask her about it, she laughs it off like it's nothing. But her energy has been way down and she has enough bags under her eyes to send a family of four on vacation to Paris."

I stopped and looked at Lionel. "What, she's still having them?"

"What do you mean still?"

We were interrupting the flow of foot traffic. A crowd of people carried candles, and we couldn't push past them.

"What the hell?" I asked.

"Caroling in Jackson Square is tonight," Lionel replied. "Fuck, I forgot. Here."

He grabbed my hand, so we weren't separated, and we stepped back against a building and stood by a stoop, so we weren't pulled along by the evening crowd. Then we resumed the conversation.

"I was having nightmares until Amy over at the Cardinal gave me a sleep charm and they went away. They started coming back when the charm wore off, so I had to go get another one. I told Verity she should get one too but she kinda blew me off."

Lionel frowned. "What were your nightmares about?"

"Usually, it's a bad memory but then it goes kinda weird. This fucking...thing appears and grabs me and I can't breathe. Then I wake up and I'm so tired I can barely keep my eyes open."

He crossed his arms over his chest and looked down at his shoes. "Is it a wraith-like figure with a gray robe and black holes for eyes?"

My blood ran cold. "Yes, it was."

"That's what Verity's been having nightmares about too. It starts out with Caleb capturing her and threatening to hurt her. But then it deviates from the memory and things get worse. Things she won't tell me about, but I can guess. Then that creature appears and she wakes up screaming."

"Oh, fuck... What do you think it means?"

"I'm not sure. But I know who we can ask. Let's keep looking for now."

We kept walking and when we got to Bourbon Street we actually held hands so we wouldn't get separated. Even during the slow season, Bourbon was always packed. The

Caroling in Jackson Square event was no help in regard to crowds. But the farther away we got from the Square the fewer people we ran into. When we reached Esplanade and walked up to Dauphine, I said, "Wait, we're doing this wrong."

"What do you mean?"

I walked until we reached an alley. I turned into it and dragged Lionel with me. I took my glasses off and handed them to him. "Hold these."

"Uh, okay."

I took a deep breath and let it out slowly. I'd been avoiding the French Quarter ever since I discovered Heather and my powers. It's the oldest section of New Orleans, where the French colony was established in 1718. And while many of the old French colonial buildings are gone, plenty of the ghosts from that period aren't. Not to mention subsequent generations of Native American, Spanish, Creole, and other immigrants.

I had been terrified I would be overwhelmed with spirits, but that wasn't the case anymore. I could feel that presence with me again, the one that sometimes followed Elias around. The one that made me feel like I could do anything with my powers. It had been with me most of the night. And now I drew on it as I called as many ghosts as I could reach.

"Holy shit," Lionel whispered.

When I opened my eyes, dozens surrounded us. Maybe even hundreds.

"I need your help," I said.

One of the ghosts rattled something off in Spanish.

"Someone who speaks English, please."

"I speak English," a woman in 1800s garb said.

"Thank you. I'm looking for a friend of mine who's

gone missing. She lives here in the French Quarter. I need to know if any of you have seen her recently."

"What does she look like?" the ghost asked.

I took out my phone and unlocked it, then swiped until I came to a picture of Verity. "This is her. Has anyone seen her today?"

The ghosts crowded around. The ones who spoke English were kind enough to translate. I heard French, Spanish, Italian, Greek, and even Gaelic. Finally, we had a lead.

"I saw her," said one young boy in turn-of-the-century clothes.

"Do you remember where and when?" I asked.

"This morning. She was walking down by the French Market. She went that way," he said and pointed in the direction of the Marigny.

"Thank you."

"Wait!"

I paused and turned. It was another woman, this one wearing a 1700s sacque gown. I was amazed she spoke English. "There was someone with her, another ghost."

"Do you know who it was?"

"Small, short girl. She had blonde hair and green eyes."

I had a thought and I dreaded asking, but I had to know. "Was she wearing a pink shirt and green shorts?"

"They were light green and light pink but yes."

I nodded. "Thank you, you've all been very helpful. You're dismissed."

The ghosts went back to their business, and I took my glasses from Lionel. "I know where to go."

"What? Where? What the hell was that? What just happened?"

"Some ghosts saw her, and I know where she was going. Don't argue with me, just come on!"

We ran the six blocks to Heather's old condo. I was out of breath by the time we got there, and my heart was in my throat. "Lionel, can you get us in?"

"If you can tell me what the hell we're doing here, sure."

"Miss Morrison?"

I spun around to see Elias and German. I wasn't sure how long they'd been standing there. Or how absolutely bugfuck insane I probably looked. But I was frantic. Verity could be in there! We needed to get her back before something happened to her!

"We need to get into this house," I said.

"Yeah, you said that but why?" Lionel asked.

"Oh, for fuck's sake," I muttered. I took my glasses off and concentrated. I called for Heather, and I could feel every ghost in the neighborhood watching me. There was a sense of dread in the air. The ghosts were afraid. "She's not here, fuck!"

"Who's not here?" Elias asked.

"I think one of the ghosts who's been haunting me isn't an ordinary ghost. I've been trying to call her since I found out Verity is missing, and I suspect I know why. This was her house when she was alive. Another ghost said he saw Verity headed this way before she disappeared."

"There's no one inside."

"Yeah, it's empty. If someone were in there, we could hear them," Lionel added.

"Damn it!"

German opened his mouth to speak, but then his phone buzzed. All our phones lit up with text alerts. They all said the same thing.

> **Reyna Alvarado:** The Court investigators are here. Everyone, please return to the Black Lily

"Shit," I muttered.

"Let's go," German said. "You can explain on the way."

"This is going to sound so insane," I replied.

Chapter Thirty-Six

WHEN WE GOT back to the Black Lily, it was to see two men I didn't know. One was a Black vampire with curly hair and deep-brown eyes. The other was a white human with strawberry-blond hair and ice-blue eyes. They weren't dressed how I expected. I thought they'd be wearing robes or something fancy. The black man was in a suit and tie, but the white guy was in a band shirt, jeans, and Converse sneakers.

"Nice shirt," I said to him, kind of as a joke since we were both wearing the same The Birthday Massacre shirt.

"Thanks. You get yours on tour?"

"Yeah, when they played the Rebel Lounge."

Lionel interrupted by pinching his cheek. "Hi, Martin. Hi, Martin's chubby cheeks."

Martin smacked his hand away. "Fuck off."

Lionel then wrapped himself around the Black guy and said, "Good to see you again, Kingston."

"You too, Lionel, but I wish it were under better circumstances."

"Yeah, me too. Don't take this the wrong way but what the hell are you two doing here?"

"We were the closest. Everyone else has been called back to the Court," Martin said.

"I haven't heard anything," Elias said.

"Excuse me," said German. "But introductions, please?"

"Oh sorry. I'm Martin, this is Kingston. We're official representatives of the Vampire Royal Court."

"You're...human," Emerson said.

"I'm a witch," Martin said. "And his life partner." He gestured to Kingston.

"Don't say that. It sounds so nineties," Kingston groaned.

"Well, excuse me but you're the one who doesn't want to get married."

"Don't start that shit again, please," Lionel sighed.

Reyna appeared and said, "Thank you for coming, gentlemen. Shall we get started?"

"Wait," said Elias. "Miss Morrison has something to say."

Everyone turned to look at me and I took a deep breath. "Okay, I want to start off by saying I lied, and I'm sorry."

"Lied about what?" Jaxon asked.

"About why I was here," I replied. "The friend who died? She was a ghost. I met her my first night in New Orleans."

"Is that the friend you asked me to locate in the member lists for you?" Reyna asked.

"Yeah, the same. Look, can we sit down? This is going to take a lot of explaining."

We ended up sitting at the large table we reserved for séances. It was the only one with enough room for everyone. Once we were seated, I began.

"So, you guys know I can see and talk to ghosts and spirits. But the reason I discovered this is because of the ghost who tore this place up when I attended my first séance. It wasn't Madame Le Blanc, it was Heather Campbell. She claimed to be a member here, more specifically an empath. That first night she claimed that she and Elias were going on a date. And it was the last thing she remembered before I found her body in the Mississippi."

"Wait, I remember hearing about that," German interrupted. "It was that woman they found on the pilings on the old wharf, right?"

"The very same. I actually found her. The reason I found her body is because I met her ghost and she inadvertently led me to her corpse. Then she was haunting me. Following me around, wrecking my house. She was demanding I investigate her death because she was murdered. I wouldn't know peace until I actually checked it out."

"What did this girl look like?" Lionel asked.

I pulled up the picture of her that was in the paper and passed the phone around.

"She's never been here," Jaxon said.

"You're sure?"

"Yeah, me and German work the door most nights. I have a great memory for faces, which makes it easier to weed out troublemakers. I've never seen her before."

"Kind of wondering how the hell she got the password then," I said. "Look, that's not the important part. After I met her, I kept having these fucking trippy nightmares and I'd wake up tired. Most of them were about the same thing. The first night I met Elias. But they'd go wrong.

"Like it would be either he didn't show up or if he did, he'd kill me himself. The whole time there was this wraith in the background. Always creeping closer and closer. Heck, I've even had one where Elias was able to mesmerize me and then killed me. Which I know wouldn't happen since it doesn't seem to work on me."

"I believe it's due to Miss Morrison's neuro-divergence," Elias said.

"We can test that theory," Lionel said. "Martin has ADHD."

"Now hold on, you're not experimenting on my boyfriend," Kingston snapped.

"Wait, you two met in Phoenix?" Martin asked.

"Yes, the night that Caleb Blake was killed and the coup was stopped. Elias saved my life, but then he tried to erase my memories and it didn't take. The thing is, Heather was convinced he was the one who tried to kill her. She couldn't prove it, and neither could I. Heather kept saying my feelings for Elias were getting in the way. And that's why I couldn't see through Elias and that he was evil."

"Sounds like gaslighting to me," said Kingston.

"That's what I thought. So much of what she told me wasn't adding up. The restaurants and the bars she supposedly worked at? Never heard of her. The club she was supposed to be part of? None of you have ever seen or heard of her. We were fighting constantly, and it got worse after Amy made the sleep charm for me. Heather started to disappear for long periods. Like she was moving on or something. The only thing that was even kind of true was her stepfather being her only living parent. Even then, she didn't tell me the whole truth.

"When I talked to Mr. Campbell, he said she was normal until her mother died. After that, she turned into a manipulative two-faced person who liked to play mind games and create drama. He also said he agreed with the coroner's report that she did kill herself. So that part didn't add up to murder. The only reason I thought it might be murder is because there was a fang mark on her neck.

"Then the other night I talked with Elias about his past, and I was convinced he couldn't have killed her no matter what Heather said. We had a huge fight about it, and I managed to take control of her and force her to leave."

"You can do that?" Jaxon asked.

"Apparently, I can now. I've compelled ghosts to do what I want three times now."

"Is that normal?"

"Hell if I know."

"Not to worry, it's normal," Elias said. "Jonas could do it. He said it took practice and a strong will, but a gifted medium can command ghosts to do their bidding. I know he didn't put it in his first book but he would have written it in his second if he'd had time to complete it."

Well, that was shiny brand-new information. Then something clicked in my head.

"You know, Heather started to disappear when I got that sleep charm from Amy," I said. "She would fade in and out like she didn't have enough energy to stay on this plane. Then for a while she solidified, and that was when my neighbor Sawyer was having nightmares. I told him where to go for a charm, and then Heather started vanishing again. But then around when Verity started looking worn out Heather was completely fine."

"What are you saying?" Reyna asked.

I took another deep breath and let it out. "I think Heather is the Night Hag. And I think she was somehow feeding off me, Sawyer, and Verity. And now I can't find Heather and I'm terrified this means that Verity is dead. I haven't been able to summon Heather since Verity went missing. I'm worried that Heather might be controlling her or has stashed her somewhere to feed on her."

Lionel snapped his fingers. "That's why you wanted to go to the condo."

"I thought she'd be there. The ghost who saw Verity said Heather was with her. And Heather lived in that building before she died."

"This is all so intense," Jaxon muttered.

"You're telling me," Emerson agreed.

"Can you try again?" Martin asked. "While we're all here, I mean. To summon Heather."

I removed my glasses and put them on the table. "Yeah, give me a minute."

I heard Kingston mutter something to Martin, and Martin shushed him.

I breathed deeply and let it out. It was harder to concentrate with everyone staring at me. I centered myself, and let in the cold, elusive power. It worked its way through every bone and muscle in my body. I could feel it tingling behind my eyes, and I heard a soft gasp from Lionel. Cold hands settled on my shoulders. Large, soft hands, as though they were there to comfort me. I tuned it all out.

I lifted my hands, palms up, and focused on New Orleans. In my head, I was over the city. I could see every ghost and spirit there was, like points on a map. But no Heather. I sighed and let the energy dissipate, then opened my eyes. "I still can't find her."

"You were fucking glowing," Lionel said.

"And your hair turned white for a minute," Jaxon added.

"Seriously? Weird. That's never happened before."

"When did you start experiencing this boost in your powers?" Martin asked.

"Ever since I yelled at the ghosts to fuck off out of my apartment. But..." I looked at Elias. "I think I'm also getting help. From Jonas."

He stared at me, and at first didn't speak.

"It makes sense. There used to be a very faint ghost that would follow you around. And ever since then, I've felt this presence. It's not malevolent, and when it's around I suddenly know exactly what to do. It's not intuition, I think I'm being guided by Jonas."

There was a sharp rap on the table.

"One knock for yes, two for no," said Emerson.

Elias swallowed, then said, "Jonas, is that you?"

One knock again.

"If you're Jonas, then tell me. Were you killed by the Night Hag?"

One knock.

"And did I have anything to do with it?"

Two knocks, so hard they actually rattled the table.

"No, it was my fault, I should have seen the signs."

Suddenly, cold energy rushed through me. My mouth opened, but a voice that wasn't mine came through.

"Elias Rothschild, don't you dare blame yourself for what happened, it wasn't your fault!"

Elias's eyes widened. "Jonas, how—"

"It's me, darling doll." My hands grabbed Elias's. "I can't do this for long, I'm burning the candle at both ends. But what happened wasn't your fault. I was targeted by something even older than you, and you did what you could. So, stop blaming yourself, you hear me?"

"I don't know if I can," he muttered.

"Try, for my sake. I love you, Elias."

"I love you too, Jonas."

Then it was gone and I was left gasping. I was so cold,

like I'd fallen through the ice into a frozen lake. I had the distant thought I would never be warm again. Elias threw his arms around me in a vain attempt to warm me. I shivered and buried my face in his chest. Then I heard Jonas's voice in my ear. When my head finally cleared, I looked up. Everyone was staring at me with various looks of shock on their faces. I gulped.

"I know how to find Verity."

It turned out to be pretty simple. We were going to have a séance. When I explained the plan, I was sure someone would protest. But after everything that had already happened that evening, they were willing to go with it. Everyone except Emerson, who said he was going to sit this one out.

"My nerves are shot," he said.

He did get some ribbing from Jaxon and Lionel, but I said I wouldn't force him to join us. He chose to sit at the bar, but he didn't want to leave. I told everyone where to sit. I would be at the head of the table with Elias to my right. Then Reyna, German, Jaxon, Martin, Kingston, and Lionel who would be seated on my left. We just needed some candles, which of course we had plenty of.

As we set them up, Lionel said, "This is crazy."

"If you have a better idea, I'm all ears," I replied. "Though I'm gonna be honest with you, I don't know that I can do this."

"You can," Elias said. "Just believe in yourself."

"Easier said than done," I said.

Once the candles were in place, Jaxon lit them, and I instructed everyone to close their eyes and join hands. Just like at a normal séance. But this was anything but normal.

Jonas said I should be able to summon Verity if

Heather merged with her spiritually. Hopefully, I would be able to command her to tell us where she was. I took a deep breath and let it out slowly. It had been a long night. I almost wished I could tell everyone I quit and go home. But Verity was my friend, and so was Lionel. I'd made this mess and I couldn't leave them in the lurch. I pushed past my discomfort and focused my thoughts on Verity.

I thought about her smile, and how her hair looked like moonlight. And she was always calm and serene and willing to help no matter the circumstances. She was a good person and a wonderful friend, and I didn't want to lose her. Not like this. I breathed in, and out, and in, and out. I listened to everyone else breathe. They were open to me, mind and soul. I could feel their thoughts and emotions flowing through me and to one another. We were all connected. We could find her, I simply had to reach out.

I cast my net wide. I drew on the feelings of those around me. When I found her, we collectively gasped. Then I opened my eyes.

Verity hovered above the table. She didn't look like the sad, sorry ghosts I'd seen since I moved to New Orleans. She was bathed in white light that glowed from within. She was beautiful but sad.

"Where am I?" she asked, scared.

"Verity?"

She looked at me. "Oh, Lyric, what have you done?"

"We're trying to find you. Can you tell us where you are?"

"I can, but I won't."

I heard murmuring from outside the circle, but I ignored it. My thoughts had to stay on Verity. I could feel she was trying to break the connection, but I couldn't understand why. "Verity, we know Heather has control over you. We think she's a Night Hag, and we want to get you back."

"You can't. If you do, you'll die," Verity replied.

"I'm not going to let you die for me."

"It's not that simple. The Night Hag went after me because the end of the dark season is approaching. Once Yule has passed it will be done. We can't let her have you, Lyric. I knew this was coming. I chose my fate."

"Without asking me if this is what I want! I don't want you to sacrifice yourself for me! Come on, Verity! You can't do this!"

"Can't I? You're my friend, and I love you. I can't let you subject yourself to her for me."

"Then tell us where you are. We can fight her together! Don't give up on your life!"

"Verity," Lionel pleaded. "We can't lose you. Please, we've lost so much already. We want to help you."

"You can't, I won't let you."

Kingston growled. "Dammit, Verity, listen to us!"

She turned her head. "Kingston, Martin? What are you doing here?"

"The same thing that Lionel and these people are trying to do. Save you," Kingston said.

"Please, Verity," I begged. "You can't let it end like this. I love you, and I want to keep you safe. Don't do this, not for me."

"I've already said you can't. I chose this. Leave me to it." Verity froze, and golden flecks of energy engulfed her. "She's found me. Break the connection or she might jump to you."

"I—"

Verity screamed as the gold washed over her, and she

vanished. The connection broke so fast, I couldn't hold myself together. It felt as though I'd been struck blind, deaf, and dumb. The next thing I knew I was on the ground.

"She's conscious," Martin said.

Elias appeared above me. "Are you all right?"

"Verity," I replied and sat up.

"Hey, take it easy, you had a nasty fall when you fainted."

"Never mind me, I know where Verity is! There was a flash of it when the connection broke. We have to go get her."

Reyna appeared at my side. She had a tablet in hand with a map of New Orleans pulled up. "Show me."

I looked over, then pointed at an area near City Park.

"That's the Masonic Cemetery," German said.

"She's there."

"Let's go."

Reyna, Emerson, German, Jaxon, and Lionel left, with Kingston hot on their heels. Elias moved to leave as well but I said, "Don't go."

"I'll be right back," he replied. "You've fainted. I'm going to get you some water." And he went behind the bar.

Martin let out a low whistle. "You okay?"

"Scary shit. You know, after Phoenix and now this I'm starting to wonder why I ever left April Oaks."

He raised an eyebrow. "How do you know about April Oaks?"

"It's where I'm from originally."

"Really? So am I!"

We stared at each other for a moment. April Oaks is a small town in Northern California with only about five hundred people if that. If he was from April Oaks, I should know him.

"Are you sure?" I asked.

"Yeah. I mean, my family died when I was really young, so I left shortly after."

"Oh my God, are you the Von Brandt kid?"

He nodded. "Guilty."

"They said your family was taken out by a Mafia hitman."

"Vampires."

I sighed. "God, I'm sorry."

"It's okay. But I've been back once or twice, I don't think I've run into you."

"When were you back?"

"About four years ago."

"Yeah, that's after I left. But you know Sheryl Morrison?"

"You mean the town drunk?"

I nodded sadly.

Martin sighed. "She's your mom?"

"Yeah."

"Fuck, now I'm sorry."

"It's true though."

"What are the odds though? Running into each other like this?"

"I don't know. I mean I haven't seen anyone from April Oaks since I moved away."

"And you moved to Phoenix too?"

"Weird choice, right? I picked it because it had a good job market and the rent wasn't too bad. At least at first. But that changed when the second tech boom started. I couldn't afford to live there now even after the coup."

"Believe me, I know. If I weren't living in Kingston's condo I wouldn't be able to afford my old place. Even Tali had to get a roommate."

I blinked. "Verity's ex? You know her?"

"Yeah. I know Verity and Tali split up, but Tali still cares about her."

"Verity does too. But I get why they couldn't make it work. Sometimes you just shouldn't mix business lives and personal lives."

"Yeah, Tali definitely learned that lesson too late. But she's on standby in case we need magical back-up."

Elias came back and gave me a glass of ice water, which I drank slowly. Then I said, "It was Heather. That golden energy we saw? That's how Heather looks whenever she manifests. It's all around her."

"Why not jump to Lyric? Verity said she could," Martin pointed out.

"I think she tried. I'm pretty sure Verity's the one who broke the connection. Heather was probably manifesting to do just that but Verity stopped her."

"I need the grimoire," Martin said, more to himself than to us. He got up from the table and walked out.

When he did, Elias took his seat and took my hand. "I have a question, and I hope you won't be angry."

"I'm so worn out I don't know that I can manage anger."

"Are you in love with Verity?"

I stared at him for a moment, confused. "Is this a joke?"

"You care about her deeply," Elias said. "And you proclaimed your love for her without a thought. Are you in love with her?"

I rubbed at my face. Well, the night was already fucked. Might as well go all the way. "I know how I feel about you. But I admit I feel something for her too. I can't put my finger on it. Like, I know I love her as a friend. But sometimes it's like there's something more there. But I haven't thought of it much since I started dating you."

Elias smiled. "You can love more than one person at a time, you know."

"I know that. I mean, I don't know that I'm polyamorous. Maybe there's just something about her. But if I do love her romantically, I'm shit at showing it. She got possessed by a Night Hag because I'm a fucking idiot."

"If you'll recall, Verity said she knew this would happen and allowed it. She wanted to spare you the pain of what Heather would do. I think, once we get her back, we should all sit down and have a nice long talk."

I laid my head on his shoulder. "Yeah, we should."

There was nothing else we could do but wait. Elias occasionally stroked my hair. Just after five in the morning, we finally got a call.

"We found her," said Reyna.

"Is she alive?" Elias asked.

"Yes, but she seems to be in a coma. Lionel is taking her back to his apartment. We can't risk taking her to the hospital if she has been possessed. Besides, it might help her if she's in familiar territory. The sun is coming up soon though, so we won't be able to reconvene until tonight."

"We'll have to do some research and come up with a plan," said Elias.

"Get with Martin on that," said Kingston. "He's got some kind of spooky book with him that can look up almost anything."

"We'll see you soon," said Reyna and she hung up.

"Spooky book?" I asked.

Martin came back into the room with a leather-bound

tome in hand. "Sorry that took so long. I packed it in Kingston's suitcase for some reason." He paused, looked at both of us, and said, "Looks like I missed something."

We filled him in on Verity.

Martin sat down and opened the book, then said to the pages, "Show me everything you have on the Night Hag."

Chapter Thirty-Seven

AS IT TURNED out, there was quite a lot about the Night Hag. To my surprise, the book added pages to itself, written in tiny print and all in English. It took a while to get through it. Martin and I got set up in the main room of the club so we could do research. We would take breaks for food or coffee, but not for long. There was a lot of reading we had to do.

At dawn, Elias had to go downstairs to the wine cellar where the spare coffins were kept along with Kingston and Reyna. Jaxon and Emerson stayed at Lionel's place to keep an eye on Verity while he and German slept through the day.

In the meantime, I reached out to my pocket friends. It was weird because I hadn't heard from them in a few days. I checked the group chat and it was pretty chill, mostly just talking about their pets and family activities. So, I messaged that I was running into an issue and there was a lot going on, but I needed any information anyone had on the Night Hag.

Psychepomp: Did you find out who it is?

EratoONine: It's Heather. It was always Heather.

Psychepomp: Fuck.

NathanaBoBanna: Most of what I have is very basic information.

DidollCarthage: Me too.

AoiManto: Is there anything specific?

EratoONine: She's possessing a friend of mine and we need to get her out.

Psychepomp: Exorcism.

NathanaBoBanna: Exorcism.

DidollCarthage: Definitely an exorcism.

AoiManto: I'll keep looking on this end but I agree with the others. An exorcism is your best bet.

EratoONine: Fuck... Okay well, thanks for trying. I'll give you guys an update when I have one.

Psychepomp: Good luck. And be careful!

By the time we came up with anything relevant, the sun had set. The vampires in the wine cellar had risen, and each looked more haggard than the last. Martin had been brewing some kind of blood substitute potion for the last hour and gave it to them when they came in. Emerson, Jaxon, and German had gone to the Cardinal to get supplies for a spell they hoped would wake up Verity.

The book told us everything we'd already assumed. Heather had forged the connection between her and me through nightmares. And she'd done the same to Verity.

She would feed on the energy of the host until she was satiated or the host died. Additionally, if the Night Hag were to feed off a human with psychic abilities, it would weaken them to the point she could take over their body.

"Is there anything about how to extract the Night Hag?" Elias asked.

"I'm not sure," Martin replied. "I'm still looking."

"Wait a minute," I said as I read over his shoulder. "Go back."

"Where?"

I reached over and flipped two pages and pointed. "Here, it mentions Yule."

Martin read aloud.

"When a Night Hag loses a vessel, it must find a new vessel before the end of the dark half of the year. Otherwise, it will wither and die one final time."

"That's what Verity meant," I said. "Today's the Winter Solstice. If we can drive her out of Verity and keep her out until midnight, Heather dies for real."

"How the hell are we going to do that?" Kingston asked.

"Well, when I asked my friends, they all suggested an exorcism. Can we do that?"

Martin flipped through the book. "Here we go. There's a ritual here to extract the Night Hag from a current host. If we do it tonight, we can make sure Heather doesn't take over Verity again. It says it takes three days for the bond to complete. Since that's also how long it takes for a Night Hag to form a connection through feeding, we'll have to hurry, or Verity's soul will be destroyed."

"No pressure," I said.

"There's a problem," Elias said. "Once we get the

Night Hag out of Verity, how do we keep it from possessing Lyric? They have a connection as well."

Martin turned to me. "Didn't you say someone made a charm for you so Heather couldn't feed off you?"

"Yeah, Amy at the Cardinal. It's where the others are now."

"Then we should get some more. For you and for Verity. The Night Hag won't have enough time to forge another connection between now and midnight."

"We'll take my car," said Elias.

We left the Black Lily and headed to the Quarter. It took us longer to get there than I would have liked, but we texted Lionel to let him know what was up. He and German said they would wait until we arrived. When we got there, we parked across the street and headed inside.

Amy was behind the counter and she said without turning to look at us, "I'm making them now."

"You don't even know what we're here for," Martin said.

"You need protection, German told me."

German shrugged. "It wasn't hard to figure out what you guys are up to. That the grimoire?"

"Yeah, and it has the ingredients we need for the ritual to get the Night Hag out of Verity."

"Great, let's grab those while Amy makes the charms."

I hugged Lionel. "How's Verity?"

"Unconscious. I left her at the apartment and Jaxon and Emerson are watching over her until I get back. We got her in her favorite nightgown and put her to bed."

"Thank you."

"No problem. So, what's the plan?"

"Exorcise Heather and put the protection charms on

Verity and Lyric. Then keep them safe until Heather is dead permanently," Elias replied.

"Simple and straightforward, my kind of plan."

Martin and German were already taking care of everything. Which left Lionel, Elias, and me twiddling our thumbs. Or so I thought. Lionel said, "Actually, Lyric, can you come with me to the courtyard? I keep hearing stories about a ghost bride and I want to see if they're true."

"Uh, sure."

I let him drag me out back. Once we were out of earshot of the others he asked, "What are your intentions toward Verity?"

I blinked. "You are the second vampire to ask me that today. Also, I hardly think now is the time."

"It's going to work, I know it will. Now I want to make sure you're going to treat my best friend right and not rip her heart out like Tali did."

I sighed and sat by the fountain. "My intention is to save her life. Once she's no longer being feasted on by a parasitic hell demon then I'll ask her if she'd like to get coffee."

"Does this mean you're dumping Elias? Because if you are, I'm going to ask him out."

I chuckled. "Be my guest. I think he might be poly."

"Really?" Lionel waggled his eyebrows. "Tell me more."

"That's all I know. But he did say when we get out of this and Verity has recovered, we should have a serious talk."

"Agreed. Now I'm definitely asking him out."

"You have my blessing."

"Awesome."

"Hey, you two."

Elias stood at the entrance to the courtyard. "We're nearly ready."

We went back inside, and Amy gave me the protection charms. They were surprisingly simple. Pendants of blue glass with an eye painted on them strung on leather cords. I recognized them as a charm against the evil eye. I put one around my neck and slipped the other into my pocket.

"Be careful," she told me. "I know my cousin would hate to lose her favorite customer."

"And what would life be without Delia's delicious coffee?"

We left, and Martin called Kingston and told him where to meet us. When Jaxon let us into Lionel's apartment, he looked wrecked. His hair was a mess, his clothes were torn, and he had a split lip plus the beginning of a shiner around his left eye.

"So, we have a slight problem."

German looked Jaxon over, eyes wide. "What happened?"

"As soon as we were alone Emerson attacked me," he said. "He used his powers to throw me around like a rag doll. He tried to leave with Verity but I managed to trip him up."

And indeed, there was Emerson. Tied to a chair with a necktie in his mouth to gag him. He glared at us with fury.

"What the fuck?" Lionel said.

Martin frowned and went over to Emerson. He put his hand on Emerson's shoulder and closed his eyes. Emerson struggled and even tried to head-butt Martin. But Kingston was there in seconds and held Emerson's head back.

Then Martin let go and opened his eyes. "He's been possessed by a Night Hag."

"So, Heather—" Lionel started, but Martin interrupted.

"No, a different one."

"There's two?"

"The boyfriend," I said.

"Excuse me?" Kingston said.

"Heather Campbell's stepfather said she had a boyfriend before she died. I didn't connect the dots at the time, but the description he gave of the boyfriend sounded like Emerson."

German sighed. "That's definitely more than three days."

"So, we've lost Emerson?"

"No, we can still help him, or at least we can try. But it is going to hurt."

"Where'd you get the rope?" Martin asked.

"It was in the closet," Jaxon replied. "I've treated the ropes with salt and bay leaves so it should keep Emerson bound without hurting him. There wasn't any more of it, otherwise I'd have used it on Verity too."

Lionel sighed. "Damn it, that was my shibari rope. You owe me."

"Excuse the fuck out of me for trying to keep our friend from clawing my eyes out."

"I didn't mean anything by it," Lionel said. "Sorry."

"Do we have enough supplies so we can exorcise both of them?" Martin asked.

"We'll have to do them both in the same ritual," German replied. "Let's get started."

"Wait, we're doing the ritual right now?" I asked.

"We need to get it done before midnight when the

Solstice ends. Heather has been inside of Verity too long already," Martin said.

When he said it out loud, it made sense.

"Okay, let's get this done."

German and Martin walked into the bedroom. Jaxon grabbed Emerson's chair and dragged him in behind them. I followed him and what I saw made me pause in the doorway.

Verity was on the bed above the covers, and the bed had been dragged to the center of the room. She was so pale her complexion was nearly the same color as her hair. I wanted to reach over and push her hair back, but German stopped me from approaching her. Jaxon moved Emerson's chair so he was a couple feet away from the bed.

"Stand over there, just to be safe," German told me.

"Should she even be here?" Martin wondered aloud. "Once we get this thing out of Verity it's just going to jump to Lyric."

"I'm not leaving," I said firmly.

When Kingston arrived, the ritual started. Mostly it was German, Martin, and Jaxon burning herbs and chanting. Nothing really happened until they started to burn the sage. Verity suddenly sat up, eyes wide open. She looked half dead already, and her eyes were cloudy like she had cataracts. She turned her head to look at Martin and lunged at him.

Kingston caught her around the middle and said, "Verity, for fuck's sake!"

It took the combined strength of Lionel, Kingston, and Elias to pin her down. And even with their vampire superstrength, they were having trouble doing so. She kicked, she screamed, and she clawed at their faces. She fought tooth and nail, or I should say, Heather did. She wasn't going down without a fight. When I saw blood dripping from Verity's nose I said, "Stop! Heather's hurting her!"

"The spell is almost done. Have the charms ready!" German snapped at me.

Meanwhile, Emerson was fighting his bonds as hard as he could. His arms and wrists bled with the effort. His eyes rolled in the back of his head, and he was sweating and pale. *God, why didn't we tie up Verity too?* There had to be some rope around somewhere. It was too late now, but on the off chance we ever had to do any of this again, restraints wouldn't go amiss. Emerson wasn't going anywhere.

I approached the bed, fear running rampant through me. Verity looked more and more like she was dying. Her skin was gray, her eyes milky-white, dark veins appeared under her skin, and her hair was brittle and completely white. How could I do this? I did love Verity; I couldn't let this thing hurt her. It was my mess. There was a sort of popping sensation when the ritual was completed, but Heather was hanging on tight. She was laughing with Verity's voice as she said, "I'll rip her apart before I'll let you have her back!"

I had the cold sensation of hands on my shoulders. I suddenly knew what to do. While everyone was distracted with Verity, I put my hands on Emerson's shoulders. I could feel that whatever had been inside him was gone. Or at least gone from his body—I could still feel it in the room, likely floating above our heads. He looked up at me, eyes wide with fear, and I put my finger to my lips. Then I slipped one of the protection charms around Emerson's neck.

I closed my eyes and held up my hands. Heather's energy twisted around Verity like a boa constrictor. The Night Hag was inhuman, yes, but still a spirit. Which meant I could control it. Elias was gonna be pissed. Lionel too probably, but this would work, I was sure it would. I reached out with my power and seized Heather. I pulled hard, and there was another *pop* once she was extracted.

I pulled the charm from around my neck, threw it to Elias, and said, "Put it on her!"

Heather seized me around the middle. She was too fast; I didn't even have time to scream. She whispered, "Got you," in my ear. The last thing I heard was someone yelling my name. Then it all went black.

It was the room again, the damp gray one with the crooked bed and moldy walls. It was my studio, but how it might look if it were allowed to rot away. This time, it wasn't the gray creature staring at me, but Heather. She was no longer in her coral shirt and mint shorts. Now she was in a long gray dress, the same one I'd seen the creature in. Her skin was paper white, with dark hollows under her eyes, and her golden hair brittle and dry as hay.

"You lied to me," I said.

"I did. So what? I've lied to a lot of people."

She moved toward me, and I moved back. Then we were circling each other, each waiting for the other to make a move.

"Who are you really?" I asked.

"Really? I've had many names. Psychics are a dime a dozen in New Orleans. But the truly gifted like you and your little girlfriend? Oh, you're a rare treat." She grinned at me, her teeth pearly white and razor sharp. "So young and vital and full of psychic energy. All that untapped potential."

"Then why not possess me? Why did you pretend to be my friend?"

Heather snorted. "You had power, but you didn't know how to use it. Hell, you denied even having it in the first place! And you were so closed off. What else could I do?"

Then it clicked. "That's why you sent me to the Black Lily. This wasn't about solving a murder. It was about me learning to use my powers."

"Exactly," she replied. "You're no use to me if you can't use all your powers. I can't unlock them myself because they're not mine to release. I needed you to learn and grow until you were nice and ripe for the taking. Though it sure wasn't easy. You're so suspicious! If I hadn't killed Heather Campbell, I would never have been able to tear your walls down and get my hooks in you. You really did a number on yourself, you know."

"Did a number on myself?" I asked.

She smiled and transformed. She was the ghost of Leticia Hamilton, just as she'd looked when she told me the gym coach killed her. She said in a whisper, "So traumatized, poor thing. You were like the psychic Fort Knox." Then she turned back.

"How long have you been planning this?"

"Ever since the first time I saw you. When you and your other friend came to visit New Orleans the first time." She walked around me in a circle, hands clasped behind her back. "It was like seeing a Christmas present, wrapped so pretty, but you were just out of reach."

"You saw me when you were still inside Heather?"

"When I was Heather. She no longer existed by that time. Poor thing wasn't really all that powerful. Her mother lasted much longer than she did."

"You didn't."

"Oh yes, I did. Mrs. Campbell was the most skilled psychometric I'd ever come across. And her daughter was just like her. But so weak and pathetic. Always worried about what other people would think or say about her. So desperate to be polite and sweet. Sickening. Once Mrs. Campbell was through, I immediately befriended her daughter. As her own mother's ghost, if you can believe it or not."

"I can, and you're sick for doing that."

"No, I'm not sick!" She grabbed me by the hair. "It's sick what was done to me! What I've had to do to survive all these years! To keep from being dragged to hell because of a man who never loved me and a fallen angel who couldn't love me enough!"

I froze. "You're the real Madame Le Blanc."

"Of course, I am. Something not widely known is exactly how a Night Hag is created. You're such a studious little thing, I'm sure you'd love to hear it before I kill you."

I pushed her away. "You won't have time, midnight's approaching."

But now, she wasn't Heather anymore. She'd changed again. This time into a young woman with rippling black curls and large velvet-brown eyes. She wore a gray velvet dress and had white chrysanthemums pinned in her hair. Another illusion, but this time of what she looked like when she was alive.

The room around us changed too. The walls were covered with emerald damask wallpaper. The floorboards were shining mahogany with plush Persian carpets laid out. Paintings in gilt frames decorated the walls as well as sconces with gas lamps attached. There was crown molding with cherubic faces in the center of the ceiling, with a crystal chandelier hanging from it. More crown molding surrounded the edges of the wall and ceiling with a similar motif.

Against one wall was a marble mantel with a fireplace, and a golden screen in front of the flames. Delicate gas lamps with crystals hanging from them decorated the mantel, along with an ornate clock, and a giant mirror hung above it. As I watched Marguerite pace the room, I could see my reflection in the mirror. Her reflection was of the withered wraith she'd become.

"Beautiful, isn't it?" Marguerite Le Blanc smirked. "The legend is mostly true, you know. But it wasn't the Devil who built my house. It was Asmodeus. Your apartment was actually my music room. I had a harp, just over there—" she pointed at the corner. "Sometimes I would play, but mostly I would wait. Oh, how I waited for him. He was beautiful, you know. The most beautiful man you'll ever meet, and I loved him with all my heart.

"But he's a busy man. Or demon, I should say demon. It wasn't once a week he would see me, but once a year. All my needs were met, except one. Companionship. It's not as though I could have visitors, and when I did leave the house, I was shunned. The neighbors wouldn't speak to me. The shops wouldn't do business with me. If I entered a room everyone pretended as though I didn't exist. They knew who I belonged to. Those self-righteous bastards wouldn't dare speak to the Demon Mistress."

Marguerite sighed as she toyed with the arms on the clock above the fireplace.

"In the beginning, Jean-Pierre and I were so happy. Asmodeus knew nothing, and we cavorted through the halls of his house. We ate his food, we drank his wine, and we made love as though there were no tomorrow. But we were doomed from the start, and we were destroyed by Asmodeus for making a fool of him. Something no demon would suffer lightly. He ate us alive."

I shuddered at the thought. I did feel a bit of sympathy, but then I reminded myself how many people had died because of her.

"When we were consumed, there was damage we hadn't considered. There wasn't enough of our souls left to go to heaven or hell. Instead, we existed, listlessly. Until we discovered we could feed on humans."

"And you extended your lives through the misery of others," I concluded.

"Exactly. Then we discovered we could possess psychics. We were even happier. Until Jean-Pierre possessed the wrong one."

I blinked. "Jonas."

"Yes, and that hypocritical vampire killed my Jean-Pierre. How were we to know a vampire could drain a Night Hag? By the time I found out what happened, Jean-Pierre was at death's door. It was only by pulling his soul into my own that I could save him. I've had to feed for two for so long, and it wears my hosts out so quickly. It wasn't until recently he was well enough to take another host."

"But he killed Jonas," I yelled. "Did you think that Elias was going to just take that lying down? Would you?"

She tilted her head to the side. "No, I suppose I wouldn't."

"I still can't believe this is the actual house," I said as I looked around. "I thought the original house was demolished."

"No, only in the legend. And believe me, I'm still very much the mistress of the house." She smirked. "Did you think it was a coincidence you ended up in my home? I arranged everything. I killed the woman who lived in the apartment before you. I made sure you found it at just the right moment, before it was even officially listed. Then, when I knew you were going to stay, that's when I killed Heather's body."

"You called her stepfather to make it seem like a suicide."

"And did a pretty good job of framing Elias for it, I believe. It was Declan Lotz who gave me a little love bite right before I did the deed. I already knew he was wanted for murder, and he'd be caught eventually and wouldn't be able to tell anyone about me. I still had a score to settle with Elias and I thought my plan was going perfectly. Then you developed feelings for him, and the plan had to change. Even worse, you locked me out! Now that really surprised me. I should have taken outside magics into account."

"Then why jump to Verity?"

"She was vulnerable and you love her. And she is a powerful clairvoyant. I thought if I could take her, I could use her to get closer to you and have another shot in the next Dark Season."

"And Jean-Pierre? Why'd you have him take over Emerson?"

"Convenience mostly. Sadly, Jean-Pierre's control of his host isn't so great since he's been weak for so long. We were going to keep an eye out for a more powerful psychic to build his strength back up. I thought we might have found one with your neighbor Sawyer. But unfortunately, his powers aren't quite what we thought. So, I suppose it's a good thing you warned him about us. We had to abandon that plan."

"I thought you were feeding on him when you

couldn't get to me."

She shrugged.

I smirked. "Jean-Pierre got what he deserved. We exorcized him from Emerson."

"It's no matter, I'll find someone else for him."

"Before midnight? I doubt it. He's toast."

"Don't you dare say that!" She lashed out and slapped me across the face.

I grabbed her hand and wrenched hard on her arm, then pushed her away. "You both deserve to die! After all the misery and suffering you've caused? Jean-Pierre didn't even love you! But you persisted in this life together because you were too chicken shit to face it alone! No wonder that demon had enough of your shit!"

"I'm going to really enjoy killing you," Marguerite hissed.

Something rushed through me. They were performing the exorcism again, and I knew what to do.

"You won't get the chance," I promised her.

Marguerite lunged; she clawed me across the face. I hit her back, and we fell to the ground punching and slapping each other. She was stronger than I'd estimated. For a moment I thought I'd bitten off more than I could chew. Until I felt the air shift. I could smell tea olive perfume, old leather, and clove cigarettes. That's when I knew. I broke Marguerite's grip on me and pushed her away.

"Now you can see what real love can do."

I held my hands out in front of me. This was my mind and my power. I could see Marguerite's energy flowing through her and out of me. I made it grind to a halt, then reversed the process. She struggled against me, but it was no use. She'd spent too much time trying to justify her actions instead of solidifying her hold on me. I was never going to be used by her again.

Once I'd drawn on my power, I yelled, "Get out."

Marguerite screamed. Her claws scrabbled against my mind. Trying to find a purchase, to hold on. Anything to prevent her expulsion. The pain seared my mind and I screamed.

Then I was awake, and something hit me in the chest, as though someone threw ice water on me. Verity, Lionel, and Elias were standing over me. Just past them, I could see what was left of Marguerite. Elias helped me to my feet, then I approached the orb. I told the others to stay back.

Tiny gold sparks of energy glittered, but they were so faint I barely registered them. There was something else in the room. It raised every hair on my body and chilled me to the bone. In the corner, by the door to the balcony, was a man. He was clothed in black and had glowing red eyes, but he was still somehow beautiful. Fear seized my heart and I was afraid to breathe. My mouth went dry. I couldn't speak. Then I realized he wasn't there for me.

"Come along, Madame Le Blanc. You've tarried upon the Earth long enough."

I glanced behind me to see if the others were watching this, but everyone was frozen. Like time itself had stopped.

He reached out and plucked the gold sparks from the air. He took out a glass bottle with a cork stopper, in which I could see more gold sparks. He shoved them inside and added, "There you are, reunited with your lover." Then he looked up at me. "It seems I owe you a favor, Lyric Morrison."

I gulped. "Uh...you're welcome?"

Asmodeus laughed. His voice was like molten chocolate. "Hold out your hand, girl."

I did as he asked, and he placed a coin in my palm. It was very old, and a strange dark energy came off it. "If you should require my intervention at any time, hold this and call to me. I will come."

"That's very nice of you, but it's not necessary."

"I insist," he said, and smiled. Like Marguerite, his mouth was full of razor-sharp teeth. "Good night, Lyric Morrison."

Then time was moving again, and Marguerite and the demon had vanished.

"Is she gone?" Verity asked.

"Yeah."

My knees went out from under me, and I fainted for the second time that night.

Chapter Thirty-Eight

SOMETHING TICKLED MY face. I tried to swipe it away with my hand, but I had trouble lifting my arm. It felt like a...feather? I opened my eyes. I was in a bed I didn't recognize. There was mosquito netting all around me, gently wafting in the breeze from an open window. It was an unseasonably warm night, but not unpleasant. I smelled water and plants. I heard the babbling of a fountain, and I knew where I was.

I sat up. Elias was sitting by the bed, his arms crossed over his chest. He parted the mosquito netting and said, "Good evening."

"How long was I out?"

"Three days. It's Christmas Eve."

"Oh fuck. Guess it's a good thing I don't work a day job anymore. Is everyone okay?"

"Yes. Kingston and Martin have concluded their investigation and have departed. They've been recalled to the Court. I've been given a temporary reprieve until you're well, then I'll have to return too."

I bit my lip. "You're not leaving forever, are you?"

"No. It's only a quick inspection. Then I'll come back to you."

"That's a relief." I looked up at him. "The Night Hag said that you drained her boyfriend. Is that why you think you killed Jonas?"

Elias sighed and ran a hand through his hair. "I didn't

know then what I know now. I thought if I were to drain Jonas, I could drain the Night Hag as well. Which I did. But when I offered my blood to Jonas to turn him, he declined. He said he loved me, but he couldn't be a vampire. He lingered for some days, then he passed away."

I reached out and squeezed his hand. "I'm so sorry. But Jonas said it wasn't your fault. It sounds like he made his choice, so you have nothing to feel guilty about."

"I don't know if I believe that, but I will try."

I smiled, then I groaned. "I feel like I went ten rounds with a grizzly bear."

"You fought off a Night Hag, that's not an easy feat. Lie back, you need more rest."

I sighed and settled against the pillows. "How's Verity?"

"She's recovered. She's up and about again. She's eager to speak with you."

"Cool. Where is she?"

"Here. She wouldn't leave your side. Neither would Lionel."

I smiled a little. "Bring them both? I think we need to have that talk."

Elias kissed my forehead and left the room. When he returned with Verity and Lionel, Verity climbed into the bed with me.

"I'm tired," she said.

I chuckled. "Me too."

Lionel waved. "Elias and I are going on a date."

"Wonderful," I said. "I felt you guys."

"What do you mean?" Elias asked. He sat in the chair again, while Lionel sat on the edge of the bed.

"When I was fighting with Heather—I mean, Marguerite—for control of my mind. I could feel all three of you. It gave me the strength to push her out."

Lionel and Elias exchanged glances. Verity didn't look the least bit surprised. I looked at her and asked, "Would you like to go for coffee sometime?"

"I think we're well past the point of coffee," she replied.

Her hand hovered over mine, quietly asking for permission. I reached for her hand and squeezed it and she smiled.

"I don't know how to navigate something like this," I said. "My dating history is...weird."

"Well, yeah, I mean you're asexual. So I imagine it's probably not riddled with lovelorn conquests," Lionel teased.

This actually made Elias laugh. "You don't know that for sure."

"Okay yeah, I don't. But still. Assumptions can be made."

"And you're right to make them," I said. "But it's kind of a combination of my autism and my asexuality. And I want us to make sure we've talked all this through before we commit to anything."

"Yeah, like, how is this gonna work?" Lionel said, gesturing to himself and Elias. "I'm like, all the way gay. And I know Verity is only into girls. So, what, your boyfriend has a boyfriend and you have a girlfriend?"

"I think that would be the simplest arrangement for now," said Elias. "Please don't misunderstand, Miss Archer, I care for you as well."

"But not how you care about Lyric," Verity said. "I get it, it's fine."

"That's pretty much how I feel too. Verity is my sister," Lionel said. "Lyric, you're cool. But seriously if you do anything to hurt her, I'm going to eat you."

"You'll do no such thing," Verity admonished.

Lionel hung his head. "Yeah, I won't. But I will give you scathing looks."

"That's fair," I replied.

My eyelids drooped, and I yawned. "I'm so sorry. I don't know what's gotten into me."

"You've strained yourself immensely. You should get some sleep, but you need to eat something first," said Verity.

"There's egg flower soup on the stove," Lionel said.

I grinned. "That's actually my favorite."

"I'll get it. Come on, Lionel, I need your help in the kitchen," Elias said.

"Like hell you do. And I don't want to miss the hot goss."

"Go on, stop being a brat," Verity said and whacked him on the arm.

Lionel rolled his eyes and sighed as though he were being put upon. "Fine. But I'm doing this under protest."

"Just go, you nosy busybody."

When Elias and Lionel were out of the room, I looked at Verity.

She was pale and drawn, and she still had dark circles under her eyes. But she looked better than the last time I'd seen her. Then I remembered the demon and I asked, "Where's that coin?"

She reached over me to the nightstand and picked it up. "This? Where did you get it?"

"The demon who came to drag Marguerite and Jean-Pierre down to hell gave it to me."

I looked it over. The coin was ancient and made of copper. There were characters pressed into it I didn't recognize. I'd have to look them up later. I opened the nightstand drawer and dropped it in there, then slammed it shut.

"You're all right now though?" Verity asked.

"Yeah. Worn out but I'll be okay. You?"

"Much the same. Thank you for saving me."

"You're welcome. But don't do anything like that again. At least not without discussing it with the rest of us. You scared the shit out of me. I thought we'd lost you."

Verity held her arms open, and I leaned against her. I let her hug me, resting my head against her breast. I listened to her breathe for a little while, her heartbeat against my ear. She was alive, and she still smelled like sweet tea olive perfume. Elias came back with the soup. Verity gave him a look I couldn't read, and he gave the bowl to her and left without a word. She had me lean back against the headboard and said, "I want to feed you."

"Oh, please don't. That would be so weird for me."

She smiled and gave me the bowl. As I ate, she asked, "So Marguerite told you the truth?"

"Yeah, about how she'd put all the pieces into place to trap me. It was trippy as hell."

"I'm sure. She took great pleasure in tormenting me with the details."

"I'm sorry."

"It's all right, it was my choice."

I paused. "How's everyone doing?"

Verity accepted the subject change. She told me about how Kingston and Martin wanted to make sure she and Lionel were okay. They passed on a message from her ex. It wasn't a plea to get back together, simply one of concern and wishing her well. Once they'd left, Reyna had gone into magical damage control.

First off, Emerson was fine, though he'd been possessed by Jean-Pierre for some time. Once he was free of the Night Hag's influence and recovered, he left New Orleans for parts unknown. Reyna did try to talk to him, but he wouldn't be dissuaded. He received a cleansing from German and another protection charm from Amy. Then he packed up and left.

Delia and Amy helped German and Jaxon with the mess. Once they were sure Marguerite was gone, they'd cleansed Lionel and Verity's apartment. By the time I was done with the soup, I was all caught up. I placed the bowl and spoon on the nightstand.

"So...I kind of confessed I loved you in front of everyone."

"I know, I was there," she reminded me.

"Right, of course. Are you sure you're okay with this arrangement? I don't want you to feel as though you're only second best or something."

"Lyric—" She scooted closer to me. "I think you'll find you have enough love in your heart for Elias, Lionel, and me. If you didn't, you wouldn't have been able to banish Marguerite."

I smiled. "I suppose you're right." I yawned. It was the fourth time since she started talking. "I'm sorry, I swear you're not boring. I'm just—"

"Drained, I know. Sleep. I'll watch over you."

We lay down, arms wrapped around each other, chest to chest and cheek to cheek. Verity hummed as she ran her fingers through my hair. Before I knew it, I was asleep. And I didn't have a single nightmare. I did, however, have a dream.

It was the same room Marguerite created, restored to what it was back in the 1800s. This time there were two

Victorian wingback chairs and a coffee table in front of the fireplace. In one of the chairs was a white man with pale-gold hair and brown eyes. He wore a charcoal three-piece suit with a white-and-blue striped shirt, navy ascot tie, brown shoes, and there was a bowler hat sitting on the table.

I sat across from him in the empty chair and said, "Hello, Jonas."

"Hello, Lyric," he said. "It's nice to meet you in person."

"You too. What are you doing here?"

"I've come to say goodbye."

My stomach dropped. "No, why? Did I do something wrong?"

He chuckled. "Not at all. But you don't need me anymore. The Night Hag is gone, and you're well on your way to having full control of your powers. You no longer need my guidance."

"Where will you go?"

"I'm not sure. Wherever I was meant to, I suppose."

"Then why did you stick around all this time?"

Jonas sighed. "I knew the Night Hag who killed me wasn't dead. And I knew it was the only way Elias would get closure. When you came to the Black Lily with a Night Hag attached to you, I knew I had to do something. As you know, mediums are unique in the supernatural community. I didn't want to see you befall the same fate as me. It took me a long time to get my strength back. Longer than I expected. But I recovered enough to help you. And to say goodbye to Elias."

"He's going to be heartbroken to hear you're gone."

Jonas got to his feet. He picked up his hat from the coffee table and brushed it off. "I've been dead for over a century. It's time I moved on. But if you could tell him one thing for me, I would appreciate it."

I nodded. "Whatever you want."

He leaned over me and whispered in my ear, "Tell him I love him, and that I'm happy he's found love again." Then Jonas kissed my cheek and added, "Thank you, for helping him heal. And for seeing Elias is not the monster that bastard Caleb made him. I hope one day he will see you as you see him."

"Thank you for saving my life," I replied. "And for teaching me how to use my powers."

Jonas stood up. He put his hat on, and I turned in the chair as he went to the door. He opened it and instead of the brick courtyard and large oak trees, there was a bright light. He looked back one last time and gave me a smile, then stepped through the door. The light grew so bright I could hardly see. Jonas began to fade, slowly at first, then all at once he was gone. Never to return.

Epilogue

One year later

"IF I SEE one more book I'm going to puke," Lionel groaned.

"Tough shit, there's three more boxes in the truck," I replied.

"Ugh, why do you have so much crap?"

"Stop complaining, at least you have superstrength."

"So what? It doesn't make it any less weird that you have so many books."

"Wait until we get to my records and CDs."

"Nerd."

"Whiner."

Verity appeared at the gate and asked, "Am I going to have to separate you two?"

"No, ma'am," Lionel said and did his best to look contrite.

"No," I said. I grabbed another box and kissed Verity's cheek. "Almost done."

"Good. Don't forget to shower, we're going to the Black Lily tonight."

"I know."

I was the last one to move into Elias's house. Lionel and Verity moved in about four months after the Night Hag incident. Lionel still owned his family's building. He rented the apartment to a married couple he knew. They were street performers who often worked in Jackson Square or by the gates to Armstrong Park. He'd thought of selling, but in the end, he couldn't. He said his Nonna would crawl out of the grave to berate him for it.

Elias treated Verity as a little sister, and I treated Lionel like the bratty brother I always wanted. While I did miss out on spending more time with them, I couldn't leave my apartment. However, I didn't go back right away. After the exorcism, German was nice enough to cleanse it for me, but I was still afraid to spend too much time there.

The house retained a lot of energy from Marguerite. It had been hell getting it out of all the nooks and crannies in the building. Jaime and Sawyer helped. My now former neighbors thought I was a little weird. But everyone could feel there was something wrong with the house. So German, Jaxon, and I went from apartment to apartment. We eradicated every bit of Marguerite's influence. And after several months the house was clean.

I never went back to my day job. I still receive emails from my old boss checking in to see if I'm okay. I was making significantly more at the séances. I was able to help more people than I would have through my old job. I was in full control of my powers and could call any ghost I wanted. I was even able to help the ones who wanted to be put to rest.

I did tell Elias about the dream I had, and that I was sure Jonas had moved on. Elias was upset at first, but he was glad that Jonas found peace. He asked a dozen questions about the dream, then he just wanted to be held for a while. I hugged him tight while he cried and sang to him to comfort him.

Elias returned to the Court as he promised. He gave a full account of what happened in New Orleans. He left nothing out; the King demanded the truth and Elias gave it to him. Once the story was verified, Elias was allowed to return home, on the condition he may be called back at any time. Elias accepted gratefully and we threw a small party for him when he returned.

Verity started her own burlesque act and was gaining a reputation around town. She decided on an interesting angle that was very New Orleans. She danced under the name Chastity St. Sinner. She incorporated a lot of Catholic imagery in her act that was very entertaining to watch. Lionel, Elias, and I would go see her perform as often as we could.

Lionel stuck with service jobs around the Quarter. Sure, the money wasn't great, but it didn't need to be since we'd agreed to pool our resources. Mostly he just liked being around people. He loved to talk, especially gossip, and he was still the nosiest person I'd ever met. It was something I came to love about him.

As for my online friends, we didn't talk as often anymore. Not that we'd had a falling-out, of course. Psyche, Nathana, Didoll, and Aoi were still my favorite people, and we talked every other day. But I wasn't spending as much time sitting by my laptop or my phone waiting for someone to message me. I know that my pocket friends love me as much as I love them, and they still have a special place in my heart.

I'd been in the process of moving in for two weeks. My old apartment was cleaned out and this set of boxes was the last. We each had our own rooms, out of necessity. I still needed my own space, and I wasn't the only one who felt that way. We would all spend time with one another, and rooms weren't off-limits. But they did require permission to enter, which was something we all held sacred. Verity and I were on the second floor of the cottage. Those were the only rooms that received sunlight. Elias and Lionel roomed downstairs.

At first, it was difficult to navigate our relationship. We had to have a lot of patience with one another, especially as none of us had been in a poly relationship before. There were a few misunderstandings, and even a fight or two. Not to mention the physical aspects of intimacy which we had to coordinate. I'm sex indifferent still. But I've had experiences of physical love and intimacy with Verity and Elias. I wouldn't trade them for anything. In the end, we worked everything out because we all understood and loved one another.

Once everything was in my room, I went to shower and dress. I'd changed my hair the week before from teal to silver with dark roots and I was still getting used to it. I hadn't cut it in ages either, and it was getting long enough I had to braid it before going to bed. Verity had teased me about copying her. But as her hair was blonde and mine was silver it wasn't really the same. Something she loved to gently rib me about.

I dressed in the same black satin slip dress and lace duster I'd worn to my first séance at the Black Lily Society. I braided my hair and twisted it into a bun; my bangs and forelocks framed my face. I put on some purple lipstick with black eyeliner and called it done. I shuffled into my boots, put on my violet glasses, and went downstairs.

Elias was in a T-shirt, jeans, work boots, and a flannel shirt. Lionel chose a sheer button-down shirt with leather pants and motorcycle boots. Verity had her hair in pigtails and wore my velvet babydoll dress. She paired it with lace knee socks and patent leather Mary Jane heels. Like me, their clothes were all black.

"You guys look great," I said.

"You too. Ready?" Verity asked.

"As ever."

We took Elias's car to the Black Lily. German waved us in and we went upstairs. We walked past the "closed for private party" sign. The tables and chairs were cleared out, and everyone was in their smartest black attire. Elias offered me his arm and I took it. Verity took my other arm. Then Lionel linked arms with Elias. We entered the room together.

"There you are," Reyna said and came out from behind the bar. "The representative will be here any minute!"

"Good news?" I asked.

"I hope so," she replied.

After the Night Hag ordeal, Reyna, Kingston, and Martin petitioned the Vampire King. They asked for the sanctions on Elias and Lionel to be lifted. They argued it was prejudicial as both vampires were no longer under Caleb Blake's sway. They'd been instrumental in dispensing with the Night Hag. So Kingston and Martin said the sanctions would be a suitable reward for their valiant deeds. Reyna agreed.

I looked at Verity. "Anything?"

Her eyes misted over for a moment, but she shook her head. "It's blurry, I'm not sure."

I patted her hand. "It's okay."

Verity hadn't escaped Marguerite completely unharmed. We'd been able to separate them before Verity's soul was destroyed. But the same couldn't be said for her powers. She couldn't see as clearly into the future or the past. She insisted she preferred it this way because she could be surprised now. German said her powers would return someday, but how long it would take was anyone's guess.

There was a lot of chatter, and we were all drawn away one by one to talk to people. Delia congratulated me for finally taking the plunge and moving in with my partners, though she was sorry I wouldn't be coming into Morning Brew as regularly anymore. We were discussing her plans to team up with the bookshop in the Rink to expand their shared space when a hush fell over the crowd.

A man I'd never seen before stood in the doorway. He had black hair and muttonchops, and he wore a red Georgian military jacket. He was flanked by none other than Kingston and Martin. Both of them were in black suits with red ties. Rather than looking pleased, however, their expressions were grave. I looked around for Elias and went to him right away. Verity and Lionel had the same idea. And we joined together as the representative moved further into the room. The rest of the crowd parted like the Red Sea before them.

Reyna joined us as well, and she curtsied. I hastily followed suit, as did Verity. Lionel and Elias bowed.

"Welcome, Viscount Hewitt," said Reyna. "We're honored by your presence."

"Rise."

We did. My heart hammered in my chest.

He looked at each of us in turn, then drew a piece of parchment out of his jacket pocket. "King Vijay is dead."

A gasp ran through the crowd and my heart leaped in my throat.

"A new king is to be selected in the coming months. In the meantime, the Court will move here, to New Orleans, Louisiana. Arrangements are being made at this time."

More gasps and a few cries of surprise.

"The Court has never come to the New World," someone muttered.

"Unusual, isn't it?" said someone else.

The Viscount waited for the room to quiet down, then he spoke again. "Elias Rothschild."

Elias stepped forward. "Present, my lord."

"You are recalled to the Court until a new king is crowned. The matter of your pardon will be decided then." Viscount Hewitt looked at me, Verity, and Lionel. "As we are aware of your...family situation, they may attend Court as well. If you wish it."

"How long do we have to decide?" Elias asked.

"Before sunrise."

Elias bowed. "Thank you, my lord."

The rest of us bowed and curtsied. Then the Viscount left. Kingston and Martin, however, stayed behind. There was a lot of murmuring, then everyone was talking at once.

Elias turned to Reyna. "May we use your office?"

"Of course."

The four of us left the room and barricaded ourselves in Reyna's office. I was the last one through the door.

"What should we do?" Lionel asked.

"We should go, of course," said Verity.

"I don't know that I'm comfortable going to the Court," Lionel said.

"It has more rules than the club, you would all be safe," Elias assured him.

Verity and I looked at each other. She'd already made up her mind, I could tell by the small smile on her face. "We'll be fine. We have two strapping escorts."

"Huh? Who? Did Kingston say something to you?" Lionel asked.

I couldn't help myself, I laughed.

Elias stepped up to me and he held his hand out. I took it and he pulled me close. He wrapped an arm around me and asked, "And you? What do you think?"

"Well, the Court's coming to us. Which is good since I don't have a passport. I could be persuaded."

"I feel it's only fair to warn you. There are standards to be met, and etiquette to be adhered to. It can be daunting."

I smiled. "Remember when I pestered you to break down the social hierarchy and protocols of the Regency era for me?"

"Ugh, I do," Lionel whined. "I thought I was gonna die of boredom."

"Hush," Verity said and smacked his arm.

Elias smiled. "Yes, I recall."

"The neurotypical world is already super weird to me. With lots of stupid rules I don't always understand. I imagine the Vampire Royal Court won't be any different. Besides, we can't let you go by yourself. You'd be lost without us."

He kissed me softly, and I smiled against his lips.

"Well, if Lyric is going, I guess that means I have to go too," Lionel said.

Elias pulled him close and kissed him too. "And you, Verity?"

She closed her eyes, then smiled when she opened them. "I'm in."

I held my hand out to her and she took it. I kissed Verity, and she sighed happily.

"Then it's decided," Elias said.

"On to another adventure," I replied.

We embraced, and as we did, I knew no matter what the Vampire Royal Court threw at us, we'd stay together. Nothing would tear us apart ever again.

Acknowledgements

There's a lot that goes into writing a book. Not the least of which is people encouraging you to keep going. Who reassure you that yes, you can write, you're just down on yourself. And of course, people who help in other and unexpected ways. Thank you to Morgan, Eden, Joanna, Kimba, Nomi, Rose, Merinda, Shane, Dan'a, and the Twitter Fang Gang, you know who you are. Y'all are the best.

Last but not least, I'd like to thank Raevyn and Liz for once again taking a chance on my story. And for helping me do what it takes to make it shine.

About the Author

Alice G. Holmes is a queer nonbinary author who lives in New Orleans, Louisiana with their cat Vanya and an aloe plant named Fenelope. They are the author of Sorcery of the Blood, the first book in the April Oaks series, and the short story The Vampire of Dauphine Street, winner of the Boutique du Vampyre Lullabies Short Story contest of 2023.

Email

holmes.alice.g@gmail.com

Facebook

www.facebook.com/theseacequeen

Twitter

@theseacequeen

Instagram

www.instagram.com/theseancequeen

Other NineStar books by this author

Sorcery of the Blood

Connect with NineStar Press

www.ninestarpress.com

www.facebook.com/ninestarpress

www.facebook.com/groups/NineStarNiche

www.twitter.com/ninestarpress

www.instagram.com/ninestarpress

bsky.app/profile/ninestarpress.bsky.social

www.threads.net/@ninestarpress